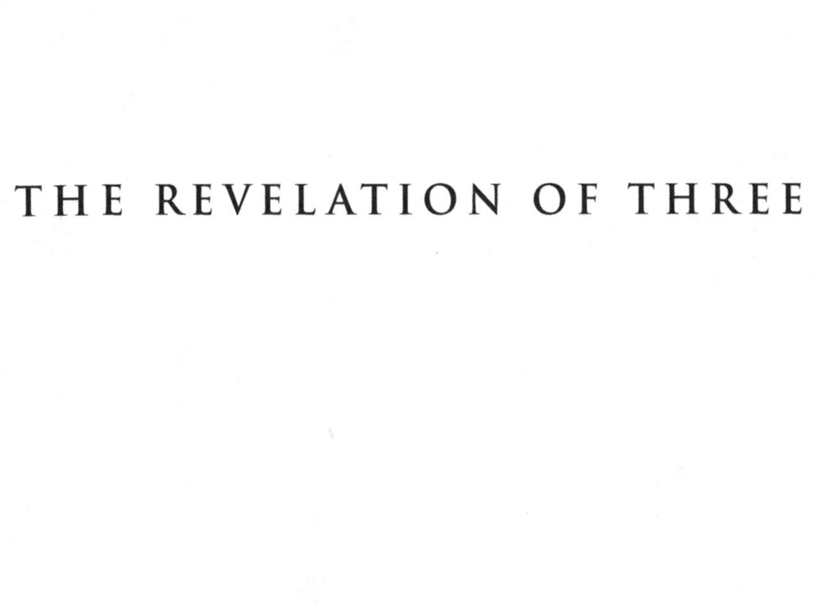

THE REVELATION OF THREE

THE REVELATION OF THREE

SARA M SCHALLER

DESIGNS BY SERAPHIM

The Revelation of Three

Published by Designs by Seraphim

This is a work of fiction. Names, characters, places, and incidents are either the product of the author's imagination or are used fictitiously. Any resemblance to actual persons living or dead, events, or locales is entirely coincidental.

ISBN 978-1-7325162-3-6 (hardcover)
ISBN 978-1-7325162-4-3 (paperback)
ISBN 978-1-7325162-5-0 (ebook)

Cover design by Sara M Schaller
Interior design by Sara M Schaller
Symbol Artwork by Adrianne Tamar Arachne
Edited by Double Vision Editorial
Maps by Lizard Ink Maps

First Edition: August 2021

www.saramschaller.com

For the readers

Thank you for your patience and support.
I appreciate you all so much.

AUTHOR'S NOTE

In this book, I've added some guides for you to use as references, specifically a cast of characters and glossary. They are not needed in order to read and enjoy the story (there's enough within these pages to keep you informed), but I wanted to include them anyway as an added bonus. If you decide to use them, they will be featured at the back.

HEAVEN
HIGH HEAVEN
MIDDLE HEAVEN
LOW HEAVEN

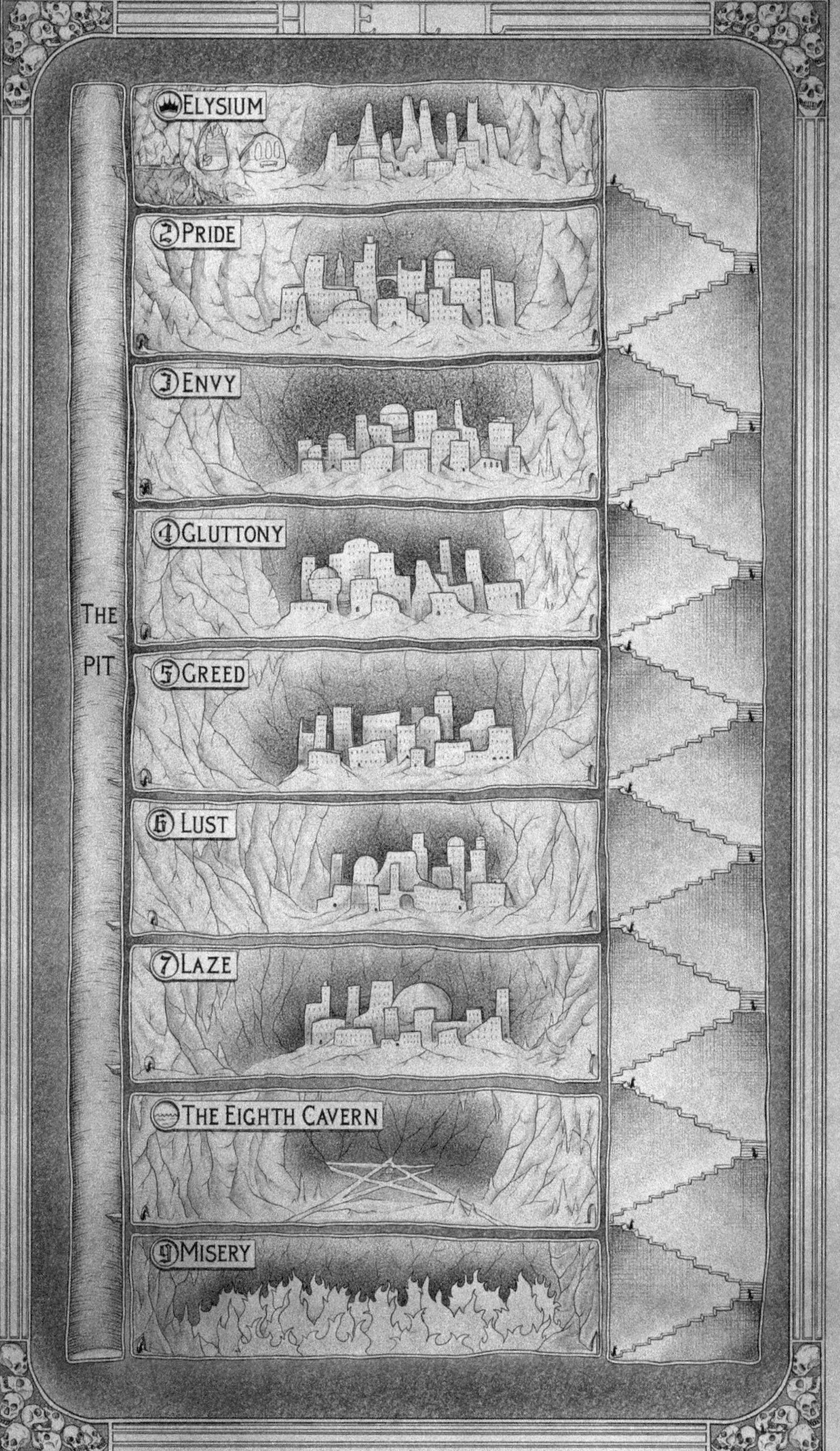
HELL
ELYSIUM
2 PRIDE
3 ENVY
4 GLUTTONY
5 GREED
6 LUST
7 LAZE
THE EIGHTH CAVERN
9 MISERY
THE PIT

YOU NEED TO FALL
BEFORE YOU CAN RISE.

1

SATAN

New York City, 3:00 pm

Nine. It had started with nine inconsequential feathers, small plumes I wouldn't miss. But in the six months since I had started losing them, the process had sped up, and now I left trails of feathers in my wake.

Yet, those plumes weren't the only thing I had lost.

The Hellfire was gone, too.

I was no stranger to loss. In my many centuries of existence, I had lost my home, my family, and my freedom. Those things were eventually found again, although in much different forms, but I feared the Hellfire's return would not come so easily. With the help of witches, I had dabbled in black magic, too ambitious to think of its cost. I had bargained my power for my freedom, and not even I, Lord Satan, ruler of the underworld, was immune to its price.

At first, I had told myself it was nothing, but deep down I'd known I was lying.

Today, it wasn't one feather or a trail. It was a whole handful.

While I might be ill, I wasn't weak. And for that reason, my ambition continued. I had plans, ones that had to be executed in a particular order. The Sacrarium, a secret society entrusted to protect the holy bloodline, had information, far too much in my opinion, and they knew about the objects I was searching for—my keys, a set of three items each archangel on the council in Heaven had been tasked to protect.

Mine had been stolen from me, before I even knew they existed, by Him—Father, the creator of all angels—but I disliked calling Him that because it gave Him authority, something He no longer had over me. Ever since I'd found out about the keys, it became my goal to retrieve them. And the Sacrarium had my most powerful key of all, the black onyx sphere. For years, I had been tracking the Sacrarium to recover it, yet they had evaded me and my efforts. But now, it was finally time to settle matters, to discover the Sacrarium and reclaim what was rightfully mine.

Gazing on the Statue of Liberty, I curled my fist around the clump of feathers in my hand, slowly easing back my fingers and letting the wind carry them away.

Why was my fight for freedom so difficult? Why couldn't I have exactly what I wanted?

An unmistakable howl rang out, and I smiled.

My hellhound must have found his prey.

The beast came loping through Battery Park, passing by humans who mistook the creature for an ordinary dog since the hound looked like a Doberman with his sleek black coat and pointy ears. He leaped over a bench, the last barrier between us, and came to stand resolutely at my side.

I knelt down and patted the hound's head. Looking into his eyes, I could tell he was locked onto a scent. Thanks to Leviathan, all the hounds were obedient. Leviathan was the one who had tamed them, the one who insisted upon training them to follow my commands. And it had paid off.

"Take me to them. Take me to the Sacrarium."

The hellhound jolted into action, weaving once again through the pedestrians in the park.

I stood and outstretched my wings, then took flight to follow.

After my chat with Michael in São Paulo six months ago, I had left Hell with the hound, determined to make the beast locate the Sacrarium. From the maps in Michael's office, I knew their headquarters was in New York, but I still needed to pinpoint their exact location.

I had returned to the burned-down orphanage, the last-known site of the Sacrarium, with the hellhound to see if he could locate a scent. It normally didn't take this long for a hound to find a reliable trail, even one that was weak and dormant, but I suspected the amulet, which allowed me to leave Hell and travel to Earth, was the cause of the problem. My strength had waned since I'd started wearing it, and the fact that my power and abilities were weakening meant my authority with the beasts was, as well.

While the hound had been away searching, I had been living in the city, free to roam as I pleased, taking a much-needed sojourn from the dark and dismal abode that was Hell. I had been locked down there for almost eighteen years, and I had every intention of enjoying the respite while it lasted.

It had been hard at first to find something to occupy me. The city had changed so much since I'd last been there, it was simply nice to explore it again with fresh eyes. Being around humans, however, was certainly the most detestable aspect of being here. I had hardly tolerated them before, but now all they did was walk around, glued to the small devices in their hands. It was a shame to see them so absorbed by technology, and it made me angry that they took the sunshine and fresh air for granted, by far the things I had missed the most while locked up in Hell.

Yet, I was also at a disadvantage. The world had changed so drastically while I had been stuck belowground that I now lacked a bit of modern knowledge. So I'd figured, why not take the opportunity to blend into this world, especially while my Hellfire was temporarily muted, to learn its new ways? I certainly wasn't going to sit around doing nothing while waiting for the hound, and perhaps gaining some insight into modern capabilities would help me with some of my enemies.

With that in mind, I'd found the one place where I would blend in the most: the gym. I had been created to be a warrior, so fighting and strength were ingrained in me, and physical training was something I prided myself on. It was there that I'd begun to learn the workings of this new world. It also had been where I committed my most frivolous act, being persuaded to add a few tattoos to my arms.

And although it may have seemed irresponsible to leave my kingdom for such a long period of time, this trip aboveground would benefit Hell in the long run by reestablishing our connection with the world.

For the past two decades since I'd been locked in Hell, I had been sending Lucifer to meet with the Nephilim, half-human, half-angel creatures, who had been my only link to modern means. Our long-standing agreement had been that I would send them weapons in exchange for technology. The Nephilim preferred to use guns and bullets, and the ones I forged in Hell were untraceable on Earth. Meanwhile, I wanted phones and trackers since we were unable to get such devices ourselves without humans asking too many questions. Overall, it had been a mutually beneficial relationship. Until I realized how trivial our deal was. The assets I had in Hell were far better than the ones they were giving me, especially since I could acquire the same technology myself if I chose to, now that I was free. It was high time we amended our agreement and reviewed our negotiations. So before I had come to Earth for my sojourn, I had sent Lucifer to negotiate a meeting with Jazema, one of the leaders of the Nephilim.

Jazema was the owner of Geneloom, a genetic testing company with worldwide reach. She had partnered with her sister, Penelope, who ran Giant Heart Healing Center, a rehab center for troubled teens in New York. Both of them were Nephilim. And from what I'd heard from Lucifer, they looked nothing alike, even though they were related.

Together, Jazema and Penelope have combined their funds and assets to operate a secret experiment, known as Operation Pure Form. The experiment's intent is to create pure-blooded Nephilim. The only way to do that was to combine the DNA of an angel with the DNA of a human. Except the former was hard to come by. Angels were not allowed to fraternize with humans in such an intimate way. Yet, centuries ago, the Watchers had. They had disobeyed the rules and had become infatuated with humans, subsequently creating the Nephilim. However, word of their wrongdoing had been brought back to Heaven, and the Watchers had been imprisoned, wiping out any chance for a future Nephilim race.

Now, the few who remained were considered weaker Nephilim, full of genetic abnormalities because their DNA no longer came straight from the Watchers but from generations of Nephilim, their blood now diluted and their abilities diminished. None of them even had wings anymore.

The purpose of Jazema and Penelope's experiment was to recreate the original Nephilim, but finding angels willing to hand over their DNA was difficult so I had no idea if they had been successful. Many angels thought the Nephilim were abominations, as I did, too sinful to be considered blessed and too mortal to be considered fallen.

As Lucifer tried to repair my shaky relationship with Jazema, the remainder of the Six—my closest fallen angels whom I had appointed as secondary leaders—were maintaining the chaos in Hell while I was away, waiting until I called on them. But now it was finally time to rid myself of the human façade I had been donning—the alias of Samuel Cross—and get back to the real work at hand.

I flew through the warm spring air, high enough to go undetected but low enough to follow the hound as he raced through the streets of New York. Many who noticed the hound had looks of alarm on their faces as he loped down the middle of the street at a freakishly fast rate. I didn't really care, as discretion was not my forte. I preferred action and results over concern for humans' peace of mind.

Abruptly, the hound stopped and let out a howl. I landed next to him to investigate the surroundings.

We were in the Brooklyn Navy Yard, an industrial part of town with a lot of activity. It was late afternoon, and most people were in the middle of their workday.

The hound sat on the sidewalk, immobile, as if something had distracted him.

I looked around. "There's nothing here."

A light breeze swept by, and the hound sniffed the air. He stood up, nose to the ground, following a scent.

Again, he stopped abruptly, ears pricked for any perceptible noise. Then he turned and raced off again, as though he had just remembered what it was he needed to do.

Sighing, I launched into the air and followed him once more. This time when I found him, he was sitting on the steps of a church.

I smirked. "Good boy."

He came closer to my side, eager for a few head pats.

The church was still in Brooklyn, but it was a nicer part of town. The building itself was big, made of brick with stained glass windows and small spires.

Unfortunately, I didn't have the ability to enter sacred ground.

I fiddled with the amulet hanging from my neck when a thought struck me.

What if the amulet has changed that, too?

Ever since I'd starting wearing it, nothing was quite as it should be. I didn't feel as strong, my power to control Hellfire and channel it as a weapon had been stripped from me, and I was molting feathers like some average bird. I wondered, though, if it changed other aspects, too. Like certain inhibitors that prevented me from entering buildings...

I walked up the steps and pushed against the door, the hinges creaking as I did so. Music came pouring out from the interior of the church, and I placed one foot inside the vestibule. No reaction. I brought my other foot through the doorway. Still nothing. I whistled for the hound to follow and let the door swing shut after him.

Here I was, inside a church, without so much as a twinge of pain.

I smiled. You had to love Astrid and Tabitha's black magic in moments like these. Surprisingly, those dithering witches had provided me with the amulet, restored my ability to travel from Hell to Earth, and exposed the foretelling of a fourteenth sphere, a celestial item with an inexplicable purpose. I had assumed its existence, but most of my blessed brothers and sisters only knew about thirteen spheres, objects powerful enough to control Heaven if combined together through a prophecy called the Union of the Spheres.

The witches, while vexatious to say the least, had been right about how to create the amulet. Could their correct inclinations be turned into action once again? Could they potentially discover the fourteenth sphere before anyone else knew it existed?

That was a thought for another time. First, I had to deal with the Sacrarium.

Entering through a second set of doors, I briefly gazed upon the ornate vaulted ceiling and the dark wooden pews of the space. The sound of singing came from behind me, up in the choir, while at the front near the altar was a gray-haired woman with wild curls speaking to a girl sitting in the first pew. Although she didn't wear a habit, I could tell the woman was a nun by her starched white shirt, long black skirt, and wooden cross necklace.

I remained in the shadows, tilting my head and drowning out the music to focus on their conversation. Besides flying, my celestial hearing was one of the few special abilities I had remaining.

"It's certainly a surprise to see you," the nun said. "I wasn't expecting you." She patted the girl's hand. "Is everything all right? Shouldn't you be finishing school?"

"I'm fine," the girl said. "I took a break this weekend because I had to come tell you something in person." She paused. "I've found it. The fourteenth sphere."

I froze and listened more intently.

Before the girl could continue, the nun stopped her. "Be careful what you say."

The girl looked around. "Why? Is it not safe here?"

"It's better to be cautious," the nun advised her. "Perhaps we should talk another time."

"Of course." The girl nodded and reached out to hug the nun. Then, soft as a whisper, the girl said in the nun's ear, "Simon Price. Upper East Side, off Fifth and Eighty-Fifth."

They pulled apart. The nun smiled. "I'm proud of you. Now, you should go. I'll be in touch soon."

I stepped out of the shadows and walked down the aisle, my presence going undetected until I clapped my hands.

The nun looked up, alarm immediately taking over her expression.

"What wonderful acoustics," I said.

"What are you doing here? How did you find us?" the nun demanded.

The hellhound growled at my side. Clearly, the woman hadn't seen the beast, because her eyes widened, not in horror but in recognition.

I smirked. "I see you've had some experience with my hounds."

The nun grabbed the girl by the arm and shoved her behind her. "Enough to know they don't easily lose a scent."

I set my gaze on the woman, her blue eyes and wild curls. "So you're the big bad Alpha of the Sacrarium. I expected more."

She ignored me and waved her hands in the air. The singing ceased instantly. "Let them leave," she said to me. "This conversation is between you and me."

I sighed. Her words held some truth. There was no use dragging in others who would only whine and weep. "Fine." It was just of matter time until I exposed her true flaw anyway. I was the Devil after all, so I couldn't let her off that easily.

"Sister Delphine," the woman shouted without taking her eyes off me, "choir practice is over for today. There's a gas leak, and we need to evacuate the building immediately."

The thumping of feet could be heard on the stairs as the choir descended and exited out the main entrance. Without turning, I could tell one of the singers was hesitating to leave just from the rigid look on the nun's face. "Delphine, go."

"But what about you?"

"I have to stay with the inspector to make sure the building's empty."

"Sister Helen—"

"Go!"

Creaking hinges indicated her exit.

My eyes narrowed as Helen pushed the girl toward the outer aisle, presumably to let her depart. There was concern and fear in Helen's expression when she looked at her.

"The girl stays," I said. My lips curled at this fortunate turn of events. I had hoped to find the Alpha of the Sacrarium, but this was even better: I had found her weakness, too.

The girl froze in place.

"Let her go," the nun said. "She has no part in this, either."

"Helen," I began.

"Sister Helen," she corrected.

"Helen," I repeated, "the girl stays, especially since you dote on her so much."

Helen backed away, closing the distance between her and the girl. "You should have let her go."

"Why?"

"Because now I won't be so cooperative." She reached for the fountain of holy water that sat next to the altar and pushed it to the ground, grabbing the girl by the arm and running down the right transept.

The hound howled as the water rushed over his paws and quickly jumped onto a pew to seek safety. Enraged, he flew over the wooden benches in pursuit of the two women.

I, on the other hand, was unharmed as the water had only washed over my boots. My rage was similar to the hellhound's, though, so I followed them all down the transept, ready to descend on my prey.

2

SOPHIA

New York City, 4:00 pm

Fear gripped my entire body as we ran down the transept and into the hallway toward the church office. Ever since high school, I had been learning the ways of the Sacrarium, at first gaining simple knowledge of otherworldly beings and then training to protect myself from them. But no amount of preparation had equipped me for being chased by a fiendish hound and an equally fiendish man who meant to harm us.

If I had to guess, I figured the beast was probably a hellhound… which meant the man had to be the Devil. My eyes widened in terror at the thought.

No wonder Sister Helen was afraid of him. I could tell she was frightened since her nails dug into my wrist as she pulled me behind her.

Claws slapped against the marble floor, the feral creature sounding like he was getting closer and closer. He suddenly came bounding behind me, his snarling jaws snapping at my legs. I screamed.

Sister Helen tugged me along quicker, her nails digging in even deeper, the intensity matching her urgency to get inside the office. Once we crossed the threshold, instinct kicked in and I slammed the door behind us. But not before the beast lodged his head through.

Pushing my back against the wood, I tried to force the creature out, but he was far stronger, easily extending the gap and advancing his front leg through the doorway. I pushed with all my might as the beast clawed and scraped. His saliva and spittle ran down the door. My shoulder gave out, and I lost my footing, the beast advancing quickly, ready to sink his jaws into my leg, but Sister Helen came to my rescue before he could. She swung a bat through the air and nailed the creature in the head.

Stunned, the hound fell backward into the hall.

Sister Helen slammed the door shut and barred it with a wooden chair from one of the desks. She reached down to help me up. "Did he bite you?" she asked.

"N-no," I stammered as the shock set in.

"Good. There's nothing worse than a hellhound bite," she said, striding toward her desk. "Paralysis, paranoia, and hallucinations quickly seize a person before they're killed by its venom."

I was stunned. My inclinations had been right. The creature *was* a hellhound. But I was still not prepared for this moment. Knowledge didn't equate action, and I definitely didn't know what to do, especially not against the Devil and a hellhound!

She turned to face me. "I probably shouldn't have told you that so bluntly, but we are working on limited time."

"Limited time? You had four years to teach and train me, yet you decided to leave out the side effects of a hellhound bite? Or the fact that I might need to run for my life from the Devil?"

"Sophia, you always knew the risks."

"No! I knew the *potential for* risks. I never knew I would be facing an actual risk before taking my oath!"

Obviously exasperated, Sister Helen shouted, "Neither did I!"

As the words left her mouth, a strong force rammed against the door, presumably the hellhound trying to make his way inside again.

Panic seized me as I realized there was no way out. "Sister Helen, how are we getting out of here? And what exactly is going on?"

Detecting the hysteria in my voice, she crossed the room and placed a hand on my cheek. "Sophia, you have a long road ahead of you before you are safe, so I need you to find the courage to carry on."

I nodded, not completely understanding her words.

She dropped her hand. "That man out there is Satan."

"I know," I interrupted.

She fixed me with an admonishing glare, and I shut my mouth.

"I don't know how he found out about this place, but he did. We've kept something from him for years—a book and a black onyx sphere—and I'm sure that's why he's here now. To seek his revenge."

"Then just give him what he wants!"

"I can't do that. What he wants is far too precious. Besides, I don't have those items anymore. I sent them away with Jordan."

"Jordan? He's involved in this?" I had grown up with Jordan at the orphanage and we were so close, we were practically siblings. I didn't know if I should feel betrayed by his secrecy, or relieved that I wasn't in this alone.

"It was his trial of trust."

"He's a Sacrarium Novice, too?"

There was another thud against the door.

"We don't have time for this!" Sister Helen strode over to the corner of the room, reached down, and pulled back the area rug adorning the floor. Underneath was a cellar door. She grabbed the circular latch and eased open the door.

Coming back to me, she passed her desk and picked up something. She held out an envelope. "Take this letter and find Jordan. Do not open it until you are with him. It has many answers, but not all of them. Unfortunately, the two of you will have to discover the rest together."

I shook my head, now understanding her intentions. "No! You're coming with me! I'm not leaving you!"

Sister Helen grabbed my wrists. "But you must. Jordan had to do this, too, and it was just as hard. I never wanted to leave either of you this way, but now you have to lean on each other."

She pushed me toward the cellar. She released my hands.

"No!" A tear escaped down my cheek. "Don't do this to me! Don't abandon me like she did!"

Another thud rammed against the door, only this time wood chunks went flying.

"Sophia, you must forgive your mother and you must forgive me. I am not doing this to hurt you. I'm doing this to protect you." She handed me a flashlight. "Now go!" She shoved me to the edge of the cellar door and forced me down the steps.

The tears flowed freely down my face as the flashbacks started to surface again in my mind.

"Sophia, go!" Sister Helen shouted one last time.

I moved down the stairs and into the cellar, and the door closed overhead, plunging me into darkness. Clicking on the flashlight, I advanced down the underground corridor and sobbed the entire way, knowing that I would never see her again.

3

SATAN

New York City, 4:00 pm

Splintered wood went flying as the hound broke through the barred door. I advanced into the office, prepared for a fight, yet all that stood before me was the unarmed old nun.

"Where is the girl?" I demanded.

"Gone," she replied.

I gazed around the interior of the office. There was no escape in sight. Only one way in and one way out. I snapped my fingers, and the hound went to work sniffing the room.

The nun turned her back to me and started fiddling with things on the desk.

"Stop!" I shouted.

She froze.

"Drop the letter opener."

She neither spoke nor faced me.

I grabbed the wooden chair from the desk to my right and placed it in front of me. "Drop the letter opener," I repeated, "and sit."

She quickly turned and used the momentum to fling the sharp object in my direction. I'd anticipated her move, though, and simply dodged it. The letter opener went flying through the air and landed with a thunk in the paneling behind my head.

The red blaze of Hellfire ignited inside me, even though I had no way to control it anymore. I grabbed her by the arm and flung her toward the chair. "Stay!"

The nun finally cooperated, letting out a sigh as her body sunk into the chair, a clear sign of defeat.

I moved past her to inspect the desk. Behind me, the chair creaked, and I let out a sharp whistle. The hellhound was on her in seconds, his front paws on her chest and his snapping jaws in her face.

She yelled out in fright.

When I whistled again, the hound eased off and obediently sat at her feet keeping guard.

Useless, nonsense papers. That's all I saw as I searched the desk. I shuffled the papers, but all that revealed was a desk calendar marked with doctor appointments. I opened the side drawer, but it only held pens and prescription bottles. Slamming it shut, I turned to face her.

"Who is the girl to you?" I asked. "Clearly not your daughter, given your holy vows."

Helen remained quiet.

"She must be one of your lackeys."

"She's not a lackey!" the nun yelled. "She's a messenger."

I smirked. "Aren't they the same thing? I think I would know since I used to be one."

"What is it you want?" she demanded, her voice laced with exasperation. "Why did you come here? We no longer have what you seek."

"I know you don't have my sphere anymore, but you *do* have

information about my other keys… And you obviously have a clue as to where the fourteenth sphere might be."

She tensed. It was easy to see she was wondering how I knew that. It was also easy to see the understanding dawn on her face as she realized I had listened in on her conversation.

"I would never tell you about your other keys. And I don't know what you heard, but the girl was mistaken. She doesn't know anything about a fourteenth sphere. She simply wanted to impress me and made up some elaborate lie."

I knew she was lying so I drew closer and whispered in her ear. "Great effort, Helen, but I don't believe you." I pulled away. "Who is Simon Price, and why does he have the fourteenth sphere?"

She was silent.

"This is no time to be quiet."

She looked me dead in the eye. "You called me Alpha of the Sacrarium before. How do you know the Sacrarium classifications?"

The nun was trying to buy time. I wasn't in a particular rush so I played her game. "Knowing the enemy is the best way to defeat them, especially if you can discover their flaws. You, obviously, are the Sacrarium's flaw. You've been the woman in charge for too long. You've grown old and weak, and you keep too many secrets. You've let your guard down, and now I'm sneaking in to ruin the establishment you've built."

She chuckled.

The reaction shocked me. "Are you…*laughing*?"

"Yes. You take satisfaction from something you had no part in. You're not ruining my establishment. The Sacrarium was already on its last legs."

Her answer made me pause. "That's impossible," I said, although I was unsure.

"Really? Look around you. Does it seem like I'm hiding in some top-secret Sacrarium headquarters? No? Well, that's because I'm not hiding anymore. There's nothing to hide anymore. There's no one of importance left but me." She stared me down. "You should know what it's like to be the leader of a crumbling foundation."

Anger boiled in my veins. "Excuse me?"

"We are both facing the demise of our power. Me, because I have no comrades in my cause left. You, because you've built a hollow crown with no true support or stability."

My eyes shot daggers at her. "Stop!"

She ignored me and smiled, ready to sow the last seeds of doubt. "Don't you think I know you can't enter hallowed ground? Something must be afoot in your kingdom if you've suddenly gained such an ability. Or perhaps something's afoot with you. Have you weakened and turned to the light again? Is Lucifer now in control?"

My hands curled into fists, and I slammed one on top of the desk, cracking the wood in two. "I'm the king! Do you hear me?"

She smirked at me as if I were a child throwing a tantrum. "Loud and clear."

"Now tell me about Simon Price," I commanded.

"There's nothing to tell." She shrugged. "I don't know who he is."

I snapped my fingers, and the hound advanced on her, placing both front paws on the nun's lap and growling in her face. Saliva dripped from his mouth and down the front of her shirt. She glared at the beast without an ounce of fear.

"Since you'd rather not talk, you leave me no choice but to find the girl."

"Leave her out of this," she ground out.

The hound inched closer. The nun scrunched her face as his hot breath washed over her.

"Do you want me to tell her you're dying?" I threatened.

Feigning ignorance, she said, "I don't know what you mean."

"Don't play games, Helen. I saw the prescription bottles in your drawer and the doctor appointments on your calendar."

She refused to answer.

"It's all right. I'll make sure she knows."

The nun pushed the hound back and launched out of the chair, ready to strike at me, but she reconsidered when the hound leaped at her. She dodged him and backed up to the desk, using the chair as a barrier between her and the hound.

"I think I'll leave you two to hash this out." I advanced toward the doorway, but a small bark drew my attention back. It drew the nun's, too. The hellhound sniffed the floor, his nose leading him to the rug, where he anxiously scratched at the fabric.

Before I went to investigate, I commanded the hound to guard the nun again. She didn't protest when I pulled up the corner of the rug and found the closed cellar door. I reached for the latch, but it was broken. She must have snapped it off before I had barged into the office.

"So that's how the girl got away," I said.

"Leave her be!" she shouted.

Instead, I came back to the hound and lifted his snout in my hand. "Find her. Find the girl."

"No!" the nun shouted.

The beast let out a howl and scampered off, happy to be on a new trail.

With the girl taken care of, it was time to go after Simon Price. Granted, finding him was a deviation from my original plan, but if he truly had the fourteenth sphere, then I would finally be at an advantage.

But first I would need backup…and to deal with the nun.

"You better watch out," she said solemnly.

I set my gaze on her. "Why's that?"

"Because you put far too much trust in those you shouldn't. I've had experience with your second-in-command in the past, and now that I've met you, I can tell you're both too stubborn, cocky, and proud for your own good. A personality like that doesn't mix with its own kind, so only one can remain. All I ask is, will it be you or him?"

The red blaze inside me suddenly ignited into an inferno. I lashed out my hand. She was now mine to deal with, mine to burn with the Hellfire.

My fingers closed around her throat, the Hellfire ready to burst from my fingertips. I could feel it, yet the blaze that lingered there would not release.

It's gone, I reminded myself.

What else must I lose for my freedom? All I'd sacrificed, and where had it gotten me? Staring into the smirking face of a woman who knew I was damaged, who knew I was *weak*.

Damn it! Damn it all!

To wipe that superior smirk off her face, I had every intention of twisting my hand and snapping her neck.

"Wait," she gasped. Her sneer disappeared, a more passive expression taking its place. Had I imagined it? Wasn't she mocking me?

"What? What do you want?" I roared quite hysterically.

"Even the Devil can be forgiven," she whispered.

"There's no point trying to save me! I'll never repent my sins!"

"I'm not asking you to. I'm only saying—" she paused, staring me straight in the eye "—I forgive you."

My whole body trembled. Weren't those the words I'd wanted to hear? Perhaps from someone else, but wasn't the sentiment the same?

What's wrong with you? a voice snapped in my head.

It was Lilith, haunting my mind with ridicule since the day she had bitten me in Eden.

Do it! Kill her!

I tightened my grasp on the nun's neck, overcome with emotion. Then I challenged the fate I had been dealt. Releasing my grip, I showed her some mercy. "Get out of my sight before I regret my decision."

She sucked in a breath and stumbled out of the office.

I'd never minded being evil and having blood on my hands, but *I* chose whose blood to dirty them with. I wasn't some psychopath who enjoyed killing people for no reason.

I still had morals…

4 Sophia

New York City, 6:00 pm

My sneakers slapped against the wet pavement of the underground corridor, occasionally making a splash as my foot sank into a puddle. The flashlight only illuminated a short distance ahead of me, and I definitely was not pointing it toward my feet, as getting out of here was my top priority.

I had come into the city for the weekend because I had finally found the fourteenth sphere and needed to tell the Sacrarium. Even though I only had two weeks of school left before summer vacation, information this vital could not wait. My college roommate, Dafne, was nice enough to ask her parents to let me stay at their condo while I was here. Little had I known that my Sacrarium training would be put to the ultimate test by crossing paths with the Devil.

I tried to shake off the thoughts. If I dwelled on it now, I'd be overwhelmed with fear and despair, and I didn't have time for that. I needed to survive.

I didn't know how long I had been down here, but it felt like an eternity. My cell phone was in my purse hanging across my body, but it was pointless to look at the time.

I need to get out.

It was so hard to see, and everything looked the same. Suddenly, I found myself at a fork in the passage and paused.

Left or right?

Fear clawed at my mind, just like Sister Helen's nails had clawed at my wrists as she forced me into the cellar.

Don't think about her. Don't think about her.

I knew what would happen if I did. The memories would come flooding back, ones that didn't make sense, ones I had buried long ago.

Don't think about her. Don't think about her.

Which way should I go?

My feet went to the left and carried me down the corridor. The laces on my sneaker caught on something, and I careened to the wet ground, the flashlight dropping from my hand. That was all it took for my mind to break the dam I had built up to hold back the trauma.

Don't think about her, the woman's voice said. *She left you. She didn't want you. You meant nothing to her. You are ours now, and we will teach you how to discover your full potential—something she feared and tried to hide.*

I freed my shoelace from the pipe it had snagged itself on, hugging my knees to my chest and squeezing my eyes shut.

No. I can't do this again.

I grabbed the flashlight and quickly stood up. I advanced down the corridor faster, needing to get out of here *now*. But in a matter of moments, all that stood before me was a brick wall.

I screamed, trapped just as I had been when I had tried to escape from that woman, the blond one who had taken me after my mom abandoned me.

I turned around. There had to be a way out. Sister Helen would never have sent me down here without a way out.

Then the voice started again.

Don't think about her. Don't think about her.

I screamed once more and, in my rage, threw the flashlight against the wall. I immediately regretted it as I saw it break into pieces before the light went out completely.

No, no, no.

My hands started to shake. My breath came out in ragged gasps. I heard every drop of water as it ran down the pipes and dripped into the puddles on the ground. But I still couldn't see anything.

I stared ahead of me into the blackness, letting my eyes adjust.

The truth resides inside. Deceit lies without. The journey to both is obscure.

That was what Sister Helen always told us.

Then the other voice again. *Don't think about her. Don't think about her.*

It was like having an angel and a devil on my shoulders, one voice encouraging me and one paralyzing me.

I shut my eyes.

Rely on your instincts.

That was what my mom used to say before she'd abandoned me at five years old. My dad had never been around. I don't know why. It was strange to remember my mother's words and listen to her now, but I did.

I stood up and reached out to find the wall. Once I did, I kept my left hand firmly planted on it and slowly made my way down the corridor. I had to get back to the fork and take the other passageway.

It seemed like ages before my hand slipped off the surface and into thin air. I had made it back to the fork. Finding the wall again,

I oriented myself and followed the new passageway for a long while until I once again reached a dead end.

What? No! There has to be a way out! This has to be it!

Panic filled my mind again as a new mantra started.

Useless. Absolutely useless. A complete disgrace.

I slammed my hand against the dead-end wall.

Think, Sophia. Rely on your instincts.

The sound of dripping water filled my ears once more.

Wait, if there was water down here, it had to be coming from somewhere…

I looked up and reached out my hands. I wasn't tall enough to touch the top, so I jumped and brushed against metal. I prayed it was a door or a latch, something that would get me out of here.

I jumped again, but this time I tried to wrap my fingers around whatever I had touched. It took a few tries before I realized what I was trying to grab on to was a metal wheel that needed to be turned to open a hatch above me.

Now I knew what I had to do. I moved closer to the right side of the passageway and quickly ran to get some momentum and jumped. My hands closed around the wheel, and I swung my feet to place them on either side of the hatch to brace myself. Hanging upside-down wasn't easy but I was acting on adrenaline.

I yanked on the wheel using all my strength, but it wouldn't turn.

"Come on!" I shouted. "Turn already!"

The wheel slowly inched to the left. I kept turning and pushing, trying to open the hatch. Finally, it swung down and knocked me to the ground. I rose from the wet floor and jumped as high as I could to grip the metal ladder inside the shoot. My hands were practically numb from holding on to the wheel for so long, and my upper arms protested when I heaved my body up the ladder. But it didn't matter. I needed to get out.

At the top of the ladder, there was another wheel and hatch. I quickly got to work prying it open, and as soon as it released, I pushed through into the late afternoon and fresh air.

I stayed where I was for a moment, my eyes readjusting to the light and my body needing a break. Eventually, I pulled myself out of the chute, sat on the ground, and took in the sight of the Brooklyn Bridge. No wonder everything had been so wet down there. The underground corridor was near the Hudson.

I pulled my phone out of my purse to check the time: *6:29 PM*. I had been in the tunnel for more than two hours.

As my phone connected to a signal, a news alert popped up on my screen. There had been an explosion at a church in Brooklyn. I tapped the alert for more information, and then brought a fist to my mouth to hold back a sob. It was Sister Helen's church, the one I had just escaped from. She had sacrificed herself for me.

As that reality sank in, so too did the leering face of the man who had killed her. Satan. The Devil.

I shuddered and, for the millionth time that day, buried the overwhelming realization that I had encountered the fallen angel who had once waged war on Heaven and brought evil into this world. I'd have to deal with it but not now. I wasn't safe yet. And safety had to be my priority. I owed it to Sister Helen and the Sacrarium. I owed it to the holy bloodline, the remaining descendant of Jesus and Mary

Magdalene, whom the Sacrarium had sworn to protect throughout time. Whether I had taken my oath yet or not didn't matter; the responsibility now fell to me as one of the few Sacrarium members left.

I gave myself a moment to take in my condition. My hair was limp and damp. My shoes were dirty and soaked through. My legs were cut and scraped in places. I had no idea what my face looked like, but I could tell my cheeks were puffy from all the shed tears. My fingernails were raw and bleeding, and I still had half-moon indents on my wrist from Sister Helen's grip.

The thought of her again made me remember the letter she had given me, as well as her instructions.

Find Jordan.

How was I supposed to do that when he was on his mission trip in Africa?

So I did the next best thing I could think of. I unlocked my cell phone and called Martha.

As far as I knew, I was the only one who actually knew about Sister Helen's real sister. While it wasn't a secret, I knew Sister Helen didn't like others knowing about her personal life, so I had never shared the information with Jordan. I'd figured if he needed to know, Sister Helen would tell him herself. And to be honest, I had met Martha by accident when I had broken my arm during a blizzard and she was the only nurse nearby who was available to help.

Martha had been retired from her profession for a few years, but once I had entered high school—and my Sacrarium training—Sister Helen had given me a phone number for Martha in case of an emergency. And this moment was definitely that. I just hoped the phone number was still valid.

When she answered, I told her everything until the call went silent.

Then Jordan's voice filled my ears. I was shocked and relieved all at the same time. "Jordan! What are you doing there?"

"Well, you're actually calling my house…and Martha's my housekeeper." He sighed. "It's a long story." Then there was a brief pause. "What's going on?" he asked.

Unfortunately, I had to tell him that Sister Helen was gone.

5 JORDAN

ITHACA, NEW YORK, 6:30 PM, PRESENT DAY

"Where are you?" I asked Sophia through the phone as the shock set in. She'd been my best friend growing up at the orphanage, and I felt like she was practically my sister. We hadn't talked since that fateful day when she had taken a train to Harvard and I had been stalked in the subway by Satan's Six, all because Sister Helen had given me a backpack with two celestial items locked inside and told me to deliver them to a particular New York City address.

Little did I know she was sending me to Archangel Gabriel. Little did I know how much my life would change from that day on. Not only traveling around the world with Gabriel to collect the other archangels and evading the Fallen at all costs, but also learning about my parents. How they were friends of Sister Helen's, most likely Sacrarium members, too. That my father had died by accident before I was born—his death certificate hadn't given more details than that—and my mother had passed away shortly after giving birth to me. The fact that they had left me enough money to go to college and keep me financially stable for the rest of my life.

Now *both* Sophia and I were caught in the crossfire between Heaven and Hell.

Except her role was even more vital than mine.

Was she aware of that?

"Sophia?" I prodded after a moment.

There was silence on the other end as if she was taking in her surroundings. "Not sure exactly, but I'm near the Brooklyn Bridge."

"Okay. Where are you staying?"

"Dafne's parents let me stay at their condo."

"Go back there immediately. Text me the address, and I'll be there as fast as I can."

"Jordan, wait!"

"What?" I asked, ready to hang up and jump in the car.

"There's more to the story than what the news is reporting. I know it wasn't a gas leak because I was there. I was there with her when Satan came. She made me go through some underground tunnel to escape. She made me leave her!" Sophia broke down in sobs.

I froze, overcome with sadness for Sister Helen and taken aback by how close Satan had been to taking away Sophia, too. "Are you hurt?" I asked, struggling to prevent my grief from consuming me. Sister Helen had been everything to me—family, mentor, protector—even the chaser of nightmares since she had been the only one who could keep them at bay when I was a kid.

"Not really. Just a few scrapes."

"Was he alone?" I asked next.

"Yes, other than the hound he had with him."

"A hound?" I repeated.

"A hellhound," Michael supplied, staring at me. Apparently, he was listening to our conversation with his celestial super hearing. "We need to leave. Now. Before the hound finds her. She can't go to the condo. It'll track her scent there right away since it's a strong trail. She has to go somewhere else. It'll take the hound some time to find a fresh lead."

"Sophia, don't go to the condo," I told her. "Go to the safehouse. I'm on my way."

The safehouse was an abandoned warehouse we'd discovered one afternoon when we'd gotten separated from our school group. It was the only place we'd had outside of school and the orphanage, but it was ours and only ours. We didn't have to share it like everything else.

I hung up, and the angels were already mobilizing. They decided Chamuel, Jophiel, and Zadkiel would stay behind with Martha, who was in no condition to be alone, while Michael flew ahead to locate Sophia and ensure she was safe. Everyone else—Gabriel, Uriel, and Raphael—loaded up in the van.

"When you find her," I said to Michael, "don't approach her. Just protect her from a distance. She doesn't know who you are and probably won't trust any unfamiliar faces right now."

"Understood." Then, right before my eyes, he spread his wings and launched into the air.

I guess we were getting comfortable around each other.

I hauled myself into the back seat of the van, and Gabriel took off down the driveway.

"Sister Helen had a safehouse for you all?" Raphael asked.

I shook my head and explained what the safehouse really was and how important it had been to us. Raphael nodded in understanding.

I sat back in my seat, adrenaline pumping through my veins. There was no way to relax during the three-hour ride from my house in Ithaca to the city when I knew Sophia was in danger. At least it gave me the opportunity to prepare myself for a fight, because it seemed our first battle was imminent.

6 SATAN

New York City, Present Day

It didn't take long to locate Simon Price. When I was in the vicinity of Fifth Avenue and Eighty-Fifth Street, I had come across a local newsstand merchant who happened to know all about the illustrious Mr. Price. Including where he lived, since his apartment building was just across the street from the newsstand. The merchant failed to mention, however, that Mr. Price was the loudest, most obnoxious man to ever grace the Earth.

When I rang Mr. Price's door, he immediately opened it and yelled, "You're late so don't expect a tip."

He obviously was expecting a food delivery. Yet, instead of a hot meal, he received a nice punch in the face.

"Oh my god!" he yelled. "You broke my nose!"

Clearly, since Mr. Price was bleeding all over himself and the floor.

"Oh my god! Oh my god! Help!" he continued to shout.

Hence how I found out he was loud and obnoxious.

I slammed the apartment door shut. "Get up," I said.

He moaned and whined some more. "What's your problem, asshole? This is my house. Get out or I'll call the police!"

"Get up," I repeated, "before I do something you'll regret."

He stood but only pissed me off more when he said, "I don't care what you'll do. Get out!" He reached out and shoved me in the chest. His effort didn't even rock my feet.

I pulled out a pocketknife from my pants pocket.

Mr. Price's eyes widened in fear. Rather than stab him, though, I strolled over to the painting hanging on his wall and sliced it right down the middle.

"No!" he shouted. "What have you done?"

"Sit down."

He hesitated.

I picked up the fancy vase on the table below the painting. "You want this to go, too?"

"All right! All right!" Mr. Price conceded and sat down on a stool along the kitchen counter.

I approached him, pulled the stool he was sitting in away from the counter, and brought it out into the center of the floor between the living room and kitchen.

"What do you want? Money? I can give you money! Just ask!"

There was a knock at the door.

Mr. Price shouted, "Help! Help!"

I smirked. He thought the delivery guy was on the other side of the door, yet what awaited him was far worse.

"Come in!" I yelled.

The door swung open, and the Six walked through.

Beelzebub was carrying a pizza box. "Found the guy with the pizza outside. Thought we'd bring it up for him. We're not ones to eat, but you have some strange tastes, fella. Pineapple and pizza is a horrible combination."

Mr. Price's face fell.

Beelzebub set the box on the counter, and Leviathan closed the door.

"Where's Lucifer?" I asked.

"Still conversing with the Nephilim," Mammon said.

"If you ask me," Asmodeus chimed in, "he's doing far more than conversing."

"What's that supposed to mean?" Belphegor asked, plopping down on the couch and turning on the TV.

"Have you seen those Nephilim women who run the operation? Jazema and Penelope? I'd want to spend as much time as I could with them. They're gorgeous."

"Asmodeus," I barked.

"What?" he complained. "I'm just stating the truth." He joined Belphegor by sitting down in a rather fancy lounge chair.

"He has a point," Leviathan said to me in a hushed tone so the others wouldn't hear.

"About what?"

"I think we need to watch Lucifer's behavior. He enjoys his visits with the Nephilim too much. They could be putting ideas in his head," Leviathan warned.

First the nun and now Leviathan? Everyone was questioning Lucifer's motives. Should I, too?

"Is anyone going to tell me what's going on here?" Mr. Price demanded.

I brought my attention back to the man. "Yes, Mr. Price, I will. You see, Beelzebub here is going to ransack the place to find something you have that I dearly want." The fallen angel cracked his knuckles and strode off to the man's bedroom. "Meanwhile, Mammon here is going to make you submit to my will." The other angel smirked and flicked out a knife.

"Wait!" Mr. Price said. "I'll give you what you want! Just ask!"

I drew closer to the man. "I know you'll give me what I want, Mr. Price. But I can see in your eyes that you're an untrustworthy bastard who'll rat on me the moment I leave, so to avoid that, we need to bend you to my will."

He looked stunned.

"Mammon," I said, stepping away from the stool, "begin."

Mammon advanced on the man. Without any bonds, Mr. Price tried jumping out of his seat, but Leviathan grabbed him by the throat. "I suggest you cooperate. The sooner you do, the sooner this will be over."

Leviathan's sheer grip brought the man back onto the stool, but the fallen angel didn't let go. Mammon drew Mr. Price's shirt away from his collar and slowly traced the knife's blade along his collarbone. Mr. Price grimaced but didn't cry out.

Mammon sheathed his weapon and stepped aside. Leviathan unfurled his hand.

Mr. Price sat calmly on the stool. "That's it? You wanted to cut me? What the hell type of criminals are you?"

I hopped up to sit on the counter. "Exactly that. The hellish ones."

Leviathan stood with arms crossed, watching Mr. Price intently. "It's started, but it may take some time," he told me.

Mr. Price glanced down, trying to get a look at his collar. "What's started?"

Small, black tendrils had begun to branch out from the wound, a telltale sign of a dark matter infection.

"That's fine. We have nothing but time," I said.

"What are you doing to me?" Mr. Price asked.

Mammon appeared again, this time with some dish towels to bind the man's wrists.

"We're turning you into a dark being," I enlightened him.

"A what?"

"A half-human, half-demonic creature who happily bends to Satan's will," Leviathan explained. Grinning cruelly, he added, "You'll love it."

Mr. Price's face contorted, and he struggled against his bonds. "I don't want to be possessed by a demon, you freak Satan worshippers!"

I lay back flat on the counter. If only he knew the half of it! But his simple human mind would never fathom it. Who needed worshippers when I had hounds, demons, and faithful fallen angels?

Are they faithful? Do you trust them?

I mulled the questions over in my mind.

Unfortunately, I was reminded once again how loud and obnoxious Mr. Price was as he complained incessantly about letting his pizza go to waste. Hopefully, he'd be more tolerable once his soul darkened.

7 SOPHIA

New York City, Present Day

I slid my phone back into my purse and wiped the tears from my eyes once more. It hurt so much to tell Martha and Jordan the news. I still couldn't believe it. But the shock and pain had to wait. I needed to get to the safehouse.

Scanning my surroundings, I spotted a subway station about a block away. Before I stepped forward on the sidewalk to head in that direction, I stopped. It felt as if someone, or something, was watching me.

My eyes darted over every person, every building, every car. Nothing seemed unusual. Then I spotted her. A girl across the street with brown skin, raven-black hair, and thick eyebrows was looking directly at me. She seemed about my age, perhaps a year younger.

I glanced down. It made sense why she was staring. I was disheveled, wet, and dirty. Certainly a sight for wandering eyes, especially since she looked much prettier and more put together than I did.

The girl kept watching me. In fact, it seemed as though she was challenging me with her gaze.

I shook off her aggressive glare and advanced toward the subway.

After a quick trip through the underground tunnels, I surfaced near the Brooklyn Navy Yard. My knees protested as I ascended from the subway. I was probably more hurt than I'd realized, but it didn't matter. Not until I made it to the safehouse.

The safehouse was an old, abandoned warehouse near the navy yard. Jordan and I had discovered it in fifth grade when our school had taken us on a field trip to the Brooklyn Historical Society and we had gotten separated from the group. Jordan had tripped over his untied shoelace, and our teacher hadn't noticed we had stopped. We'd tried finding her once Jordan fixed his shoe, but we were only ten-year-olds and had no sense of direction.

We had stumbled upon the old warehouse, and it had immediately become our sanctuary. It wasn't large, just two floors, but it had a beautiful view of the river and the bridges. We'd spent the whole morning there just talking and enjoying the view until our stomachs had started to growl. We had headed down to the street only to run into two police officers who had been canvassing the area to find us.

Sister Helen had been worried, but once we had been rescued, her worry had turned to fury. Naturally, we had been grounded and had to do extra chores around the orphanage. But we hadn't cared. We had found our safehouse, our home away from home. We had returned to the safehouse weekly for about a year, until we entered middle school and I got swept up in clubs and other extracurricular activities.

Our meetings had always taken place during the daylight, usually after school. We'd kept waiting for someone to claim the warehouse for storage or renovate it into lofts. But no one ever had. Now, with the area and the building shrouded in early-evening darkness, it looked creepy and eerie.

Maybe it had always been that way, and I had just grown old and wise enough to finally notice.

Sighing, I approached the front door, the one we had always used to enter the building, but in the many years since, someone had bolted it shut. Probably to keep out prying kids.

I contemplated calling Jordan back to tell him to meet me somewhere else, but I was running out of daylight and knew that darkness would only bring out more predators than the ones already chasing me. So I went down the side alley to the fire escape. I paused briefly, as my body did not want to perform any more acrobatics today, before jumping into the air and grabbing hold of the ladder. I pulled myself up, rung by rung, until I was safely on the scaffold.

When I reached the second-story window, I tried unsuccessfully to push it open. Maybe someone owned the building now and had locked it up good and tight, but peering through the window, it didn't look like it was occupied.

I leaned my head against the window frame. Exhaustion, pain, and adrenaline were all pumping through my body. I desperately wanted to stop moving, and I succumbed to my inner instincts and did the only thing I could think of: I pulled off my sweater, wrapped it around my hand, and punched my fist through the windowpane. The glass shattered, and shards fell to the ground.

I extracted my fist and used my foot to clear away the rest of the glass. Then I climbed inside and eased myself down to the floor. Closing my eyes, I rested my back along the wall. Finally, I could stop moving.

"Sophia?"

My eyes flashed open. "Dane!"

I remained frozen on the floor, stunned to see Jordan's former roommate from the orphanage. Jordan and I never shared the warehouse with him—it was no secret that the two of them could barely tolerate each other—but I supposed it would be arrogant to think we were the only ones who knew about it.

I narrowed my eyes. "How did you know about this place?"

"I followed you," he supplied. "Yeah, yeah, I know it's creepy. But I was curious about what you and Jordan were up to when you didn't come back to the orphanage after school. I guess I kept waiting for you to invite me to join you, but you never did."

We hadn't invited him on purpose. Well, Jordan hadn't invited him on purpose. I would have been open to the idea. But looking back, maybe I should have made more of an effort.

"Your hand's bleeding," he said, changing the subject.

I didn't glance down. Instead, I got to my feet and closed the distance between us in seconds, then enveloped him in a hug. It was so good to see a familiar face, to not be alone, that I didn't care it was Dane.

At first, his whole body was stiff, but then he awkwardly brought his arms around me to return the gesture. I closed my eyes, relishing in the comfort of his presence and the warmth of his skin, the hard muscles beneath my arms.

That's when I realized he had no shirt on.

I stepped back in a flash. "Why are you not wearing a shirt?"

He smirked. "Why did you break my window?"

I fumbled with my words, not sure what to say. "I…I…I didn't have a place to go so I came here."

His smile vanished, and a look of understanding filled his eyes. "I get it."

Glancing around the room, I saw clothes and blankets scattered around. "So you live here?"

He nodded.

"What happened to your apartment? Your job?"

He sighed. "It's a long story."

I shrugged. "Well, I have time."

"What happened to Harvard?" he countered.

"I'm still at Harvard, about to finish up my freshman year. I love my classes, and all that hard work in high school paid off since it helped me get a full-ride scholarship. I have a roommate named Dafne and we get along great. That's about it. Now you."

He gestured for me to sit so I sat down on the floor in the middle of the room and faced the large bay window, the one with the beautiful view.

A blanket suddenly appeared around my shoulders, and Dane sat down next to me on the floor—this time with a shirt on.

"I got paint on it," he said, reading my thoughts as he rummaged through a first aid kit.

"You paint now?" It was getting dark inside the warehouse so it was hard to see any of his supplies.

"Yeah, it's hard not to when you have a view like this."

I glanced out the window at the city. The water, the buildings, the bridges—the lights were beginning to illuminate everything.

"Can I see your hand?" he asked.

I eased it out from under the blanket and held it out to him. "I'm surprised you have a first aid kit."

He huffed out an awkward laugh. "Me too. But I learned the hard way it's better to have one than not."

"Are you ever going to tell me what happened?" I asked.

"Are you?" he challenged, inspecting my hand.

My fingers were caked in dried blood from my struggle in the tunnel, and my knuckles were cut up from the broken glass. I guessed my sweater had been too thin to successfully shield my skin.

"Not really," I said. "I'd rather you talk about painting."

He took out an antiseptic wipe and brushed it over my hand. I flinched as it stung.

"Sorry."

"It's okay." I paused. "Please tell me," I said, since he refused to speak.

He forced a smile. "The job I had, the one at the tattoo shop, was a shit show."

"Language," I teased him.

He rolled his eyes. "They wouldn't let me do anything other than clean the shop and manage the phones. I get that I had to learn how to use the tattoo gun, but they wouldn't teach me. They didn't even let me draw for them. But that's not the worst of it."

"What was?" I asked.

"They wouldn't pay me!"

"At all? Even for the cleaning and the phones?"

"No, they were bastards. I can't believe I let them talk me into working for them. I mean, we never talked about pay, but I thought they were my friends and would treat me right. Anyway, since I wasn't getting paid, I couldn't afford my rent and my landlord kicked me out. I didn't have any money for a new place so I came here. I had nowhere else to go, either." He wrapped a gauze bandage around my knuckles and then packed up the first aid kit. "That should help for now," he told me.

"Thanks. So how did you get those?" I pointed at the tattoos covering his arms.

He sighed. "I traded for them. Working at the shop at least afforded me the opportunity to meet some other artists so I let them tattoo me in exchange for teaching me how to tattoo since my so-called friends wouldn't bother."

"You let people just tattoo whatever they wanted on you?"

"No! Not just anything. They all mean something. They're things I wanted."

"All right." I still didn't like the idea. "So now you know how to tattoo?"

"Yeah, but I don't have any credentials or a portfolio of work. So I decided to change tracks. Venture into some other artistic avenues."

"Like painting," I guessed.

"Yeah." He shrugged. "For now, I've been working at the local boxing gym around the corner. The pay is decent, and I'm trying to save up for school."

My head whipped around. "You want to go to school?" I was shocked. Dane had always called me a sucker for my higher learning aspirations.

He smirked and shook his head. "I know it's sounds ridiculous, but yes, I want to go to art school."

I touched his arm. "That's not ridiculous, Dane. I'm really happy you're thinking about it."

"Thanks."

"What brought you to a boxing gym, though? That seems random."

He crossed his arms. "That was the part I was trying to avoid sharing."

I narrowed my eyes at him. "What did you do?"

"The guys at the tattoo shop made me close the store every night by myself and I was really upset with them, so one night I stole some money and left. I wasn't planning to go back."

"But…?" I anticipated.

"But," he continued, "they found me. Pretty much mugged me and beat the crap out of me."

My jaw dropped slightly. "What? Were you okay?"

"Not really. One of them stabbed me with a knife. To be honest, I thought I was going to die because they left me there to bleed out."

My eyes were wide in shock. I didn't know what to say.

"Someone must have found me, but all I remember is waking up in the hospital. Every time I think about it, the whole thing seems unreal, but I always have this reminder," he said, lifting up his shirt to show me a jagged scar on his abdomen. "That's how I learned a first aid kit comes in handy. Changing the bandages on this thing was terrible.

"Anyway, I had never felt so vulnerable before, and I realized I didn't really know how to defend myself. I always put on this tough-guy act, but I couldn't follow through with it. So I found the gym. Asked if I could work there in exchange for using the equipment. The owner agreed. He's a really nice guy. He actually pays me now and still lets me use the gym. I also met this cool guy there…kinda like a mentor. He let me tattoo him in exchange for training me and teaching me some defensive moves."

So that's where the muscles came from.

Surprised by the thought, I forced it out of my head. "I'm glad everything worked out. You should be more careful, though."

"I know. I've changed a lot since the last time you saw me."

I glanced at him and found him looking back at me. "I like this Dane. It reminds me of the good times we shared as kids. It's a shame you and Jordan never got along. We all could have hung out more."

At the mention of Jordan, he turned away.

"What happened between the two of you?" I asked. "It never made sense that you just hated him all of a sudden."

"I never hated Jordan," he was quick to say.

"Really? Because you didn't act that way."

"I don't want to talk about it. It's too personal."

I shook my head in frustration. "You say it's too personal, and he says it's not his story to tell."

"Because it's not," Dane said. "I was going through a lot when we were kids. Had a lot of insecurities. I took it out on Jordan to make me feel better. He always had nothing to worry about. Everything was handed to him, and he was always doted on. I figured being bullied would be the one thing that stood in his way of having a perfect life. But I realize now what I did to him only made me a shitty person, especially after what he did for me." He absentmindedly fiddled with a loose thread on his jeans.

What did Jordan do for him?

I wanted to know, but I could tell he didn't want to talk about it anymore. He'd already told me more than he'd initially wanted to. "What brought about this change?" I asked instead.

"Sister Helen."

My head whipped around, my gaze clearly questioning when it met his because he was quick to explain.

"She was there when I woke up in the hospital after being stabbed. I never updated my emergency contact information so they called her. We had a real heart-to-heart. She told me I had to get my act together, that she knew the person I was pretending to be wasn't the real me. I was defensive at first, but she was right."

I nodded and tried to swallow the lump in my throat.

She's gone. You need to tell him she's gone.

But the words wouldn't come.

"She didn't know who found me, either," he went on. "I wanted to know so I could thank them, but it remains a mystery."

I smiled. "That is a very Jordan thing to do."

He laughed. "Yeah, I've been trying to steer my moral compass in a direction he would approve of."

"He's coming here, by the way," I told him. "To get me."

Now it was his turn to whip his head around. "Really?"

"I'm sure he'll be glad to see you."

He looked less sure.

"Where is this painting you've been working on?" I asked, trying to take his mind off Jordan. "I'd love to see it."

He stood up and headed for the corner of the room. I followed. It was hard to see since there was no electricity and the sun was setting outside, but I could see the easel set up in the corner. It wasn't until I moved closer to the canvas that I gasped. The painting was absolutely beautiful—the colors, the brushstrokes, the details. It truly captured the view before me in paint.

"Dane, this is amazing," I said, peering even closer.

He shrugged. "It's a good attempt."

I stared at him. "This is not a good attempt. This is a masterpiece. Believe me. I studied enough art this past year to know." Turning back to the painting, I admired it some more.

"You study art?" he asked.

I nodded. "Art history and conservation. That's my major."

"Wow, I never knew that," he said.

His tone had changed so I tore my gaze away from the painting to set it on him. He was looking at me again, but I couldn't tell what he was feeling. Admiration? Friendship? An artistic connection?

Or perhaps something more?

It was as if the thought had been whispered in my ear. This was ridiculous. I was putting too many expectations on the meaning of his gaze. *This is Dane,* I reminded myself. *Mean, defiant Dane.*

Still…

Even if I wasn't reading too much into his gaze, did I want it to be true? Did I want Dane to feel something for me? Did *I* want to feel something?

I could admit that I'd had a crush on him when we were younger, but it had been an innocent one, a passing one. Every girl had been crushing on him in grade school. He was the only cute guy in our class. But ever since the rift between him and Jordan, I hadn't given him much thought.

Jordan was my brother. Dane was his bully, even though he had been relatively friendly toward me. I couldn't choose. It would have only hurt Jordan if I had.

Didn't you choose, though? Jordan over Dane?

Suddenly, I realized I *had* picked sides. I *had* chosen between them. No wonder Dane had retaliated at the world. He had felt overlooked, maybe still did.

I turned away and moved past him, back to the middle of the room. I took my place on the floor again and resigned myself to staying right there and waiting for Jordan. I'd lost Sister Helen, nearly been killed myself, and had come face-to-face with Satan. On top of that, I might still have a hellhound on my trail. I couldn't handle deep right now; I'd fall apart.

As if he could sense the turmoil raging inside me, Dane appeared next to me and extended a deck of cards. "You want to play while we wait?"

I smiled. "Of course."

He started dealing them out for a game of War.

"Do you remember the day I came to the orphanage?" I asked him.

He grinned. "Yeah. You were all alone in that holding room."

I rolled my eyes. "It wasn't a holding room! It was a playroom."

"No, it was more like a waiting room with toys. A waiting room where your fate got decided for you."

"You make it sound so harsh," I chided.

"Because it was!"

"*Anyway*... I remember that day because I was all alone and really upset and you came in to cheer me up by playing a game of War."

"And we played a few rounds until we were laughing so loudly that the nuns came in and shooed me away."

"Yes, but you let me keep the deck."

"I did."

"Which I came to learn was a nice gesture coming from you since I've never seen you without a deck of cards."

He smiled and rubbed at one of the tattoos on his arm. It featured symbols from each suit in a deck of cards. "What happened after I left that day?" he asked.

"I played Solitaire until Jordan came in and persuaded me to play UNO instead."

"And the nuns didn't kick him out?"

"No."

He shook his head. "Figures. He was always their favorite."

"That's not true. You were just a mischievous hellion."

A huge laugh escaped from his mouth, one I hadn't heard in ages. Then he grew serious, donning a poker face. "You ready to play?"

After years of practice burying my feelings, I buried the horror of the day in the same deep place I hid my feelings about my mother's abandonment. There would be time to process everything later. For now, I grinned, more grateful for the mundane distraction than I could express.

"You bet. Just don't be upset when I beat you," I said, whipping down my first card.

8 JORDAN

New York City, Present Day

Gabriel could hardly stop the van before I was jumping out onto the sidewalk. Michael flew down from his perch on the roof and said, "All clear. No Satan. No hound."

Without hesitation, I approached the door to the safehouse, only to find it padlocked. Uriel was right behind me, pushing me aside and kicking down the door.

I raced through the doorway and up the steps, not bothering to look over my shoulder at the angels. I knew they'd be forming a protective circle around the entrance and preparing for a possible attack. All that mattered right now was Sophia. I had to find her. I had to keep her safe.

When I reached the top of the stairs and barged into the wide-open warehouse, I hadn't expected to find her playing cards with Dane. I stopped short.

"Jordan!" she shouted, throwing off a blanket and getting up from the floor. She crossed the distance between us in seconds to give me a hug.

I returned it, then quickly pulled away to look at her. She was hurt. Not majorly, but she was still hurt. "We need to leave. Now," I told her. Then I looked at Dane. "And you're coming with us."

He stood up. "What do you mean I'm coming with you?"

"You're not safe here," I said without explanation.

His brow furrowed. "Safe from what?"

I ignored him. "How much did you tell him?" I asked Sophia.

She looked at her feet. "Nothing."

"How much did she tell me about what?" Dane demanded.

I approached him. "There's no time to explain everything. Will you just trust me?"

He gave me a once-over, from my set jaw to the wild and determined look in my eye. There was only one other time he had ever seen me this way. And it's one we never talked about anymore, not that we really talked at all anymore.

Dane nodded. "All right." He hurried to pack up his things around the room.

My gaze landed on the view outside the bay window. It hadn't even been a full year since I was chased by Satan's Six through New York, yet here I was in fight-or-flight mode again. Except this time, I wasn't worried about myself. I was worried about protecting the ones I loved. I had already lost Sister Helen. I was not about to lose my friends, either, despite my rocky history with Dane. We had grown up together, so, in a way, we were family.

Dane swung his bag over his shoulder, ready to leave. Sophia, however, was delaying us, lugging a gigantic canvas from the corner of the room.

It was a beautiful painting of the view outside the bay window. But it didn't make sense why she wanted it. "What are you doing?" I asked her.

"Sophia, just leave it," Dane said.

"No, I can't. It means a lot to me," she confessed.

She had always been sentimental like that. "All right," I said. "Grab it and let's go."

Sophia went down the stairs first with the painting, Dane close behind as he assisted her. I took one last look at the room. They had left the deck of cards. I swept them up off the floor as a precaution. It seemed hellhounds had a strong sense of smell so there was no reason to leave behind things that would make it easier for them to track us. Then I trudged downstairs, right into an argument.

"Who are these guys?" Dane demanded, gesturing to the angels.

I brushed past him and Sophia, who had an equally defensive look on her face, and opened the van's back door. "Our ride. Load in."

"You know them?" Sophia asked.

"Yes, I met them on my mission trip." I gestured for her to hand me the painting, which I hauled into the van.

Dane kept his bag with him, and the two of them settled in the back seat.

I slammed the back door shut and turned to look at the angels.

"We came for Sophia," Uriel said. "Who's the other guy?"

"He was my roommate at the orphanage. I didn't know he would be here. I made him come with us so the hellhound wouldn't find him."

Michael sighed. "I understand. But I don't like it. We're involving too many people."

"I agree. But I couldn't leave him."

Gabriel placed a hand on my shoulder. "You did the right thing. Now let's leave."

The rest of us piled into the van.

As Gabriel started the car, Dane leaned over and asked, "Where are we going?"

"Somewhere safe," was all I told him.

"Wait, we can't go anywhere until I go back to the condo," Sophia piped up.

"Whatever you left there can be replaced," I countered.

"No, not this." She gave me a meaningful look. "It's Sacrarium business."

My eyes widened. She knew about the Sacrarium?

Well, I suppose she should since she's the bloodline, right?

My stomach sank. Great. I had been tasked with carrying *The Book of Prophecies* and Satan's black onyx sphere, so God only knew what she may have been tasked with carrying.

"What the hell does that mean?" Dane protested.

Sophia placed a hand on his arm. "I'll explain later. I promise."

I could feel Michael's gaze on me, and a quick glance at the rearview mirror confirmed it. I knew the longer we stayed on the streets, the more dangerous it would be, but I couldn't say no. "Where's the condo?"

"Front Street and Peck Slip."

Without a word, Gabriel quickly changed direction and steered us to the condo's location.

"Is anyone staying with you?" Michael asked Sophia.

She shook her head. "No. Dafne's parents only use it when they need to."

Michael was clearly relieved. I didn't blame him. It seemed like all we kept doing was involving more and more people.

When Gabriel pulled up across the street from the condo and parked the car, I leaned forward into the driver's seat. "How do we go about doing this?"

"In and out," Michael said.

"Preferably one trip," Uriel added.

Gabriel gave me a pointed look. "With you staying in the van."

I glanced over my shoulder at Dane and Sophia. They were both staring at our little huddle, and I could tell they were upset with me, their expressions a mix of confusion and worry.

"That might be fine and good, but it looks like we might have company," Raphael cautioned.

My head snapped around to follow his gaze to the open front door of the condo building.

Crap!

Thinking quickly, I said, "Better plan. Me and Sophia go up with three of you as protection while the other stays here with Dane."

They contemplated for a moment, and then Michael gave a curt nod. "Let's move," he commanded.

Gabriel, Michael, and Uriel jumped out of the van. Raphael stayed put to watch Dane.

I met Sophia's eyes. "All right, Sophia, let's go get whatever you need." I turned to Dane. "You stay here with Raphael," I said. "We'll be right back."

Sophia and I exited the van and waited for a signal from the angels. They were already stationed inside the doorway and on watch. Nothing seemed unusual so they motioned us forward.

We entered the lobby. "What floor?" I asked.

"Third," Sophia whispered.

The angels nodded, and we approached the elevator. I pressed the button, and we waited a few seconds before it dinged. The doors opened and out sailed the hellhound, aiming right for Sophia. I pushed her out of the way.

The hound landed gracefully on the floor and was quick to reorient himself, setting his sights on her once again. Before the beast could attack, the angels were on it, Uriel intercepting his advances and deftly fighting him off while Michael and Gabriel guided us toward the stairs.

"What about Uriel?" I asked.

"He can handle it," Michael replied.

The four of us entered the stairwell and climbed them two at a time. When we reached the third floor, Sophia pulled out her key as we ran down the hall. Just as she inserted it in the door, a loud ruckus echoed from the stairs. Michael pushed us into the condo and followed behind, slamming the door shut and leaving Gabriel out in the hall on watch.

Once inside, Sophia and I remained quiet while Michael peered around the condo in the dark.

None of them had ever told me they could see in the dark, but it wouldn't have surprised me if they could.

Sophia reached for the light switch, but Michael stopped her. "We're not alone."

She blanched.

Slowly, he reached behind his back and pulled out a short sword from beneath his jacket.

Sophia, eyes wide, turned to me. "You have a lot of explaining to do."

A lamp clicked on in the living room, and I tensed, expecting to see Satan. Except it wasn't.

"Lucifer," Michael growled.

The fallen angel smirked and beckoned to Michael with a small gesture. That was the only sign he needed. The two launched at each other.

I grabbed Sophia's arm, and we raced past the kitchen toward the bedroom.

9 MICHAEL

New York City, Present Day

The blade of my sword whizzed through the air as I executed swipe after swipe at Lucifer, who simply dodged my attacks. He was playing games, wanting to draw out my moves to find a weak point. But I wouldn't let him. Instead, I stopped swiping and simply cracked him in the head with my fist.

The move was unexpected and certainly caught him off guard, his head flinging backward. He spit blood onto the floor, the smirk erased from his face. "It's about time you used a valiant weapon."

I sheathed my sword. "Blades not good enough for you?"

"No. Guns are better. But since I have none on me, brute force will have to do."

He ran at me, and we smashed into the television unit before tumbling to the floor. Punches met their marks—mine in the face, his in the ribs. The blow winded me, giving him the advantage to stand up and kick me while I was still trying to recover.

His boot met my ribs again, over and over in succession. Before he could do more damage, I grabbed his foot and yanked, slamming him to the ground. We wrestled on the floor, wrecking the living room and breaking everything in sight.

We had each other by the throat when I finally realized how similar we looked. Blond hair. Blue eyes. Similar strength and fighting capability. He had replaced me. My brother had replaced me with a mirror image of me, a mere shell that somewhat resembled me on the outside but was nothing like me on the inside. Lucifer was evil. I could see it in his face, in the murderous look in his eye. I could smell it on him—the scent of fire and ash, of blood.

My face contorted. "What did you do?"

A psychotic smile crossed his face. "What Satan should have done." He let out a soft whistle, and two hounds beat down the door and rushed into the apartment.

Several thoughts ran through my mind at once.

Gabriel must have been holding off the extra hounds in the hallway.

Is he hurt?

How does Lucifer have control of them?

Jordan and Sophia need me!

Distracted, I went flying through the air as Lucifer tossed me across the room. I landed among a set of decorative plants, the large terra-cotta pots smashing under my weight.

Lucifer advanced on me, but not before an arrow came flying through the doorway. One that was slightly off its mark since it merely grazed the fallen angel's arm.

I glanced back to see Uriel standing in the hall, unsteadily aiming his bow with one eye squeezed shut. "What's wrong with you?" I asked.

"I suffered a head injury. Can we please save the chitchat for later?"

He was right. I eased up off the floor to head toward the bedroom to save the kids, but Lucifer came after me first, grabbing my collar and pulling me back. I reached behind me and grabbed his arms, then swung him over me and onto the floor.

The breath hissed out of him as he landed on his back.

"Stay down! You're outnumbered," I urged.

The sword on my back came unsheathed. Turning around, I saw Gabriel had taken hold of the weapon. At first, I was worried he was suffering from the paranoia of a hellhound bite, but instead of using it on me, he smashed the hilt down on Lucifer's temple several times.

While angels couldn't fall unconscious, they could still feel the effects of a concussion, which was what Lucifer should have been feeling now.

Raphael stumbled through the door. "Do you have them? Are they safe?"

The four of us looked at one another and ran down the hall together. Except when we got to the bedroom, no one was there. All that greeted us was the breeze from the open window.

10 JORDAN

New York City, Present Day

As soon as we were inside the bedroom, Sophia grabbed her backpack and threw some clothes in it. Then she pulled out a small cosmetic bag from the front pocket and shoved it in her purse, finally zipping the backpack shut and swinging it over her shoulders.

"That's it?" I yelled.

"You don't understand. It's taken me almost a year—"

Suddenly, a large weight came crashing down on me from behind. I didn't realize there had been a hound hiding in the bathroom until his teeth were snapping in my face. The only thing holding him back was the mere coincidence that his leg had gotten caught in a phone charging cable.

Rolling away from the hound, I righted myself and got to my feet again.

"Are you all right?" Sophia asked, concern in her eyes.

I nodded and grabbed a pillow from the bed, throwing it at the hound. It hit the beast in the head, drawing his attention away from his caught leg. He tore into the pillow, spewing feathers everywhere, and it gave me the opportunity to rush at the distracted hound and push him back into the bathroom. I slammed the door, and several thuds shook the wood from the other side.

"Sophia, grab that chair!"

She stood there frozen, just staring at the door.

"Sophia!" I yelled.

She turned to me, and I realized she must have been reliving the hellhound's attack from this afternoon. "It's going to be okay, but you have to give me that chair."

Sophia glanced at the desk and moved like a robot, picking up the chair and placing it underneath the bathroom doorknob.

I let go and rushed over to the window. "We need to keep moving." I sent up a prayer as I spied a fire escape outside. Unlocking the window, I pushed it open as far as it would go, which wasn't very far since it was meant for emergency purposes only.

Drawing close to my side, Sophia said, "That's not the same hound as the one downstairs."

"What do you mean?"

"There was only one at the church. That one was downstairs in the elevator. But this one is a different color." The sound of splitting wood had her freezing again. She vigorously shook her head. "No! This can't be happening again!"

Clearly, the buried trauma of this afternoon was beginning to surface. "Hey, look at me."

She set her eyes on mine.

"You're going to be fine," I said.

She nodded and squeezed out onto the fire escape, approaching the metal stairs and then starting to descend.

A deafening shock reverberated through the condo, and two hounds suddenly appeared in the doorway. They charged in, just as the one in the bathroom tore through the door.

I climbed through the window after Sophia, easing through the small gap on my back rather than my stomach, but I wasn't fast enough.

One among the three hounds was quicker than the others and immediately snapped at my leg, latching on to my jeans. Thankfully, his bite didn't pierce my skin, but I was still caught within his jaws.

I kicked out with my free leg, tried punching him with my fist, but he wouldn't let go. I grabbed the window frame as he started pulling me back into the room, the other hounds ready and waiting to sink their teeth into me.

Throughout my journey with the angels, I had been caught in a few situations where I couldn't estimate the outcome, but this was by far the worst. Now there was no one to save me, and although I had trained with Michael, he had mainly prepared me for hand-to-hand combat, not to fight a bestial pack of infernal dogs.

The hound that had my jeans in his mouth started shaking his head back and forth, and I began to lose my grip on the window frame. I suddenly heard a hissing sound as someone reached around me from outside and sprayed an aerosol in the hound's face. He cried out and let go of my jeans, tearing a hole in the denim.

I pulled myself through the window as my savior slammed it shut.

Glancing up, I saw Dane standing above me. "What are these things?"

"Hellhounds," I said. We descended the fire escape. "You were supposed to wait in the van."

"I did. Until that Raphael guy left me to help the others. He gave me this canister of holy water and told me to use it if something attacked me. Then Sophia came running to the van saying you were in danger, so I came to rescue you."

"Thanks," I said, jumping off the fire escape and onto the sidewalk. Sophia was there waiting for us.

"I don't know what the hell is going on," Dane said, "but I assume I'll get an explanation?"

I nodded. "We'll tell you everything when we can, but now is not the time."

"Are you all right?" Sophia asked me, her voice weak. "I'm so sorry. I just froze."

"It's okay." I turned back to Dane, who jumped down, too. He handed me the aerosol can and I put it in my pocket.

"Now what?" he asked.

"We wait in the van," I said. The angels were nowhere in sight so I supposed waiting with the doors locked was the best course of action.

"Uh…I don't think that's a good idea," Sophia commented.

"Why not?" I asked.

"That's why." She pointed to the van across the street, which was currently being ransacked by a hound who had broken in through the windshield. He spied us and let out a howl, alerting his pack to their prey.

So I suggested the one thing I knew how to do best. "Run!"

11 SATAN

New York City, Present Day

It had been hours since we'd arrived at Mr. Price's apartment, and my patience was growing thin.

"Mammon!" I yelled from my position in the kitchen.

"What?" he shouted back from the couch, where he had upturned all the cushions to see if anything was hidden beneath.

"Why did you have to cut him so far away from the heart?"

The angel turned to me. "You didn't have a problem with my cut an hour ago."

He was right. I was just trying to pick a fight because I was bored and wanted to move on. Thankfully, Asmodeus had shut Mr. Price up, finding some duct tape and placing a piece over his mouth.

I jumped off the counter and grabbed a magazine from the rack next to the table. Because I clearly had lost interest in him, Mammon returned his attention to the couch.

I flipped through the pointless magazine, then stopped as I felt someone staring at me. "Yes, Belphegor?" I peered over the publication at him.

"Sorry, sir." He averted his gaze.

I glanced back at the pages, but I could still feel him looking at me. "What is it?" I demanded.

"Well...I can't help but notice all the art-related things here."

"Meaning?" I asked.

"The paintings, the fine objects, the proximity to the Met just down the street, that *Smithsonian* magazine you're reading..."

I checked the cover. Sure enough, he was right. Although Belphegor could be lazy and dense sometimes, he certainly had his moments of perceptiveness.

"Your point?" I set down the magazine.

He shrugged. "Maybe we should be asking Mr. Price some questions. Like what he does for a living."

"That's the plan, Belphegor, but not before he turns. Anything he says could easily be a lie without him under my sway." I paused. "Good observations, though. They may come in handy."

"Of course, sir." Belphegor nodded and returned to his seat on the couch.

I pondered his words. If Mr. Price had an art background, it might make sense that he was able to locate the sphere. Such an object would be fascinating to humans, certainly if they discovered it in a remote or obscure location.

But would he have it here? Perhaps not, but he could still give me information.

"Sir," Leviathan cut in. "I think we have a problem."

I pulled my attention away from my thoughts and looked at Leviathan. He pointed at the TV across the room. One of them had put on the news. Moving away from the counter, I approached the couch to get a better look. The headline across the screen read PECK SLIP

RAVAGED BY RABID DOGS. As I peered closer, it was easy to tell that those were no rabid dogs. They were my hellhounds.

The red blaze ignited inside. What I had suspected was true. Even my stupid dogs weren't taking my orders.

Beelzebub came in from the bedroom puffing on a cigar. He pulled it out of his mouth and said, "Look what I found. A Met museum ID card. Apparently, Mr. Price is the curator of the Department of Ancient Art and Antiquities."

I grabbed a bottle of alcohol off the wet bar and threw it at him.

He dodged it, and it shattered against the wall. "All right, then. Didn't mean to upset you."

"All of you just be quiet!" I yelled.

They obliged.

"Did you do this?" I asked Leviathan.

"The hellhounds? No."

I paused to think the matter over.

"You didn't send the hounds?" Leviathan asked.

"No. I sent one hound after one girl. That was it."

"What command did you give the hound?" he asked.

"Why should that matter?"

"Please, just tell me."

"I told the beast to find the girl and come back when he did." I froze. "The damn dog never showed up."

"Exactly what I feared," Leviathan said, rubbing his brow. "The hellhounds have been acting strangely, not following orders. I trained them to follow you and you alone."

I sighed. "All right, but that doesn't explain who sent more."

"It might," Leviathan disagreed. "If someone else has learned to command them, it would be very easy to summon a whole pack."

My jaw tightened. There was only one possible person it could be. *Lucifer.*

If the hounds weren't listening to my commands because of the amulet, that meant they were taking orders from someone else, someone with power. And who better to turn to than my second-in-command?

Slamming my fist into the wall, I yelled, "Damn him!"

They all stared at my outburst.

I stepped over to Mr. Price, who lifted his head from his chest and stared at me with a weak gaze. His hair was soaked through with sweat, and his wrists were a bright shade of red as he had been struggling against his bonds for the past few hours.

I ripped the duct tape from his mouth.

"What do you want from me?" he whispered.

I drew close to him and pulled back his head by his hair. Looking into his eyes, I knew we didn't need to wait much longer. The irises were almost entirely black. I let go, and his head dropped.

"How does the wound look?" I asked Leviathan, who had followed me.

He approached Mr. Price and pulled back the collar of his shirt. The small cut was festering near the man's collarbone, black lines escaping from the wound and traveling down his chest.

"We're getting close. Only a few more minutes. Five at the most, I'd guess. He's giving in, and considering how drenched he is, the fever must be close to subsiding."

"Please let me go," Mr. Price begged.

I knelt in front of him. "Why don't you let go instead? It'll make this much easier. End your suffering. You see, once the dark matter completely consumes you, you'll have no choice but to do what I want."

Leviathan appeared at his left side and whispered in his ear. "Give in. Let the darkness take over."

Mr. Price suddenly gasped. The black lines along his neck slowly receded as the dark matter running through his bloodstream overwhelmed his heart.

"Look at me," I commanded.

Mr. Price set his gaze on me. His eyes had returned to their natural blue color, and his veins were normal once again; however, inside, his heart was black.

The process was complete. Mr. Price was now a dark being completely under my control.

I stood up, glanced at Asmodeus, and demanded, "Cut his bonds."

"Finally," Asmodeus huffed. He drew a dagger from the inner pocket of his jacket. Approaching Mr. Price, he sliced through the dish towels around his wrists and released the man.

"Mr. Price," I said, setting my attention on him. "Do you truly work at the Met?"

He nodded. "Yes."

"Interesting. Have you recently acquired any fascinating objects?"

"You'll have to be more specific. I've encountered several fascinating objects over the past few weeks. We're opening a new exhibit."

I glared at him. "Fine. Have you recently acquired a sphere?"

His eyes lit up. "Of course. You should see it. It's absolutely mesmerizing."

My eyes narrowed. A strange look had entered his eyes when he talked about the sphere. He almost seemed…hypnotized.

Shaking off his odd reaction, I asked, "Mr. Price, can you get me the sphere?"

He laughed. "Certainly not. It's been catalogued in the collection. We're centering our whole new exhibit around it. If I gave it to you, it would cost me my job."

I grinned cruelly. "Well, then, maybe it's time you start looking for a new one. I want that sphere. And you're going to get it for me."

Mr. Price was nervous. "H-how?"

I leaned over and whispered in his ear. "You're going to steal it."

Before I could say anything else, the apartment door opened and Lucifer stumbled through. He was out of breath, beaten up, and unsteady. I stood up. "Lucifer, I see you have graced us with your presence. Where have you been?"

"More importantly, how did you find us?" Leviathan asked, his eyes full of suspicion.

Lucifer answered my question first. "You sent me to set up a meeting with the Nephilim and told me not to return until I did."

"It's taken you six months to do that? And it's left you this…flustered?" I raised an eyebrow at him.

He ignored the second part of my question and placed a hand on his forehead. "Jazema isn't too happy with you. She refused every time I asked. I had to coax her into agreeing."

"And why exactly is she mad at me?" I asked.

"She's mad," Lucifer continued, "because she's tired of your antics. First you want an alliance with her, then you don't, then you do… You're constantly changing the terms of your agreement, only to settle on the exact same thing. She feels offended and betrayed so she wanted to give you a taste of your own medicine, drawing this out for as long as possible."

Exasperated, I said, "Could she be any more childish?"

Lucifer shrugged. "There's no need to dwell on it. She's agreed to finally meet."

"When?" I asked.

"Tomorrow at 11:00 AM at the Empire State Building."

"Good. Now answer Leviathan's question. How did you find us?"

"Really? Can't you see I need a minute?"

I glared at him.

"Fine," he ground out. "Asmodeus told me where you'd be."

"Oh, did he?" I turned and set my sights on him. "And how did you know where Lucifer would be, considering Jazema keeps her whereabouts secret?" I glanced at Lucifer. "Or did you think I would forget?"

"What's with all the questions?" Lucifer demanded. "Besides, there are such things as cell phones. He simply called and told me."

He had never been this defensive before, this brazen before. If anyone knew the early signs of change and mutiny, it was me.

Is this how He felt? Doubtful of my loyalty so He got rid of me before I became a problem?

Lucifer was my most efficient fallen angel. I told him everything so he could manage things for me. I didn't want or need to deal with the insignificant problems, especially when he could do that for me. I had been banished from Heaven for asking questions and vowed I wouldn't hold those in Hell to ignorance the way He had. I was more powerful than Lucifer. A second-in-command was just that: inferior to the first in command. His question shouldn't bother me.

Yet, it did. It challenged the foundation on which I had built my kingdom. In fact, all his behavior bothered me. The missing time. The hounds. The rebelliousness.

So I decided to test him. "If you have a phone, then you must have seen the news. The hounds are running rampant. Why shouldn't I question you when things clearly aren't as they should be?"

He shrugged. "What do the hounds have to do with me? If they're anyone's problem, they're Leviathan's."

"Deflecting blame will get you nowhere," I warned. He opened his mouth in protest. "But no need for more explanations." I had gotten what I wanted—a sign of disloyalty. "I believe we're done here." I turned to Mr. Price. "We'll be in touch."

The man winced, clearly not looking forward to it.

"Leviathan, Beelzebub, you're coming with us tomorrow. The rest of you, return to Hell."

Everyone began to shuffle out. Leviathan stopped me. "Are you satisfied with Lucifer's explanations?"

"Of course not. But that won't stop me from moving forward." In fact, his betrayal would only make me demand more, for who knew how deep his deceit had spread.

12 JORDAN

New York City, Present Day

Our feet pounded the pavement as we ran as hard as we could away from the pack of hounds chasing us. Outrunning the fallen hadn't been easy, so I knew this wasn't going to be, either. The hardest part was that I wasn't alone this time.

Sophia, Dane, and I all tried to match one another's pace because none of us wanted to leave the others behind. Sophia was in front, her long legs carrying her swiftly along the pavement. I was in the middle since my running skills had become exceptionally better in the past several months. But what can I say? I've had a lot of practice. Meanwhile, Dane was in back trying his best to keep up. He was in good shape, but he wasn't a fan of running. Never had been.

Thankfully, we had a head start since it had taken the hounds some time to regroup. But once they'd accomplished that feat, they were quickly gaining ground on us.

It was only a matter of time before they overtook us, so we had to come up with a plan fast. I racked my brain for any information I had learned about hellhounds from Zadkiel. He wasn't one to dwell on underworldly beings, but I remember him telling me something about the creatures.

What was it?

Thunder rumbled overhead—the normal kind, not the fallen kind that indicated a portal to or from Hell was being summoned—and then it hit me. Hellhounds were unable to track their prey if the scent went cold, and the only way to do that was to wash it away with water. Meaning either we needed to get wet or we had to get them wet.

I looked up at the darkening clouds as I ran.

Please let it rain. Please let it rain.

We couldn't hold out for natural forces, though. We had to get to the river fast.

"Follow me!" I shouted, veering to the left toward the piers.

Sophia and Dane followed my lead.

The East River loomed just across the street. Granted, I was leading these hounds straight into a tourist sight, but at this point, it was our only option. My hope was that they'd be so focused on us, they'd leave innocent bystanders alone.

We came to the intersection of Maiden Lane and South Street. Ahead was the pier with a number of boats and a small patch of trees. Luckily, the light was green so we raced through the crosswalk and under the highway overpass.

It was dark under the bridge as night had already set in so none of us saw the hound lurking there. Neither did we anticipate his mighty leap into the air, aimed right at Sophia.

The beast tackled her, but Sophia managed to roll out of his way once they hit the ground. She reached for a fallen tree branch near her arm and used it as a shield as the hound came back at her, snapping his jaws.

Instinct kicked in, and Dane and I ran over to the patch of trees, grabbing massive branches. As we approached Sophia and the hound, she managed to stick the branch between his jaws so he couldn't bite her.

Without thinking, I swung my branch through the air like a bat, aiming for the hound. It hit the beast, stunning him. Dane took a swing next, leveling him to the ground. He reached for Sophia's hand to help her up.

Once she was standing, her eyes widened, and she shouted, "Jordan, watch out!"

Of course, I wasn't paying attention, far too focused on the well-being of my friend instead of on our surroundings.

A pack of four hounds slammed into me all at once. I distinctly remembered the f-word being dropped by Dane, before snarls, slobber, and warm breath enveloped me. I grunted in pain as my forehead met the concrete. Something was dripping down the side of my face, and I figured it must be blood.

It didn't take long for Dane and Sophia to start swinging at the hounds, taking out two, maybe three of them, but they kept coming back, undeterred by the wooden branches. One hound was snapping at my legs again, but I managed to kick him in the face. The other I held off by gripping his neck in my hands. I scrunched my face as bad dog breath flooded my nostrils.

With all my strength, I pushed the hound back, away from my face, and quickly reached into my pocket for the holy water aerosol Dane had used earlier. I sprayed it into the air just as the hound recovered and was preparing to attack again. He started sneezing and shaking his head.

Just when I thought I had fought them off, I saw another out of the corner of my eye. It was huge and ready to pounce. The atmosphere filled with an electric energy, and thunder boomed overhead. Lightning struck the sky, illuminating the hound's hideous face. The muscles in his legs were poised to strike, and as he launched into the air, the hound's eyes shifted away from me to a dark figure approaching in my periphery. It was Dane, gone completely wild, as he grabbed the hound around the neck midleap and yelled, "Stop!" His shout echoed under the overpass.

The other hounds halted, and the one in Dane's arms seemed to melt like butter at his command, turning into a sweet house pet rather than a feral dog.

Thunder boomed again, except this time, rain fell with it. One of the hounds, presumably the leader, let out a howl and ran off. The others followed—four in total—until Dane let go of the one in his arms.

Sighing, I let my head fall back to the ground. We were safe. For now.

Dane knelt beside me, completely drained and stunned. Sophia, her eyes wide, came to kneel at my other side. We were all thinking the same thing, but no one wanted to say it.

The two of them looked down at me. "Are you all right?" they asked in unison.

Oh... Apparently, we hadn't been thinking the same thing because I was wondering why the hounds had listened to Dane. There was no logical explanation for what had just occurred.

I glanced down my body, doing a quick inspection for injuries. Nothing seemed hurt or broken. Pressing a hand to my forehead, I winced when my fingers met the aching wound. I drew back my hand. It was smeared with red.

"Yeah, I think I'm okay," I said, about to get up. But I stopped when I noticed Sophia staring at me. "What's wrong?"

"Nothing." She smiled faintly. "You've changed in the nine months since I've seen you. That's all."

"How so?"

"You're a lot braver than I remember," Sophia said.

"Yeah, and you just beat the shit out of a pack of feral dogs unscathed," Dane chimed in.

"Language!" Sophia teased.

He rolled his eyes.

"Look who's talking, Mr. Dog Whisperer," I said to Dane.

"What?" he asked. "I didn't do anything. It was the storm."

Except I knew it wasn't. It couldn't be. The hounds had submitted the moment Dane had commanded them to stop. Unless it was a coincidence?

Before I could dwell on it, the unmistakable sound of beating wings filled my ears.

I pulled my attention away from Sophia and Dane and looked toward the sound. Michael and Gabriel stood there, wet from the rain with wings fully outstretched, matching expressions of condemnation on their faces.

Dane rubbed his eyes. "Do they—"

"Have wings?" I supplied. "Yes. Though now's—"

"Not the time," he finished. "I get it. 'Cause they look pissed."

He was right. They certainly did look pissed.

But we were finally safe, protected.

And in so much trouble.

13

JORDAN

New York City, Present Day

I had never seen Michael and Gabriel so silent before. I could tell they were upset, perhaps even mad, so I kept quiet, too, as did Sophia and Dane. All that was spoken was Gabriel's command, "Back to the apartment. Now."

I shuffled to the nearest subway station since the van was nowhere in sight and the angels weren't too keen on flying with humans in the best of circumstances. Rather than fly ahead, though, the angels followed in our wake, keeping a watchful eye on the three of us.

I felt like a kid again as Sophia, Dane, and I descended the subway steps in shame. At least that's how I felt. I knew I had let them down. But what was I supposed to do? Hellhounds had been chasing us, and I hadn't been prepared to fight them. I wanted to explain that to Michael, but now didn't seem the time. They had already risked exposing their wings for us. Arguing about hellhounds in public would only make things worse.

The subway ride to Gabriel's apartment was long, much like the night the Six had chased me, as we had to make our way from Lower Manhattan to Central Park. I had no idea what time it was, but it was definitely late. The city was encased in darkness, and since it was a Friday night, the subway was packed.

By the time we entered the lobby of the apartment building, my stomach was beyond growling. I was going to be sick if I didn't eat something soon.

Benny, the garage worker turned footman, greeted us as we entered. "Welcome home, Mr. Maestro. I see it's a late night."

"Thank you, Benny," Gabriel responded, ignoring his comment and heading right to the elevator. Michael, Sophia, and Dane followed. Benny stopped me. "What'd ya do, kid?"

I sighed. "Got in trouble with my friends."

The elevator chimed.

"Jordan!" Michael called.

"I better go," I told Benny.

He patted my shoulder. "Good luck, kid."

The elevator trip upstairs was quick. When we arrived at the penthouse, Gabriel unlocked the door and we all proceeded inside. Raphael and Uriel were waiting for us, the former much more sympathetic and the latter more furious than Michael and Gabriel combined. I actually wished Chamuel was here to combat Uriel's wrath, but he was back at the house with Martha, Zadkiel, and Jophiel.

"Do you have any idea what you put us through?" Uriel yelled. He held an ice pack to his head. "Taking on a pack of hounds and completely disappearing!"

Before I could say anything, Raphael jumped in. "All right, all right. I know we're all a little upset, but we survived. Now let me see your injuries."

Sophia and Dane turned to me, but I shrugged them off. "Take care of them first," I told Raphael, approaching the table where his medical bag sat. He had taken out gauze, bandages, and a bunch of other things and spread them about the table. I swiped a pad of gauze and held it to my head to stop the bleeding.

Dane brushed off the request, too. "I'm fine. Nothing's bleeding, nothing's broken. I just want a hot shower."

"The guest bathroom is that way." Gabriel indicated down the left hall.

Dane grabbed his bag from the living room—the angels must have retrieved it from the van along with the painting—and retreated to the guest room.

"I'm not too hurt, either," Sophia said, although Raphael was inspecting her hands.

"Did you fall?" he asked.

"Yes, earlier today."

"How did you cut your hand?"

She cringed. "I broke through a window."

He looked up at her when she said that but didn't ask questions. I could tell he knew she had been through a worse predicament than just the hellhounds, but he didn't push the topic. I didn't, either. At least, not yet. Eventually I wanted to know what had happened today, but it could wait.

"Other than your hands, are you hurt anywhere else?" he asked.

Sophia bent down to touch her right knee. "I hit my knee when I fell, but I think it's fine."

Raphael took a look. "You definitely scraped it, but I don't think anything needs stitches. Why don't you wash up and then I'll give you some medicine to put on?"

"Okay." Sophia left Raphael's side.

"There's another room down the hall you can take," Gabriel said.

"Thanks." Sophia slipped off her backpack and carried it down the hall. She retreated the same way Dane had gone. In fact, the two must have bumped into each other in the hallway as we all heard a loud, "Sorry!"

All that left was me. I sat down in a chair at the dining table where Raphael had spread everything out.

"Let me see," he said, and I lifted away the gauze pad.

He lightly placed a finger under my chin to raise my head. "Nothing too serious. Although you have to stop banging this head of yours."

"I know."

I looked over at Michael, Gabriel, and Uriel. They silently stood in the kitchen.

"I'm sorry," I said.

The words unleashed a storm.

"What happened to your training? Everything I taught you? Where did that go?" Michael demanded. "Because you completely ignored it and got yourself hurt."

My jaw dropped, and I turned my head away from Raphael's ministrations. "In my defense, you never taught me how to defeat a hellhound! Zadkiel's teaching saved me this time more than your combat moves. I was trying to be rational. I was trying to *save* them. Because other than the seven of you, I don't have anyone else!"

That silenced Michael, but Uriel took his place. "Who is that guy anyway? I thought we came here to help Sophia."

Raphael grabbed my chin and turned my head back toward him. "His name is Dane," I said. "He was my roommate at the orphanage."

Silence yet again. I glanced at Gabriel. He came over to stand in front of me. "A lot has happened today and there will be time to share, but not right now. All that matters is you and your friends are safe."

"Thanks. What about you all? Are you okay?"

"We're fine. Michael has a few bruised ribs. Uriel has a head injury. But no one was bitten." He glanced down at his suit, which was full of tears from the hellhounds. "Even though it may look like I might have been."

I sighed in relief.

"Yeah, we can take a lot," Uriel said.

"Just not a frying pan to the head," Michael joked.

Uriel glared. "It's not funny!"

"A frying pan?" I asked.

Gabriel explained. "The hound in the elevator tore through some woman's condo trying to evade Uriel. Uriel followed after it, but she was none too happy and took a swing at him with a frying pan thinking he was a burglar."

"Oh, she hit her mark all right," Uriel added, holding his head. "I've never seen stars like that before. It stunned me for a good minute."

"How do we explain this?" I asked. "The attack, I mean. Everyone saw those hounds."

"We don't have to explain anything," Uriel said. "Humankind tends to make explanations for things themselves, whether they're right or wrong."

"True," I said.

"All right, you're done," Raphael announced.

"Thanks." I stood up. "I can't wait to take a shower after all that dog breath and slobber in my face."

"You can use the master bath," Gabriel said, pointing down the right hall.

"Okay. I'm just going to get some clothes." I went down the left hall to the guest room where I usually stayed. The last time we were here, I had left some clothes behind just in case I ever needed them when I came back. Clearly, that had been a good decision.

This time, I knocked before entering since the door was closed and Dane was presumably inside. He opened the door, towel drying his hair.

"You mind if I come in to get some things?" I asked.

He stepped aside. "Not at all." He sat down on the bed while I rummaged through the dresser. "Jordan, what's going on? Who are those guys? You know I saw their wings earlier."

I turned to him. "I know."

He rolled his eyes. "So enlighten me a little. I'm not stupid, you know."

"I never said you were." I sighed, unsure how to explain. "But before I say anything, I think Sophia should be here because I'm sure she has the same questions."

"Fine. But I want answers."

I left the room, clothes in hand, and paused momentarily in the hall. I'd always known there was another door at the end, but I hadn't known it led to another bedroom. I wanted to go inside and reassure Sophia that I would explain everything, but it seemed she was in the bathroom instead, since I heard the shower on.

Sighing, I retreated the way I had come and headed to the master suite to take my shower. I was cautious walking into the room because this was Gabriel's private domain, but then I remembered he never slept so it didn't feel as weird as I'd expected. The bedroom actually looked like a guest room since there were no personal touches at all. The same went for the bathroom.

As I shrugged out of my shirt, the closet on the other side of the bathroom caught my eye. I peered inside and smiled. This was unmistakably Gabriel. Row upon row of suits filled the space, as well as fancy ties and dress shoes. At least some part of his personality was able to shine through. Stepping away from the closet, I set my sights on the shower.

After washing up and putting on my sweats, I returned to the kitchen area with the full intent of talking to the angels about what to tell Sophia and Dane. Instead, the two of them were already waiting for me in the living room with their questions. They were seated on the floor in their lounge clothes, staring at a sealed envelope that rested on the coffee table.

When I entered the room, they turned their gaze to me. I joined them at the coffee table, sitting between the two of them. The angels sat at the dining table behind us, clearly wanting to be present for the ensuing conversation but being respectfully distant to give us some privacy.

"What's that?" I asked, nodding toward the envelope.

Sophia looked glum. "It's a letter from Sister Helen. She told me not to open it until I was with you."

I hesitantly reached for the letter, knowing whatever was inside were Sister Helen's final words. "Maybe we should open it first, then."

"Not so fast." Dane swatted my hand away. "We need some explanations first."

"I agree," Sophia said, "but I think we *all* have something to tell one another tonight." She gave Dane a pointed look.

"Fine," he said. "I'll share, too, but Jordan goes first."

My stomach growled. "I can go first, but can we eat something while we launch into this lengthy conversation?"

Sophia patted my arm. "We already ordered Chinese. It should be here soon."

"Good." I scratched my head. "Where do you want me to start?"

Sophia was quiet for a moment, seemingly getting her thoughts in order. Then she unleashed them like a torrent. "Why didn't you tell me you were a Sacrarium Novice? Was your mission trip a trial of trust? Why didn't you write? Why didn't you call? Were you too busy to do those things?"

It didn't take her long to start asking the hard questions.

"Sophia, calm down," I said.

"Don't tell me to calm down! I have every right to be frustrated with you!"

I guessed she had a point. "Fine, be mad at me if you want, but here's the truth. I'm not a Sacrarium Novice. I didn't even know what the Sacrarium was until I met Gabriel, and at that, his explanation was very limited because he doesn't know too much about it, either. None of them do. They know its intended purpose—to protect the holy bloodline—but they know nothing about its inner workings. Which means I don't, either. As for my mission trip, it was a hoax. Sister Helen made the whole thing up. She needed me to do something else for her."

Sophia's brow furrowed. "Like what?"

"I can't tell you that part. All I can say is she needed me to help some...people remember their purpose."

Dane jumped in. "People? Ha! That's rich. *They* are not people," Dane said, pointing to the angels.

Sophia's eyes widened in shock. Her gaze skipped back and forth between me and the angels. "Oh my gosh! Sister Helen told me she gave you something to hide, but she never told me that she assigned you the ultimate trial of trust."

What is a trial of trust?

Confused, I shook my head. "I have no idea what that is. Sister Helen never told me about a trial of trust, just like she never told me about the Sacrarium." I sighed. "This is getting too complicated."

"*You* think this is too complicated? How do you think I feel?" Dane said.

"Oh, just be quiet for a second," I said. "Sophia, I don't know what you're talking about but let me finish my story and then you can ask questions."

She pressed her lips into a thin line and nodded.

I twisted around and looked at Gabriel, questioning him with my eyes, asking him if I could tell them. "Go ahead," he said, reading my thoughts.

Turning back to Sophia and Dane, I said, "If you haven't guessed by now, they're angels. There are three more currently living at my house in Ithaca. And before you ask, it's my parents' house."

Saying those words aloud was a relief. I didn't like lying or keeping secrets—just the thought of doing so made me feel uncomfortable. So with that off my chest, I jumped right into everything that had happened over the past nine months. The chase through New York. The backpack. The Sacrarium. The world travels. Meeting the angels. The various attacks by the Fallen. Satan. My parents' house. Martha. The Nephilim. *The Book of Prophecies*. The spheres. All of it.

The only thing I left out was the presumption the angels and I had about Sophia's involvement.

"Well?" I asked the two of them when I was done.

Dane studied me. "When did you suddenly become a badass?"

I laughed.

"No, really? I would like to know," he joked.

I nudged him in the shoulder, and he nudged me back. We had

never been this close. We had never been friends. I didn't know what had brought about the change, but I liked it.

Sophia narrowed her gaze on us. "Can we stop joking around for a second and take this seriously?"

I turned to her. "Of course."

The doorbell rang, announcing the arrival of our dinner. Gabriel stood and approached the door. I jumped up to get my wallet.

"Where are you going?" Michael asked.

"I want to pay for the food."

"We already took care of it."

I sighed. This was their latest expression of overprotection. They insisted upon paying for everything. Chamuel even insisted upon doing my laundry when I had told him several times I could do it. The angels weren't my butlers. I hadn't expected them to be my protectors, either, although I certainly appreciated it. If anything, they were my family, and I wanted them to feel that way.

Besides, I had been dependent on everyone while I was at the orphanage. I may have done my own chores, but my meals and clothes had been provided by Sister Helen. I certainly hadn't been able to pay my own way. Now that I knew about the money my mom and dad had left me, I could finally do my part. I *wanted* to be helpful.

Michael smiled. "Next time."

"Right," I said sarcastically, knowing full well they wouldn't let me pay next time, either.

I grabbed some utensils from the kitchen just as Gabriel deposited the bag of food on the coffee table.

"Thank you," Sophia and Dane said at the same time.

"You're welcome," Gabriel responded, heading back to the dining table with the others.

"Do you want us to eat at the counter?" I asked him.

He looked over his shoulder at me. "No, you're fine there."

I shrugged and sat down on the floor again. We spread out the Chinese food and dug in, Sophia daintily scooping up some orange chicken with her chopsticks and Dane shoving noodles into his mouth with a fork.

I grabbed an egg roll with my fingers, took a bite, and resumed our conversation. "So what do you have to say about my story, Sophia?"

"A part of me isn't surprised by the presence of angels since I was tasked to work with some myself. But, Jordan, you have to understand, the trial of trust you were given was not supposed to be carried out by a Novice." She shook her head in disbelief. "Sister Helen always told me that she would have to go on a trip soon to gather others from around the world so they could help her stop the Sacrarium's enemies once and for all. I always thought she was referring to some top-notch Sacrarium members I never met, but she was referring to *them*. To the angels. It was a task that was supposed to be carried out by her and her alone. The fact that she gave it to you shows how much trust and faith she has in you."

"Well Sister Helen did know my parents, so maybe she thought I was like them."

"Your parents were Sacrarium members?" Sophia asked.

"I believe so," I told her. "What exactly is a trial of trust anyway?"

"A trial of trust," Sophia began, "is something every Sacrarium Novice must complete before they take the oath to protect the holy bloodline. Most Novices are young, so the oath-taking happens at the age of twenty. Prior to that, a Novice starts out by being taught basic Sacrarium knowledge in addition to self-defense. Once those skills are mastered, the Novice is then given a trial of trust to prove they're dedicated and trustworthy. Every Novice gets a different trial so no two are the same."

I nodded. "Makes sense. How far along are you?"

Sophia shrugged. "I thought I had finished my training and had only my trial of trust left to complete but I'm realizing how unprepared I am."

"You can't blame yourself, Sophia," Dane said. "From what I've heard and experienced so far, none of this seems easy."

I agreed. "He's right. Being taught something is not nearly as hard as putting it into practice."

Sophia smiled. "Thanks."

"So were you given your trial?" Dane asked.

She nodded. "Yes. I was tasked with meeting members of the Triune to help them find a few items that went missing. Triune members are angels, too, but ones with a different purpose. They are largely stationed on Earth to protect the bloodline and anything pertaining to it."

Sophia recited their purpose like a definition, clearly one ingrained in her from her training.

"There are three main leaders of the Triune, each an angel who represents a different faith. Aziza represents Islam, Yadira Judaism, and the third leader, Katriel—or Kat as many called her—represents Christianity. The items I was tasked to find were three scepter pieces and the fourteenth sphere. Since I was interested in art history, Sister Helen thought this would be a good assignment for me. It didn't hurt that I was beginning my studies and seeking out internships. She thought perhaps through those studies and internships, I might find clues or information about mysterious or unknown objects. Essentially, she wanted me to keep an eye out for anything that was remotely related to what the Triune was looking for."

She took another bite of chicken and chewed it before continuing. "I accepted the mission because I wanted to complete my trial in time to take my oath. After working a short time with Aziza and Yadira I had thought my trial of trust was futile, merely something to keep me busy and fulfill a Sacrarium requirement."

"What made you think that?" I asked.

"Because when the objects went missing so too did Kat. Aziza and Yadira believe she went into hiding with them. Meaning I was tasked to look for information on objects that would never surface unless their beholder decided to reveal herself."

"Why would Kat go into hiding? Who is she hiding from?" Dane asked.

"Satan," the angels and I answered together. I turned to them and could tell they wanted in on our conversation. I waved them over, and they came closer to sit on the couch and love seat.

"Wait a minute," Dane interjected. "Satan? Like the Devil? Like the monstrous creature stuck in Hell and full of evil?"

"No," I responded. "Satan who escaped Hell and is now walking around Earth unleashing hellhounds on us."

Dane opened his mouth as if to speak, then shut it.

"I know, it's a lot to take in," I offered. Turning back to Sophia, I said, "Sister Helen gave me the backpack for the same reason—to protect it from Satan. I imagine Katriel might be doing the same thing with these objects."

"Possibly. But Sister Helen and the Sacrarium thought differently. They thought it was mere coincidence that the objects and Kat had gone missing at the same time. Instead, they believed the objects were hidden around the world and it was only a matter of time before someone stumbled upon them. Hence my mission."

"Doesn't that sound familiar..." I glanced at the angels.

"Quite," Uriel replied.

Raphael nodded. "It sounds like our keys."

Sophia and Dane didn't know what those were so I explained. "Each of the angels has three keys. One is an actual metal key, another is a gemstone, and the final one is a sphere. Their keys were hidden at different wonders of the world, and they're all needed to complete a prophecy called the Union of the Spheres."

Sophia raised an eyebrow. "Really? I've never heard about any prophecy before. I guess the Sacrarium doesn't know about it."

I shook my head. "They do. One of the items in the backpack Sister Helen gave me was Satan's sphere."

"Oh... That wasn't part of my training." Sophia's face fell. "Just goes to show you how much I still don't know."

I patted her hand. "It's okay. We'll figure everything out together."

"Why would the scepter pieces be hidden like our keys?" Gabriel suddenly asked.

"Because the scepter pieces are needed for the prophecy, too, and hiding them in different places will only make it harder to complete the prophecy," Michael responded.

Gabriel paced back and forth. Whenever he did that, it was a sign he was trying to think something over. "I suppose. But who's supposed to find these missing objects? We don't know about them, and the Triune doesn't seem to, either."

"I'm sure somebody knows. They just haven't surfaced yet," Raphael said.

Sophia disagreed. "I'm not too sure about that. I actually found someone who does know about them—well, at least the fourteenth sphere—which is what changed my mind about my mission being futile. Now I'm doing everything I can to complete it."

"Meaning?" Dane asked.

"Meaning," Sophia elaborated, "that I found a curator named Simon Price who works at the Met. We were first introduced when I attended a lecture of his at the museum over fall break. I was fascinated by his research in ancient art and antiquities, which is his specialty, so I asked him afterward if I could interview him for one of my school assignments. He agreed, and during our meeting, he mentioned that he would be traveling to Antarctica in January. That surprised me so I asked him more about it. He told me a scientific research team had contacted him after locating a strange object in one of their ice samples."

I observed the others. They all looked as rapt as I felt.

"We lost touch after that," she went on. "Until a couple of days ago when he guest-lectured at my university. That's when he told me about the object found in the ice, a mysterious sapphire sphere that had no logical explanation for how it got there. I had found the fourteenth sphere—I knew I had. But I didn't know what to do. I still don't entirely know what to do. All I know is Simon Price is creating an exhibit around the sphere that opens in two weeks. The museum has hyped it up so much, they're actually holding a gala for special guests and donors before it opens. I brought all this information to

Sister Helen at the church because that's what I'm supposed to do as a Novice." She grew tense and solemn. "But that's when he showed up," she said, her hands visibly shaking.

"When who showed up?" Dane asked.

"Satan," I said. "And a hound."

Dane stared at Sophia, but she wouldn't meet his eyes. "You've been running from those hounds all afternoon?"

She nodded, and a tear fell down her cheek. I reached out and put my arm around her shoulder, pulling her closer.

"Don't get me wrong, I know those hounds are scary, and I'm sure Satan is even worse, but I get the feeling I'm missing something," Dane said.

I sighed and looked at him. "There was an explosion at the church. Sophia made it out in time. But—" My voice cracked. I couldn't say it.

"But what?" Dane asked, fear filling his eyes.

Sophia brushed her tears from her cheeks. "But Sister Helen didn't."

His lip trembled slightly, and his eyes welled up. "What?"

I let go of Sophia, anticipating Dane's reaction. "She's gone."

"How can you say that so calmly?" he exploded, shoving me back.

"Dane! Stop! It's not his fault," Sophia defended.

"It's not your fault, either," I added, knowing Sophia all too well.

She shook her head almost violently. "Don't say that."

"It's the truth," I insisted.

"She sacrificed herself for me. That is something I have to live with now," she said. "It only happened this afternoon so give me some time to process."

She was right. I backed off and focused on Dane instead. "Dane," I said.

"Leave me alone." He clearly was forcing himself not to cry, subsequently shutting down and drawing back inside his isolated shell. What scared me was that the Dane sitting before me wasn't the mean, retaliative one. It was the hurt, alone one.

"Hey," I said, scooching closer to him. "Don't hold it back. Your feelings matter. Let them out."

But he wouldn't listen. He was self-destructing.

I grabbed his shoulder and forced him to look at me. "*You matter.*"

He knew what I meant. He knew what I was alluding to. I could see in his eyes that he had transported back to that night when he had made the worst choice of his life.

14 DANE

New York City, Six Years Ago

I lay awake in my bed, watching the minutes tick by on the clock.

12:49 AM.

Only one more minute.

When the red numbers finally switched, I knew it was time to go.

Meet me at the playground at 1:00 AM.

Those had been my father's instructions.

I had met him at the park after school one day. He had come to help me after I had wiped out on my skateboard. It was there he told me he was my father and had been looking for me for years after my mother had given me up. He even knew my birthday to prove it.

I had pinched myself to make sure I wasn't dreaming, because that's all I ever wanted my entire life: for someone who cared about me to show up and take me away from the nuns.

Don't get me wrong, they were better than nothing, but they had too many rules. Plus, in their eyes, I was second best. And I didn't want to be second best.

My father didn't think I was second best.

Throwing back the covers, I quietly slid out of bed. Jordan wasn't a light sleeper, but I knew if I woke him up, my plans would be ruined. He was nosy and annoying. There would be no chance of running away if he caught me. He would either pester me with too many questions or run to tell the nuns.

Thankfully, the socks I wore on my feet didn't make a sound as I carefully crossed the room to my closet, purposefully avoiding the floorboards that creaked.

I had prepared ahead of time, wearing clothes to bed that I could escape in, but I still needed my jacket and shoes. Slowly, I eased open the closet door and reached inside to pull out a hoodie and a pair of sneakers. I slipped on the hoodie but kept my shoes off. I would put them on once I was outside.

Reaching inside the closet again, I grabbed my backpack. I had packed it with a change of clothes, lots of snacks, and my most prized possession: the deck of cards I had saved my money to buy. It had taken me three months of chores just to get enough. But it was worth it because I finally had my own pristine set that wasn't a hand-me-down.

Ever since I had seen a talent show on TV where magicians made their cards disappear into thin air, I had wanted to learn their tricks. It would be incredible to have magic like that right at your fingertips.

I had gotten pretty good with making the cards disappear but only if I had on a long-sleeve shirt. I still needed some practice to perfect the trick, but I couldn't wait to show my dad. He would be proud of what I had learned so far.

He had told me I didn't need to bring anything with me, that I was his to take care of now. But it seemed weird not to bring along a few things that I liked, especially my cards.

I slipped the backpack over my shoulders and picked up my sneakers, only briefly setting them down again when I arrived at the window. I released the latch and tried lifting it open without making any noise, but it was old and screeched as it went up.

Unfortunately, the window was on Jordan's side of the room so the sound had his eyes flashing open. He squinted at me in the dark. "Dane? What are you doing?"

"Go back to sleep."

A slight breeze swept through the room, and Jordan shifted in his bed, sitting up and pulling the blanket closer. His gaze landed on my backpack and shoes. "You're running away?"

"No!" I said defensively. "I'm meeting some friends."

He glanced at the clock, then turned back to me. "We're thirteen-year-olds. What friends do either of us have that want to meet at one in the morning?"

"You wouldn't know. You're not mature like me. Now go back to sleep." I climbed through the window, but before I could close it, Jordan appeared on the other side.

"Can I come?" he asked.

Sighing, I sat down on the fire escape and put my shoes on. "No, you're not invited."

"How come?"

"Because we're not friends."

"That's your choice, you know. I would be your friend."

I opened my mouth to shout, *I don't want you as my friend!* but decided against it. It would only hurt his feelings, and then he would definitely go tell the nuns I was sneaking out.

Instead, I leveled with him. "If you promise to go back to sleep and not tell anyone about this, I'll do your chores for the next two weeks."

Obviously, I wouldn't be here. I would be with my dad. But he didn't have to know that.

"Make it three, and we have a deal," he bargained.

"Fine."

We shook on it, and then he slammed the window shut.

I climbed down the fire escape and jumped to the sidewalk. I peered down the street. Everything was so dark and deserted. Maybe this wasn't a good idea. Maybe I should just go back inside and crawl into bed.

I looked up at my room.

No, you have to do this, I told myself.

Taking a deep breath, I started walking. The park was close to the orphanage. I only had to go a few blocks before I could see it across the street. But everything was so dark, and the park was a maze. The sidewalk was surrounded by bushes, and at night, they made it hard to remember how to get to the playground. Plus, the park was near the pier so the occasional sound of boat horns kept making me jump.

When I finally found the playground, there was no one there. I didn't know what time it was since watches were for adults and cell phones weren't allowed until we were in high school. One of the nuns' many rules.

I figured I was early so waiting seemed the best idea. I spied some chalk on the ground and made myself comfortable on the concrete, doodling to pass the time.

After a short while, I heard someone say, "Wow, that's impressive."

Glancing over my shoulder, I saw my dad standing there. I smiled.

"Thanks." I dropped the chalk and brushed the dust from my hands. Standing up, I went over and hugged him, just tall enough to reach his waist.

He patted my shoulder. "You ready to go?"

I nodded.

Grabbing my hand, he asked, "Would you like to walk along the pier before we leave? I bet you've never seen it this late at night."

"Sure," I said, eager to agree.

"Wait!" someone shouted, rushing out of the bushes.

It was Jordan.

Outraged, I yelled, "You followed me!"

"I had to! Well, I didn't *have* to," he backtracked. "I was really just curious. But now I'm glad I did because this guy is kidnapping you!"

"He's not kidnapping me! He's my father!"

Jordan paused, thought it over, but ultimately didn't like it. "If he was your father, don't you think he would have come to the orphanage to get you?"

I hesitated. Jordan had a point. I thought about it for a second, though, and realized the one person who would try to mess this up was the person who had always messed everything up for me, the person who always made me second best.

I let go of my dad's hand and screamed, "Why do you always ruin everything?"

"I'm not ruining anything! I'm trying to help you!"

I rushed over to Jordan and shoved him to the ground. "I don't need your help!"

Suddenly, police sirens echoed through the night.

Great! Jordan probably told the nuns.

Or he had made such a bad getaway that they realized we were missing. My dad and I had to leave.

"Let's go, Dad," I said, turning away from Jordan. But no one was there. "Dad!" I shouted. "Dad, where are you?"

"He's gone," Jordan said. "Because he's not your dad."

I faced Jordan and launched at him, wrestling him to the ground and punching him in the face.

A police officer came running over to us. "Boys, stop!" He pulled me off Jordan and said into his radio, "I found them."

When Sister Helen arrived, Jordan's eye was already purple and his lip was swollen. She made sure he was all right before coming over to me. Of course he would be the victim in all this.

"Dane, what were you thinking?" Sister Helen asked. "I've told all of you kids never to listen to or follow strangers. You're lucky that man didn't hurt you or take you."

Head down, I picked at my bloody knuckles. "He wasn't a stranger. He was my father."

Sister Helen shook her head. "I'm sorry, Dane, but he wasn't."

I looked her in the eye. "You're wrong!" A tear fell down my cheek.

She reached out to console me, but I moved away. She had to be wrong. Because if she wasn't, that meant no one wanted me.

"Dane, look at me," Sister Helen said.

I refused.

"Dane." Her tone was serious now, so I glanced up at her. *"You matter."*

I didn't know how she had known those were the words I needed to hear, but I was glad she had. I sobbed and hugged her tightly. She held me close until I was ready to pull away.

Brushing the hair out of my eyes, Sister Helen said, "The policeman needs to talk with you, to see what you remember. I'll be right here the whole time."

I nodded, and the officer came over to us. He pulled out his notepad. "Your name is Dane, right?"

"Yeah."

"Well, Dane, can you tell me what the man looked like?"

I shrugged, trying to think.

"I know it was dark so it might have been hard to see his face," the officer remarked. "At least, that's what Jordan said. But you were holding his hand. Was there anything you noticed?"

I had been holding his hand. I rolled my eyes thinking about what a childish mistake that had been for someone my age who didn't need their hand held anymore. But I had seen something Jordan didn't. "He had a ring on. It was a black cat with its mouth like this—" I opened mine wide, showing my teeth.

"All right, that's helpful." He jotted something on his notepad.

I grabbed it from him. "But it wasn't an ordinary cat. It was a big cat, like a cougar or something." I started drawing. "And this wasn't the only time I saw him. I first met him when I fell off my skateboard after school. He had golden hair. Light eyes. Maybe blue." I was almost finished. "And he told me his name was Luc, spelled *L-U-C*." I handed over the notepad.

The officer glanced down at the drawing, stunned. It showed every last detail of the ring exactly as I remembered it. Sister Helen seemed surprised by my talent, too, and smiled approvingly at me.

"Did the man say what his last name was?" the officer asked once he took his attention away from the drawing.

I shook my head. "No."

The officer flipped the notepad closed. "Thanks for your help, Dane." He looked at Sister Helen. "The boys can go home now. Let us give you ride."

It would have been more exciting riding in the back of a police car if I hadn't been so tired. When we arrived at the orphanage, the other kids were still sleeping so Sister Helen quietly made us wash up and go straight to bed. But I couldn't fall asleep, even though I was exhausted.

Deep down, I knew Sister Helen was probably right. That man hadn't been my father, and I was lucky he hadn't taken me.

But it didn't change anything with Jordan.

I stared at his sleeping form in the bed across from mine. He would always meddle and ruin everything. He was why I was always second best.

So I made a promise to myself never to be his friend, never to be nice to him again. Right now, he lived a perfect life, but going forward, I would do everything I could to make it imperfect.

15

JORDAN

New York City, Present Day

Dane erupted into tears, but rather than pushing me away and succumbing to the oblivion of his sobs, he clung to me with a hug—one I returned.

"I'm sorry," he said. "For everything I've done."

"I forgive you," I told him. "And I'm sorry, too."

We left it at that, letting the past go.

Sophia came over and joined in for a group hug.

It was several moments later when we separated and regrouped around the coffee table, our food long forgotten. The angels were still seated behind us but remained silent as we worked through this together.

"She was the one who got me to clear my head and change my ways," Dane whispered.

"Who? Sister Helen?" I asked.

He nodded.

"You should tell him what happened," Sophia said to Dane.

So Dane did exactly that and told me what had occurred in the months since we had left the orphanage. The crappy job, the homelessness, the near-death experience, and Sister Helen giving him the advice he needed to turn his life around.

"I'm sorry that all happened," I said.

"But he's going to art school now," Sophia added, looking to the bright side.

Dane grinned. "*Trying* to go to art school. I haven't applied yet."

"Is that why you wanted that painting? It's his?" I asked Sophia.

She brightened. "Yes! It's a meaningful piece since it's his first. When he's famous one day, you'll thank me for saving it."

I laughed. "Understandable." I turned to Dane. "It makes sense now where all the tattoos came from." Since he was wearing a tank top, both his tattoo sleeves were on full display.

Dane quickly glanced at his arms, then poked me in the shoulder. "It makes sense now where all this muscle came from. You were always the scrawny one, but I guess fighting fallen angels changes you."

"Ha! That and an intense training program," I commented, looking at Michael.

He smiled. "I can't take all the credit. You're a good pupil." Then he grew serious. "I'm sorry about before. I was too hard on you. I was just...worried."

"It's okay. I mean, you were right. I hardly used any of my training."

"I'm not too sure. You remained calm and rational. You acted bravely. Besides, you were right. I never taught you how to fight a hellhound."

"Wouldn't that have been helpful," Sophia teased.

"How did you manage to get rid of them?" Uriel asked.

The three of us looked at one another. "Well my plan was to head for the river since Zadkiel had told me once about how the hounds can lose a scent if the trail went cold and the only way to do that was to get wet."

"So, what? You were planning on jumping in the river?" Raphael asked.

"Well, yes, actually," I said.

Dane's head snapped toward me. "You wanted us to jump in the river?"

I shrugged. "Yeah. It was the only idea I had."

"Good thing that storm came," Sophia added.

Gabriel pondered her comment. "The storm would have been a good deterrent, but neither you nor the hounds got wet."

I looked at Dane, and he rolled his eyes. "It was the storm. I didn't do anything other than command them to stop."

"And they listened?" Michael asked, eyes wide.

"Yes," I said hesitantly.

He shook his head. "Something's not right. Lucifer was able to command them at the condo, too."

"What are you thinking?" Raphael asked.

"I'm thinking something's going on with Satan. That he and Lucifer are not on good terms, that Lucifer—" He broke off. "Never mind. It's been a long night. I wonder if your display of dominance was what stopped them."

"Yeah, let's go with that. My display of dominance," Dane agreed, but I still wasn't fully convinced.

Sophia was quiet.

"You okay?" I asked.

She sighed. "Yeah, it was just an exhausting day."

"How did you make it out of the church?" Dane asked suddenly.

"Sister Helen sent me through some underground tunnel," Sophia replied. "It was dark and damp, and I thought I would never make it out of there. That's where I fell," she told us.

"And what did Sister Helen have to say about the fourteenth sphere?" Gabriel asked.

Sophia shrugged. "She was happy I had a lead, but we never got the chance to talk about it. I was hoping to suggest to her that we should go to the gala to see if the sphere is actually real." She paused. "Simon Price did give me three tickets. That's why I insisted on going back to the condo to get my cosmetic bag. I hid them in there, and know they're irreplaceable."

The angels exchanged looks.

"You're going, aren't you?" I asked them.

"We have to," Gabriel said. "Sophia is right. We have to confirm if the sphere is credible."

Michael glanced at Sophia. "This is your mission. I don't want you to feel like we're taking it from you. I don't want you to feel obligated to give us the tickets."

"But I should," she said. "I wanted so bad to go and see the sphere for myself. I thought it would be right for me to go since it is *my* trial of trust." She shook her head. "But I'm in over my head. It's not safe. So you should take them."

We were all silent for a moment, until I saw Sister Helen's envelope still sitting on the coffee table among the now-empty takeout cartons. "What about the letter?" I asked.

"I suppose we should open it," Sophia suggested. She picked up the letter, then paused, looking thoughtful, and handed it to me. "You do it."

"Are you sure?" I asked.

She nodded. "I don't want to."

I took it out of her hand and quickly broke the wax seal. When we had been kids, Sister Helen always sealed her stationery with wax. At the time, it had been purely fascinating to watch the flame melt the wax and see her press the metal sealer to the sticky bubble.

Now I realized that all those letters must have contained Sacrarium information because the crest in the wax was a fleur-de-lis, which I had come to know as the official symbol of the Sacrarium.

I slid out the letter, discarded the envelope on the coffee table, and unfolded the pages.

"Read it aloud," Sophia said.

I cleared my throat and began. *"Dear Jordan, Sophia, and Dane…"* My eyes flicked to him as he gasped. None of us had been expecting his name to be in the letter.

Ignoring the interruption, I focused back on the letter and continued, *"I hope the three of you are together. If not, you must find one another immediately. The bond you share is the only thing that will get you through this. And if you're reading this at all, then it is my final goodbye. I haven't much time, and when I say that, I mean it literally. In the last year, I've neglected to tell you that I've been diagnosed with terminal cancer."*

I paused as the words knocked the wind out of me. I forced myself to press on. *"I didn't tell anyone, not even Martha, because I was determined to fight it,"* I read. *"I also didn't want to disrupt your senior year of high school with such troubling news. So fight it I did, until my efforts were doing nothing other than exhausting me. I was prepared to tell you all in person, even Martha. But as part of my clandestine operations, I must always be ready to explain events, even if I'm no longer around, hence the letter.*

"However, I recognize how dangerous it is to leave a paper trail so they never include compromising information. Perhaps coded occasionally, but never without a way to decode it. I only say this because there is so much I wish to tell you that I simply cannot because it would put you all in danger. Instead, you must help one another find the truth and solve the mysteries

together. I love each of you. Never doubt that. And always remember, the truth resides inside, deceit lies without, and the journey to both is obscure. With all my love, Sister Helen."

I glanced at the line written below her name. Thanks to Zadkiel, I knew it was in Latin. *"Neque heredis exponere,"* I read aloud.

Dane scrunched up his face. "What's that supposed to mean?"

"It's Latin. It means, 'Do not expose the heir,'" I said, glancing at the angels.

"It's the Sacrarium motto," Sophia explained. "All the members know it, even the Novices. Once you're initiated, you're told who the heir to the bloodline is and are sworn to never tell another so as not to expose the heir and put them in danger."

"That makes sense," I said, thinking over the phrase.

"I've heard that the heir doesn't even know they're the bloodline," Sophia added.

"What do you mean?" I asked. "The heir of the bloodline doesn't know they're the heir? What good does that do?"

"Supposedly, whoever the previous heir was did know, but it put great strain on the family. That's why the current heir no longer knows they're the bloodline—to alleviate some of the pressure and stress."

"That's ridiculous!" I exclaimed. "The heir has a big responsibility to complete the prophecy and end this war. They have a target on their back regardless. Don't you think it would be better if they knew so they could prepare themselves?"

Sophia and Dane stared at my outburst. The angels, meanwhile, knew why I was so upset. We presumed Sophia was the bloodline based off a mysterious letter Michael had found, yet here she was sitting right in front of me totally oblivious to her fate. Everything the Sacrarium prided itself on—the secrecy, the lies—would be its ultimate downfall because Sophia was not prepared to face this fight.

"Sorry," I said. "That's just frustrating to me."

Sophia nodded. "I get it."

"What exactly *is* the Sacrarium?" Dane asked.

Sophia explained the secret society's purpose and intent to him.

Shocked, Dane said, "And we were living among the society at the orphanage?" He shook his head. "I feel bad for this heir. I mean, it seems like they have to save the world."

"Not save the world but end the war," Sophia disagreed.

Dane rolled his eyes. "Still."

"Whoever the heir is, they're not totally helpless," Sophia said. "They're given guides and mentors to train them."

"But wouldn't they know who they are, then?" Dane asked.

"No, because they're trained in basic Sacrarium knowledge and treated like any other Novice," she explained.

Dane crossed his arms. "But once they take the oath, what happens?"

Sophia shrugged. "I'm not sure. Typically, when a normal Novice takes the oath, they are told who the bloodline is, but I'm not sure if it's the same for the heir."

I sighed. It was frustrating how none of us knew the same information—whether we had been told differently or not at all. Luckily, moving forward, that would change.

"So if Jordan isn't a Sacrarium Novice, then why would Sister Helen send him to get the angels?" Dane asked.

"Personally, I think she was running out of time and options, especially if she was so ill herself," I said.

Sophia nodded. "I agree. The Sacrarium was already struggling to survive with the few members they had left. Now with Sister Helen gone it's near impossible. Besides, no matter how it happened, Sister Helen was ultimately trying to get Jordan to one of the angels."

She had a point. It didn't matter whether I'd met Raphael or Gabriel first. I would have traveled with either of them around the world to find the others.

"I wonder why she didn't send me instead," Sophia said distractedly. "She must have thought I wasn't ready."

I could tell Sophia was on the edge of self-destructing so I grabbed her hand and met her eyes. "What's done is done, Soph. You can't question it. And don't doubt yourself. You *are* ready. In fact, your trial might be more important than what Sister Helen had me do. If we don't find the scepter pieces and whatever this fourteenth sphere is, we might not be able to complete the prophecy and stop the Fallen," I said. "With or without these guys." I gestured to the angels.

Uriel took the ice off his head. "Although your chances are far better with us."

I smiled. "Of course they are. Let's just hope the Fallen don't wield frying pans like that woman tonight."

The others laughed.

Uriel put the ice back on his head. "Still not funny," he grumbled.

It felt good to be here with the angels and Sophia and Dane. It felt like coming full circle. It felt like home.

Sophia yawned.

"Perhaps it's time you three got some sleep," Gabriel suggested.

I nodded. "That would be good."

As we cleaned up our dishes, Raphael and Uriel sat in the living room watching the news, Gabriel retreated to his office, and Michael went out on the balcony continuing his watch. After saying a quick goodnight to everyone, we went to bed—Sophia and Dane to their respective guest rooms and me to Gabriel's master suite.

I climbed into the king-size bed and snuggled against the pillows. Even though we lost the woman who'd raised us today, we had found one another again. Her last wish was for the three of us to be back together, to succeed as a team, and I would do everything in my power to fulfill that wish. Her sacrifice would not be in vain. We would finish this fight together.

16

SATAN

New York City, Present Day

"Remind me again whose idea it was to meet here?" I asked Lucifer as we stood in a serpentine line waiting to get to the top of the Empire State Building.

"Mine," he said proudly.

"And why, pray tell, did you suggest this god forsaken place full of people?"

"Because I thought the more public the place, the better. Jazema is furious at you, and there's no telling what she might do. If we're surrounded by humans, then maybe whatever she has up her sleeve won't be so lethal."

My eyes turned to slits. "You're expecting an attack."

Lucifer shrugged nonchalantly. "It's possible."

I grabbed him by the collar of his shirt. "What are you up to?"

He raised his hands in the air. "Nothing. Now I suggest you let go before other people notice."

I released him, fuming. I needed this meeting, even if I was walking into a trap. For years, I had been trying to change our deal, but like each time before, I refused because the price was too high. Jazema wanted me to be a part of her experiment—she wanted my DNA—and I

simply refused to succumb to such a level. I wouldn't let her get the satisfaction of creating a Nephilim abomination from me. So now it was time to take back the power and shift the scales in my direction.

It was nearly our meeting time when we arrived at the elevators. The wait was longer than the quick trip to the top, and the tourists that surrounded us eagerly scrambled out as soon as the doors opened. We exited at a much more leisurely pace, walking through the double doors and out onto the viewing deck.

Crossing my arms, I gazed at the sight around me, the whole city laid out before me. The Empire State Building was a tourist trap, but admittedly, I understood why because it was one of the few places where you felt bigger than the world around you. It was hard not to lift my eyes a little higher to the sky above. I wondered who was on watch. Cassiel? Ariel? Sandalphon? They would have been standing on the parapets of the Watch Tower with the golden sun shining on their face and the slight breeze ruffling their feathers.

It was funny to think I used to wonder what it was like to be down here on Earth, and now I was here, wondering what it would be like to be back up there.

A female voice interrupted my thoughts. "Is the Devil remorseful about his rebellion?"

I smirked, hiding my true feelings. "Never. Does the Nephilim regret her fall for man?"

She chuckled darkly. "Hardly. And it wasn't a fall for man. It was seizing an opportunity for the Nephilim race."

I turned to face her. "Jazema."

Gazing at the Asian woman, you wouldn't know she was a Nephilim.

She blended in so perfectly with her long, straight black hair and light skin, her nails manicured and painted red. She was wearing a white suit with fancy gold heels. All interests a normal human might have in the way they presented themselves. Except she was far more lethal than she let on.

"So I hear you're furious with me," I said. "I can't imagine why. I've been such a good friend."

"Really? Because you've kept none of your promises."

"The only promise I haven't kept is meeting with you face-to-face, but I sent Lucifer in my stead since I was otherwise indisposed."

She pursed her lips. "You're sticking with that explanation?"

I laughed. "You think I was lying about being trapped?"

"I've had my doubts, but let's not dwell on the situation. I've enjoyed Lucifer's company far more than yours."

Small sparks of anger ignited inside me, but I refused to show her how much her words irritated me. "I called this meeting because I want to change our agreement."

Her eyes narrowed. "I thought you called this meeting to get back in my good graces and reestablish our shaky alliance. Now you tell me you want to change our agreement?" She paused. "I'm slightly pleased we're finally on the same page, but can I even trust you anymore?"

"Could you trust me to begin with?"

Her lips twitched into a smile. Even though she apparently hated my company, she certainly was enjoying our banter. "Probably not. I'm willing to overlook it, though. You have assets I desperately want." She ran her eyes over me.

"Those assets aren't on the table."

Her fingers played along the collar of my shirt, close enough to feel the heat of my skin but far enough away not to touch it. She obviously thought my Hellfire was still active.

Good. Better she doesn't know.

"Why not?" she whined.

"You know why not."

She rolled her eyes. "Because you hate being controlled." She chuckled and pulled back. "What an ironic thing when Lilith is clearly still controlling you."

My anger ignited. "Jazema, I suggest you tread lightly regarding the topic of conversation."

"Or what?" she demanded.

I gazed around the observation deck and quickly spotted her Nephilim accomplices. They meandered through the crowd, mixing in well with the tourists. Unless you knew what you were looking for: agile grace, quick reflexes, and a calculating gaze.

"Or we make this an all-out brawl," I replied.

She sneered. "Oh please. You'd never make a scene. Not in a place so public." She analyzed my face, realizing that her conclusions were inaccurate. "So quick to anger. So quick to deny that her venom is truly what changed you instead of your own free will."

I froze. Was that true? Had my rebellion been spurred on by her bite? I thought it over a moment, realizing it had been. That was the whole point of sending someone to Eden that day—to bait Lilith and have someone succumb to her.

Had I done that, though? Had I fully yielded to her power, her control? I didn't feel like I had. Ever since she had bit me, I had made my own decisions, my own choices. But then why was she the voice I heard inside my mind, the one always doubting me and questioning my actions.

I shook my head. This wasn't the time for self-reflection. "Are we here to negotiate or to throw insults?"

She flicked her hand as if she were swatting a nonexistent fly. "You're here to negotiate, but you refuse to give me what I want, so I don't see how we can carry on."

"Fine. Then we're done."

Her mouth dropped. "Excuse me?"

"It's not hard to understand, Jazema. You need my assets more than I need yours."

"Oh really? Have you tired of the technology I've given you?"

"No, I've just come to see how worthless it is. It doesn't really give me an advantage." I raised my hands. "Not when what's running through my veins is a hundred times more powerful. Besides—" I shrugged my shoulders "—you would never give me the good stuff anyway, the tech you keep for yourself and your experiments."

"Then what can I give you to keep the agreement in place? The weapons you provide are untraceable since they're forged in Hell and not made in some ordinary factory."

I smirked. "I'll keep giving you weapons and bullets forged in Hell—" I paused "—as long as you give me the locations of my keys."

Her eyes flashed. "How would I know where they are?"

I crossed the small distance between us and backed her up against the balcony railing, barring her way by placing my arms on either side of her. "Don't play with me, Jazema. You make it your business to know every dirty little detail about someone so you can have leverage over them."

"I'm not playing." Her tone grew serious. "I've heard of your keys, but I don't know where they are. Some dirt is hard to find when they're God's secrets."

I felt an object placed at the middle of my back, right between my wings.

"Back off," a deep voice said from behind.

"Why?" I spit over my shoulder.

"Because I'm the person who can give you answers. Not her."

I dropped my arms without turning and let Jazema ease away from the balcony.

She dusted off the sleeve of her white suit. "Satan, allow me to introduce you to the Sentinel, my hitman who kills people and ties up loose ends."

I turned around to meet the man. He wore a hooded black cowl that covered his face, but I could see the color of his eyes was a chestnut brown. How he had gotten up here was a mystery, between the suspicious appearance and the weapons strapped to his body. He obviously hadn't walked through the front door. The only sign of a personality was his cocky stance, a telltale sign of arrogance.

"How the hell would you know where my keys are?"

His brown eyes stared me down. "Because I betrayed the Sacrarium."

That made me pause. Could that really be? Had the mighty secret society had a betrayer among their ranks at one point? The nun had hinted at some internal downfall, but was this man telling the truth?

"Why should I believe you?" I asked.

He shrugged. "Believe what you will. I don't have to prove myself to you when I know what I say is true. I was just trying to help your negotiations."

"Fine," I conceded. "Then tell me where my keys are."

"Uh, uh, uh. Not so fast," Jazema said. "If he tells you, you have to keep our weapons deal *and* give me a pint of blood."

My eyes narrowed to slits. She was such a conniving woman. Like hell would I agree to such a thing. I had no choice but to refuse. I wouldn't walk away empty-handed, though. No, I would get what I wanted.

Suddenly, a thought struck me. If what the Sentinel had said was true, all I had to do was get something from him, a personal object of some kind, and then I could have the witches do their magic. They could extract the location of my keys from it since it would be tied to him. It was just a matter of finding the right object.

My gaze landed on the Sentinel's hand. The gun. Surely that would do. As a kill man, it would be a prized possession. It would also be caked in fingerprints and DNA. What better binding entities than those in black magic?

I mischievously smiled and unleashed the Devil within.

My wings came out as I spun around behind the Sentinel and grabbed his arm. The move caught him by surprise, but he quickly regained his focus. We struggled over the gun in his hand, and a shot rang out. An innocent pigeon dropped dead at our feet.

At the sound, paranoia reigned as the tourists started screaming and running. Jazema disappeared into the stampede, along with some of her Nephilim accomplices. Two remained behind, ready to assist the Sentinel, but Lucifer and Beelzebub blocked their path and engaged them.

What a pity to cause such a scene. It would be over soon, though. Just a twist of his human arm was all it would take to break the bones and get the gun…

The Sentinel landed a roundhouse kick to my abdomen.

I let out a rush of breath as the wind was knocked out of me and a rib cracked. I fell to one knee, slightly stunned by his force.

Glancing up through the hair that had fallen in my eyes, I analyzed my opponent.

"You think I'm some average human," he said. I could tell a cocky grin was plastered across his hooded face just by the tone of his words.

He pointed his gun at me.

It was my turn to give him a cocky grin. "A man like you should know that won't work on me."

"I know." The gun shifted slightly to my left. "But it would work on her."

My eyes darted to the teenage girl cowering behind me. She had brown skin and raven-black hair. As he pulled the trigger, my body reacted before my mind could, and I found myself yet again saving a human soul instead of sacrificing it.

There had to be a reason to kill, and in this circumstance, just like with the nun, there was none. This girl was innocent. The nun had been far from it, but she would get a punishment far greater than death, for she would suffer from her illness and atone for her secrets. That seemed like a good case of revenge. While this... This was pure insanity.

I took the bullet in the back as I leaped in front of the girl. Her jaw dropped as my wings snapped out. She was clearly stunned, both by the rescue and the sight of my wings.

"Get out of here!" I yelled at her, wincing in pain.

She jumped up and ran off to get away from the crossfire.

"Well, well, well... I guess Lucifer was right. You have grown soft."

The Sentinel's words unleashed my anger. I threw myself right at him, taking another gunshot to the chest and leveling him to the ground. I brought my foot down on his knee, snapping it. He howled in pain.

Grabbing him by the scruff of his shirt, I dragged him over to the coin-operated telescope and smashed his hand against the metal. He grunted but wouldn't release the gun, so I kept repeating the action as he tried to kick out his good leg and trip me up. The small effort was no match for me.

In my anger, I slammed his hand one more time and shouted, "Give me the gun, damn it!" His bones were beyond broken at this point, but I finally felt his fingers release.

Dropping his hand, I looped my finger through the trigger and spun the gun around. "Such horrendous weapons," I said, teasing him. But rather than writhe in pain, he stared at me with white-hot anger. Our fight wasn't over.

Time was running out, though. Security guards and police would be here any moment.

As I flung the gun in the air, the Sentinel's eyes widened. Clearly, he was dearly attached to his weapon. Yet, rather than let it fall to the pavement below, Leviathan swooped by, caught it, and flew off.

Reaching into my jacket, I pulled out a knife. "I'm old-school."

The Sentinel chuckled, easing up off the ground to stand unsteadily on his good leg. "Old-school? You're ancient." He whipped out a dagger and resumed our fight, lunging first.

I dodged his thrust and brought my knife around, cutting him in the shoulder and tearing his long-sleeve shirt. He staggered back and spied a glance at his wound, which was already streaming blood.

My eyes followed his and widened in surprise to see what was hidden beneath his shirt. "You bear the mark of Lilith. Why is that, when Jazema hates her with a fiery passion?"

He swiped the blood from his arm. "Because she's the one who created me. And I'll always play sides for her."

He launched himself at me again, but the attempt was futile with the number of injuries he had sustained. I could tell he wouldn't stop, though, and I was prepared to end it. All I needed was one more well-placed blow. But just as I kicked out, something out of the corner of my eye distracted me. It seemed that Beelzebub had slain his Nephilim attacker and was barring the doors so no authorities could come out on the observation deck. Yet, whoever that teenage girl was, she was a clear genius because her earlier surprise was all an act as she approached him from behind, ready to attack. What drew my attention was the fact that Lucifer was standing by, his opponent defeated, simply watching as the Nephilim girl stalked toward Beelzebub.

"Look who's finally showing his true colors," the Sentinel remarked, lashing out with his dagger again.

I ducked, but instead of parrying his next move, I hurled my knife through the air, its mark the girl's raised hand. The knife collided with her gun, knocking it away. Her raven-black hair blew into her face, but there was no mistaking the shock etched on it.

As she faltered again—for real this time—the Sentinel came at me with a killing strike. Except instinct took over and I turned my body, moving my wing to block the blow. The knife tore through my feathers and nicked my arm, a small prick of blood beading up. I raised out a hand and caught the rail of the balcony as I fell. Pain erupted, not in my arm but in my wing, the most sensitive spot for any angel, fallen or otherwise.

Slumped against the concrete wall, I saw the Sentinel back off, sheathing his dagger. "The no-good, rotten bastard is more of a turncoat than I am."

I eyed him. "Your insults will only egg me on!"

"I wasn't talking about you," he said with a sneer. "I was talking about Lucifer."

That damn scoundrel must be betraying everyone. But what did Lucifer have to do with the Sentinel?

Confusion must have flashed across my face.

The Sentinel chuckled. "How little you know…" He turned his back on me to shuffle away.

I swiped the Sentinel's knife from the ground and kicked him down from behind. Kneeling on top of him, I lifted back his head and put the blade to his exposed neck. "What should I know?"

"Maybe that he chose to meet at the Empire State Building because he knew your sphere used to be hidden here and thought it would be a good way to humiliate you, given you know nothing."

My grip tightened on the dagger. That son of bitch!

"What else?" I demanded.

"Maybe that he's working for Lilith, just like I am."

My hand trembled with rage. I knew I couldn't trust her. But she had been sabotaging me all along!

Then a thought occurred to me. "Why tell me this?"

"Because the bastard's ready to betray Lilith, too, and it's high time to end him. But why not make it a competition between you and me to see who does it first? He'd be better off if it's one of us anyway, since she'll tear him limb from limb when she returns."

Returns? Lilith was coming back? From where, I didn't know, but none of this boded well.

I was about to slide the blade across the Sentinel's throat when Leviathan swooped down and careened into me.

"What do you think you're doing?" I yelled at him. My knife whizzed through the air and landed on the ground behind the Sentinel, where I had been mere seconds before.

"Saving you," Leviathan stated.

The Sentinel had distracted me on purpose so the Nephilim girl could use the knife I had thrown at her on me; however, thanks to Leviathan, their plan hadn't worked.

Nonetheless, they did get away. The Sentinel shuffled over to the girl, covering his arm to hide the mark, while also trying to stop the blood. She stretched out her wings, speckled brown in color, and grabbed his good arm, launching them both into the air.

"Hey!" the remaining Nephilim yelled. "What about me?" He clearly did not possess the same gift as the girl. Hardly any Nephilim did anymore, which meant one thing: Jazema and Penelope had been successful with their experiment. But how they had done it, and how many they had created, still remained a question. One for another time.

Beelzebub raced over to us. "We gotta leave, boss."

"I know," I said, grimacing as my adrenaline dropped and I started to feel the effects of my wounds.

Behind him, Lucifer took flight after his temporary allies. Damn him!

He better not return or I will slay him where he stands.

The police started pounding the doors, and Beelzebub grew anxious. "We really gotta go. Grab on," he said, knowing I couldn't fly considering I had a gaping hole in my wing.

I took Beelzebub's outstretched arm, making sure to grab his shirtsleeve. Even though my Hellfire was no longer working, no one needed to know that other than me.

We zoomed off just as the police broke down the doors. The remaining Nephilim was the only soul left on the observation deck, and the police dragged him to the ground before he could plead his innocence.

Somebody had to take responsibility for the attack. Just like somebody had to pay for Lucifer's treachery. But not until we were back in Hell…

17 JORDAN

New York City, Present Day

"Jordan." The word was a whisper, echoing through my mind. "Jordan," the voice said again, beckoning me.

There was silence and darkness. Then a persistent tapping against my forehead right between my eyes, almost like a bird pecking at me.

I wanted to move my arm, to shoo off the irritating sensation, but it was paralyzed at my side. Before I could panic, I was freefalling through darkness, unable to shout or move my body. The drop seemed endless, until suddenly I hit the bottom, or rather, jolted back into my body. Opening my eyes, I was still surrounded by darkness, except now I could move my limbs. I pushed myself up to my knees, wondering where I was and how I had traveled beyond Gabriel's apartment.

Suddenly, the temperature dropped and a wind gusted about, tearing at my body. I crossed my arms to warm myself but couldn't keep my teeth from chattering. I tried to move my feet, to get out of the chill, but they were frozen in place as ice started to form over them.

"Hel-help!" I stuttered. "Help!" I sank to the icy ground, knowing there was no one to help me.

The wind rushed through my ears, and I closed my eyes, succumbing to the cold. Then I heard a noise, someone shuffling across the icy tundra.

I pried my eyes open and peered through the snow that had started to fall. "Hel-hello?"

No one answered. Instead, I heard laughter.

"Well, well, well," a female voice said.

"Wh-who's there?" I asked weakly.

"I thought it would never work," I heard the voice say.

"Sh-show yourself." It was getting harder and harder to speak.

Silence.

They must have left.

"Boo!"

I jumped as the word was shouted directly in my ear. The laughter started again, coming from a figure that stood before me. It was a woman shrouded in a long, hooded cloak. I couldn't see her face, but she looked warm.

I shivered. "Wh-where am I?"

She knelt before me. "In a place frozen in time." She lifted her hand and touched my face, her fingers adorned with claws. She ran one of them across my cheek, close enough to feel it along my skin but not hard enough to draw blood. The claw trailed down, along my neck, and stopped to rest right above my collarbone. "No wonder it finally worked," she remarked. "You aren't wearing any protective wards."

I scrunched my face in confusion and blinked a few times, realizing I might have been having some hallucinatory trip, potentially evoked by the massive amounts of hellhound breath and saliva that had been spewed in my face all night.

Unable to stay upright, my body collapsed from the cold, falling to the thick ice. I was covered in snow, and the shivering was so strong I couldn't even speak.

The woman stroked my face again, as a mother would a child's. "My poor dear."

I opened my mouth and wheezed out a tiny, "Help…"

She venomously smiled. "Oh sweetie, I wish I could, but this isn't a dream. It's a nightmare."

In that moment, I knew whatever was happening had nothing to do with the hellhounds. I should have known better because this is exactly how I used to feel as a kid. Except I had Sister Helen to save me then, and now I didn't.

Lying there on my side, I tried to get a glimpse of the woman's face, but it remained beneath the shadow of the hood. Who was this woman? Why was she so mean?

My eyes sunk closed. I guessed I would never find out.

I thought I might have finally found my peace until there was pressure on my chest again. "No! Leave me alone!"

"Jordan!" A voice, familiar and urgent, called my name.

I wanted to listen to it, I wanted it to guide me out of the nightmare, but I couldn't rise from the darkness.

18 DANE

New York City, Present Day

"Good morning," Sophia said to me as I entered the kitchen.

I stopped rubbing the sleep from my eyes to gaze at her. She wore pajama shorts and a T-shirt, and her long, wavy blond hair was loose and tousled. Her face was bare, as were her feet. I couldn't help but think how beautiful she looked.

For years I had secretly crushed on her, wanting to draw every swoop and curve of her face, but I knew the odds of us ever being a thing were slim. She didn't feel the way I did, and I doubted she ever would. I was damaged goods—too rough around the edges. She deserved someone a hell of a lot better than me.

When we were younger, I'd figured it was just a childhood crush, but the moment she had crashed through my window yesterday, all those feelings had rushed back stronger than ever.

I had always teased Jordan about liking her because I'd known it would torture him. He hated expressing feelings for girls because they confused him—both the feelings and the girls. I knew he and Sophia were close, but they were like brother and sister. I guessed a part of me had teased him to deflect my feelings. Or maybe I secretly had hoped he would call me out on the fact that I was the one in love with her. But he never did. No one did because no one cared about how I felt. No one cared about me.

All my life, I had felt uncomfortable with myself. I felt trapped in a body that didn't match my soul. I felt like my true self was locked away somewhere, waiting to come out, except it never had. Who knew if I would ever find that self, find that place where I belonged, but I sure as hell would keep searching for it. In the meantime, I was creating a new path to leave behind the Dane who was always angry and who couldn't forgive. It was time to seek the new Dane—or rather the original one who had enjoyed having friends, the one who could help a secret society fight Satan, whatever that meant.

But why not give in to the darkness? What had doing right ever brought me but being second best?

Sitting down at the kitchen counter, I rubbed my forehead. This was how it always was: a voice on each shoulder leading me to light or dark. The dark always had been louder, always stronger.

"Dane? Are you okay?" Sophia asked.

I looked up at her sparkling blue eyes, wishing the concern on her face hinted at something more.

How do you know it doesn't? the kinder voice whispered. *Maybe she does like you. She's been through stuff, too. Who's to say she doesn't have baggage? Who's to say you can't have a second chance?*

I smiled. Maybe this *was* my second chance. For once, I listened to the light, optimistic voice and drowned out the dark side.

"I'm fine, just a little tired still," I said to her. "And confused, but I guess that's to be expected given everything that happened yesterday."

"I can relate." She was vigorously stirring something in a ceramic bowl with a wooden spoon. "You didn't have to get up. Jordan hasn't yet."

I was about to ask her what she was doing when I stopped. "Jordan's not awake?"

"No." She set the bowl down and licked some kind of batter off her finger.

I pulled my eyes away from her lips. "Has anyone checked on him?" I asked.

She looked at me. "No," she said slowly. "Why?"

I shrugged. "He never sleeps in late."

"Well, like you said, a lot happened yesterday." She brought her attention back to the bowl. "I'm making pancakes. Your favorite are chocolate chip, right?"

"Yeah... How'd you know that?"

She smiled at me. "Because we grew up together."

"I know that," I laughed. "It's just...you remembered."

"I remember a lot of things." She dumped some batter into the frying pan on the stove.

"Yours are blueberry, right?"

"Mm-hmm."

"And Jordan's are cinnamon." The voice came from the hallway opposite the kitchen, the one on the left side of the penthouse. It was one of the angels, the one who owned the apartment. Gabriel, I think his name was.

"Sorry to interrupt," he said. "I heard voices so I wanted to check on you. Did you sleep well?"

"I did. Thank you," I told him.

"I did, too," Sophia said. "And thank you for going shopping this morning. I figured it might be nice to make breakfast instead of ordering out. It was a nice distraction from…well, everything." She slid some pancakes onto a plate and set them before me.

"Thanks," I said. "Did you happen to make coffee?"

"It's over there." She pointed at the steaming pot.

I stood up and grabbed a mug from the cabinet. I poured myself a cup and took a big sip without adding anything to it. Catching the time on the microwave out of the corner of my eye, I nearly spit it out. "Is that the time?"

Gabriel glanced over her shoulder. "Yes. Why?"

Because it's 11:30 AM *and Jordan isn't awake,* I wanted to say. But instead, I shrugged it off. "No reason." I glanced down the hallway toward the master bedroom.

Jordan was an early riser, always had been. Sometimes to the point of being a pain in the ass when we were younger, flicking on lights and creaking open his closet door when I was still sleeping. So I couldn't help but shake the feeling that something was wrong. I also knew that he *hated* being woken up. Ironic given how much he had done it to me. I figured leaving him alone was the best thing to do. I was probably overreacting anyway. He was probably just exhausted from yesterday like the rest of us.

Sighing, I returned to my seat with my coffee and started eating.

A few minutes later, Sophia had finished making the rest of the pancakes and had hopped onto the stool next to me with a plate of her own. Just as she reached for the syrup and I was about to take my last bite, the other three angels raced into the apartment, slamming the front door abruptly.

"What's wrong?" Gabriel asked.

"There's been another attack," Raphael said.

The TV flicked on to breaking news, which announced an active-shooter alert at the Empire State Building.

"When did this happen?" Sophia asked.

"About half an hour ago," Michael said.

Everyone huddled around the TV in the living room, and I stood to join them. But I had a sinking feeling in the pit of my stomach. I looked down the hallway again, to the room where Jordan was sleeping. The door was shut.

The harder I stared at it, the worse the nagging feeling got. "Something's not right," I said, more to myself than anyone else. I crept down the hallway, inching closer to the door. I reached for the knob. My fingers curled around the smooth metal, and just as quickly, I pulled back as the handle froze my skin.

"Shit!" I yelled, waving my hand in the air to drive away the burn. Then I slammed my body against the wooden door with all my strength, ready to break it down to get inside.

Between my loud curse and the sheer noise I was now making to get in, everyone came running down the hall.

"What's wrong?" Sophia asked.

"The knob is frozen," I told her, ramming my shoulder against the door.

Michael pushed me aside and raised his foot, bringing it down on the handle. With the sheer force of the blow and his celestial strength combined, the door swung open easily, the lock completely broken.

Inside, Jordan lay curled in a fetal position on the bed, blankets completely thrown off. He was shivering so bad you'd think he was outside in negative-degree weather.

I raced to his side, and the others followed. Placing my hand on his chest, I tried nudging him awake. "Jordan!"

Nothing.

One of the angels reached out to touch his arm. "He's ice to the touch."

I focused on his lifeless face, too alarmed that he wasn't coming back, to notice who had spoken. "Jordan! Jordan!" I shook him now, but there was no reaction.

A hand appeared on my shoulder, leading me away. "Let Raphael attend to him."

Stepping aside, I looked up at Gabriel. There was concern on his face. There was concern on everyone's face, but he was trying to remain calm.

Raphael inspected Jordan to no avail. "I don't understand what's wrong. I've never seen anything like this before."

"What? Can't you do something?" Sophia pleaded.

"I'm going to try," Raphael replied, a determined look in his eye. "Uriel, gather some blankets. Michael, help him warm them with the space heater. We need to get his body temperature up."

They nodded and left the room.

"How can I help?" Gabriel asked. Clearly, he couldn't stand by helplessly. I understood the feeling because I was getting antsy waiting for them to help Jordan, too.

"Keep close," Raphael said. "I might need you." They shared a secretive look.

Sophia drew my attention away as she came closer and reached for my arm. "He's going to be okay, right?"

I sighed and set my jaw. "Yeah, he's going to be okay." But I couldn't look her in the eye when I said it.

Raphael pulled up the covers and tucked Jordan in. Soon, Michael and Uriel returned with some heated blankets, which they placed atop the bed. "This will have to do for now," Raphael said.

"That's it? There must be something else you can do," I said.

"Dane, I'm sorry, but I've never seen anything like Jordan's condition before," Raphael said. "I don't know what could have brought it on, but right now, the best thing we can do is get him warm."

"You think it's hypothermia?" Michael asked.

Raphael shrugged. "It seems to be more like that than a coma."

"It seems like he's stuck in a dream. You can see his eyes moving back and forth," Uriel commented.

His words echoed through my mind, and suddenly, I remembered that this wasn't the first time this had happened. I moved closer to Jordan again, leaning over and pulling down the collar of his T-shirt.

"What are you doing?" Raphael asked.

A plain silver cross lay around his neck. "Damn it!"

"What's wrong?" Sophia asked.

"He's not wearing his necklace," I said, exasperated.

She scrunched up her face, confused. "What necklace?"

"The fleur-de-lis," the angels said together.

I nodded. "Yes, where is it?"

"At the house in Ithaca," Michael replied.

"What does the necklace have to do with Jordan's condition?" Raphael asked.

Without answering, I sat down on the bed next to Jordan and leaned over him, pressing my thumb firmly to his forehead. I hoped I was doing it right because I was basing this trick off what I had seen Sister Delphine do in the past, not anything I had ever done.

Come on, Jordan.

Suddenly, he gasped and slowly peeled his eyes open. He blinked a few times, trying to focus his vision. His lips were nearly blue, and they trembled as he tried to smile. "Wh-what ar-are you doing?" he stuttered.

I released the breath I'd been holding. "Just trying to wake you from your beauty sleep," I said, hiding my relief with a joke.

He tried to chuckle but coughed instead, snuggling farther under the blankets. "Wh-what's g-going on? You all l-look concerned."

"We couldn't wake you up. You were shivering and ice to the touch," Raphael explained.

"I c-can believe that because I'm absolutely f-freezing."

Michael pulled the warmed blankets tighter around him while Gabriel retreated to the closet and returned with a beanie that he slipped on Jordan's head. "I never found much use for it anyway."

The room fell quiet, the only noise the sound of Jordan's chattering teeth as he tried to control the shivers.

"Where did you go this time?" I asked.

He shook his head. "Somewhere strange and cold. There was a woman there. I couldn't see her face, and she wouldn't help me."

"Your dream," I said. "You were stuck in it, like when we were kids."

He shrugged it off. "It was only a dream." But he didn't seem convinced.

My eyes hardened. "One that sent you into a hypothermic coma."

"It was hardly that bad," he said. He looked to the angels. "Right?"

"Unfortunately, it *was* that bad," Gabriel said. He turned to me. "Would you mind explaining now what the necklace has to do with his condition?"

"What are you talking about?" Jordan asked.

Shaking my head, I said, "I don't know exactly. What I do know is that Jordan has weird dreams—vivid dreams, night terrors—whatever you want to call them. He's been this way ever since we were kids. At first, it was nothing, but one night when we were six, I heard this loud noise and woke up to find Jordan on the ground. He had fallen out of bed, and I figured the fall must have woken him up so I rolled over to go back to sleep, but then he started having some kind of seizure."

Jordan's face crumpled in confusion. "I did?"

"Yes, I'll never forget it. I ran and got Sister Helen. She came back to our room with Sister Delphine, as if she knew what was really happening. Sister Delphine pressed her thumb to your forehead and brought you back to consciousness. Once you were awake, Sister Helen settled us back to bed, but before you fell asleep again, she gave you your fleur-de-lis necklace."

"Right, she told me it would protect me," he recalled aloud.

"Well, yeah, but it does a lot more than that," I said. "It keeps your dreams away."

"Like a protective ward," Jordan whispered.

"A what?" I asked.

"A protective ward. The woman in my dream… She said I finally wasn't wearing any protective wards. My necklace must be one of them."

Sophia shook her head. "But why? How?"

No one had an answer.

Jordan glanced at me. "How did you know about my necklace? And why didn't you ever tell me any of this before?"

"Sister Helen asked me not to. She said she'd handle it… As for the necklace, I don't really know how it works, but after you started wearing it, you never had a nightmare, bad dream, or incident again while we lived together. That can't be a coincidence."

Jordan looked puzzled. "I guess you're right. I'd never given it much thought before. I don't really remember what happens to me. I hardly even remember the dreams."

"I think Dane's theory is very credible," Raphael said. "I had no idea what was wrong with you or how to treat you because I hadn't seen anything like it before. I almost asked Gabriel to peek inside your mind."

I tilted my head. "Excuse me?"

"Not that again!" Jordan exclaimed.

"I said *almost*. It was a last resort," Raphael clarified.

"Allow me to explain," Gabriel said to me. "Some angels have gifted abilities. One of our fellow brothers has visions while I can transmit thoughts."

"Yes," Sophia said, "angels have abilities. But right now, our main focus needs to be making Jordan feel better. What else can we do?"

"She's right. You're still shaking," Raphael said.

"Maybe some food?" she offered hopefully. "I'll bring you some pancakes."

His face brightened. "You made pancakes?"

"Yes, cinnamon ones, especially for you."

"Thanks," he said, smiling.

Sophia left the room and went back to the kitchen.

"There's something else you might want to know," Gabriel said to Jordan.

"What is it?"

"There's been another attack."

Jordan froze, and within seconds, he was back to being himself, the ever-responsible hero. Except in the time we'd been apart, he had grown even more mature.

Flipping back the covers, he jumped out of bed and raced down the hallway to the living room and the TV. We all followed him, the angels protesting and trailing warm blankets after him.

Jealousy flared in my chest. It seemed no matter what scenario we were thrown into, Jordan was always the one doted upon.

I went back to my cold coffee and pancakes, gazing over at Sophia, who was looking out the window. "You okay?" I asked her.

She blinked and tore her eyes away from the view. "Yeah, I'm just worried about how intense Jordan's dream was. I mean, was it the cause of the doorknob being frozen?"

I hadn't thought about that.

"That sounds so insane, right? I mean, it couldn't have been that," she said. "Dreams can't turn into reality."

"I don't know, Soph." She looked so scared and worried, almost like she was concerned about something else. I touched her hand. "You sure you're okay?"

She smiled weakly. "Absolutely."

But she didn't look me in the eye when she said it. Instead, her gaze was rooted to the TV and the devilish menace haunting New York.

19

SATAN

HELL, PRESENT DAY

On my return to Hell, I secluded myself away in the portal room, the place where I traveled back and forth from Hell to Earth now that I had the amulet, dropping the Sentinel's knife on the worktable. Glancing over at my wing, I could tell it wasn't going to heal. The wound would have started to close by now, but it remained open.

I peeled off my shirt, dug the bullets out of my chest and back, and inspected my arm. The small cut was nothing compared with the damage done to my wing. Although it wasn't healing, either.

I pounded my fist on the stone table. "Damn it!" I needed those obnoxious witches.

Someone cleared their throat behind me.

"What do you want?" I demanded without turning around.

"I came to bring you the gun," Leviathan said. He deposited the weapon on the table.

"Good."

He lingered.

"What?"

"There are some things that need your attention, sir."

Facing him, I asked, "Like what?"

"Well, what would you like me to do if Lucifer returns?"

My anger rose to the surface. "Confine him and bring him to me immediately. His behavior must be dealt with."

"All right."

"What else is wrong?" I asked.

"Haborym wants to speak with you."

She was the fallen angel who had helped me manipulate divine light to create my portals, barriers, and shields. Now she was the one who forged our weapons.

"About?"

Leviathan shrugged. "She didn't say."

"Fine. Anything else?"

"There is a small problem in Envy."

I frowned. There were nine levels in Hell, the bottom being Misery, where the spirits were forced to complete their sentences of torment, and the top being Elysium, where my brethren of fallen angels resided and where I ruled. Between these were the Eighth Cavern—home to the five rivers of Hell—and six other levels that housed cities named after the deadly sins. The cities each had a designated leader, a member of the Six, so I didn't have to deal with the insignificant woes of the spirits who resided there, the ones who had completed their sentences.

Which is why my anger was flaring because Leviathan, who was the leader of Envy, should be able to control his own city.

"A problem you can't deal with?"

"I can, but I want to know how best to proceed. You see, Astrid and Tabitha are becoming a little…boisterous."

Those damn witches needed to learn their place. "It's about time I paid them a visit."

I left the portal room and made a short trip to my private quarters for a clean shirt, then reconvened with Leviathan in the throne room. Stepping over to the Pit, I was about to launch into the open air when I remembered my wing. It still hurt but I had grown numb to the pain.

"I can take you down," Leviathan offered.

"No!" I strode over to the steps leading down from the throne room.

Leviathan followed. "It'll take longer on foot."

"I don't give a damn. I need a good walk anyway."

"I'll come with you, then."

"No." I turned around on the steps to face him. "I don't need your help in this endeavor. What I need you to do is tell Haborym I'll meet her in the throne room once I'm done. Then track down Lucifer. See if he's truly with Jazema."

"Of course."

I left him and made my way into the city of Elysium. It was bustling with fallen angels, many of them acknowledging my presence as I passed. My excursion was uneventful as most of the angels knew not to disturb me, unlike the spirits. Once I made it through to the other side of the city, I entered the cave that connected to the other levels and traveled down the stone steps in relative darkness. There were sconces placed along the wall where flames rose out, illuminating the way, but the firelight wasn't very bright.

It was odd how quiet the caves were. Not many hellish beings journeyed through them but the hounds roamed them constantly, usually creating a cacophony of sound.

Finally, after three flights of steps, I entered Envy. This area of the city was less populated than the rest, more for spirits who simply wanted to live out their afterlives in as peaceful a way as possible. Various stone dwellings, dingy and dilapidated, were carved into the cave, some spirits peeking out their windows and quickly moving deeper inside their homes once they saw me.

As I drew closer to the central part of the city, loud noises filled my ears—laughing, arguing, bartering, even screaming.

I stopped momentarily and braced myself for the onslaught of demanding spirits. It was inevitable that they would stop me and want my attention.

Stepping into the street, I headed to where I had originally found Astrid and Tabitha. Sure enough, the spirits detected my presence.

"Hello, sir! Thanks for joining us down here today."

"It's good to see you!"

"Help! Help, Lord Satan, sir! She's stealing my money!"

I ignored them all and continued through the city until I made it to the place known for magic and divination. Unlike the last time I was here, there was a massive crowd of spirits in the street blocking my path. "Move! Move! Get out of my way!" I demanded.

They slowly parted, initially frustrated by being bothered until they noticed who I was.

"I'm terribly sorry, sir," one spirit said. "Everyone," he yelled, "make way, make way! Our Lord Satan is coming through!"

The masses parted even farther, and I swiftly walked through the horde. When I came closer, I realized Astrid and Tabitha's usual table was gone. Instead, it had been replaced by a large tent with a sign that read The Witchcraft Sisters, selling potions, divinations, and magical wares.

One spirit exited the tent with a big smile on his face and floated past me, stroking a necklace that looked exactly like my amulet.

The anger inside started to boil. "You're all here for this?" I shouted.

"Yes, sir," one female spirit said. "The Witchcraft Sisters are the best around. They guarantee good prices and satisfying results. It also helps that they have your full endorsement." She pointed to another sign erected outside the tent: PERSONAL SORCERESS AND SEER OF OUR LORD SATAN.

That's it!

I shoved through the remaining crowd and burst into the tent. There were spirits everywhere, browsing the merchandise. In the far corner, a voice captured my attention.

"Get your amulets here! Exact replicas of our Lord Satan's! A tried-and-true testament to our handiwork!" It was Tabitha, eagerly drawing in spirits and passing out amulets.

In another corner, an unmistakable screeching gasp filled the air as Astrid read a spirit's palm and launched into some prophetic divination. Yet, I could tell she was faking, since her hair still concealed her face. Whenever she had a true vision, it would blow out of the way, exposing her face and blind gaze.

I stepped closer to Tabitha. "This is what you do with my money?"

She looked up, and her face fell. "Sir! I had no idea you were here!" She abruptly hid the amulets and pushed through the spirits crowding around her. "How can I be of assistance? Perhaps you'd like a love potion to help with your lady lover friend." She grabbed a bottle off the nearest shelf and offered it to me.

I slapped it away. "Get everyone out of here! Now! Before I start harming your customers."

Alarmed, Tabitha raced around shouting, "All right, everyone! It's time to go! We're closing for lunch and will reopen later!"

I glared at her.

"Get out!" she screamed urgently, my sinister presence obviously doing the trick.

All the spirits exited the tent, and I was left alone with Tabitha standing before me.

"What are you doing?" Astrid shouted, coming closer to her sister. "You're getting rid of paying customers!"

"Enough!" her sister yelled. "We have far bigger problems."

"What do you mean?" Astrid asked.

"She means I've discovered your little business," I said. "You dare betray your Lord with treachery and backstabbing?"

"No, sir. It's not," Tabitha pleaded. "We're just being entrepreneurial."

"Yeah," Astrid agreed, donning her fake bravado.

"Entrepreneurial? So you're using me and my ailments to make a profit."

Tabitha's jaw dropped slightly, realizing her poor choice of words. "No, sir. No, I promise."

"Then why are you selling my amulet?" I shouted.

"Because the people love you," Astrid chimed in.

"It's not real, only an imitation," Tabitha explained. "We just thought it would be a great way to advertise our work, since we were able to help you with a task so important. Our intent wasn't to be treacherous. If anything, the amulets were a way to idolize you."

My glare hardened. "I'm done with your excuses."

Despite my warning, Tabitha opened her mouth to protest.

I raised my hand to silence her. "But I'm prepared to make a deal with you."

The sisters' eyes grew wide, even Astrid's cloudy ones.

"You can keep your business as long as you stop selling amulets, fake or not."

"Of course, sir," Tabitha agreed.

"Now I imagine you want to keep your good name?"

"Absolutely," Astrid said.

"Well, then I have another task for you. But first, I need answers."

They nodded.

"And absolute secrecy. I swear if anyone finds out, it's straight to the rivers with both of you."

They both made a zipping motion across their lips. I knew it was all for show. Spirits didn't end up in Envy because of their trustworthiness. Then again, no one in Hell was truly trustworthy.

I paused, weighing my options. I knew they would have the answer to why my abilities had diminished, but telling them would make me vulnerable to their chatty gossip, and *no one* could know. I already had problems with Lucifer. I could only imagine if the rest knew I was weak. I could easily decimate the witches if they spoke out of turn, but how much damage would their loose tongues do before they were vanquished?

Fumbling with my amulet, I knew the advantages outweighed the consequences. I chose my words carefully. "There have been some… unusual side effects since I began wearing this amulet. Do you know why?"

"Side effects, sir?" Tabitha asked. "Such as?"

I stopped. They didn't need to know everything, especially not that my greatest strength was gone. "I've lost feathers. I'm taking a bit longer to heal. And the Hellfire isn't *quite* as strong as it was previously, although still strong," I added, protecting my secret. "What's causing these changes?"

Tabitha shook her head and tsked. "Every magic has a price. Your blood and feather contributed to two-thirds of the potion so the amulet weakens you because it's drawing on the energy of the items it was created from. Since they came from you, it's straining you. The longer you wear it, the worse the effects will be."

"Why didn't you tell me this sooner?" I yelled, reaching to take it off.

"I wouldn't do that if I were you," Astrid warned.

I stopped. "Why not?"

"If you take it off," Tabitha explained, "the amulet is no longer viable, meaning we would have to create you a new one. But there's no guarantee the ingredients or the process will be the same. In fact, the price will probably be more exacting."

"So I leave it on and what? Deal with my wounds, my...*side effects*?"

"If you want to keep traveling to Earth," Tabitha said, "then yes."

"Maybe you should start focusing on finding that holy bloodline and—" Astrid paused to run a finger across her neck "—you know, take care of business."

Having Astrid tell me what to do irritated me, but she was right. I was focused on everything but locating the bloodline whose existence trapped me down here. But after the havoc I had wreaked, I needed to finish what I started before Jazema and the Nephilim came knocking on my door.

"I have some things I need to attend to first," I told them. "But meet me in the throne room after you close for business."

Astrid and Tabitha saluted me. "Yes, sir."

"And keep your damn mouths shut!" I thundered, putting the fear of the Underworld into them. My powers weren't so weak that I'd lost my gift of intimidation.

I left, running right into a spirit on the way out of the tent.

"Sorry, sir," she cowered.

"It's all right." I stepped aside so she could go in.

"No, Sire, I don't want to go in there," she told me. "Those sisters have dealt me a rough deal too many times." She shook her head. "No, I go to Abbadona now. She doesn't trick you with black magic." She skirted around me and continued her journey.

Abbadona. In the Eighth Cavern of Hell. The level that I liked least.

Still, maybe I should go see her.

20

SATAN

HELL, PRESENT DAY

I retraced my steps through the city of Envy, my journey calmer and uninterrupted now that the spirits had dispersed after my outburst. I returned to the stone steps and continued down several flights to the eighth level of Hell, where the rivers resided.

Since there were still no hellhounds in sight, my trip was quicker, but the fact that they were gone was alarming. They were a defense against spirits traveling between cities, and if they didn't return soon, anarchy would ensue. And not just among the spirits. The demons and fallen angels would soon follow when they realized my sway over the hounds had diminished. It wouldn't be long before they realized how weak I had grown, and then mutiny and usurpation of my throne wouldn't be far behind.

I stopped briefly before the entryway into the Eighth Cavern, curling my hand into a fist and gazing at it. I needed to fix *me*. I needed to take control.

So I dropped my hand and strengthened my resolve as I stepped into the Eighth Cavern to find Abbadona and face the merciless allure of the rivers.

As soon as my feet touched the stone floor, the rivers' whispers started, tempting me closer to their waters.

Come, my king.

Wash away your sins.

Return to your full glory.

I closed my eyes and fortified myself. I had faced worse than the waters. I had faced the Hellfire and walked again with the ache running through my veins.

Opening my eyes, I moved deeper into the Eighth Cavern. I could see Abbadona's hut situated a short distance ahead of me. It stood high above the rivers, erected atop a stone hill. I drew near, but my attention was quickly consumed by a familiar voice.

"Help!" Lilith wailed. "Help me!"

I turned to the right, toward the sound of the voice.

"Please, Satan, help me!"

My feet moved closer and closer, until I stood near the edge and peered into the waters.

"Free me!" the voice screeched, but it was no longer Lilith's. It was now a deep, demonic voice.

I moved back, but my foot was caught. Below me was a solid stream of water wrapped around my ankle like a vise. It pulled, nearly knocking me to the ground. I stood strong, but I could see the river waters shifting and swirling, ready to surge and pull me under. Yet, I did not panic or try to flee. The waters calmed me, soothed me, dazed me into complacency. And as they rose high, shaping into a monstrous creature ready to consume me whole, I smiled faintly thinking about how nice it would be to let go and release myself from this hellish life.

Suddenly, a figure lashed out at the slippery beast with a wooden staff, slashing it in two. There was an ear-piercing scream as the waters dropped back down to the river below.

Someone firmly gripped my arm and pulled me away from the river's edge as I returned to my senses.

I was being led up the steps of the stone hill to the hut by no other than Abbadona herself. We entered the small interior. "Sit," she demanded, motioning toward a series of rugs and cushions that covered the floor. I obliged, mainly because I was still disoriented from whatever spell the river had cast over me.

The interior of the hut was rather dark. Only a few small lanterns interspersed throughout illuminated the space. All sorts of fabrics and textiles were draped along the ceiling, insulating the hut and keeping in the small amount of heat since the entirety of Hell was always freezing cold. Their intricate patterns matched the rugs and cushions I sat on. There was an herby smell that permeated the whole space, reminding me of long-forgotten apothecaries.

Across from me, in the middle of the hut, was a large wooden worktable strewn with bottles and other supplies. A large book was open on the table and sat upon a stand. Beyond the table, a curtain was drawn back to reveal row upon row of jars, which contained herbs and other elixirs. Abbadona moved about the hut, mixing something with a mortar and pestle. She picked herbs as she went, some from open jars on her worktable, others from bushels that hung from the ceiling.

Her skin was the color of midnight, and her black hair hung in long braids adorned with gold beads. She wore a black corseted dress, the skirt long and her shoulders mostly bare save for two thick straps. A shawl was draped over her, hanging around her elbows. About each wrist was a gold cuff that glowed in the lantern light.

She was a vision of black and gold as she mixed her concoction, the muscles in her arms contracting with her motions. Abbadona was quite beautiful, something I had never realized before. Perhaps I hadn't been in her company enough to recognize it, or perhaps something in my mind had veiled her beauty from me. Either way, I was aware of it now.

She placed the pestle down on the worktable and moved toward me, stopping briefly on the way to reach into a jar for a pinch of salt, which she sprinkled among her mixture.

"Here," she said, kneeling down. "Smell this. It will help reorient you."

I took the mortar from her and put it close to my nose, breathing in deeply. It smelled earthy and spicy. I wasn't sure what was in it, but it certainly helped clear my head.

Her piercing gray eyes were watching me. I could tell she wanted to say something. "Speak," I urged her.

She tsked. "I don't mean to question your motives, sir, but why didn't you tell me you were coming? I would have assisted you through the cavern."

I sighed, handing her the mortar. "I don't need assistance."

She chuckled. "Really? That's not what I hear." She stood to bring the mortar back to the table.

"What *are* you hearing, then?" I questioned.

She turned away from the table to look at me. "Gossip, rumors."

"About?"

"You." She said the word so nonchalantly.

"Care to elaborate?"

She shrugged. "Certainly. But you must first tell me what brought you here."

I glanced at my wing. "I'm not healing as I normally do. A spirit suggested you might be able to do something, since Astrid and Tabitha can't."

Abbadona skirted around the table to get a closer look. She knelt before me again. "Did Astrid and Tabitha tell you why you're not healing?" She stared at my amulet.

I lifted it away from my chest. "Yes, they did."

She tsked again. "What are you doing playing with black magic, sir?"

"You're familiar with Astrid and Tabitha's gifts, then?"

"Most certainly. Since they can't travel aboveground, I supply them with herbs and such that I collect during my journeys."

I smirked. "I didn't realize you were invested in their business."

Abbadona returned my sarcasm with a glare. "I'm not. Supplying them helps take some of the work off me. You'd be surprised by how woeful spirits can be."

"Are you trying to tell me something, Abbadona? Perhaps how I should rule?"

She grew frustrated. "Don't you see? You don't rule. You dictate."

"What's the difference?"

"Ruling requires partnership and alliance. Dictating is purely demanding and demeaning. You don't build trust when you dictate."

"No, you build fear," I said, my anger rising. "Is there any better way for people to follow you than if they fear you?"

"But they don't fear you," she said. "That's what I've been told, at least."

My face fell, her words quashing my anger and replacing it with a fear of my own. "What do you mean?"

She shook her head somberly. "Satan, there is mutiny brewing."

My head snapped back in surprise. Not by the mention of mutiny but by the fact that she used my name—not sir, not sire, not Lord Satan. Just Satan. No one ever called me by name alone.

"The hounds have all but disappeared. They follow someone else's command."

I had a guess, but I asked anyway. "Whose?"

"I don't know. But there's more. There are whispers of rebellion among the fallen angels. They are beginning to question your rule, your strength. The demons are siding with them."

"The demons are loyal to no one, so naturally they will join the dissenters. They follow whomever has more power," I pointed out.

"Yes, but the spirits are beginning to hear these rumors, too, and are uprising. Misery is about to explode in chaos. If you don't do something to take control soon, their hatred will spill over into the cities and war will be inevitable."

"How do you know all this?"

"Because I watch and listen. Some of it I must deal with firsthand. These months that you have been gone have been the most difficult. Without the hounds, many spirits are escaping."

"Why didn't you tell me this sooner?"

Abbadona was outraged. "Because you don't listen! This is exactly my point! You only intervene when it's too late. I've tried many times to meet with you, but you never prioritize my reports. For years now you've been doing this so I stopped trying altogether, especially when it put me in danger. And since no one else thinks about me, I must think about me."

Alarm filled me. "Did someone hurt you?"

She looked me in the eyes. "Why do you care? You never have before."

"That's not true."

Her gaze hardened. "Really? Because I've never seen you show an ounce of pity."

Strangely, the thought occurred to me that something else might be going on here. So I asked her, "Why did you fight with me in Heaven? Why did you take my side?"

Her eyes flashed. "Why does it matter?"

"Just answer me," I demanded.

She looked down, and her words held a defensive tone. "I fought with you because I thought your cause was worthy. Angels should be able to express their free will. They should be able to be who they want."

"Your gifts, your knowledge… He suppressed them," I clarified.

She nodded. "There are plenty in Heaven who have gifts. They just use them how He would like them to be used."

I gazed around the hut. Unlike Astrid and Tabitha, Abbadona did not practice black magic. She simply practiced the healing arts, ones based in water and energy, and she had been disgraced for it.

"That's not the only reason," she said softly.

I returned my attention to her.

"You were quite charming. It was hard not to follow you. I knew in Heaven such feelings were sacrilege, but I thought things would be different in your new kingdom. Then Lilith appeared, and my chances with you soon vanished."

I opened my mouth to speak, but she continued. "When I realized you didn't return my feelings, I regretted my insurrection. But I was stuck here no matter what, relegated to the Eighth Cavern to deal with the rivers because I have immunity over them like no other, and that's only because my gift allows me to control them."

I thought back to how the river had captured me. "Has anyone ever survived after being dragged through one of their depths?"

"The majority who succumb to them don't. Or rather, what I should say is that they never return. What I have learned about the rivers is that every person is drawn to their allure for different reasons. Oftentimes, only one river is truly tantalizing to a person, revealing their deepest fears and desires. The only commonality among them all is that they all promise pain, both physical and psychological. If, however, you are able to overcome it, the rivers also promise the chance to be reborn. At least, that is what the waters tell me."

She stroked the black feathers along her wings. That's when I realized something.

"They finally turned black. For the longest time they were still white, even after our fall."

She nodded. "They did. I have now accepted my fate. I never had a chance of going back, but I don't care anymore. I always have, and always will be, your most loyal follower."

Surprised by her words, I reached out and placed my hand on her cheek.

She flinched, anticipating the Hellfire. Then her eyes grew wide, and she grabbed my hand with both of hers. "This is worse than I thought." She met my eyes. "It's gone, isn't it?"

"Yes. In addition to my inability to heal, I have no Hellfire." I shouldn't have told her, but something had changed between us.

"No one must know. If they do, we'll be fighting by tomorrow."

"I agree. Now tell me who harmed you."

She sighed and stroked my hand. It was nice to feel another's touch.

"The whole incident was very strange," she began. "After making my rounds about the cities, I returned here to find a gift left for me on the worktable. It was a beautiful gold bracelet. There was no way to tell who it was from, but I convinced myself it was from you. But the moment I put it on my wrist, I blacked out."

My brow furrowed. "That's impossible. An angel, no matter blessed or fallen, cannot lose consciousness."

"Right, but I did. And when I awoke, the bracelet was gone."

"Nothing else?"

"Not from the hut. There was a trail of water from the River of Fire, which was the only peculiar thing."

"Why is that strange?"

"Because the stone only gets wet if the waters try to take someone, and even then it doesn't leave a trail from the river's edge to the entryway steps."

"You think someone stole some of the river water?"

"I *know* someone stole some of the river water. I just don't know who, why, or how."

"From the River of Fire?"

She nodded.

"Isn't that used for the ore from which we make our weapons?"

"It is."

My jaw hardened. "When did this happen?"

"A few days ago."

"Damn it!" I pulled my hand away from hers.

"What's wrong?"

"Lucifer is behind all this. I had a meeting this morning with the person I trade weapons with. I broke our alliance. Lucifer arranged the whole thing. He must have known my intentions and had the foresight to steal some of the water to give to her. Now she can make the weapons without me."

"Did you tell him your intentions?"

"No, I haven't told him any of my plans."

"Then you must discover how he knows."

"Yes, and I must discover where he got this special bracelet. If it has the ability to incapacitate us like that, then I have far greater problems."

"But first, you must be healed," she reminded me.

"Right."

She inspected my wing. "I see you were shot."

I nodded.

"Have you been losing feathers, too?" she asked.

"Lots." Her gaze shifted to the amulet. "I know what you're thinking, but if I take it off, I can't go to Earth."

"We can find another way to get you to Earth," she began.

"No." I was adamant. It had taken me long enough to get this far; I was not about to go backward.

"Fine." Her eyes narrowed on my arm. "Where did this come from?"

I glanced at the wound from the Sentinel's knife. "A fight. It's not important, merely a scratch."

"You're mistaken. You've been poisoned."

"Poisoned?" I twisted to examine my arm.

"Don't worry, you're immune to it."

"How?"

"Well, based upon the fester marks and the scent, it's a snake venom from a very specific kind of snake." She stood and gathered ingredients. "And you were bitten by a certain snake, were you not?"

"You mean Lilith."

She looked at me over her shoulder with a sassy glare.

"I didn't know her bite was poisonous."

Abbadona abruptly stopped what she was doing. "Seriously? You do remember what it did to you, don't you?"

"Yes, but I didn't perish."

"Because you are strong, not because she's not poison." She resumed mixing up her ingredients into a salve.

"There's nothing between us, Lilith and me."

"How do you expect me to believe that when I hear you're looking for her?"

I shook my head. "Astrid and Tabitha better keep their mouths shut."

"How did you know I heard from them?"

"Because that's all they like to ask me about. Besides, I'm not looking for her to rekindle a romance that never happened. In fact, as of today, I'm not looking for her anymore at all. I've learned Lucifer's been on her side the entire time."

Abbadona came back to me with the salve and spread it over the knife wound. Her face was close to mine as our eyes met. I'd never had someone I could talk to so freely, someone I knew I could trust deep down. Not since my fall.

She stopped spreading the salve and set the bowl aside. "Why were you looking for her, though?"

"Because she has answers."

"Who's to say I don't have answers?"

"I never said you didn't."

"Then I need you to rely on me more. It's time to diversify your group of six."

"You want to be a part of the Six?"

"I didn't mean it that way. I just meant you need to start relying on a chosen few other than them...preferably a few females."

I smiled. "Why is that?"

"Because we tend to see things a little more clearheaded."

Chuckling, I said, "All right. Whom do you have in mind, other than yourself?"

"Haborym. Perhaps Nehema."

"Why Nehema?"

"She's a fierce fallen angel, just like Haborym, who's taken on a lot of responsibility while you've been away, all for the sake of saving your kingdom."

I nodded. "I'll consider it."

"Good. Also, while Astrid and Tabitha do bring about results, I wouldn't use them anymore. They dabble too much in magic that comes with consequences."

"Fine. I'll personally come to you, then. Any other requests?"

"Just one more." Her tone grew serious. "Never, and I mean *never*, trust Lilith."

"Speaking from experience?" I joked.

Her glare was venomous. "She is the mother of blood magic, a force stronger than black magic."

My sense of humor vanished. "All right." How had I not known this? Probably because Lilith hadn't revealed anything about herself to me during the short time I was in her company. I would have to take Abbadona's word for it.

Sensing that I was heeding her advice, she said, "Now lie back." She stood and went to retrieve something from one of her shelves.

I hesitated. "What are you doing?"

"I'm trying to heal your wing," she said, gathering a handful of gemstones. "I'm pretty certain it will work, but I'm sorry to say I can't do anything about the Hellfire or your healing abilities. Those will only return when you take off the amulet."

Satisfied with her explanation, I lay back on the cushions.

"Close your eyes," she said, once more at my side.

I eyed her skeptically.

"If I wanted you dead, I would have let the river take you."

Good point.

I shut my eyes. It was hard to tell what she was doing, but I got the sense that she was waving her hands over me.

"You're out of alignment," she said.

My eyes flew open. "How is aligning my chakras going to heal my wing?"

"There is power in balance. Now *close your eyes.*"

I did as I was told. Several moments later, I felt something placed between my eyes.

"Relax," Abbadona urged. "It's only a gemstone to channel energy." She placed six more stones down the length of my body, each one on a chakra.

I lay there in silence for what felt like a very long time.

"Focus on your wing," she said. "Envision it healing."

I followed her command, envisioned my wing healing, the feathers growing back, the hole healing up, even the wind blowing against it as I flew.

She picked up the stones. I could feel the absence of each of them as she took them away. Then she said, "Open your eyes."

When I did, it took me a few moments to orient myself. Sitting up, I blinked a few times to adjust to the dimness of the hut. Abbadona had retreated back to her shelves and worktable.

I glanced over my shoulder at my wing. Sure enough, it was healed. "What did you do?"

"Nothing that will cost you, unlike those witches."

I rose from the ground.

"Let me lead you out," she said. "I don't want you falling in again."

She walked with me among the rivers, her arm linked in mine so I wouldn't stray. Instead of guiding me to the entryway cave, though, she took me to the Pit, knowing full well that I would want to fly back up now that my wing was functioning.

At the precipice, she let me go, and I strode over to the edge. Before launching into the air, I turned back to her. "I'll be needing more of your assistance soon, but I'll wait until you've regained your strength. I know what you did took more out of you than you're letting on."

She smiled faintly.

"And one more thing." I met her gaze. I wanted to reassure her about how she felt, but the words wouldn't come. Instead, I simply said, "I appreciate your help."

Then I stepped over the ledge and stretched my wings, flying back up to Elysium.

21 SATAN

HELL, PRESENT DAY

When I landed back on the familiar ground of my throne room, Haborym and Nehema stood before my throne, awaiting my presence.

"Ladies, how can I assist you?"

They both looked at each other and said at the same time, "You first." Then they glared at one another.

"I don't need your disagreements to play out here. I'm very busy, so speak or leave."

"We both have important information to relay to you, and we're unsure if you want the other hearing," Haborym explained.

"Fine. Haborym, follow me." I led her down the short hallway connected to the throne room, past my private quarters, and into the portal room. "We can't be overheard in here. Now, what is it that troubles you?"

"Our weapons, sir. We can't make anymore. As you know, the ore supply comes directly from the River of Fire, and we had devised a method of transporting the water from the Eighth Cavern to the Forge in Greed through a well so as not to endanger anyone. But it's either dried up or severely blocked. I'm inclined to think more of the latter, since the river itself still has plenty of water in its depths."

"A blockage? Where do you think it starts?"

"I'm unsure at the moment. I need to complete my check of the well in each city below it, but I need Abbadona's help and she's been very busy as of late."

I sighed. "Tell her I said to make it a priority. Are we low on supplies?"

Haborym shrugged. "Our condition is not dire, but Jazema's last shipment has depleted us more than I would like."

My eyes narrowed. "When was this shipment filled?"

She thought a moment. "Probably only a few days ago."

"And who authorized the shipment?"

Her brow furrowed. "Lucifer. He told me you gave him the command."

My hands curled into fists. "I did no such thing."

Wide-eyed, Haborym said, "I'm sorry, sir. I thought he was speaking on your behalf."

"You are not at fault, Haborym. He is technically my second-in-command so you were doing what you thought was right. But listen to me now. Lucifer can no longer be trusted. Do not listen to him or take his commands. You will do only what *I* tell you to do. I am asking that you get my verbal permission from now on, and please tell the other fallen angels they need my personal authorization, too."

"Of course."

"Also, if you see him, do not let him think you have betrayed his trust and report his presence to me immediately. Tell no one of this conversation, and do *not* fulfill anymore of Jazema's shipments."

"Is all of this temporary?" she asked.

"No, it's indefinite." I met her gaze. "Understood?"

"Yes, sir. I will attend to the well forthwith and go seek Abbadona's help." Her eyes trailed over to the knife sitting on the table. "May I?" she asked.

"Sure."

She picked up the Sentinel's knife and analyzed the blade. "Do you mind if I take this?"

"No. Just watch out. The knife is poisoned."

"I know. That's why it intrigues me."

From anyone else, that would be alarming, but from my weapons master, it wasn't.

With matters settled, I followed her out to the throne room. Haborym didn't linger. Instead, she extended her wings and launched into the Pit, on her way to see Abbadona.

I set my sights on Nehema. "And what is it that troubles you?"

"My new appointment."

"Your what?"

"Asmodeus said you were appointing me leader of Misery. I've been down there for months now trying to keep the peace. Murmur and Mulciber, those two irresponsible fallen angels who you entrusted to contain the chaos, are nowhere to be found, and the spirits grow restless. Abbadona has been helping me in my efforts, but it's an impossible task."

The absurdity of her words gave me pause. What in Hell's name had transpired while I had been gone?

"Nehema, I did not sanction that appointment."

"You mean, Asmodeus lied to me?"

"Yes."

Her jaw clenched. "That lustful bastard! I only listened to him because I thought he was conveying your command. As far as I'm concerned, I'm washing my hands of it." She turned to leave.

"Wait," I commanded.

She faced me, her brow creasing. "Please don't make me."

"Make you do what?"

"Stay down there. Quell Misery into peace."

"How did you know I would ask?"

"Because the thought is written clearly all over your face."

I smiled at her competence. Maybe Abbadona had been right. Maybe I needed some fresh blood among the Six. In the time I had returned, the three of them—Abbadona, Haborym, and Nehema—had been more enlightening than any of the others.

"What made you listen to Asmodeus? Other than the fact that you thought it was my will."

She sighed. "I've wanted a position of command, but only a little."

It was nice to finally meet an angel with a similar ambition to mine. "Just a little?" I asked.

Her lips curled upward. "Fine, maybe a lot."

"That's what I thought. Which is why I would like you to stay in Misery. You've been dealing with the spirits for a few months now so you know how to somewhat control them."

"But I don't want to stay down there. I want more."

I laughed. "You have to start somewhere before you can get more."

"So you're saying there's a chance?"

"Possibly. I'm afraid I won't have any open positions among the Six until there's a vacancy." However, given the treachery I was discovering among the Six, I was sure I would be talking with her again soon. I paused. I'd never interacted with Nehema much, but it turned out she was pleasant company. "By chance, did you happen to be an angel of the home?"

"What made you guess that?"

"I can tell you're a people person. You have a natural gift in playing to others' wants and needs in exchange for your own benefit."

"That's not quite what an angel of the home does," she commented.

"True. An angel of the home attends to people's wants and needs. Yet, the fallen counterpart twists people to their will. You're devious, cunning, and persuasive, as well as diplomatic."

"Please stop, sir, your flatteries will make me blush," she joked, batting her eyes.

"You'll be very useful indeed."

"For what, might I ask?"

"For revenge."

At the words, her eyes gleamed in happy anticipation. "Just tell me when."

"I will." I rubbed my knuckles. "Keep an eye out for Murmur and Mulciber while you're down in Misery. I would like to speak with them if they happen to resurface."

"Yes, sir."

"Does that mean you're keeping your position?"

She smiled. "Anything for you, sir."

"Good. And just so you know, Lucifer can no longer be trusted. Do not listen to him or take his commands. Same goes for any of the fallen angels. You must get permission straight from me. Now if you see Lucifer, report his presence to me immediately. Also, keep your acquaintance with Asmodeus. See what information you can get out of him, without being too obvious."

"Certainly. Do you think he's working with Lucifer?"

I raised an eyebrow. "I never told you what Lucifer was doing."

"No, but I hear rumors. And I see how you two interact. He's quite envious of you—or rather, of your power."

"Well, stay connected to the rumors. I want to know everything you hear. And yes, I believe Asmodeus, as well as Murmur and Mulciber most likely, are working with Lucifer."

Who else would have been able to outsmart Abbadona other than the two angels who interacted with her most often? Murmur and Mulciber were constantly moving between Misery and the cities to escort spirits back and forth. And, of course, there was no way to do that without passing through the Eighth Cavern, meaning they needed Abbadona's help to navigate the rivers. They must have been the ones to devise a way to steal the water, possibly even block the well, because other than Abbadona, they were the only ones who traversed that cavern.

"Is there anything else I can do for you?" Nehema asked.

"No, you've done well. That will be all for now," I said. "But tell no one about this. We must keep absolute secrecy."

"Of course." Like Haborym, Nehema spread her wings and launched into the Pit.

Finally sitting down in my throne, I contemplated all I had heard. It seemed I had far more problems than a mutiny brewing. I had to restructure. I had to find answers. I had to return to my former self before my kingdom crumbled.

22 JORDAN

New York City, Present Day

"Jordan, wake up! We need to leave. Now!"

Prying my eyes open, I stared at the face of Sister Helen as she shook me awake. My confusion must have been clear because she said, "There's no time to explain. We have to leave."

She left my side and approached the door to my bedroom. I rubbed my eyes, pushing away the drowsiness to make sure this wasn't a dream. "You're alive?" I asked.

"Of course I'm alive," she said. "Now come on. We have to go."

I sat up in bed. "Go? Go where?"

"I'll tell you in time. For now, show some haste." She picked up a shirt from the floor and threw it at me.

Putting it on, I jumped out of bed to follow her to the door.

Wait.

I stopped. Why had my shirt been on the floor? I never left clothes on the floor. Chamuel always reprimanded me when I did that.

"Sister Helen, something doesn't feel right. Where are you taking me?"

She turned and grabbed me by the throat. Struggling against her tight choke hold and gasping for air, I realized it wasn't Sister Helen anymore.

Those bottomless black eyes and intense grip belonged to someone else.

"Do you fear me yet?" Satan asked.

My eyes widened.

"You should. Because nowhere you go is safe. I will find you. I'll find all of you, and I will wipe out every last person you love to get what I want."

He tightened his grip, and my eyes closed as the last breath of air escaped my lungs.

Moments later, to my surprise, I opened my eyes again. But I was no longer in my room at my parents' house. Instead, I was back in my bed at the orphanage.

"Don't worry. You're safe." An indistinct figure leaned over and brushed my cheek.

"M-mom?" I asked, unsure of how I knew it was her.

"Lie down. Rest." She placed a hand on my chest. "I'll sing you a song to put you to sleep."

She softly hummed a calming tune, some lullaby that pulled at my memories. My eyes closed once more. I was finally in a place where I knew I could sleep, but suddenly, the hand on my chest grew heavy as she pressed me to the bed.

My eyes flew open as the woman singing the lullaby morphed into another, my mother's face replaced by one I didn't recognize. She had long black hair and hollow cheekbones and wore claws on her fingers. When her eyes landed on mine, they were an unnatural mix of colors.

"You again?" I demanded. Even though I hadn't gotten a glimpse of her face the first time, I knew this was the same woman from the icy tundra.

"I guess your mind is stronger than I thought," she said. "You were able to see through my illusions quickly." She paused. "You get that from your mother. She resisted me for years."

"What did you do to her?" I demanded.

She stared into my eyes. "Nothing she didn't bargain for."

I wanted to move. I wanted to defend myself, defend my mother. But I couldn't. The woman held me to the bed, her heavy hand full of an emanating power.

Sighing, she said, "This won't hurt. I promise you."

"What?"

Then I felt a pinch on my arm, but I couldn't pull my eyes away from her hypnotizing gaze. "Who are you?"

She raised her clawed hand to her mouth and sneered. "What a pity… I can't draw your blood. It would have made things far easier." Leveling her eyes on me again, she made gestures with her hands. I didn't know what she was trying to do, but clearly it hadn't worked because she yelled out in frustration. "Damn it!" She grabbed my throat in her grip, resting her clawed thumb on my chin.

I could tell she wanted to kill me. The desire was there in her eyes. Somehow, though, I knew that wasn't her true intent. Not yet anyway. She wanted to torment me some more. So she opened her mouth wide, and sharp, fang-like teeth descended on my face.

I screamed.

The noise echoed in my ears as I jolted awake. My head was leaning against the car window. I lifted it and peered around. Clearly, I had screamed aloud because the car was pulled over and Michael, Gabriel, Sophia, and Dane were all staring at me.

I sighed and rubbed my eyes. It was just another nightmare…

"I'm all right," I told them. "Just…just a dream."

They obviously didn't believe me, but Michael steered the car back onto the road nonetheless. It was early morning, and we were headed to Greenwood Heights, a town in Brooklyn near where Sister Helen and Martha had grown up. Today was the funeral, and we were headed to the church. It was hard to believe all the arrangements had been made in two days, but Sister Helen had organized everything before she'd died.

At first, the angels were a little hesitant to let us attend the funeral. They didn't want us out in the open, exposed to more danger, especially since they weren't entirely sure the hounds and the Fallen were off our backs. But we wouldn't stand for it. We needed to be at Sister Helen's funeral. She was the closest thing the three of us would ever have to a mother.

Thankfully, Raphael was quick to turn to our side. He had pointed out that going to the funeral could bring about a kind of healing that nothing else could. Once they heard that, the other angels agreed to let us go—but only if we followed their every precaution and command. It was a fair trade in our eyes. After all, Sister Helen had died to keep us safe. I don't think she would have been pleased if we were captured or killed while attending her funeral.

Besides, the past two nights had already been traumatic enough. And I wasn't only talking about what had happened with Satan, Lucifer, and the hellhounds. I was talking about how I had been haunted in my sleep by a string of nightmares.

The one I'd just had in the car was by far the worst. Satan. That strange woman again. My mom. None of it made any sense. The only commonality was the beginning. Each nightmare always started with Sister Helen waking me up and telling me we had to leave. I could understand why that part kept replaying because the last time I had ever seen her, she had told me the exact same thing: I had to leave, I had to go, I had to run.

Why did those have to be her last words to me?

Why did she even *have* last words?

Thinking about it made me want to punch something, but that wouldn't do any good in the car so I tried to calm myself, to control my anger, as much as I could. It was hard to do since I was anxious and felt like I was going to fall apart any minute.

Glancing over to my right, I looked at Sophia and Dane. They both sat silently, lost in their thoughts. Sophia was fiddling with her hands in her lap. Dane was flipping a playing card with his fingers. We were all a mess, dreading the day that stretched out before us.

I wish I'd had more time with Sister Helen. I imagined each of us did. Instead, all we had were memories, and even those were hard to hold on to, especially when I'd thought I had so much time left. In the three days since I'd received the devastating news about Sister Helen, I quickly realized I had taken my remaining time with her for granted.

I had never thanked her for all she had done for me. I'd never hugged her goodbye one last time. I'd never told her just how much she meant to me.

Clearing my throat, I tried to hold back my tears. Focusing on all the things I never said or did wouldn't help. It would be better to just remember her.

Her kind face. Her unusual smile. Her habit of putting out plain old peppermints on her desk like the other sisters did but keeping the good stuff—like the mini chocolate bars—hidden in a secret compartment in the left drawer of her desk. How she smelled of lavender, and how she always chased the nightmares away, not just for me but for the other kids, too.

The thought of her made me reach for my fleur-de-lis necklace, the one that no longer lay there. Instead, I fiddled with the plain silver cross.

Ever since the angels had discovered the mysterious power of my necklace and how much I desperately needed it, they were set on returning to my parents' house. But I'd refused to go until after the funeral. Paying our respects to the woman who'd raised us took priority.

Gabriel had suggested that he fly to the house to get it, but with the hellhounds still on the loose, Satan walking among us, and random attacks happening in the city, the angels ultimately decided it was better for him to stay and help guard us. Instead, Zadkiel would bring it with him when he arrived with the others for the funeral.

In the meantime, I was horribly sleep-deprived, holding myself together by a thread.

The looming steeple of a church pulled me away from my thoughts. We had arrived at Sister Helen's childhood church, St. Michael's, where a ceremony would take place before the remarks at the cemetery. Martha and the others would be waiting for us here. Raphael and Uriel had flown ahead this morning since there wasn't enough room in the loaner car we had been given while the van was getting repaired.

I wasn't entirely sure what I had been expecting, but seeing the crowd of people amassed outside the church hadn't been what I had envisioned. Nuns, priests, friars, and ordinary people were among the group here for Sister Helen. She truly had touched a lot of people's lives.

Michael pulled up to the curb and let us out, handing us over to

Raphael and Uriel who were already waiting. Then Michael drove off with Gabriel to park the car.

As soon as we started toward the church, all eyes were on the three of us. Many of them merely glanced over to see if they knew us, but a select few actually recognized us. Suddenly, we were transported back to our childhood where the label *orphan* hung invisibly over our heads.

I didn't associate myself with that word anymore, not since I had met the angels, discovered my parents, and reconnected with my friends. I wasn't sure if Sophia and Dane felt the same way, but I could tell they dreaded the way these people were looking at us, too.

"I thought we might be able to avoid this until the cemetery," Sophia whispered.

"Avoid what?" Dane asked.

"Talking to people, mingling, reminiscing, whatever you want to call it," she replied.

Dane said something back to her, but I wasn't listening. Instead, I was looking for Martha. I hadn't seen her since we had seen the news on TV about the explosion.

Michael and Gabriel's return distracted me from my search.

"Did you find the others?" Gabriel asked.

I shrugged. "I don't see them anywhere."

"Jordan!"

At the sound of my name, I scanned the crowd to see who called me. Near the parking lot full of cars, I saw some hands waving in the air. Sure enough, there was Martha standing with the others.

We all headed in their direction, and as soon as we were close enough, I enveloped Martha in a hug.

She returned the hug just as fiercely and patted my back. "Oh, don't start already. I can barely keep it together."

I drew back. "You don't have to keep it together."

She smiled weakly as her lip trembled.

"How are you?" I asked. "I missed you."

She chuckled. "I missed you, too, sweet boy. And I'm as good as can be expected. You left me in fine company, though." Martha gazed at Chamuel. "He's been such a great support."

"I bet he has." It was Chamuel's specialty, after all—taking care of others whether in their time of need or not.

"Listen," Martha said, "there's something I want to ask you." She glanced over my shoulder. "Perhaps Dane, too, but I don't know him very well, so maybe you can ask him."

"What is it?"

"Will you two help carry in the casket? I already asked some of the angels to assist, but I want the two of you to do it. Helen would want it that way."

Tears came to my eyes, but I forced them back. "Of course we will."

Martha patted my hand and strode over to the parking lot to meet the hearse.

"Dane," I said.

"Yeah," he came closer to my side.

"Martha wants us to carry in the casket. Some of the angels are going to help us."

He nodded. "All right."

"I'll go help Martha," Sophia said, leaving us.

Once everything was settled, it all seemed to happen so fast. Dane and I flanked the casket, him on the left, me on the right, while Michael, Gabriel, Raphael, and Chamuel assisted us. As we began to walk, Martha followed behind, arm-in-arm with Sophia, whom she'd taken to as quickly as she'd warmed to me, while Zadkiel, Uriel, and Jophiel came after them.

The crowd that had been amassing outside was now sitting inside among the pews, and it wasn't long before we joined them after depositing the casket at the altar.

There was a sermon and a lot of prayers. Some family friends spoke, as did some nuns Sister Helen had worked with in the past. Every single person talked about her kindness and charity. The final speaker, Sister Delphine, was one the three of us knew well, as she was a nun who helped operate the orphanage. Her speech held a similar tone to all the others.

I glanced over at Sophia, who stared wide-eyed at Sister Delphine as she stepped off the altar and retreated down the aisle.

Placing my hand on hers, I whispered, "You okay?"

A tear fell down her face. "She was there." Sophia paused. "Sister Delphine was there in the church the day—" Sophia broke off, unable to finish. The organ started up, drowning out whatever else she had wanted to say.

We all rose as the church erupted into song, the ceremony ending. Dane and I exited the pew to carry the casket again, along with the angels. Sophia grabbed Martha's arm, and we all walked out of the church.

Once the casket was back in the hearse, it was time to follow it to the cemetery. Dane, Sophia, and I walked quickly to the car, following behind Michael and Gabriel.

"Do you think Sister Delphine knows something?" Dane asked.

Sophia's head whipped around fast. "Why do you say that?"

Dane shrugged. "She's always been the one lurking in the shadows. People like that usually know more than they let on."

I chewed on Dane's comment as we entered the car and made the quick trip to the Greenwood Cemetery, where Sister Helen would be peacefully laid to rest.

We all gathered around the grave as the priest said some final words, surrounded by others who had come to show their support. As the last flowers were placed on the casket and it was lowered slowly into the ground, Martha covered her face with her hands and wept. I put my arm around her and drew her to my side. I noticed Dane was doing much the same with Sophia, though he was trying to keep back his own emotions.

Meanwhile, I didn't know what to feel. A mixture of numbness and detachment filled me. I supposed they were the beginning stages of grief starting to set in. Everything still seemed so surreal.

I spied movement out of the corner of my eye. The angels had gotten up from their seats and were approaching the grave. They were a sight to see, all seven of them dressed in suits with somberness and stoicism plastered across their faces. Each of them knelt around the grave and bowed their heads, softly whispering a prayer in Latin. When they were done, their heads lifted in sync.

Gabriel reached out and touched the left side of the tombstone. "Rest in peace, our sister."

Across from him, Michael did the same, placing his hand on the right side of the tombstone. "For we will avenge you."

They rose and approached Martha as one. She stood to meet them.

"We share our deepest condolences for your loss," Chamuel said, handing her a rose.

"Her sacrifice will not be in vain," Gabriel added.

"Our brother did this, and I assure you, he will pay for it," Michael finished.

Martha grabbed Michael's hand. "Thank you." She looked at the other angels standing around her. "All of you."

As other attendees approached Martha to express their condolences, I stood up and retreated away from the others.

"Jordan," Dane said as I brushed past.

I didn't respond. I had to leave. I had to flee.

The thought brought a sharp pain to my head. I pressed my hands to my temples.

Flee, a voice inside my head said. *Do you know how many times I've had to flee?*

I swayed on my feet as scenes of hardship flashed through my mind like a movie. Regaining my balance, I made it to the nearest tree just as the pain in my head brought me to my knees.

My entire life I've been running. And that has been centuries for me. But I will run no more. I will have my vengeance—beginning with you.

It was her. The woman from the nightmares.

For disgracing me, death shall follow thee.

The words were hailed as a curse. They echoed again and again through my head.

Death shall follow thee. Death shall follow thee.

I covered my ears, praying the chant would stop, until suddenly everything ceased. I gasped and grabbed at the tree in front of me to steady myself. I sobbed uncontrollably, tears streaming down my face.

What was happening to me?

Had that woman cursed me in some way? Was I to bring death to those I loved? Was I responsible for Sister Helen? Was her blood on my hands?

Like a flood, the emotions I had bottled up spilled out in a tsunamic wave. The grief overwhelmed me, leaving me shaken and distraught.

"Jordan!" There was alarm in Raphael's voice as he rushed to my side, holding me in his arms and inspecting my face. "What is it? What's wrong?"

"It's all my fault! She died because of me! I'm cursed!" I grabbed at my head again as the pain returned.

Clarity crossed Raphael's face. "Jordan, stay here and try to keep calm. I'm going to find Zadkiel. You need your necklace."

As he ran off, my mind took me somewhere else, to a place that was brutally cold, the place frozen in time where the wicked woman resided.

I tried running, but I slipped along the ice. I slowly pulled myself up from the ground and peered through the frozen water. Something was under the surface…

A face pale as death appeared with raven-black hair and a set of furious eyes. "Let me out!" she shrieked. Her wail cracked the ice, shattering the flimsy ground I stood upon and dragging me under into an icy torrent.

When I surfaced, gasping and choking, she met me there, in a dark place filled with nothing but silence.

She stroked my shivering face. "I'm glad you finally found me."

"What do you want?"

Her smile was full of menace. "All I ever wanted was to be free, to have the power to do as I pleased. Those privileges were taken from me the day I was created." She paused and vehemently spit out her next words. "And I was punished for trying to save myself!" A dark look crossed her face. "I vowed never to live in another's shadow, be it man or woman. I vowed to find my own power and become a creator, producing beings who I would never put to shame." She stared longingly at her hand, as if she could feel the power she was alluding to thrumming beneath her skin. "I vowed to vanquish my enemies, enact my revenge, and do whatever it took to usurp the divine throne."

Like a serpent, her hand coiled around my throat and she hypnotized me with her gaze, slowly squeezing the life out of me. "Except your parents stood in my way."

She released my neck, and I sucked in a breath, unable to take my eyes away from her. Stroking my cheek, she said, "You look so much like her, the beloved Evangeline." Her fingers stopped and moved to outline my eyes. "Yet you have the Conway eyes." She grew serious. "I wonder if you have the Conway mind."

I yelled in pain as she pressed her thumb between my eyes. She grinned excitedly and traced an invisible shape along my skin. "That should do nicely. You are now mine to torment until I get what I want."

Scrunching my forehead, I yelled, "What do you want?"

She slapped me across the face. "Have you not been listening? I want to be free!"

"I would never do that! I would never free you, you she-devil!"

Suddenly, I knew who she was. Uriel had used the exact same word to describe her.

Lilith.

But my realization didn't matter now. I had made her angry, and her rage spurred on far more lethal consequences.

Her hand eased back. "You have now been marked, Jordan Conway. And no one escapes the mark of Lilith."

A sharp pressure between my eyes drew me out of the waking nightmare, along with a soothing voice. "There, there. Just breathe."

Gazing into her brown eyes, I convinced myself my mother was here to save me, her red hair vividly bright in the sun. Instead, as I came to my senses, I stared into the green eyes of Sister Delphine, who had her thumb pressed firmly against my forehead.

I opened my mouth to speak.

"Easy now," she said. "The visions take a lot out of a person, especially when you're untrained and they're unchecked."

"Y-you know what's wrong with me?"

She smiled faintly. "You have ancient blood, my dear. On both sides. I tried warning your parents, but they didn't listen. You are unbalanced, and I believe your only options now are to wear your necklace forever or learn how to control your gifts."

My brow creased in confusion. "Gifts?"

"Hush. Now is not the time." She eased her thumb away from my forehead and brushed the hair out of my face. "I will return and reveal all to you when I'm able to do so." She rose and briskly walked away.

I lay there on the grass beneath the tree, wondering if I had just imagined her presence. That's how Zadkiel and Raphael found me, just lying there observing the spring leaves and listening to the song of birds.

"Jordan, are you all right?" Raphael asked.

I sat up. "I don't know. I think so."

Zadkiel reached into his jacket pocket and pulled out my necklace. "Here." He offered it to me.

I took the silver chain in my hands and lifted it over my head to hang it on my neck. Immediately, I felt its effects like never before. A sense of clarity and control overcame me, as if I were waking from a dream. I finally felt protected again. And I needed that now more than ever before since Lilith had marked me. I raised a hand to my forehead and winced. Nothing was there visibly, but when I touched it, an immediate pain erupted behind my eyes.

I had to tell the angels it was her. They needed to know because I think she posed a threat. But I would wait until later, when the funeral was over and we could talk in private.

"How do you feel?" Zadkiel asked.

"Better. Much better." I braced myself as I rose to my feet. They grabbed each of my arms to steady me. Once I was sure-footed, they let go. I brushed away the blades of grass from my jacket, straightened my tie, ran a hand through my hair, and rubbed my tearstained cheeks, trying to pull myself together.

When I was ready, we walked back to the grave site together and joined the others. I was sure my episode had made us late for the repast, but it seemed Martha was still conversing with some attendees. In fact, she was talking to Deborah and Peter Barnes, my neighbors. It was nice to see them here.

I wonder if Naomi's with them.

Just as the thought entered my mind, her voice graced my ears. "I've been looking for you everywhere."

Her arms came around and enveloped me in a hug. I returned the gesture, taking comfort in her embrace. Technically, Naomi was my neighbor, too, except we'd grown close over the past six months

I'd known her, certainly becoming friends and potentially becoming something more.

Zadkiel and Raphael shared a smile, leaving the two of us alone and returning to the others.

Naomi pulled back. She was wearing a simple black dress, her hair in the usual bun. "I'm so sorry for your loss, Jordan. When my parents told me, I was devastated because I knew she meant a lot to you."

"Thank you."

She cupped my cheek with her hand. "I've missed you. A lot."

I stroked her wrist. "Me too."

"I thought it would be enough just hearing your voice and seeing you through video chat, but it's not. It doesn't compare to being with you here in person."

"I know," I said.

As the words came out, I knew they were the wrong ones to say. My tone lacked enthusiasm. But that was probably because I still hadn't fully recovered from my waking nightmare, not because I didn't want to spend time with Naomi in person.

She dropped her hand away from my cheek.

"Naomi, I'm sorry. I'm not myself, and I've had a rough day." I reached for her hand. "But having you here means the world to me, and seeing you has made the day much better."

She smiled and squeezed my hand.

"Are you going to the repast?" I asked.

She frowned. "Unfortunately, I can't. I have to get back for a group project I'm working on, and we have a drive ahead of us. But I wanted to come for you, and I certainly wanted to see you before we left."

"Well, I appreciate you coming. Your parents, too. Tell them I said hello."

"I will."

She started to ease her hand away from mine, but I gripped it tighter. "I'll be home soon. So maybe once the summer starts, we can see each other more?"

Her wide smile brightened her face. "I'd like that."

This time, when she eased her hand away, I let her go. Martha was ready to leave anyway as I saw her head to the car, and Naomi's parents were waiting for her, standing off in the distance watching us.

I joined the others, and we loaded up in the cars again to go to the repast, which was taking place at a restaurant nearby. When we went inside, my stomach growled. Clearly, I had forgotten how hungry I was.

Before I could find a seat, Sophia grabbed my arm. "There's someone I want you to meet." She whisked me over to a girl standing by herself in the restaurant. Even though she was alone, she stood with confidence.

"Jordan, this is Dafne, my roommate and friend from Harvard. I don't know where I would be without her, helping me move in and letting me join her family for the holidays."

In that moment, I realized once again how horrible a friend I had been to Sophia, completely missing her birthday last year, as well as Thanksgiving and Christmas. I had been traveling much of the fall, and when we had returned for the holidays, I had been so wrapped up in myself that I hadn't thought about Sophia. I couldn't believe how selfish I had been, but it wasn't going to happen again.

Bringing myself back to the moment, I looked at Dafne, noticing her big gray eyes, her long brown hair cut in a stylish way with bangs. I smiled at her. "It's great to meet you. I've heard so many wonderful things about you. I know Sophia was very excited to meet you last summer, and I'm glad she has you as a friend."

"Thank you. That's kind to say." Although her words were nice, her tone was slightly guarded. Her smoky eyes searched mine. "Sophia has mentioned you a lot, too. I'm happy I can finally put a face to the name."

Before another word could be said, Dane arrived. "Excuse me, sorry to interrupt. I need to borrow Jordan for a minute."

"Wait, before you go, I want you to meet my friend Dafne," Sophia said.

Dane glanced at her. "It's very nice to meet you." Pleasantries were not his strength, and it showed as he left the conversation at that and pulled me away.

"What's wrong?" I asked.

"Well, considering we have seven angels here who must put on a show of eating in public, I figured you'd want to be clued in to the situation."

Abruptly, I stopped. How had I forgotten to think of them, too?

"Don't start blaming yourself." Surprised he knew what I was thinking, I met his eyes. "I know you a lot better than you think. Anyway, you're sleep-deprived and being haunted by a strange woman. I don't think anyone will blame you for forgetting."

I nodded, and we approached the angels. "Guys, I'm sorry I didn't think about this ahead of time. Maybe if you just sit with us no one will notice."

"It's all right. Uriel has a plan," Jophiel said.

I gawked. "*Uriel* has a plan," I repeated, disbelieving.

Jophiel nodded assuredly.

"Okay," I said, unable to stop the smile from spreading across my face for the briefest of moments.

We all sat down at a large table, Sophia joining us, along with Dafne.

Somehow, she was seated across from me, her gaze challenging mine. Clearly, she did not like me.

As the waiter came around to get our orders, each of the angels declined.

"We're fasting," Chamuel explained in his goodhearted way.

At the waiter's questioning glance, and Dafne's, Uriel brusquely added, "It's a religious vow we have taken."

With that, the waiter left. I couldn't help but smile since Uriel's way was always a little tactless.

As salads were placed in front of us, Dafne looked at Dane. "So, Dane, how do you know Sophia?"

He swallowed hard and said, "We grew up together. All of us did."

"You were at the orphanage, too, then?" Dafne clarified.

"Yep, my whole life."

"And what do you do now?"

"Dafne," Sophia chastised her, but with a friendly gleam in her eye.

"What?" She smiled mischievously. "I just want to know him a little better."

Sophia forked a clump of salad into her mouth, trying to hide her blush. I looked back and forth between the two of them, trying to figure out what was going on. Why was Sophia blushing? Was she embarrassed?

Glancing at Dane, he seemed aware of the situation but was not playing into Dafne's game. "I'm an artist. Right now, though, I work at a gym. I'm saving up for art school."

"Well, isn't that dreamy," she said, pointedly staring at Sophia.

Not liking her tone or the games she was playing, I decided to put the pressure back on her. "And what is it you do, Dafne? You're at Harvard. What do you study?"

"Economics. I'm supposed to help run the family business once I'm done with school."

"What's the family business?" I asked.

"We're vintners." She paused. "We own a vineyard."

"Oh..." I'm glad she clarified that because I had never heard the expression before.

"That's not all Dafne does," Sophia said, lowering her voice. "She also is the best fashion designer I've ever met."

Dafne laughed. "I'm the only one you've ever met."

"True, but I still mean it."

"Thank you, Soph." Dafne smiled sheepishly.

That was the first time I saw her trade her guarded demeanor for a genuine expression of emotion. But soon it vanished and she sighed.

"My parents don't approve of fashion design so we don't talk about it much." She challenged me yet again with her gaze. "What do you do, Jordan?"

"I've just finished up a mission trip. These guys actually were my travel companions."

Obviously, I was slightly stretching the truth here to make up an explanation for the angels' presence. Their actual jobs they had when I met them were vastly different from missionary work: Michael was a private investigator, Gabriel was a violinist and New York socialite, Raphael was a doctor, Uriel was a wildlife research specialist, Zadkiel was a professor, Chamuel was a chef, and Jophiel was an archivist.

"I wanted to take a break from school," I continued, "and I like helping people so I was interested in going on a mission trip. I'll be attending Cornell soon, though. I've deferred my acceptance so I can do a bit more traveling before focusing on school."

"So when you go to Cornell, what are you thinking of majoring in?" Dafne asked.

I met her rebellious gaze. "Not sure yet."

"By the way," Sophia asked, "who was that girl at the cemetery?"

"Yeah, the one you nearly kissed," Dane teased.

I glared at him. "We were *not* about to kiss. We haven't kissed. We aren't even dating." I stopped because I was obviously getting flustered. "Her name is Naomi. She's my neighbor. We've been talking and hanging out occasionally. Nothing more."

"But you like her?" Sophia asked, beaming.

"Yes, I like her."

Dafne was grinning at me now, too.

"What?" I asked.

She shook her head. "Nothing. You're just cute when you're flustered."

I ignored her comment and concentrated on my food.

Our lunch passed along with happy conversation and reminiscing over our childhood. It was nice to end the day remembering Sister Helen's spirit rather than focusing on the physical lack of her person. It seemed to help Martha, too.

As we left the restaurant, I felt better than I had in days. I knew I wasn't miraculously cured of my grief. It would come and go in waves for all of us, I was sure. But Sister Helen wouldn't want me to get swallowed by grief. She would want me to finish the mission she had given me, even if it meant facing a reality without her in it.

23

JORDAN

New York City, Present Day

After the repast, we went back to Gabriel's apartment to regroup. Martha had returned to my parents' house with Chamuel, Zadkiel, and Jophiel while the rest of us figured out what to do. We couldn't possibly stay at the apartment any longer—not all three of us plus four angels. There wasn't enough space, and it would be nice for each of us to have privacy. Going back home was the most logical choice, but Dane and Sophia had lives that they couldn't just leave behind. There had to be a compromise.

"So what do we do now?" Sophia asked. "I'd only planned to stay for a long weekend, and I don't think I can go back to school with hellhounds and fallen angels chasing after me."

"The best option would be for you both to come back to Jordan's house with us," Michael said.

"How long until summer break?" I asked Sophia.

"Two weeks."

I thought for a moment. "Can you finish your classes virtually?"

"Possibly," she replied. "A lot of them are dual classes anyway, both in-person and online just in case students are sick or miss a class. I'd have to talk with my professors and the registrar. It might not be impossible, though, especially with Sister Helen passing they might make an exception."

"See what they say. If they let you, then you can come stay with us at the house." I turned to Dane, knowing he would be the harder one to persuade to join us. While he wasn't in school and didn't have a place to stay to begin with, he did have a job. Besides, he had always been adamant about not taking handouts, and this would seem like a handout.

"I appreciate the offer," he said, "but no. I have a job."

"Which you can quit," I pointed out.

"Yes, but then I would just need to get a new job."

"Get one near my house."

He paused. "And what, have an angel come to work with me every day as protection?"

I glanced at the angels.

"We would be willing to do that if we could have all three of you under the same roof," Gabriel said.

Dane's eyes widened. "I was joking."

"You're the one being stubborn here," Uriel remarked. "Choosing your pride over your safety."

Dane crossed his arms over his chest. "Excuse me?"

They sized each other up.

"Enough already," Sophia interrupted. "Dane, you're being ridiculous. Your life matters more than a job, so just come to Jordan's house. You don't even have a place to live anyway."

He sighed. "Fine. You're right."

"Then it's settled. We're going back to Ithaca." I looked over at the angels. "Can we leave today?"

"I don't see why not," Michael said. "There's nothing left for us to do here. Not until the gala, which we can prep for at the house."

All of us changed our clothes, and Sophia and Dane packed up the few belongings they had with them. Then we headed downstairs to the parking garage where we all loaded into the repaired van.

"I thought this thing was a goner after the hounds," I said.

"We had to replace the windshield," Michael explained. "And it could use some more exterior work, but otherwise, it still runs."

We settled into the drive, Sophia and Dane falling asleep and me trying not to by counting trees out the window. I knew I had my necklace back, but I was still afraid to test it. Lilith meant business. She had marked me and vowed to torment me until I freed her. And I think she would do whatever it took to get around the protective ward of the necklace. So resting my mind was not a safe thing to do right now. Fortunately, the drive passed quicker than I had thought it would.

Hearing the familiar sound of gravel crunching under my feet as I exited the van made me happier than it would most people, since it had become a feeling I associated with returning home. I reached in my pocket for the house key when the front door opened and the other three angels stepped out.

"Welcome back," Zadkiel greeted.

I smiled. "Thanks. It's nice to be home." I turned to Chamuel. "How's Martha?"

He shrugged. "Upset. Sad. We got home around dinnertime, but she didn't want to eat anything. Just went right upstairs. I checked on her a little while ago. She was thinking about taking a trip."

"Where?" I asked.

"Anywhere, really. She just wants to get away."

I nodded, understanding she needed time to herself.

We all entered the house together, but soon the angels slowly dispersed, retreating to their usual areas. I was ready to go upstairs myself when I realized Dane and Sophia were frozen in the massive entryway.

"This is your house?" Dane asked in disbelief.

"I can give you a tour once I show you to your rooms," I offered.

Sophia beamed. "I'd like that. It's so stunning I want to see everything."

We ascended the main stairs, and I took them to the left wing of the house, where the guest rooms were located.

"The angels use some of the rooms on this side of the house, so don't be surprised if you run into them up here. Also, Martha's suite is at the end of the hall," I explained. "These two rooms here should do." I indicated the ones with open doors.

"Thanks," Sophia said, stepping inside one of the rooms. "This is huge."

"Everything's huge," Dane said, dropping his bag in the other room and coming back out. "Where's your room?"

I pointed in the opposite direction. "Down there."

"Can we see?" Sophia asked.

"Sure."

We walked down the hall, and I stopped before my parents' room. "That was my mom and dad's room. Mine is up here." I led them up a short staircase, opened the door, and stepped inside.

"This is so cool!" Sophia exclaimed.

"Yeah, it still feels a little weird that all of this is mine," I admitted.

After spending some time in my room, I took them through the rest of the house, showing them the library, the kitchen, and the entire downstairs. Then we all settled into our rooms for the night.

I changed into my pajamas and got into bed, ready to fall asleep, but I just sat there. I was totally exhausted but so scared to close my eyes.

There was a knock at the door. "Come in."

Gabriel entered and closed the door behind him. He sat down in the comfy armchair and opened a thick novel he had brought with him.

Our eyes met.

"Raphael told me what happened at the cemetery today. We'll get to the bottom of this, I promise. In the meantime, I'll be your chaser of nightmares."

Finally, after three days of torment, I got some sleep.

24

SATAN

HELL, PRESENT DAY

I was in my private rooms contemplating my next steps when I heard two familiar voices out in the hall. I rose from my seat and approached the archway to the throne room.

"He's obviously busy," Astrid said. "We should come back another time."

"He's the one who wanted us here once we closed for the day," Tabitha pointed out. "I'm just following orders. If he's too busy to see us, then he can—"

"I can do what, Tabitha?" I cut in, appearing before them.

"You can…you can," she spluttered, surprised by my presence.

"Have us wait on you all day," Astrid supplied.

Tabitha smiled widely, squeezing Astrid to her side. "Yes, we can wait on you all day, for we have no other better ventures to attend to."

I smirked, entertained by their groveling. "While I appreciate your attentiveness, I no longer need your services, so you may return to your other *ventures*."

Tabitha, who was growing unruly again, let go of Astrid. "What do you mean no longer need our services? Who else could you find to replace us? We're the best Hell has to offer."

"Perhaps," I said. "However, I did pay Abbadona a visit. Her success is much more guaranteed than yours, especially since it comes with no consequences."

Astrid rolled her hazy eyes. "Pfft…Abbadona. She thinks she's so much better than us."

I strolled over to my throne and took a seat. "Doesn't she supply you with products? I wouldn't be too hasty to condemn the hand that feeds you."

"We would never do such a thing," Tabitha backtracked. "We're just a little outraged that you promised us work and are now dismissing us so flippantly."

"Quite right," Astrid agreed. "We had prepared so many wondrous goods, knowing full well the quality you expect."

"*Goods* provided by Abbadona," I stated.

The sisters paused, taking a moment to study each other and silently come to an agreement.

"Fine," Tabitha conceded. "You don't want our help anymore, then don't come begging." She whipped around and headed to the stairs.

"We're too busy anyway," Astrid added, following her sister.

I heaved a breath of relief, finally rid of those dithering witches. At the sound of rushing air, I glanced over at the Pit, knowing someone was flying up. Haborym and Abbadona landed on the ground, and neither of them took a moment to pause.

"We've unblocked the well," Abbadona reported.

I nodded. "Good. What was blocking it?"

"This." Haborym handed me a weapon.

It was a chakram, a sharp, disklike weapon that separated into two identical pieces. This particular weapon had belonged to a member of the Triune. Lucifer had confiscated it from her when he had captured her. Except I was only looking at one piece.

My eyes widened. "Shit!" I ducked as the other piece came flying out of the portal room and lodged into the stone wall above my head.

Abbadona and Haborym were ready to attack, the former wielding energy at her fingertips and the latter drawing out a knife from the holster attached to her leg.

I raised my hand, staying their attack and focusing my attention on the unsteady figure standing in the stone archway.

"Kat," I said. "I see you've escaped."

She set her amber eyes on mine. They were full of anger and hinted at the strength she used to possess before she had been imprisoned here for eighteen years. Reaching behind me, I pulled the chakram out of the wall. Normally, I wouldn't be able to hold it. It was a light energy weapon and no fallen angel could wield one, just as no blessed angel could wield a dark energy weapon. But it seemed the list of how I had changed because of the amulet kept growing.

Kat wasn't surprised by my new ability. Why would she be when she had been there when the amulet was made, banging incessantly in the portal room to deter the witches from completing the process.

I swiped the air with the weapon, marveling at how I could feel the light energy again. "Did Lucifer give this to you?"

She cleared her throat, not having spoken much in almost two decades. "Some demon threw it in my cell. Told me it was a gift from Lucifer." She hoarsely laughed. "How ironic when he was the one who took it from me." She raised her hands. "I cut through my shackles and tore through the divine light barrier, but I wasn't strong enough to summon a portal. So I waited for you to return." She glared at me. "When you did, it was a matter of striking when you were alone."

Her eyes shifted to the other female angels. "But you're never alone anymore. Why is that? Scared someone's going to stab you in the back?"

I lashed out, grabbing her throat. She didn't so much as flinch, let alone show surprise at my lack of Hellfire. "This charade is pathetic, Katriel. You know you're not strong enough to fight me."

She sneered. "Your threats are what's pathetic. You know you can't kill me because it will alert the Triune."

I gritted my teeth, hating that she was right. "Abbadona, fix the barrier on the cell."

Without a word, she skirted around us and entered the portal room.

I threw Kat to the ground and stood over her as Haborym bound her hands with new shackles.

"I don't know what Lucifer expected," I said. "Did he really think you could kill me?"

"Maybe if I weren't so weak," Kat commented. Then she defiantly smiled. "I don't think I was anything more than a distraction, though."

My eyes flashed as a loud ruckus came from the portal room. "Haborym, stay here!" I yelled, rushing to Abbadona's aid.

When I entered, she had already slayed six of the ten demons that had attacked her. I quickly sliced my way through three more with the chakram, just as she finished off the last one.

Clutching her side, she wavered on her feet. I dropped the chakram and held her up, spying the blood escaping from her wound.

But it wasn't an ordinary injury. No, it was infected with demon venom, which they secreted from their claws. It wasn't as lethal as a hellhound's venom, but it was still a pain in the ass. Hallucinations and fevers were the typical symptoms, and they usually lasted for weeks.

"Get me to my hut," Abbadona whispered.

I lifted her in my arms and went out to the throne room. "Secure the prisoner and clean this up," I demanded, passing by Kat and Haborym and jumping into the Pit.

It wasn't long before I landed in the entryway cave to the Eighth Cavern. Without hesitation, I strode through into the wake of the rivers' domain. But unlike last time, their whispers didn't call to me.

Not because they didn't try. Believe me, they did. But I refused to listen because I was far too concerned about Abbadona.

I mounted the steps to her hut, went inside, and gently laid her down on the cushions.

She pointed to her shelves, where vial upon vial of medicines and herbs sat. "Second shelf, third row, eighth vial in."

Following her instructions, I grabbed the correct vial and returned to her side.

"You need to clean and dress the wound with the antidote," she said, indicating the vial.

I nodded, rising to find some bandages along with some clean water. Locating the first was easy, the second not so much. Then I spied a full pail in the corner.

"Is this usable?" I asked her.

"Yes," she whispered, giving me the smallest of nods.

With all the supplies gathered, I came back to her and attended to the injury. The gash marks were deep and tender, and the wound was still bleeding. It wouldn't stop as I washed it clean, but once I started applying the antidote, it finally ceased.

I wrapped her wound with bandages, being careful not to pull too tight. When I finished, she seemed more comfortable, the pain subsiding. However, she was in for a long fight.

I looked down at my hands, stained bright red from her blood. I poured water from the pail into a bowl to wash them, not wanting to contaminate the whole pail since I would need more water to quell the fever that was sure to come.

Once everything was cleaned up, I sat down next to her, taking her hand in mine.

She smiled weakly. "You can go. I'll be fine on my own."

"No, I'm staying right here." I squeezed her hand. "I'm not leaving you."

25 SOPHIA

Ithaca, New York, Present Day

Bang! The sound of a gunshot. The thump of a body falling. The repeated wail of "What have you done?" And finally, the sight that would haunt me forever: me being carried away in my mother's arms, moving quickly into the warmth of a nice May evening. But no amount of late-spring air could have chased away the chill inside my body.

The taxi ride was short. The library visit was, too, as that was where my mother had brought me and, ultimately, left me. My shouts of "Mommy! Wait! Mommy don't leave me!" echoed in my mind, mixed together with a voice in a court room yelling, "Liar! She's lying!"

And then I was back outside the library, stumbling down the steps on my short five-year-old legs, trying to catch up. She vroomed off in a taxi and subsequently left me without so much as a backward glance. The tears came hot and fast. Panic and shock set in as those giant stone lions loomed above me. But worse were the stares of strangers, none of whom had the courage to console an abandoned child.

Except the slender woman with the blond hair. She was nice. Too nice. I should have known her rescue was masked in deception.

The memories came in waves—thick, huge, drowning waves.

Flashbacks of the lab. Those female scientists. All they wanted was my blood. All they wanted was for me to understand my full potential. Those poor other kids, like the one with wings sprouting from her back. "You can help them," the blond woman said to me. "You just have to let go."

My hands full of feathers and blood…

Then he came and saved me, the man who knew my name. He was strong as he picked me up in his arms. He reassured me everything would be all right. And as I cried into his chest, the five-year-old me latched on to his gold St. Michael medallion, the only thing I had to remember my savior by.

I jerked awake when a hand touched my arm, and the beeping of my alarm brought my mind out of the nightmare and back to the present. Looking over my shoulder, I saw Chamuel's kind face.

"Sophia, are you okay?" he asked.

I nodded. "Yeah." Then I reached over to stop the alarm blaring from my phone.

"You sure? Because it seemed like you were having a nightmare again. They've been coming every night for the past two weeks, ever since the funeral. I wonder if yours and Jordan's are related."

Sitting up in bed, I shook my head. "No, mine are from past trauma. I'm reliving actual moments that happened while Jordan is being haunted by things that aren't real." I stopped, realizing I had confessed more than I had meant to. "Anyway, I promise I'm all right. I hope I didn't bother you, though."

He shook his head. "No, I had just finished the laundry when you started mumbling in your sleep." He tapped his ears, indicating his celestial hearing. "You sounded distraught, and I wanted to make sure you were all right. You're sure you don't want to talk about it? You seem to relive the same moments over and over again. At least on the nights I know you actually sleep."

I gazed at Chamuel. He had a genuine look of concern on his face. Out of all the angels, he was the one I was drawn to the most, the one I felt comfortable talking to. But he was prying into the part of my life I never talked about. My childhood. My trauma. My nightmares. My insomnia.

"I know you're dealing with a lot right now," he continued. "Your last final is today, and you haven't had much time to process the Satan attack, let alone grieve Sister—"

"I'm fine, Chamuel." I cut him off before he could say more. "Really."

"Okay." He reached down for the laundry basket. "Just know I'm here if you ever want to talk about it," he said before leaving the room.

I slid out of bed and approached the closet to grab my towel, catching a quick glimpse of my reflection in the mirror on the wall. The girl who peered back at me looked like she had just raced down those library steps in a panic. Yet, that had been fourteen years ago.

Most days I was able to conceal that girl behind a mask, able to hide the trauma and act like every other free-spirited nineteen-year-old. But today was not one of those days. At least, not without a hot shower and several cups of coffee.

The last two weeks of school had gone by in a flash. Thankfully, my professors had let me finish out the year online so I didn't have to worry about going back to campus other than to return my textbooks and collect my things from the dorm. I had completed those tasks last week—with the protection of two angel escorts, obviously—packing up my things and saying goodbye to my friends. Dafne was the only one I kept in touch with over the phone, texting and calling each other nonstop. I was grateful for her. She was such a good friend. She hadn't even asked me about it whenever I'd had bad dreams at school. She had just carried on like normal.

It was strange to end my freshman year at Harvard in such a peculiar way, but I valued my life and safety over my education, and I was happy I had found a compromise. Now I only had one final left until summer vacation. Maybe then I could try to help the angels prep for the gala, which to my knowledge hadn't even been mentioned since we'd left Gabriel's apartment.

My mind trailed off as tears streamed down my cheeks. I glanced over at the mirror again and watched them fall. It was petty to be upset about my anticlimactic freshmen year, but I was. It had been taken away from me, just like…

Just like Sister Helen.

It's all your fault, the tiny voice inside my head told me, even though so many had tried to reassure me it wasn't.

A loud sob escaped me, and I sunk to the floor. Covering my face with my hands, I wept.

It was all too much. For years, I had been plagued by the trauma of my childhood, the half memories of what had happened to me when my mom had left. None of them made any sense, probably because I didn't truly remember what had happened, but every night, the nightmares would come, as if my mind was trying to make me remember, to show me something from my past. Yet they triggered nothing other than half-truths and me doubting if what I saw in my mind was even true. The only way I could deal with them was by never actually going to sleep. But some nights it was hard to fend off the drowsiness.

Except, recently, instead of being transported back to my five-year-old self, I was carried to the church where Sister Helen had sacrificed herself for me, pushed me into that underground tunnel where I'd thought I would never see the light of day again. All the while being chased by snarling dogs, the coldhearted laugh of the Devil taunting me in my sleep.

Luckily, last night I had been spared that terror.

I tried breathing deeply to push away the panic attack but to no avail. The sobs choked out my breath.

Why? Sister Helen, why did you have to leave me like my mother did?

Sister Helen was the only one who had loved me and accepted me. And now I was alone. Again.

It's all your fault!

No one cares.

No one wants you.

My mind was stuck in a tailspin of self-betrayal, and just when I thought it was going to drag me under completely, there was a knock on the door.

"Soph? Can I come in?"

Dane.

I wiped the tears from my cheeks and approached the door. When I opened it, confetti was thrown in the air and a kazoo sounded.

"Congratulations! It's your last day of school!"

The gesture brought a weary smile to my face. I had thought the feelings I had for him were a childhood fantasy, one that would dissipate with time and maturity. But seeing him standing there with confetti in his perfect hair—who I am kidding, just being with him—made me realize how much I had been fooling myself. If anything, he had only grown more attractive.

Fortunately, he was also a balm to my panic attack, and the pressure lifted from my chest. I knew my face still displayed the lingering effects, though. And he saw it, too.

He frowned. "What's wrong?"

I shook my head. "Nothing. I don't want to make you late for work."

"Forget work. You're more important."

I invited him in, and we sat down on the edge of the bed to talk. I told him how I was feeling, and of course, it had me crying again.

He wiped the tears from my cheek. "You have every right to feel the way you're feeling about school. And it's also natural to have survivor's guilt. But what I want you to remember right now is neither of those things." He stopped and grabbed something from behind his back. It was a present. "Just push those aside for today and remember how proud I am of you that you finished your first year of college."

My lip trembled at his words, and new tears started to fall.

"That was not supposed to make you cry more," he teased.

I laughed and reached for the gift, untying the bow and slipping off the paper. I gasped when I caught a glimpse of what was beneath. It was a small painting of a snowy owl, every feather executed with expert detail.

Looking up at Dane, I said, "You painted this?"

He nodded. "Owls are symbols for wisdom, and your name *means* wisdom, so I thought it would be a cool way to commemorate your first year at Harvard. Since, you know, you're there to learn and everything..." He awkwardly trailed off.

I closed the distance between us and squeezed him in a hug. He had no idea how much I would cherish this painting. Well, maybe he did since I had been so sentimental about the first one.

Pulling back, I looked him in the eye. "Thank you."

"You're welcome." He stood up. "I should leave. I don't want to make you late, either."

"No need to worry. I have a lot of time. My final isn't until later this evening. I got up early so I could study some more. But I know you have to go so I'll see you later."

I followed him to the door and watched him retreat down the hall.

Yep, I definitely had a problem where Dane was concerned. But I couldn't think about him now even though I wanted to. I had to think about graph theory and algebraic equations, and get ready to tackle my last final of the semester.

26 JORDAN

Ithaca, New York, Present Day

The persistent chime from my 10:00 AM alarm woke me up. Peering bleary-eyed at the screen, I tapped it to turn it off.

I rubbed the sleep from my eyes and leaned back against the pillows. Life had been strange over the past two weeks. Even though we were all together, everyone seemed a little distant. Sophia was here finishing school. Dane had found a job at the local art supply store—Jophiel always went with him to keep watch—and I had been nightmare-free and catching up on some sleep. And although we had found a new normal, we were all internally struggling with Sister Helen's death. The only one who was externally struggling was Martha. She had gone on vacation, never giving us a firm date as to when she would return.

The angels were also taking the loss harder than I'd thought they would. Michael had fallen into a state of silence. Gabriel would lock himself away during the day with his violin. The others were solemn and quiet, retreating to their parts of the house and occasionally helping out with whatever they could, mainly household tasks. I supposed this was their way of grieving. I knew all of them felt responsible for Sister Helen's death, wishing they had put a stop to Satan before he could do any harm. I also knew they wanted to avenge her, but so far, no plans or action had been taken.

Grabbing my phone from the charger, I crawled out of bed and headed downstairs. The smell of cookies hit me immediately, which meant Chamuel was baking. The scents of brown sugar and melting chocolate filled my nose as I entered the kitchen. Those ingredients could mean only one thing: chocolate chip cookies. My favorite.

The timer on the microwave beeped, and Chamuel opened the oven to pull out a baking sheet. He set it on a cooling rack and removed his oven mitts. He turned away from his confections and finally noticed me. "Good morning."

"Morning."

"Did you sleep well?" he asked, plopping balls of dough on a new baking sheet.

"Yeah, I've been fine ever since Zadkiel gave this back to me," I said, fiddling with my necklace. Actually, I had been fine ever since Sister Delphine had done her weird forehead-mojo trick on me, but I hadn't told the angels about that. Not because I didn't want to but because I had forgotten.

"Good. We were all really worried about you." He said the words, but they held no emotion. Chamuel was focused on his task and stuck inside his head.

This obviously wasn't the time to mention it. Instead, I set my sights on the warm cookies and reached for one from the cooling rack.

"Watch out. Those are hot," Chamuel warned.

"I know," I mumbled, my mouth full of cookie. I swallowed. "That's the point. They're better this way."

A loud thud, followed by a gigantic bang, sounded from downstairs.

"What's going on down there?" I asked.

"Training," Uriel stated, entering the kitchen with a laundry basket.

"Who's training?" I asked.

"Well, more like fighting to get out the rage," Uriel clarified. "But to answer your question, Michael and Raphael."

"Where's Gabriel?"

A musical note reverberated through the house, and within seconds, a violin ballad had commenced, its tone full of melancholy.

I guess that answers my question.

I reached for another warm cookie.

"So, Chamuel," Uriel said hesitantly, staring at the laundry basket, "I think we might have a problem."

Chamuel's head snapped up from the oven. "What did you do? I gave you one simple task. You couldn't have messed it up."

"I did what you asked. I put the white clothes in the wash when my load finished."

"And?"

"And I forgot to take out my red shirt by accident."

Chamuel reached for the basket and held up a pink sock. "One. Simple. Task."

"I'm sorry," Uriel apologized. "It was an accident."

I full-out laughed like I hadn't in days.

"You think this is funny?" Chamuel asked. "Your socks are pink, too. All our socks are pink!"

Smiling, I said, "First off, Chamuel, you don't have to do my laundry for me, but thank you. Second, you like the color pink so just forget about the socks."

He sighed and threw the pink sock back in the basket. "You're right. I was just trying to help everyone, but I think I should let you all fend for yourselves. Can you bring this back upstairs? I'll take care of it later."

"No problem," Uriel said, grabbing the basket from him.

I set my phone on the counter and headed to the pantry for some cereal. While I could have eaten cookies for breakfast, I knew it would annoy Chamuel if I ate any more of his creations before they cooled.

Just as I had gathered everything and brought it back to the counter, my phone chimed. One glance at the screen, one look at the name that appeared, made me grin.

"That must be Naomi," Chamuel said.

My head snapped up at his comment. "How did you know?"

"The joy she brings you is written all over your face," he explained.

Uriel scrunched up his face. "Yuck."

"Uriel," Chamuel chastised.

"What?"

"Be more mindful of others' feelings."

"Oh please. I'm leaving now." He left the kitchen with the laundry basket and trudged back upstairs.

"Don't mind him," Chamuel said. "This is the first time I've seen you genuinely smile in the past two weeks, and I would rather you enjoy the moment."

I picked up my phone, unlocked the device, and opened her text message: *Hey, you! I had to share the news. I got an amazing summer internship at a cutting-edge lab. Eee! I'm so excited!*

Smiling, I typed back, *Congrats!*

Thanks! I might be a bit busier than I thought this summer.

Which means we wouldn't have much time together.

Setting the thought aside, I replied, *That's okay. We'll make it work.*

Good. Because I'd still like to see you. Talk soon!

I sighed. Our summer was already getting away from us. As much as I wanted to see Naomi, I knew both of us would be busy—her with the internship and me with lying low from the Fallen. Besides, I felt like the best place I could be right now was here. The angels weren't acting right—none of us were acting right—so maybe it was time to confront everyone about their feelings. Maybe if we all shared how we felt, we would feel better.

"Is everything all right?" Chamuel asked.

I puffed out a breath. "How could you tell this time?"

He lifted a finger to his forehead. "Your brow is all furrowed. A telltale sign of stress."

"Are my emotions really that obvious?"

He shrugged. "You have a very expressive face."

I nodded. "Well, Naomi got an internship for the summer, and I'm really happy for her, but I don't think we'll be seeing as much of each other as we would have liked."

"You can still talk, right?" the angel asked.

"Yeah, but that's all we ever do. It's better to be with the person."

"Maybe you can find some time."

"Maybe." It seemed unlikely given the celestial battle looming over us. "There's so much going on, I feel guilty worrying about this."

"Why? You need to live your life, Jordan."

"Yeah, but it's too early to move on," I told him. "We're in the thick of it now, and none of us have been acting like ourselves. I feel like we need an intervention. You know, clear the air and get us all on the same page again."

He brushed off my suggestion. "Regardless, I think you should keep in touch with Naomi. I mean, eventually this will all be over." Chamuel returned to the cookies.

He had a point, but would Naomi still want to be around when I was ready to involve her in my life? That was the hard part: I couldn't tell her anything.

In that moment, a woeful violin note reverberated through the house again.

Gabriel had such impeccable timing.

I settled in my seat and prepared my bowl of cereal. After breakfast, I went back upstairs to make my bed and shower. Since the angels weren't in the mood to do much of anything, and Sophia and Dane were preoccupied, I went downstairs to spend the day in the library.

There were so many books inside—all of which had belonged to my parents—that I decided to peruse the shelves to see what I could find.

Zadkiel was in the library when I entered, his head buried in *The Book of Prophecies*. Without looking up, he asked, "Is everything all right, Jordan?"

"Yeah, just wanted to look through some of the books."

He acknowledged my answer by nodding his head.

I walked along the shelves, scanning the spines as I passed. Occasionally, something would grab my attention and I would stop to pull the book out and flip through the pages. The library was enormous, feeling almost like a maze, but I was happy to get lost in its depths.

My first great discovery was a book about ancient cryptography and code breaking. I thought it would be really interesting to learn about that so I set the book aside. After adding a few more titles to the pile, my search stopped as I got distracted by a dictionary of symbols. I read the first few chapters about symbology and its significance. Then I started flipping through the pages of the large book, stopping once in a while to read about particular symbols.

When I finally decided to take a break, the clock read 6:30 PM. I had literally spent the entire day with my head in a book.

You needed that every now and then.

Standing up, I decided to put the symbol book back on the shelf, knowing I would be able to find it later since it was so huge. I was in one of the back corners of the library and knelt down to place the book back on the bottom shelf when something caught my eye. Three shelves over, there was a book with its pages facing out rather than its spine. I put the symbol book where it belonged and walked over to the other book in question. I pulled it from the shelf only to discover it was a worn copy of John Milton's *Paradise Lost*.

I flipped through the pages, which were littered with highlights and notes in the margins. One passage near the beginning stood out to me: *Awake, arise, or be forever fallen.*

I snapped the book shut, holding it tightly in my hand. I knew what the book was about, how it depicted Satan as a sympathetic hero. But he would never get any sympathy from me. Not after what he did.

He had killed Sister Helen to satisfy his revenge on the Sacrarium. I couldn't help but wonder about my parents. They had been Sacrarium, too. Had Satan killed them, as well? Were their causes of death mere cover-ups so I wouldn't go around asking questions?

You give him too much credit.

I raised a hand to my head. Oh no. She was back.

He didn't kill your parents.

I squeezed my eyes shut, trying to drown out her voice.

I did.

My eyes flew open in shock, and her diabolical laughter rang through my mind in endless waves. Shaking my head, I tried to make it stop.

That can't be true. Lilith couldn't have killed my parents. She had been locked up.

Correction: that was why *they locked me up.*

Sudden rage and hatred ran hot through my veins. I wanted so bad to take out my emotions on her, but she wasn't tangible, only a voice inside my head tormenting me. I reached for my necklace. Why wasn't it working?

Did you really think I wouldn't find a way past your protective ward? Month by month, as we get closer to Samhain, the veil grows thinner. It's just a matter of finding the holes until then to keep tormenting you.

The terms she was using were familiar, but I was by no means an expert in what she was talking about. If anything, her words only frustrated me more, so much so that I wanted to throw the book down the row of shelves and hear the satisfying thump as it hit the ground.

But then my mind took a darker turn.

Burn it. Burn it like he burned the church. Burn it like he burned her.

I covered my mouth to silence the sob that wanted to escape. Lilith was poking at the hole in my heart that Sister Helen had left behind. Lilith was in my head, trying to influence my thoughts and actions. I had to get her out.

Without thinking, I cocked my arm and threw. The book flew

through the air and made a satisfying thump after all as it landed across the room. But a small clink of something metallic along with that thump was unexpected.

I gazed at the book, which lay faceup, its pages spread open. My eyes grew wide as I noticed a large hole in the paper. I crossed the room and picked up the book again, inspecting the inside. Sure enough, someone had carved a perfect rectangle into the book.

But why?

I looked up from the book, my eyes landing on a metal key lying on the floor before me. I reached out and picked it up. It was a medium-sized brass key with an ornate design.

What was a key doing in a book? What did it open?

And then I remembered Martha's words from last fall: *There are so many keys hidden in this house. Your parents hid them so no one could get in.*

My mother's studio and my father's office! I bet this key opened one of them. But which one?

Neither! You're wasting your time. You need to focus on freeing me!

I clutched my head and yelled, "Get out!"

Hurried footsteps rushed over to me. "Jordan, are you all right?" Zadkiel asked.

I glanced up at him through my hands, and worry twisted his expression. It was time to tell everyone that Lilith was the one haunting my mind. She obviously wasn't leaving anytime soon.

"No," I whispered. "I'm not fine." Then conviction filled my entire being. "Wait here. We need to talk. All of us. I'll go get the others." I left the library and headed to the kitchen. On the way, I slipped the key into my pants pocket.

"I need you in the library," I said when I found Chamuel. He was pulling out ingredients to start cooking.

"But I have to get dinner ready," he stated.

"It can wait!" I shouted.

I didn't stick around to hear his response or see his shocked expression. Instead, I raced to the foyer and ran down the steps to the lower level. The music room was my first stop. Rather than knocking, I barged into the room, knowing that Gabriel would hear me anyway with his celestial hearing.

He stopped playing immediately. "Jordan, is everything all right?"

"No, we need to talk. Meet me in the library."

Leaving Gabriel behind, I strode down the hall and entered the gym. Although I knew I would find the three remaining angels here, I did not expect to witness a full-out wrestling match. Just as I entered, Michael body-slammed Uriel onto one of the mats on the floor and twisted his arms behind him like a pretzel.

"That's enough!" Raphael yelled, acting as referee.

Before I could agree with Raphael, Uriel used his legs to push himself up and then smacked his head backward into Michael's face. The move stunned the warrior angel, but it did not loosen his grip on Uriel's arms. Frustrated, Uriel repeated the same move again and again until Michael jerked back, letting him go.

"All right! It's over!" Raphael shouted, stepping between the two of them.

"I'm bleeding." Michael wiped his nose. "You fight dirty."

Uriel shrugged. "So do the Fallen. A little blood in the face is the least of your concerns when it comes to them."

Michael gave him a hard glare.

Before they could go at each other again, Raphael intervened. "I think it's time to stop for the night. Besides, it seems Jordan may need us."

All three of them planted their eyes on me.

"I need to speak with all of you," I said. "We're meeting in the library."

"About what?" Uriel asked.

"I'd rather tell you all at once. But it's important."

Uriel and Raphael left the gym and headed to the library.

"Are you coming?" I asked Michael.

He hesitated. "Perhaps you should go on without me. My judgment has been questionable lately."

"What do you mean? You're the only one who makes actionable plans."

"Exactly. Ones that put us in danger, lead us into Satan's trap." He paused. "Ones that get people killed."

"Sister Helen's death is not on your hands," I told him.

"Really?" His face was contorted with anguish. "I led him right to her! He saw the private investigator work I was doing in Brazil. He saw the map I had of the Sacrarium's past whereabouts. How am I *not* responsible?"

"Michael, that happened six months ago. Clearly, Satan didn't understand whatever you think he saw. So you can't do this. You can't self-destruct. You can't blame yourself."

"But I can because she wasn't the first," he whispered solemnly.

Confused, I asked, "Who else?"

"Allen Clark. I promised to help him, too, and now he's nowhere to be found."

"You don't know he's dead."

Michael gave me a hard stare. "Allen didn't just go silent. He *disappeared.* There's a high likelihood he's dead."

There were no adequate words to say so I changed the subject in hopes of distracting him. "Don't you want to know what's going on? I have a lot of information that could lead us down new paths to new answers. You vowed on Sister Helen's grave you would avenge her. Are you really just going to stand aside and let the others do it without you?"

I could tell my words pulled at his courageous heart. He wanted to listen, he wanted to come to the library with me, but something was holding him back.

"What are you afraid of?" I asked. Somehow I knew it was fear making him hesitate.

He crossed his arms and shrugged.

"Everyone is afraid of something. Gabriel is afraid of change. Raphael is afraid of loss. Even you must have a fear."

He was still silent so I kept talking. "I'm the king of fear. I fear change. I fear loss. I fear love, or feeling too little or too much. I fear failure. I fear my hopes and my dreams because I sometimes think I'm not good enough to aspire to such things. I fear the future and the unknown. I fear the nightmares that plague my sleep. I fear my own mind." I paused, thinking of Lilith, then continued. "But even though I fear many things, I'm not afraid of fear itself because it helps me learn and grow. So even you must have a fear." I sat down on the floor across from him. "Tell me what you fear."

He shook his head. If angels could cry, I imagined he would have been in tears just then.

Sensing what might be the cause of his hesitation, I delicately brought up the subject. "Although I fear Satan, my love for Sister

Helen outweighs my fear because she deserves justice. You taught me that being knowledgeable about the enemy allows us to defeat them. Well, you know Satan better than anyone. You're the best angel to defeat him. If we don't have you, we're all screwed."

Michael sighed. "But that's the problem. My biggest fear *is* defeating Satan. I cannot slay him because he will always be my brother. Even though it's the right thing to do, I cannot bring myself to do it."

I was surprised by his confession—the part about how he was afraid to vanquish Satan. Yet, I supposed I would feel a similar way if I were in his place. I could never bring myself to harm Dane, even though we had a history of opposition.

"Then we don't defeat him," I said. "We neutralize him."

"How?" Michael asked.

"In this particular moment, I'm not sure, but I think once we talk everything over in the library, we might have more answers."

He nodded. "Okay, I'm coming."

We made the trek back upstairs, ready to join the others.

27 JORDAN

Ithaca, New York, Present Day

Thankfully, Michael and I ran into Dane and Jophiel as they walked through the front door after a day at work.

Before any pleasantries could be exchanged, Jophiel asked, "What's going on?"

"How did you know something was amiss?" Michael asked.

"It's written all over Jordan's face," Dane supplied.

I sighed. "We're meeting in the library. We have a lot to talk about."

Dane nodded. "Did you get Sophia?"

"Get me for what?" she asked, walking down the steps.

"A meeting in the library," Dane said.

She shrugged. "First time I'm hearing of it."

"Me too." He stared at her. "So how'd it go?"

She scrunched up her face. "Fine. Probably better than fine, but it's math and now I have a headache." She smiled. "At least school's over." Then she grew serious. "Enough about me. Let's go deal with whatever's going on."

Together, we walked down the hall to the library, where the other angels were already waiting. There was too much unsaid among us so I strode to the center table where *The Book of Prophecies* rested and jumped right in to enlightening them about what I knew.

"First off, Sister Delphine is more involved than she lets on," I said. "Dane was right about her knowing things."

"The nun we met at the funeral?" Raphael asked.

I nodded. "Yes, she helped Sister Helen operate the orphanage. In fact, she's been around our entire lives now that I think about it, and I don't think it's a coincidence."

"Why's that?" Gabriel asked.

"Well she helped stop whatever was happening to me at the funeral. It was like I was having nightmares but was fully awake. She pressed her thumb to my forehead and made it all go away, just like Dane had said she did when we were kids. She told me I had gifts, visions. She said something about warning my parents but that they didn't listen. She promised she would return and reveal everything, but I haven't heard from her since."

"Visions? That's the word she used?" Zadkiel asked.

I nodded.

"Hmm..." He drew closer to *The Book of Prophecies*. "I've been reading the entirety of this book, and most of what is documented inside originated from a group of angels who specialize in visions."

"What do you mean?" Jophiel asked.

Zadkiel rubbed his forehead. "It seems they occupy another realm and are known as the Ishim. They document divine messages and prophetic visions, many of the angels having these visions themselves."

"But there have been other angels like that. Metatron is a perfect example. What makes this group different?" Uriel asked.

"Because they were once Watchers." Zadkiel's lips curved into a sad smile. "The only ones who actually obeyed Father and remained good. They were renamed the Ishim so as not to associate with the negative reputation the Watchers now hold. It's also why they are unknown to the world."

"What does this have to do with Sister Delphine and my 'visions'?" I asked, using air quotes on the last word.

"This group of angels was sent here centuries ago to teach humans the knowledge of the universe," Zadkiel began. "There were five of them, and each angel found two worthy pupils to share their knowledge with, the intent being that the pupils would pass it down through the generations of their family. Much of that knowledge is gained and taught through visions and conditioning of the mind, but many can no longer access these teachings."

He paused for a moment before continuing. "I wonder if Sister Delphine belongs to one of the ancient families connected to these angels. It would explain why she knows how to help you, and it would explain her interest in you. If what you are experiencing are indeed divine or prophetic visions, then you are a rarity, since many no longer have such a gift."

"Could it be possible that one of Jordan's parents had a similar gift?" Sophia asked. "Sister Delphine did mention them, right?"

My eyes widened in shock. I had never thought of that possibility before.

"I mean," she continued, "it might explain their involvement in all this. Especially if one of your parents was part of this group and the other was part of the Sacrarium."

"You make a very valid point, Sophia," Zadkiel agreed.

"Maybe we should find Sister Delphine," I suggested, desperately wanting answers.

"I'm worried that might be a hard task," Gabriel said. "If she wanted to be found, she would have shown up here already. If she said she would return with answers, then perhaps we should wait until she's ready."

"Something must be keeping her away," Dane said. "She's been with us our entire lives and *now* she decides to tell Jordan about who he is? Why wait so long?"

"It might just be a vow of secrecy," Jophiel said.

I sighed. "I'm starting to get tired of secrecy."

"Me too, kid," Uriel chimed in.

"In any case," Zadkiel interjected, "Sister Delphine is an asset we need to keep in mind because it seems she might be the key to unlocking the past."

"Speaking of keys and unlocking the past…" I reached into my pocket and pulled out the key I had discovered. "I found this today hidden inside a book."

"A book in this library?" Gabriel asked.

I nodded. "A copy of *Paradise Lost* to be exact."

Michael chuckled. "How ironic."

"I think it opens either my father's office or my mother's studio. I haven't tried it yet."

"What are you waiting for?" Uriel demanded.

"Uriel!" Chamuel chided. "We've discussed this!"

"Yeah, yeah, mind the feelings of others," he recited, brushing off Chamuel's concern.

"It's all right, Chamuel. I didn't try the key yet, but I'm going to now." I didn't mention that Lilith's internal torment was what stopped me. I knew I should tell them about her. It was more important than the key

I'd found. But honestly, it felt like every time I tried to, my mind would just get distracted. I wonder if Lilith's mark had anything to do with it...

Anyway, after hearing Sophia's theory about my visions being related to my parents, I couldn't get the key off my mind.

I stood and walked over to the office door and inserted the key in the lock. Although it fit, it wouldn't turn.

Removing the key, I said, "It obviously doesn't open the office."

"Then let's try the studio," Michael said.

I looked at him. It was nice to see conviction return to his face. Nodding in agreement, we all headed downstairs.

The studio was across the hall from the music room, and as we neared the door, I suddenly grew anxious. What if the key didn't open this door, either? What if this was all some elaborate scheme to throw us off locating the real key?

Calming the voice inside my head—it was entirely my own this time—I reached for the knob and inserted the key. Sophia, Dane, and the seven angels stood behind me, and I could feel their tense energy as I turned it in the lock. The gears actually moved, and the lock ticked open. After removing the key and returning it to my pocket, I grabbed the knob and twisted, the door swiftly opening.

The room was dark, only illuminated by the rising moon shining in through the bay windows. It reflected off the lake at the back of the house, creating a picturesque scene. I fumbled along the wall for a light switch and flicked it on once I found it. Entering the studio was like seeing the world through my mom's eyes. There were paintings on every inch of wall space, depicting scenes from locations across the globe. The counters in the room were covered with supplies—paints, brushes, palettes, mixing trays.

It seemed my mom also experimented in other mediums. A pottery wheel and kiln were set up in the far corner while there were racks of fabrics for quilts and patchworks. It was amazing to see. I felt like I had finally met the person she truly was, in a place that was full of her energy. Her personality showed through in other parts of the house, but here I could finally *feel* her presence as if she were alive and standing next to me.

Although the studio was neat and tidy, a blanket of dust covered everything, probably because this room had been locked for close to nineteen years. I vowed I would start cleaning tomorrow and restore the room to its former beauty.

"I've always noticed this room from outside, but you could never see in the windows. And there was no urgent reason to try to break them to get in," Jophiel commented. "Who would have known what magnificence lay behind them?" The angel of art walked slowly about the room, his eyes wide and curious as he scanned every piece of artwork. Dane was in a similar state, walking silently around, his eyes full of wonder.

Jophiel was right, though. From the outside, there was no indication of what the room held. The windows must have been specially treated. I wondered if the same went for my father's office since, from the outside, you could tell there was a window in that room but couldn't see through it, either.

I walked over to one of the windows to look outside at the night.

Jordan.

It was as if someone had whispered my name in my ear. Startled, I scanned the room. The others hadn't seemed to hear it. Just as I was about to set my sights back outside, my eye caught something sitting in the corner. From the door, it was blocked from view by the kiln, but standing so close to the window, I could easily see it. It was covered with a sheet, though, so it was hard to tell what was underneath.

I approached the covered object, grabbed the cloth, and pulled it back. Dust went flying, forcing my eyes temporarily shut. When I opened them, what lay before me was a tapestry loom upon which a large square of fabric sat. It depicted a tree, presumably the Tree of Life, its branches woven in three colors—red, green, and blue. It seemed the square had been cut from a larger piece of fabric, its edges frayed and loose.

To anyone else, it was simply a tapestry patch, but to me, it was so much more. The threads hummed, not just with voices but with power. However, the whispering voices were hard to hear, their words incoherent, as if something was blocking what they had to say.

I reached out to touch it when the excruciating headache returned. I dropped to my knees and cried out in pain.

Everyone raced to my side.

"Jordan, what is it?" Sophia asked.

I clutched my head, the pressure unbearable. "My...head," I managed to force out.

"Put your thumb to his forehead," Uriel said. "Isn't that what we're supposed to do?"

Raphael did as Uriel suggested, but when his thumb touched my skin, searing pain spread through my head. I yelled out, and Raphael let me go.

"It's not working!" the angel of healing shouted in obvious frustration.

"How did this even happen in the first place?" Gabriel asked. "He's wearing his necklace."

I lifted my eyes to the easel again, but a figure blocked my view.

Lilith.

She was standing there in ethereal form, only visible to me. She was the one doing this, using her power to block all the things that protected me, like the necklace and the thumb trick.

You're getting distracted, Jordan, Lilith urged. *It's time to unleash me so I can finish what I started.*

Words wouldn't form so I adamantly shook my head back and forth, denying her.

She lashed out, grabbing hold of my neck. I choked, gasping for air.

You need to find the fourteenth sphere, Lilith continued. *That is the only way this will end.* Her hypnotizing eyes grew wide, filling my entire gaze. *Make this easy. Take off your necklace so I can fully control you.*

Clawing at my neck, I grabbed hold of the fleur-de-lis necklace, ready to yank it off and end this misery.

"Jordan, no!" Gabriel clutched my arm, preventing me from tearing off the piece of jewelry.

I wheezed.

"Gabriel, stop!" Michael demanded, kneeling in front of me. "Can't you see it's suffocating him?"

"But what if that's what they want?" Gabriel reasoned. "To trick us into thinking taking it off will help him!"

"What who wants?" Michael asked, outraged.

As soon as Gabriel said, "I'm not sure," Dane shouted, "How are you not sure? She's standing right there!"

The angels stopped for a second to look at one another, completely stunned. They couldn't see Lilith, and I hadn't thought anyone else could, either, but it seemed that wasn't the case…

"Who's standing right there?" Michael asked.

Dane didn't respond. He lunged forward, grabbing hold of Lilith's arm, and forcefully prying her fingers from my throat.

Her hand released, and I gulped in air, trying to recover from her death grip.

Lilith's eyes shifted away from me, breaking her hypnotizing spell to stare at Dane. Utter shock was etched across her face. She was so shaken that she escaped from his grasp and disappeared before our eyes.

Everyone surrounded me, but I didn't hear them, couldn't hear them, because a bright light lit up my surroundings, and I swore I heard the song of angels.

Jordan.

It was the voice I had first heard when I looked out the window, a small whisper in my ear. I closed my eyes to listen closer.

You must be untouched. A soft pressure brushed the space between my eyes, pecking and pecking at my mind. *Until you are, you cannot receive the message you need to hear.* Finally, the pressure eased and I knew Lilith's mark was obliterated. I could feel it.

My eyes snapped open. Without taking notice of anyone else, I rose from the floor and gazed upon the tapestry. I could hear the whispering voices again, but they were still muted. Glancing down, I reached for my necklace and slipped it off. As soon as I did, the voices grew louder and coherent, their song no longer suppressed. I touched the fabric, and as the soft threads brushed my fingertips, my eyes rolled back in my head—not in pain but in trance.

I felt my mouth move but couldn't control it as the words came pouring out:

"Bloodlines tied betwixt you three
Threads sealed and woven in a tree.
Find the one destined to thee
Your family tree you cannot flee.

"In boughs of cypress, spruce, and oak
Lies the blade you must uncloak.
Assume your role, discover your power
For you will need it at the fateful hour.

"Children raised together
Must follow the feather.
Red, green, blue in hue
They will guide you anew.

"Wisdom, blood, and balance
Will each be challenged.
Not one, not two, but three shares
So goes the Prophecy of the Three Heirs."

As the last word escaped, I collapsed into unconsciousness.

28

JORDAN

ITHACA, NEW YORK, PRESENT DAY

When I came back to my senses, I was no longer in the studio. Instead, I was lying on the couch in the living room, my necklace sitting securely around my neck and the scent of pasta wafting toward me.

I sat up quickly, trying to understand what had happened. But that was a mistake as a crushing headache came pounding through my temples. Groaning, I eased back down on the couch and closed my eyes.

"How are you?" Raphael asked.

Contorting my face, I said, "Not so good."

"I imagine. Why don't you try to eat something? It will make you feel better."

Without opening my eyes, I knew Chamuel had arrived with the pasta, as the smell of tomato sauce and garlic had drawn closer. I cracked open my eyes, grabbing the bowl of spaghetti and digging in. I must have been hungrier than I'd thought because I shoveled forkfuls of pasta in my mouth, scarfing down the food quicker than I, or anyone else, had anticipated.

Chamuel handed me a napkin, and I wiped my face. "Thanks," I said. "For everything."

"No problem." He stood and took my bowl.

"Are we going to address what happened downstairs?" Uriel asked.

Across the room, Chamuel shot daggers from his eyes. Uriel threw his hands up and mouthed, *What?* back to Chamuel.

Ignoring them, I asked, "What exactly *did* happen?"

Michael crossed his arms. "You don't remember?"

"Not really. All I remember is uncovering the loom and seeing the tapestry." I stopped, transfixed on the piece of fabric.

"Don't think about it!" Uriel shouted. "I don't know if I can handle you experiencing another vision."

"Is that what it was?" I asked.

The angels were hesitant to answer. Finally, Zadkiel said, "Yes, it was. I've seen enough of them to know. I had to watch over Metatron in Heaven whenever he had one. They are draining and debilitating for even the most skilled."

"So what do we do now?" I asked.

"Find the freaky nun," Uriel said.

Jophiel rolled his eyes. "You're acting immature."

"Immature?" Uriel replied, outraged. "I can handle a lot, but I didn't sign up for humans having creepy mystical trances."

Worried, I asked, "Was it really that creepy?"

Uriel's head tottered back and forth. Raphael shoved him in the arm.

"I would use the word *startling*," Gabriel amended. "None of us were expecting it."

"Did anyone write down what I said?"

Jophiel reached into his shirt pocket and offered me a folded sheet of paper. "I did. What you said was extremely important, and it's not every day you witness a vision."

I took the paper from him and read.

"Do you have any idea what it might mean?" Chamuel asked.

I nodded. "I have a gut feeling Sophia, Dane, and I are the three heirs." I glanced at my two friends, who remained silent. They looked just as drained as I felt.

"We were thinking the same thing, but we didn't want to overwhelm any of you," Gabriel said.

"I also think it's telling us how to find out who we are." I looked at Dane and Sophia. "Any thoughts?"

"Other than 'holy shit what did I sign up for?'" Dane blurted out.

"Dane," Sophia cautioned.

"What? I know you saw her, too—that woman suffocating Jordan."

"I did… She was so scary I felt paralyzed." Sophia crossed her arms as if to shield herself from the memory.

"She's not just any woman. She's Lilith," I said.

The angels' attention snapped to me.

Sophia shook her head. "Before we go there, let's talk about the tapestry."

"What about it?" I asked.

"Well, that was only a piece of it, right? I mean, tapestries tend to be much bigger than that," Sophia said. "So where's the rest of it?"

Shrugging, I said, "No idea."

"We need to find it," Sophia said. "There has to be more to it than just the tree. It needs to be put back together. The fabric is already unraveling after so many years, it needs preservation. If there's more to the message, it could be lost forever if we don't take care of the tapestry."

I hadn't thought of that.

"The colors mean something, too," Dane added. "Red, green, and blue are the three primary colors of light."

Sitting there, I was proud of both of them. Their passions for art were coming through, but more than that, their knowledge bases would be integral to solving this mystery. With everything that had occurred in the past few weeks, I had never stopped to appreciate their presence. I wouldn't trade it for anything, and if I could, I would keep them with me as long as possible on this journey. Because I couldn't do this alone. That had been my problem in the past. I had thought Sister Helen's secrets were my burden, that I had to find the answers and fix everything on my own. Of course, I knew the angels would help, but knowing Sophia and Dane were not just on my side but invested in this fight, too, was like a weight lifted off my shoulders.

"Now can we talk about Lilith?" Michael asked. The three of us nodded, and he went on. "How do you know her?"

"I don't," Sophia and Dane said together.

Then everyone focused on me.

I sighed. "You all know I've been haunted in my nightmares by a strange woman. At first, I had no idea who she was. It wasn't until the funeral when she came through while I was awake that I learned her identity. She keeps insinuating a connection to my parents, some confrontation or wrongdoing they had with her, and she claims that she killed them."

They all looked at me, various states of shock on their faces.

"Did she tell you what she wants?" Michael asked.

I nodded. "I'm not entirely sure what she means, but I do know she wants to be freed."

"She's locked up?" Zadkiel asked. "Where?"

I shrugged. "I don't know. But this time she mentioned that I had to find the fourteenth sphere." I met Sophia's gaze, and she shuddered.

"Before we deal with the sphere," Gabriel said, "I want to know how Lilith got past the necklace."

I nodded. "She did tell me the necklace is a protective ward, but tonight she also told me that, even though we're still months away, as we get closer to Samhain, the veil grows thinner."

"What veil?" Dane asked.

"The veil between worlds," Zadkiel supplied. "Samhain is essentially Halloween. On that night, transitioning from one dimension to another is very easy, as the barriers that are typically in place are lowered. There's a reason why ghosts and ghouls can wander the streets on Halloween. It's because they can escape from Hell."

"But the same goes for all the realms," Jophiel added. "Hell, Earth, and Heaven."

"How do you keep them out?" I asked. "At least, from Heaven?"

"We fight them," Michael said. "Though the only beings we need to worry about are fallen angels, since no one else could even get to Heaven, and most of the Fallen don't even try. They like being in Hell too much."

"But Lilith could get there. She breached Heaven before by disguising herself as one of us. She could never complete her plans, though," Gabriel said ominously. "That's probably why she wants to be freed. She wants to finish what she started."

"She did say that," I confirmed. "Not the Heaven part, but that she wanted to finish what she started."

"On my birthday," Sophia commented.

"You were born on Halloween?" Chamuel asked.

Sophia nodded.

Dane and I knew that, but we never knew the day was connected to Samhain.

A moment of silence passed among us.

"So do we have to worry that Lilith will keep tormenting you?" Raphael asked.

"I don't think so. At the funeral, Lilith marked me." I rubbed the spot on my forehead. "It gave her some kind of power over me, which is why the thumb trick wouldn't work. But right before my last vision, I heard angels singing. One of them erased her mark so that I could hear the prophecy."

"An angel? Who?" Sophia asked.

I shook my head. "I don't know."

Dane rolled his eyes. "There's a lot we don't know. I think we should focus on what we do know. Lilith wants this fourteenth sphere, and obviously to return to Heaven, so we need to do something about it."

"He's right," Michael said. "Which means we need to follow the only lead we have right now: the gala. Sophia laid the groundwork, so we need to follow through."

"Okay, but how do we get the sphere?" Jophiel questioned.

"We steal it, I suppose," Uriel said.

"We're not stealing it," Raphael chided.

"Fine, we *borrow* it," Uriel amended. "Although, they're the ones who technically stole it since it's actually ours."

"Do we even want it?" I asked. "I mean, what do we do with it?"

"We'll decide when we see it. As angels, we can easily detect celestial energy, and once we get a reading, that will determine our course of action," Michael said.

"What do you suggest?" Gabriel asked.

Michael gave him a knowing glance, the two already conspiring and putting together a plan.

"We already have access to the gala since we have the tickets Simon Price gave to Sophia. Now it's a matter of confirming if the sphere is real," Michael said.

"And if it is?" Sophia asked.

He chewed his lip. "Then we keep it safe. I expect we won't be the only ones there trying to gain access to the sphere. Not with the Fallen being as rampant as they have been," he said. "Which means we need backup if anything goes wrong, and from now on, I'm always planning on something going wrong because Satan is on the loose."

I remembered our conversation from earlier. Michael knew Satan better than anyone else, and although our aim may no longer be defeating him, we still had to neutralize him. I supposed anticipating his plans would put us one step closer to thwarting them.

"So how many of us do you need inside the museum?" Raphael asked.

"We only have three tickets, but I would like five of us on the inside. The others can wait outside," Michael strategized.

"With intel and the getaway car," I joked.

"Exactly," Michael agreed.

I stared at him. "You're serious?"

"Completely. You never know what could happen."

I thought I had gotten to a point where the angels could no longer surprise me, but that apparently wasn't the case.

"I think I could get two more of us inside," Chamuel said.

Michael raised his eyebrows. "How?"

Chamuel shrugged. "I might know the caterer. I'll have to ask around, though."

"Perfect. Gabriel, Raphael, and I can attend as guests while Chamuel and Uriel help out in the kitchen. That leaves Jophiel and Zadkiel outside, ready to assist if the need arises," Michael said.

"Do I really have to be on kitchen duty?" Uriel asked. "You know how much I hate chores."

"Would you rather be outside, away from the potential action?" Michael asked.

Uriel sighed. "Of course not, but why can't I be a guest?"

"Because Gabriel is a socialite, Raphael organizes foreign-aid projects, and I need to lead the operation without distraction," Michael pointed out. "And to be honest, Uriel, you're not very diplomatic."

"Fine. I don't really like talking to people anyway. I'll take kitchen duty," Uriel conceded.

"What about us?" Dane asked.

The angels all turned to look at him.

"You'll stay at the apartment in New York while we're at the gala," Gabriel said. "It's not safe for you all at the museum, especially since we don't know what will happen, and the apartment is sanctified and warded against the Fallen. We certainly aren't leaving you all here in Ithaca unprotected."

Dane opened his mouth to protest but stopped, probably realizing Gabriel was right. It wasn't safe for us to go to the gala.

And although Gabriel hadn't said it, I knew he preferred having someone watch over me because of my visions, which could potentially harm me. Hopefully, I was beyond that, though.

"All right," Zadkiel said. "Is there anything else we need to discuss right now?"

"I certainly hope not. It's been a lot for one night," Jophiel said.

"You're right, it has. Luckily, that's everything I had to tell you when we gathered in the library," I added.

Gabriel nodded. "Good. Don't let it bottle up next time, no matter how melancholy we are."

"Yeah, no more secrets," Sophia emphasized adamantly, meeting my eyes.

"I promise," I assured them, yawning. "I think it's time I went upstairs and relaxed a little before bed."

"Let me come with you," Gabriel said, obviously not convinced Lilith was gone.

I was grateful for his protection. I wasn't sure yet myself if the she-devil had left for good or just retreated to prepare for her next attack.

29

SATAN

Hell, Present Day

Abbadona was no better. Shortly after I had bandaged her up, the hallucinations had kicked in, along with a slew of other symptoms. My intent had always been to stay with her, but after seeing how vulnerable she was to the delusions that pulled at her mind, I realized she wouldn't have survived on her own.

Especially since the rivers had called to her, too.

With her abilities weakened, the waters were taking advantage of the opportunity, knowing there was no one around to keep them in check. So much so that they even tried playing games with me. I wouldn't stand for it, though, so with the help of Haborym and Nehema, I relocated Abbadona to my private quarters, where I could still keep watch over her but without any pestering from the rivers. It was the safest decision for both of us.

Except peace and quiet was hard to come by. Now that Kat had successfully escaped once, she was hell-bent on doing so again—and getting far beyond the bounds of Hell this time. The banging in the portal room was incessant. I was surprised she didn't tire herself out.

After two full weeks of it, however, it was beginning to get on my nerves.

"Sir, I came to see how Abbadona is doing. Is there anything I can do?" Nehema asked, peeking her head inside my private quarters.

My head snapped up from the museum brochure I was analyzing. I had been thinking about Simon Price and his soon-to-be theft of the fourteenth sphere. Now my full attention was on her.

"Actually, yes." I rose from my seat. "Stay here with Abbadona. It's about time I take care of our unruly prisoner."

I marched to the portal room and strode right through the invisible barrier of Kat's cell to confront her face-to-face. "What do you want?"

She dropped her raised arms as she was preparing to bang against the wall again. "My freedom."

"I've kept you down here for close to two decades. What makes you think I'm eager to be benevolent?"

She smirked. "Your recent change of heart."

I smacked her across the face. She went flying to the ground.

Spitting out blood, she rubbed her jaw and leveled her gaze on me. "After all these years, don't you know violence doesn't intimidate me?"

I knelt in front of her. "Yes, that's why I decided to let you rot."

Her shackles jangled as she crossed her arms. "And I am content to rot. But I am not willing to let my sacrifice go in vain. All those years ago, I willingly followed Lucifer down here, knowing there was a good possibility I would never leave again. I did so because what he and Lilith had planned would completely destroy the world as we know it, throwing it into evil and darkness."

"What's wrong with that?" I joked.

"There was no place for you in it. They had every intention of usurping your throne and making you suffer a long, painful death."

My anger was boiling beneath the surface. But she didn't need to see that.

"So what, I should be thanking you for preventing it?"

Her jaw tightened. "No, not everything is about you," she ground out, seemingly trying to calm herself. "I did whatever I could to sabotage them. I captured Lilith and thwarted Lucifer from enacting her plans, even though I knew it would ultimately land me here. And now I will not sit by and watch everything I did unravel before me."

"Meaning?"

"Meaning," she continued, "I'm going to help you."

Her sudden honesty intrigued me. "I'm listening."

"I know the fourteenth sphere has been discovered. I know it's sitting in some museum ready to be put on display. I know you intend to have some dark being steal it, just so you can use it as leverage to get the locations of your keys."

My patience was wearing thin. "Why are you telling me everything I already know?"

"Because I'm willing to reveal those locations to you. But *only* if you retrieve the fourteenth sphere and destroy it."

I pondered her words. She had never wanted to give me information before. She was too stubborn. So why the sudden change? Examining her face, I could tell she was speaking the truth. She was willing to make a deal with me to preserve her past actions. But she was also doing it as her last act. Katriel was an angel, a blessed angel living in a fallen world. She had put up a good fight for almost twenty years, but her energy was waning, her life force was waning. She simply could not survive down here in a place so unsuited for her.

I was ready to take her deal, but it all depended on one lingering question. "Why do you want me to destroy it?"

She met my eyes. "Because I locked Lilith in the fourteenth sphere, and if you destroy it, there's no way she can be freed. There's no way she can take what is yours ever again."

Liking the sound of that, I smiled wickedly. "Count me in."

30

JORDAN

New York City, Present Day

Two days had passed since the night Lilith had appeared and I'd spoken the words of a strange divination. Since then, the angels had been planning for the gala. Chamuel had secured a spot for himself as a waiter and for Uriel as a dishwasher. All that was left to do was reconnaissance. Each of the angels took turns flying to the city and scouring the interior of the Met. Michael had done a good analysis of the outside and the perimeter, too, drawing up diagrams and formulating the best way for Jophiel and Zadkiel to remain nearby.

Meanwhile, Sophia, Dane, and I watched from the sidelines, trying to decipher the Prophecy of the Three Heirs. Sophia was also hoping to figure out a way to help me with my visions. While the necklace was working and the visions had seemed to stop, she still thought it would be worthwhile to learn how to harness them. I suspect some kind of training would be involved, but what did that look like? Meditation? Reading palms or crystal balls? Who knew really? Perhaps Sister Delphine, but she still was nowhere to be found and I wasn't going to rely on her. Besides, we needed to get through the fourteenth sphere predicament first before we could focus on fixing me. That object could not fall into the wrong hands.

"We're here," Gabriel announced, pulling me away from my thoughts.

Here was a brownstone in Brooklyn. Early this morning, we had all left the house in Ithaca and headed to the city for the gala, which would be taking place tomorrow night. Before we went to the apartment, Gabriel wanted to make a quick stop to see his friend Tony, the man he had called his assistant when I had first met Gabriel the night of the subway chase. Apparently, Tony had supplies they needed for the gala. What those were, we would soon find out.

Gabriel parked the car on the street right in front of the house, and we exited the vehicle. The others came walking up to meet us after presumably landing in an alleyway nearby. Together, we mounted the steps to the front door, where Gabriel rang the doorbell. Several moments later, an old man opened the door. He was tall and had silver hair. Gold chains graced his neck and wrists, and a few gold rings were also on his fingers. He wore a black velour jogging suit with comfortable-looking Velcro sneakers.

The moment he saw Gabriel, he heartily greeted him. "Gabriel!" the man said, enveloping him in a hug. They patted each other on the back, then drew apart. "Let me get a look at you! Still the same after all these years."

"Of course," Gabriel replied with a sly grin. Then he grew more serious. "How are you, Tony? Feeling good?"

"Ah!" He waved off Gabriel's concern. "Nothing knocks me down. Not even appendicitis." They both laughed. "Come in, come in, all of you," Tony urged.

We all trudged through the door into the foyer. The inside of the house was beautiful. The floors were marble, and the wooden staircase in front of us looked original. Tony led us through the hall, passing by an immaculate living room. "Perfect timing. The family's here for lunch. I know you don't eat, but they'd still like to see you anyway."

"As I would like to see them," Gabriel said. "Though, I'm sure the kids may be hungry for some lunch." He gestured toward me, Sophia, and Dane.

Tony planted his eyes of each of us in turn. "Which one of you is Jordan?"

I raised my hand. "I am, sir."

He slapped me on the back, the force incredibly strong given his age, and walked with me. "It was a surprise to hear that Gabriel had a young boy show up on his doorstep after being chased through the subway. Sending over some food the morning after was the least I could do since this guy can't cook to save his life. Besides, my daughter's food is impeccable. She's a caterer, you know."

Before I could say anything, we had arrived at the kitchen where all eyes were turned on us. "Gabriel!" they all shouted in welcome.

"Come here! Come here! Let me kiss you," a woman with gray hair said, squeezing Gabriel in a hug and kissing him on the cheek. Her name was Francesca. She was Tony's wife.

We were all received in the same manner, with side hugs and cheek kisses, introductions being made as we went through the lineup of Tony's big Italian family.

"Claudia!" Francesca yelled to her daughter. "Get some glasses and give the kids some lemonade!" She turned to us. "Sit here, dears, and have some lunch. We have fresh rolls and cold cuts from the deli."

"What about you boys?" Claudia asked, now holding the lemonade pitcher.

Tony threw his hands in the air. "Claudia, I told you! They don't eat!"

"All right, Dad, all right. I didn't want to be impolite," she responded, exasperated.

Although we had been instructed to make sandwiches, one was made for each of us instead, stacked high with Italian meats and cheeses. I took a big bite and delighted in the delicious taste.

"You want some pasta salad, hon? I made it this morning." Even though it was a question, the answer was determined for me. "Claudia! Get the pasta salad!" Francesca sat down for a minute before another idea struck her. "Claudia, get my cheesecake, too!" She turned to Dane. "You have to have the cheesecake," she said to him. "It's to die for."

In the few short minutes since we had arrived, we were quickly filled up with food and sweets. Tony's family was so kind and generous, they made you feel like a part of the family. I wondered how Gabriel had met Tony. They seemed to know each other so well.

I glanced over at the older man, who was conversing with the other angels. Even though none of them had met Tony prior to today, they were all talking to him as though they had known him for years. Meanwhile, Gabriel was chatting with Francesca in the other corner of the kitchen.

"So, Jordan, you have a girlfriend?" Claudia asked me.

My eyes widened in terror. I was not about to be subjugated to more matchmaking. Martha had been relentless when I first met her. "Uh...kinda." I wasn't sure what Naomi and I were other than friends, but there might be a chance for more.

"Mmm." She seemed unconvinced. "Well, if you're ever looking, my daughter Angelica is a sweetheart."

"Claudia!" Tony yelled.

She held her hands up innocently. "What?"

"Leave the kid alone!"

She huffed out a breath and rolled her eyes, standing up from the table and leaving us be.

Gabriel crossed the small kitchen and returned to Tony's side. "You ready?" the old man asked.

"Whenever you are," Gabriel responded.

"What do you want to see first?"

Gabriel smiled. "Let's go visit Nonna Bea."

Tony chuckled. "I should've guessed."

He rose from his chair and exited the kitchen. We followed him back down the hall and up the wooden staircase, the steps creaking as we went. We stopped at the second floor, although there were more steps that continued up. Skirting around the bannister, Tony walked to a room at the front of the house, its door slightly ajar. He knocked and walked in, saying, *"Ciao, Mama!"*

"Ciao, Antonio," said an old woman hunched over a sewing machine. Her back was turned to us as she sat there nimbly feeding fabric through the needle. The afternoon sun shone in through the big window, illuminating her face in sunshine.

"Mama, we have guests," Tony said.

The woman slowly turned in her seat, her face lighting up in awe. *"Gli angeli!"* She stood from her seat, and for a woman who had to be in her nineties, if not older, she moved quickly to greet each angel and kiss their hands.

"Mama," Tony chided abashedly. "Show them the clothes?"

She brightened, approaching the closet and sliding open the door. She reached inside and pulled out a garment bag. Bringing it to the other side of the room, she hung it on a hook and unzipped it.

"Per Gabriel," she said, drawing a suit out of the bag.

Gabriel drew closer. *"Grazie, Beatrice."* He kissed her hand, then reached for the suit to admire it.

"Per Raphael," Beatrice said, pulling another bag out of the closet.

The angel of healing accepted the suit, showing his gratitude in the same way Gabriel had.

"E per Michael." She brought out one more suit.

He was the one who looked the most surprised. *"Grazie, Beatrice,"* he thanked her. Then he walked over to Gabriel and whispered, "You made us suits?"

"Of course," Gabriel said. "We have to dress the part, and Beatrice is the best seamstress."

Michael clenched his teeth. Keeping his voice low, he said, "I don't like wearing suits."

"Well, you don't have a choice." Gabriel slapped him on the back.

Michael raised the garment bag to eye level, grimacing at it.

"I bet you want to be the dishwasher now," Uriel teased.

"Shut it," Michael said, plastering a smile on his face.

"You don't like it?" Tony frowned.

"It's not that, sir. In fact, I am very appreciative, and it is quite beautiful. It's just, in my line of work, I don't typically wear anything so fancy," Michael explained.

Tony shrugged. "I can understand that."

Satisfied, he escorted us back downstairs, this time with Beatrice in tow. We headed back to the kitchen, depositing the suits in the living room on the way.

"*Mama, mangia,*" Tony said, helping her sit down at the table. Then he said, "Enzo, come with us."

A boy about our age, with shoulder-length wavy hair, followed us out the back door. He must have been Tony's grandson.

Stepping outside into a little backyard oasis full of hanging bistro lights and Adirondack chairs, the city was full of sun and humidity, and I felt both the moment my feet touched the ground.

"This way," Tony instructed. "The rest of what I have for you is in the cellar."

He approached two metal doors built into the ground, secured with a combination lock. Tony spun the little dial, inputting the code, and took off the lock once it opened. Setting it on the ground, he opened one door while Enzo opened the other.

"Follow me," Tony said as he descended the cellar stairs.

We did as instructed, though why we'd be going into the cellar I couldn't determine. I assumed Tony was going to gift us some wine. Why, I wasn't sure since the angels didn't drink and we weren't old enough to do so legally, but when he raised his hand and clicked on the light, I realized how wrong my assumption had been.

Instead of a wine cellar, we were standing in the middle of a weapons arsenal.

"What could you possibly need down here?" Sophia asked in bewilderment.

Tony innocently looked at her and shrugged. "You never know."

Shocked, I stared at the angels, wondering what they were thinking.

"We're not here for weapons," Gabriel reassured us.

"We have plenty of those," Michael clarified.

My emotions were riding a roller coaster right now with the way they were handling this.

"We're here for tech," Jophiel said. "Specifically, communication systems."

"We want to be able to speak with one another, regardless of whether we're inside or out," Zadkiel added.

"I see," I said, the words slowly escaping from my mouth.

"Enzo, explain the technology," Tony told his grandson.

The boy enlightened Jophiel and Zadkiel on how to operate it.

"I also have a van you can use," Tony said. "It's untraceable, just in case."

"And where did you get that?" Dane asked.

Tony shrugged again. "I know a guy."

Dane turned to me. "Are you hearing what I'm hearing? They're getting help from the mob!"

"Who said anything about the mob?" Michael asked.

Dane sputtered. "Seriously..." He stopped and flat-out asked Tony, "Are you in the mob?"

"Who's asking?" he responded.

Dane slapped his hand against his forehead.

"Dane, relax," Gabriel said. "We know what we're doing."

"Do you?" he countered. "You're not above the law."

"No one said we were," Gabriel replied.

"Well you're acting like it. I mean, you're anticipating a confrontation, but what about the aftermath?" Dane asked. "You think you'll be able to waltz out of there after likely destroying the place and combatting supernatural beings in front of a bunch of humans?"

"Dane," Uriel chided. "Not in front of *him*." Uriel held up a hand and pointed at Tony.

"I know more than you think, buddy," Tony said. "So don't worry about me."

Michael interceded, trying to reason with Dane. "We've made scenes in public before, and while I'm not condoning them, there are ways to get out of them."

"Like relying on human ignorance, right?" Sophia added.

The angels all stopped.

"What's going on with you three? You're acting strange," Gabriel said.

Sophia, Dane, and I exchanged glances.

"It's just... We're worried about you all," I confessed. "You're heading into the unknown, and we can't do anything to help you."

Gabriel came closer and brought a hand to my shoulder. "We'll be fine." He glanced at Dane and Sophia. "I promise." Then he brought his attention back to Tony.

About an hour later, we entered the kitchen again from outside, bidding Tony's family goodbye. We passed through the living room to retrieve the suits and walked out the front door.

"Good luck," Tony shouted as we loaded up the car. "And call me if you need anything."

Waving farewell, I couldn't help but hope that everything went according to plan at the gala.

31 JORDAN

New York City, Present Day

When we had arrived at Gabriel's apartment last night, Sophia, Dane, and I had settled in, then decided to start binge-watching a show with several seasons since we had needed something to carry us through tomorrow.

Well, tomorrow had arrived, and we had completed the entire series, but it had only gotten us to 7:30 PM.

"What now? The angels haven't even left yet, and we finished it," Dane complained.

"We order Chinese food," I stated.

Sophia grabbed the remote from Dane. "And we start a new show."

They argued about what to watch next while I placed the takeout order. Settling on the couch again, I asked, "What did you decide?"

Before they could tell me, Gabriel walked in the room. "Okay. We're leaving."

The three of us turned our attention to the angels.

"Good luck," I said. "And be careful."

"We will," Gabriel assured me.

Grinning, Dane said, "Nonna Bea did good!"

“Right?” Gabriel agreed, flaunting his charcoal suit.

“It’s quite exquisite,” Raphael added, admiring his brown one.

Michael sighed, the deep blue of his suit accentuating his eyes. “I have to admit,” he confessed, “it’s pretty comfy.”

“You all look so dashing,” Sophia said. “All eyes will be on you three.”

Raphael grew bashful, looking down at his feet. “I’m not so sure about that, but thank you for your kindness.”

“You two look dashing, as well,” Dane teased.

Chamuel smiled at his joke. He looked natural in his starched white shirt and black waiter’s vest. Uriel, on the other hand, glared. Even though he was a dishwasher, he was forced to wear a similar outfit to Chamuel’s.

“Where are Zadkiel and Jophiel?” Sophia asked.

“They already left with the van to monitor the perimeter at the Met,” Michael replied.

“If anything happens,” Gabriel said, drawing my attention back to the matter at hand, “call or text the number in this phone.” He placed it in my hand.

“You got a burner phone?” I laughed.

He grinned slyly. “It’s all part of the operation.”

“Of course,” I said. “Now get out of here before you’re late.”

The five of them sauntered out the door, and silence filled the apartment.

“It’s weird,” I said.

“What is?” Sophia asked.

“Ever since they’ve come into my life, I don’t think there’s been a day that I haven’t been with the angels.”

Sophia gave me hug. “They’ll be okay.”

I nodded.

"Let's start the show," Dane suggested. "It'll take your mind off it."

"Yeah, maybe," I said.

As soon as he pressed "play," there was a knock at the door.

"I guess the Chinese is here." I stood up to answer.

"Wait!" Dane paused the show and jumped over the couch. "What are you thinking? You can't just answer the door. We have to make sure it isn't someone—or something—dangerous."

He had a point. I glanced around the apartment and spied a kitchen knife sitting in the butcher block on the counter. I grabbed it and approached the door.

Quietly peering through the peephole, I was surprised to see who was on the other side: Sophia's roommate, Dafne.

I unlocked the door and opened it. "What are you doing here?"

Dafne stepped back in shock at the sight of the huge knife.

"Oh, sorry." I slipped it behind my back. "Come in."

She stepped inside, and I shut the door.

While I returned the knife to the butcher block, I heard Dane ask Sophia, "Did you invite her?"

"No," Sophia said. "Dafne, how did you find us?"

Dafne set down the garment bag she was holding. "My grandfather told me where you would be."

Rejoining the group, I asked, "Grandfather? Who's your grandfather?"

Sophia was the first to put two and two together. "Tony's your grandfather!"

Dafne nodded. "Yes. There is a lot to explain about my family, but we have no time. Just know we are your allies, not your enemies." She paused. "Where are the angels?"

"How do you know they're angels?" Dane asked.

"Because my family has been associated with angels for centuries."

A bell rang in my head as I remembered Zadkiel's story. "The Ishim?"

Dafne raised her eyebrows, surprise written across her face. "Yes. Not many know about them, though, so I'm curious how you do, but that'll have to wait, too. Where are the angels?"

"They left for the gala," Sophia said.

"Already? I was hoping I would catch them."

"Why?" I asked Dafne.

"Because my grandfather got word that there was going to be a Nephilim attack at the gala tonight. My parents are trying to stop it," she explained. "And when I heard your angelic friends were involved, I figured I should come warn them as an extra precaution. My grandfather told me where Gabriel lived, but I guess I'm too late."

Panic flooded me. We had to tell the angels, but I couldn't think straight.

"Jordan, didn't Gabriel leave you a burner phone?" Dane asked.

Of course! I ran over to the couch, searching the coffee table for the phone. When I found it, I typed out a quick text: *SOS. Nephilim are attacking the gala. Be on your guard.*

I hit "send," my anxiety decreasing.

Then a sudden vibration could be heard from the dining room table.

Oh no...

Rushing over, I saw the other burner phone, the one Gabriel should have taken with him, sitting on the table.

I picked it up. "Guys, we have a problem."

Sophia turned to Dafne. "I hope you had a backup plan."

Dafne grinned, exuding confidence. "Of course, I did." She walked over to the garment bag. "Why do you think I brought these?" She unzipped the bag to reveal two suits and two dresses.

"You want us to go to the gala?" Sophia asked. "Are you insane? It's not safe."

"Is there really any other choice?" I countered. "The angels are in danger. We have to help them."

Sophia and Dane looked at each other, gearing up for the inevitable. "Fine," they said in unison.

"How do we get inside, though?" Sophia added. "I gave my tickets to the angels."

"That's where the artist comes in," Dafne said, handing a laptop to Dane. "Do you know Photoshop?"

"Yeah."

Dafne pulled out her phone from her pocket and tapped on the screen. Then she showed it to us. It was a picture of a gala ticket.

"Can you replicate this?" she asked Dane.

He nodded. "Sure."

"Then get to work." She grabbed the dresses from the garment bag and looped her arm through Sophia's.

"Wait, you want me to forge them?" Dane asked.

"Yes, I do," Dafne responded. "Now let's get ready."

The girls disappeared down the hall.

Dane was clearly stunned, but he opened the laptop. "How do we print them?"

I shrugged. "I don't know. Ask Miss Mastermind."

The doorbell rang again, this time surely the Chinese food. Instead of worrying about arming myself, I approached the door and opened it. The delivery guy handed me the food and I paid him, then slammed the door shut and brought the takeout bag inside.

Depositing it on the kitchen counter, I yelled, "Food's here." Though I highly doubted any of us would eat it.

I approached the garment bag and pulled out one of the suits. "I'm going to change."

Dane was too focused on recreating the tickets to respond.

I headed to the master suite since the girls had claimed the other bathroom, and I shut the door. I pulled off my T-shirt and was reaching for the dress shirt when I heard a quick knock at the door. Before I could say anything, Dafne walked in.

"I just realized I forgot to bring you a tie," she announced, catching a glimpse of me half-dressed. She stared at me wide-eyed and openmouthed for a moment, then regained her composure. She cleared her throat. "Do you mind if I grab one of Gabriel's? I want to make sure it matches."

"Sure." I pointed behind me. "They're in the closet."

She brushed past me, and I slipped on the dress shirt. Soon she returned with a tie she thought was acceptable, placing it next to the jacket. She fingered the fabric of the lapel fondly. There was such awe, desire, and thrill in her eyes.

"Did you make the suit?" I asked, remembering her hidden talent.

She nodded.

"Why didn't you go to school for it?"

Surprised, she concentrated her attention on me. "Fashion design?" She chuckled sardonically. "My parents would never let me. They want me to be a part of the family business. They want me to do something practical."

"But you love fashion design."

She turned back to the suit. "Yes, I love it. I wish I could be a designer."

"You still could."

Our eyes connected. "How?"

"Transfer. Or wait for grad school. It's not impossible."

"Maybe for you. My parents would never let me leave Harvard."

"But if you had another school in mind, a plan to convince them, then they might let you do it."

She grew defensive. "Don't you think I've tried? Besides, why do you care so much?"

I frowned. "I'm sorry. I didn't mean to upset you. I just think you should do what you love, no matter what anyone else thinks. Even your parents."

"Easy for you to say…" she started and then stopped.

"Because I have no parents?" I finished.

She cringed. "I'm sorry. It came out before I could stop myself."

"It's all right. I'm used to it."

We stood in silence.

Then she whispered, "Parsons. That's the school I would go to."

I nodded in recognition. "I've heard of it."

The two of us fell silent again.

"We should get going, so…" she trailed off and turned to leave, running right into Dane.

"Tickets are done," he said, placing his suit on the bed. "Not sure how you plan to print them."

"E-mail them to me," she responded, retreating down the hall.

Dane elbowed me in the side and smirked. "Since when did you become Casanova?"

"What do you mean?" I asked.

"I mean, she's into you," he said, walking into the closet.

"Who?" I asked, alarmed. "Dafne?"

"Yes, Dafne." He laughed. "Did you not realize she was just ogling you?"

My head snapped back. "I wouldn't call it ogling."

"Of course, you wouldn't." He shook his head. "Now finish getting dressed."

We changed into our suits, and I couldn't help but admire Dafne's handiwork. She really knew what she was doing, even though what she had made was wildly out of my comfort zone. It was a black suit, but it had zigzag accents of metallic-gold thread woven through the jacket. Dane's was similar in that it was a black suit, but his jacket had electric-blue accents. I suspected our jackets would complement their dresses.

I sat down on the chaise in the closet to put on my shoes while Dane meticulously gelled and combed his hair. Running a hand through my own hair, I asked, "What should I do with this?"

He glanced at me in the mirror. "You want to tame your mane?"

I shrugged. "It seems like the thing to do."

"It's better than letting it go wild and free."

"Hey, don't hate on my waves," I said. "They're hard to manage. You wouldn't know with your straight hair."

He chucked a bottle at me. "Put some of this in it. I'm going to e-mail Dafne the tickets and find my tie."

I squirted some of the gel in my hand and ran it through my hair, quickly realizing my mistake. I raced out of the bedroom and into the kitchen. "Uh, Dane? I think I used too much," I said.

He turned and shook his head, shutting the laptop and approaching me. He pulled a comb from his pocket. "You have to style it in. It's mousse, not gel."

"Do you always keep that in your pocket?"

"What?" he asked, exasperated. "A comb? Of course, I do. Now stand still."

I did as I was told, letting him fix my hair.

"There," he said, standing back and admiring his work. He washed his hands at the sink. "And *you* can help me with this." He shoved the tie at me.

Looping it around his neck, I started making a knot.

"You two clean up nice," Sophia said.

Both our heads whipped to the left. The girls stood in the kitchen decked out in gowns, jewels, and makeup. Much like I had predicted, their gowns matched our suits—Dafne's a metallic gold and Sophia's an electric blue. They looked so fantastic, Dane and I were essentially speechless.

"Wow," Dane whispered, eyes glued to Sophia.

"Wow," I agreed, consumed by the sight of Dafne. I pulled on the tie, unintentionally yanking it so tight I nearly choked Dane.

"Hey! My neck is still attached to my head, you know!" he exclaimed.

"Sorry," I said, forcing my focus back to the tie and finishing it off.

Dane stepped over to the girls, complimenting them, while I hung back.

What was wrong with me? Seeing Dafne in her dress and talking to her before made me feel unsettled. I couldn't have feelings for her. I *didn't* have feelings for her. Dane's comments were just getting in my head. I could have a friend who was a girl. I mean, Sophia was one.

But why did this feel so different?

I shook my head. I was just missing Naomi. That's what it was.

Joining the others, I asked, "Ready to go?"

"You bet we are," Dafne said. "Let's go warn some angels."

32 JORDAN

New York City, Present Day

Before we arrived at the Met, Dafne made a detour to Times Square. She hopped out of the Uber, grabbed my hand, and pulled me after her.

We wove through the crowds of people, heading to the TKTS ticket booth. Rather than wait in line, she went right to the front and cut the next person.

"Hey!" a red-haired woman shrieked.

I cringed. "Sorry!" Then turned to Dafne. "What are you doing?"

She ignored me and focused on the girl behind the counter. "Carmen, did you get the file?"

The girl smirked and slid four tickets under the glass. "Hot off the presses, just like you asked."

Dafne reached out to grab them, and Carmen drew them back. "You owe me."

"I know," Dafne assured her. "Whatever you need, it's done."

Carmen pushed them forward again and let Dafne take them this time.

With our fake tickets secured, we rushed back to the Uber and climbed into the back seat.

When our driver pulled up in front of the Met, I wasn't sure what to expect. Certainly not all the flashing cameras. Yet, that was the scene we were thrown into as soon as the car door opened.

Sophia and Dane were the first out, walking arm-in-arm down the line of journalists like some celebrity couple. They were probably too focused on getting inside to realize where they even were.

I scooted out of the car and turned back, offering my hand to Dafne. She stared at the hubbub beyond me and hesitated.

"Hey," I whispered.

She met my eyes.

"You ready to strut this catwalk?" I asked.

Beaming, she placed her hand in mine and exited the car.

The four of us received more attention than I thought we would, someone even stopping to ask who I wore.

"Delucci," I told them. "It's a new designer."

Dafne pinched my arm as we walked off. "Why did you say that?"

"Because it's the truth. Have you ever thought about that? Your label name? It could just be Delucci, or Dafne Delucci, or DD."

She full-out smacked me.

"Ow!"

"No one calls me that," she snapped.

"What? DD?"

"Yes. Only my great-grandma can call me that."

"All right, all right," I said. "Well, either way, you have a cool name so anything would work."

We stopped at the end of the carpet and reconvened with Sophia and Dane. Dafne pulled out the fake tickets from her purse and showed them to the guard at the entrance. He checked them briefly, then waved us through.

As we entered the museum, Dafne leaned into our group and said, "We need to find the angels before the exhibit opens."

"I suggest we break off in pairs. That way we cover more ground," Sophia said.

We agreed and stepped inside, right into a surreal experience. Everything was lavishly decorated, and there were waiters milling about in fine black vests and starched white shirts, carrying trays of hors d'oeuvres and drinks.

Dafne snagged a glass of prosecco.

"Why are you drinking?" I asked.

"Because I'm nervous."

"We're underage," I reminded her.

"You're talking to the daughter of a vintner. You're crazy, if you think I haven't drunk wine."

"That's your family's wine?" I asked.

"Yeah. You haven't heard of Delucci wine?"

I shook my head.

She pulled me over to the bar. "Excuse me, what wine are you serving? Can I see the bottle? It's delicious."

The bartender reached down and fulfilled Dafne's request. Sure enough, *Delucci* was written over the label.

"Wow, I had no idea," I said.

She shrugged, and we returned to our search. Glancing around the huge, crowded interior of the room, it was impossible to spot the angels anywhere. Dafne and I did a few turns about the room with no luck.

"Maybe we should try the kitchen," I suggested.

"We just came from there," Sophia said, rejoining us with Dane. "Chamuel and Uriel weren't anywhere. They must actually be working."

I gazed around the room again and zeroed in on the large staircase. "We could always try upstairs."

"It's worth a shot," Dane agreed.

We approached the steps and mounted them, flashing our tickets to the guard at the top. Dafne and I passed through but stopped when Dane and Sophia didn't follow.

"Soph, what's wrong?" Dane asked her.

Sophia remained frozen at the top of steps, staring down at a tall, slender blond woman who had just arrived. The attention of the whole room had turned to her.

Dafne grabbed my arm. "We need to leave."

"Why?" I asked.

"Because we're too late." She looked down fearfully at a dark-haired woman standing next to the blond one. "My grandfather warned me she was the instigator of the attack."

Before I could respond, Dane came over to us and said, "Sophia wants to go back downstairs. She said for you two to search up here without us."

"What? Why?"

"I don't know, probably to make sure we find the angels," Dane retorted.

He hadn't snapped at me like that since we had lived at the orphanage.

"Dane, I think we should *all* leave," Dafne said.

"No," I told her. "We need to see this through. The angels are still in danger." I handed Dane one of the burner phones and kept the other one. "Just in case." Then I grabbed Dafne's arm and led her away from Dane.

I heard his footsteps as he walked back down the hall to the stairs.

"Who is that woman?" I asked Dafne again.

“She’s from Geneloom,” she whispered.

I froze in shock. Geneloom? Why did they want the sphere?

“Ah,” a man said, striding over to us. “You must be the new donors. My boss told me you were young, but I wasn’t expecting to find such a youthful couple as this.”

Dafne and I exchanged confused looks.

The man introduced himself. “I’m Simon Price, curator of ancient art and antiquities.” He gestured to the woman next to him. “This is my assistant, Bianca. We’d love to give you a tour of the exhibit before everyone comes inside.”

Dafne shook her head. “Unfortunately, we—”

I don’t know what came over me, but I cut her off before she could finish. “We’re actually much older than we look.”

Her eyes snapped to mine, questioning me through her gaze.

The whole point of the angels coming was to see if the sphere was real. They were nowhere to be found, and we were here, suddenly handed this opportunity to do what they had come to accomplish. And while I couldn’t detect celestial energy like they could, I’d still had experience with divine objects before, so we had to take this chance.

Simon and Bianca laughed, taking my words as a joke.

“It’s a pleasure to have you both here,” Simon said. “And we thank you very much for your generous donation. Let’s get started, shall we?”

Dafne and I followed Simon and Bianca into the exhibit. They showed us around the room, explaining the historical context. Walking past display case after display case revealed that the sphere was nowhere in sight. Simon and Bianca took us into the next room, and as soon as we entered, I stopped dead in my tracks.

"Isn't it wonderful?" Simon commented, seeing my reaction.

We drew closer as Simon tried to explain the sphere's origin. I had completely tuned him out, totally enthralled by the object. It seemed to be the correct size—about as big as a grapefruit—since it looked just as large as Satan's sphere, and its deep-blue color was mesmerizing. It certainly was a solid ball of sapphire, but how did I know if it was really the fourteenth sphere?

I knew there was a way to tell. I tried to remember what the angels had said as I walked in a complete circle around the pedestal the sphere sat on. Yet, nothing called to me. I wasn't even sure what I was trying to sense. I had felt it when Zadkiel had pulled *The Book of Prophecies* and Satan's sphere out of the backpack. There had been no mistaking they were special.

This, though, was so spectacular to see on its own, I was trying to decipher whether what I felt was intuition or mere excitement.

Bianca came closer to the pedestal. "It is quite magnificent. It's like it hypnotizes you."

Her choice of words had me frozen in place. All Lilith did was hypnotize people with her serpentine gaze, and she had commanded me to get the sphere for her when she was stuck in my head. But why? I stared at the sphere, and suddenly I could feel its pulsating energy—almost like the thought of her had activated it. In that moment, I knew the sphere was real. And it seemed Lilith's power was connected to it somehow.

Bianca stepped even closer, bumping into the pedestal and toppling the object from its perch. Horror crossed Bianca's face as the sphere fell toward the hard floor.

My reflexes were slow, and I had little time to react, but maybe that was a good thing as my memory finally kicked in and I recalled Chamuel's warning from last fall: *Humans can't touch celestial objects.*

Well, I guess that was goodbye to the fourteenth sphere.

Except, instead of shattering, it landed in the palm of Simon Price's gloved hand.

Where had those come from? He must have slipped them on when he'd been talking and I hadn't been paying attention. But how had he known he needed them?

"That was a close call," Simon said, admiring the sphere. But rather than place it back on the pedestal, he kept it in his hand.

"What are you doing?" Bianca asked. "Put it back."

"I can't," Simon said.

"Why not?"

"Because Satan needs it," Simon answered honestly.

Did he just say…?

That would explain how he had the gloves. Yet, why was he working for the Devil? Satan could hardly tolerate humans unless he could control them.

Then everything clicked into place.

Simon Price *was* under Satan's control.

As Simon and Bianca argued, Dafne drew closer to my side. With the sudden distraction, I reached into my pocket for the burner phone and tapped out a text message.

SOS. We're in the exhibit. The sphere is real. We need help.

I hit "send" and slid the phone back in my pocket.

"Jordan," Dafne said, her voice full of concern.

"Yeah," I replied.

"Why didn't the security alarms go off when the sphere fell from the pedestal?"

We looked at each other.

Then the sound of a gunshot rang out.

33 Dane

New York City, Present Day

I followed Sophia as she raced back downstairs after the blond woman. Catching up to her, I grabbed her by the arm and pulled her into an alcove.

"What's going on?" I asked, searching Sophia's eyes. Something wasn't right. That same haunted look had returned to her face.

"It's her," she whispered.

"Who?"

"The woman from the library." She stared, faraway and dazed. "The woman who kidnapped me."

Her words halted everything. The whole room seemed to freeze. "Kidnapped you?" She wouldn't look at me so I grabbed her face in my hands and made her meet my eyes. "You were kidnapped?"

She nodded slowly. "I was only five years old, and the memory plagues me every night when I close my eyes. I was reported missing, even though my mom let her take me. I don't know who cared enough to find me, but someone did." She reached for her necklace and rubbed it.

My hands moved away from her face and cupped the backs of her arms instead. "We should leave. You're not safe here."

She shook her head and tore out of my grasp. "No, I want to see her. I want to confront her." She pushed away from me and faded into the crowd.

"Sophia!"

I fought through the mass of people, desperately trying to get a glimpse of her wavy hair or blue dress. It was as if she had disappeared entirely, seamlessly blending in. By my right arm, there was a group of people who were already tipsy. One bumped into me forcefully, knocking me back into the man behind me.

"Sorry," I apologized, only to see it wasn't a man I had bumped into but an angel.

Thank god.

"What are you doing here?" Raphael asked, suddenly flanked by Michael and Gabriel.

I ignored his question. "I've lost Sophia, and I think she's in danger."

"Let's get to the kitchen," Michael said. "We need to regroup."

They easily parted the crowd with their powerful presence. As we walked through the swinging doors, someone shouted, "If you have more dishes for me, I'll squirt you in the face."

"Uriel, calm down. It's us," Gabriel said.

He turned around. "Thank the Heavens. Can we leave yet?"

Gabriel shook his head. "No. The kids are here. We have to help them."

"Great," he said, casting the sponge into the sink. "Where's the battle?"

"There's none yet. And hopefully, there won't be," Raphael said.

The doors opened again, and Chamuel came in with an empty tray. Before he could ask what was going on, Michael raised a finger to his ear and spoke in the comms unit. "Jophiel, Zadkiel, get to the building. The kids are here, and I'm getting a bad feeling."

"Where have you all been?" I demanded.

"They're actually making Chamuel and me work," Uriel explained. "They even sent me to take out the trash."

"And we've been trying to cover the room to see who's actually here, checking for the Fallen and hellhounds. There are a lot more people here than we expected," Raphael added.

"Well, you left behind your burner phone and we needed to warn you, so we came in-person," I said.

Michael froze. "Why did you need to warn us?"

"There's going to be a Nephilim attack here tonight. Dafne came to tell you at the apartment, but you were already gone. It turns out she's Tony's granddaughter."

There was a persistent buzzing in my pocket. Reaching inside my jacket, I pulled out the burner phone and read the message aloud.

"It's from Jordan," I told the others. "It says, '*SOS. We're in the exhibit. The sphere is real. We need help.*'"

Then, the sound of a gunshot rang out from upstairs.

Outside the kitchen, people started screaming and running.

"Chamuel, get him out of here!" Michael ordered as he and the others ran out the door.

"Come on," Chamuel urged. "We can go out the back."

"No. Not until I find Sophia," I protested. I turned to follow the angels, but my path was blocked when a dark-haired woman stumbled through the doors, almost falling to the floor.

Chamuel grabbed me and hid us behind the prep counter.

"You ridiculous trollop!" a female voice yelled. "You're jeopardizing our company by bringing him here!"

I peeked around the corner. It was the blond woman Sophia had recognized, standing before the dark-haired one. She must've shoved her through the doors.

"Don't talk to me like that!" the other woman lashed back, standing taller. "At least, I'm *doing* something. Mobilizing the Nephilim and bringing them here to retrieve the sphere will finally give us leverage."

"Says who? You? Or Lucifer?" the blond woman challenged.

Chamuel pulled me back, concern written on his face.

"Me!" the dark-haired woman shouted.

"Jazema, when will you realize he's using you?"

"Stay out of it, Penelope! I can handle myself."

"Fine, do as you like. But your place at Geneloom will be compromised."

"Are you threatening me?"

I tried peeking again, but Chamuel restrained me. I elbowed him to stop, but all he did was push me behind him, taking a look for himself. He quickly whipped back and reached for a knife from the counter.

One of the women chuckled. "Looks like we have a stowaway."

Chamuel flung the knife with a marksman's precision, and it would have hit its target had the woman not ducked freakishly fast.

"Stay here," Chamuel whispered, running the length of the prep counter and picking up cutlery as he went.

"So you want to have a knife fight?" the woman named Jazema said. She twirled a blade between her fingers. "I'm game."

I hunched in place as I heard the whooshing of knives being thrown through the air. Each must have scored a hit on the other as Chamuel let out a yelp and Jazema hissed in pain. Peeking out from my hiding place, I saw that her sleeve had ripped where the blade had struck her.

Suddenly, I was pulled up by the collar of my jacket. The blond woman, Penelope, leered down at me over the counter. "Why, hello, boy."

I swung a punch and nailed her in the nose. She screamed, letting me go. Dashing for the door, I stepped out of the kitchen, back into the deserted museum, only to skid to a halt in front of a girl with raven hair and a gun.

I raised my hands in the air, but she just smiled viciously. Her finger slowly pulled back on the trigger. But before a shot could ring out, a shadow attacked, tackling the girl.

It was Sophia. She wrestled the other girl on the ground, smacking her hand against the floor and forcing her to drop the gun. Then Sophia punched the girl in the face, dazing her.

"Help me tie her up!" she yelled to me.

I picked up the unconscious girl and dragged her over to the bar where Sophia ripped the hem of her dress to use to bind and gag the girl.

"Where did you learn all that?" I asked.

She shrugged. "The Sacrarium taught me self-defense, but I never felt confident enough to use it until now. It was like instinct suddenly kicked in."

"Where did you run off to before?"

She briefly stared at the girl as if she recognized her before walking over to the gun and picking it up. "I was looking for the blond woman. Then the gun went off and I got stuck in the stampede."

"We have to get out of here," I said.

She stared at the gun.

"Soph, what are you doing?"

She met my eyes. "Ending her." Sophia rushed to the kitchen door.

"No!" I shouted, following.

We were already inside when I finally caught her in my arms. She squirmed and fought. "Dane, let me go!"

A loud crash drew my attention away as Chamuel was flung across the kitchen and careened into the prep counter, sending it sailing back against the stove. The angel had been beaten, his eye swollen and his lip bleeding. He struggled to stand when Penelope came over and grabbed him by the hair.

Sophia took advantage of the distraction, aiming the gun at the blonde. I swung her around, taking away her shot. She yelled at me and squirmed again.

Then I heard the most earsplitting crack as Jazema and Penelope double-teamed Chamuel and struck him in the leg with a meat tenderizer, breaking the bone cleanly in half. He yelled out in agony.

Just when I thought it couldn't get worse, the back door burst open and a clear ball of liquid went sailing through the air. On impact, the ball exploded, sending water everywhere.

If anything, the intrusion stunned Penelope and Jazema, temporarily distracting them.

I pushed Sophia through the swinging door, knowing the momentum would send her staggering back into the museum. I figured I would beg forgiveness later because Chamuel desperately needed help. I rushed over to him to pull him out of harm's way just as two more pairs of arms appeared.

Peering past the hair that had fallen into my eyes, I saw Jophiel and Zadkiel had arrived to rescue us.

"It won't work!" Chamuel yelled.

"We're getting you out of here, even if we have to carry you," Zadkiel demanded.

"Not that!" He winced in pain. "The grenade! It won't work. They're not Fallen."

"Then what are they?" Jophiel shouted as the three of us heaved Chamuel to the door.

"Watchers!"

To make his point even more poignant, a raging scream filled the air, and then a butcher knife was sailing our way. Clearly, Jazema and Penelope had lost it. But it didn't matter because the knife didn't meet its mark. A fire extinguisher, thrown so perfectly and precisely, knocked it off course, sending it to the ground.

Sophia stood in the doorway, chest heaving from exertion and anger.

Penelope dropped the butcher block in shock. "It's you. My darling, I thought I'd never see you again."

"You shouldn't be pleased to see me," Sophia spat. "Not when I have every intention of causing you pain." She aimed the gun and fired.

34 JORDAN

New York City, Present Day

Bianca flinched at the sound of the gunshot. She went to let out a scream, but Dafne covered her mouth. "Quiet," she whispered. "They don't know we're here."

I motioned them to the exit on the left, until the security gates started to drop. I rushed over and caught one before it closed. "Dafne!" I winced as the pressure came down on my shoulders. "Get something to hold it open."

Simon was the first to move, grabbing an acrylic display box and shoving it under the gate. I let go and it came down hard on top of the box, leaving a small gap underneath.

Quickly, Dafne grabbed Bianca, who was frozen in place, and joined us in the alcove. We huddled together, listening.

"We're not leaving until we find it!" someone shouted. The voice sounded oddly familiar. I didn't know from where, but one thing was clear: the Nephilim attack had begun and they were here for the sphere.

Without a word, I motioned with my hand for Dafne and Bianca to crawl under the gate since they were small enough to fit through. Bianca began easing herself under when another shot rang out.

I flinched, not expecting others to be outside the gallery, and Bianca screamed as the bullet lodged in her shoulder. Dafne grabbed her legs and pulled her back under.

Instinctively, I reached out, applying pressure to the wound to stop the bleeding.

Bianca started sobbing. "I'm going to die! I'm going to die!"

She was making so much noise, we had little time before we were discovered.

"Shh," Dafne said. "You're not going to die."

I knew Bianca needed a tourniquet for her arm so I glanced at their dresses. Bianca was in a knee-length one; Dafne was in a gown. "Dafne, I'm sorry to ask, but can you rip the hem of your dress?"

I thought destroying her creation would crush her, but she didn't hesitate. She handed me the torn fabric, and I wound it tightly around Bianca's shoulder, tying a good knot. Her teeth started chattering so I whipped off my jacket and draped it over her shoulders.

"Why is she shivering?" Simon asked.

"The shock is setting in," I told him. "Come here. Put your hand on the wound. It still needs pressure."

Simon scooted away, refusing to help and clutching the sphere.

Dafne came closer and did as instructed to help Bianca.

Gunshots rang out again in the hall as if an all-out battle had commenced.

"What's that?" Simon asked, terrified.

Yet, I wasn't frightened. A battle could only mean one thing: reinforcements had arrived. "Simon, is there another way out of the gallery? One not near the main staircase?"

He nodded. "Yes, you need to go to the right instead of the left."

"All right." I met Dafne's eyes. "Here's what you're going to do. You're going to slide under—"

Dafne adamantly shook her head. "No! They're still out there."

"But they're distracted. This is our chance," I said. "Now, you're going to slide under and you're going to take Bianca and get her out of here. She can't wait until this is over. She needs to get to a hospital. You hear me?"

"What? No, I'm not leaving you."

"The angels are here. I'll be fine."

Her face scrunched up, almost like she was going to cry. "Jordan, no," she whispered.

"Dafne, please go," I begged her. "I can't handle this if I'm worrying about you."

"How are you handling this? And who's to say I won't be worrying about you?"

"I know you're scared. I am, too. But everything is going to be fine."

Dafne shook her head.

"DD," I said firmly. "Go."

Her lip trembled as she broke eye contact. Lying back on the floor, she slowly shimmied under the gate. She peeked around the pillar, making sure the hall was clear, and gave a thumbs-up.

Then I guided Bianca under. Dafne threw Bianca's good arm over her shoulder and lifted her. The assistant could barely stand on her feet, but Dafne didn't care. She half limped, half dragged her down the hall and out of sight.

As soon as they disappeared, Simon tried wiggling under the gate, but his shoulders were too large to make it through. Before I could tell him it was pointless, I was grabbed from behind and he was pulled back by his feet.

"Well, well, well. If it isn't the pestering boy and the dark being..."

I knew this "man" was one of the Six, the skull tattoos on his hands a clear indicator of that. And while I didn't know his name, I figured this had to be Lucifer. Who else would Satan send to get the sphere?

Then my forehead scrunched in confusion. Why did Satan need Simon Price if he was going to send Lucifer?

The fallen angel flung me from the collar of my shirt, sending me gliding across the marble floor. "I'm not surprised you're here," Lucifer growled. "You seem to be everywhere. Yet, unlike Satan, I have no qualms about killing you."

"He doesn't, either, believe me," I said, rubbing the hidden scar on my shoulder.

Lucifer struck quickly, grabbing me by the front of the shirt and placing a knife against my throat. "But did he play with his prey? Nothing's more thrilling than the hunt and the chase. I should know. I pursued you throughout the city."

"And you lost me," I reminded him.

He pressed the blade harder against my skin, almost drawing blood.

"You know something," I said, unafraid of his threat. "After being chased so much, the prey becomes wiser."

I kicked out my leg, utilizing the moves Michael had taught me. It tripped up the fallen angel but only briefly. He came back swinging with his fists and the blade.

Duck. Duck. Strike.

I remembered the mantra Michael had said during training.

Duck. Duck. Feint.

I followed it faithfully, anticipating Lucifer's moves.

Duck. Duck. Hit.

I nailed him in the back with my fist in the most vulnerable spot for angels, right between the wings. He fell to his knees, stunned. This was the one series of moves I had mastered because it reminded me of Duck, Duck, Goose. However, I had yet to learn how to handle a double-team, so when another person came up behind me, they lifted their gun into my periphery and knocked me out cold.

35

GABRIEL

New York City, Present Day

My heart was in my throat when I heard the gunshot ring out. I was out of the kitchen and racing up the stairs before Michael could command Chamuel to get Dane out of there. All I could think about was Jordan.

I needed to find him. I needed to protect him.

And I would pulverize whoever stood in my way.

Flashbacks of the war came to mind as Michael joined me on the main stairs, both of us wounding assailants as they launched themselves down the steps. This time with bare hands instead of weapons. This time not caring who we harmed, for our brothers and sisters were no longer the enemy.

Each opponent had a gun, which meant they were Nephilim. The Fallen did not fight with firearms. They were too much like us, too old-school, to have any desire to wield modern technology during combat.

Uriel and Raphael followed us from behind, the four of us fighting together seamlessly as a group, knowing one another's moves and anticipating them. We had trained for this. Not only in Heaven but every night since, whether we were together or miles apart.

Quickly, we reached the top of the stairs where a guard lay on the ground bleeding out. "Raphael!" I shouted. But he was already there, kneeling down to help the man.

Sirens blared outside, probably as police and paramedics arrived on the scene.

"Watch out!" Michael yelled, trying to intercept the lone assailant who had arrived in the hall. He was pointing a gun and ready to shoot when an expertly thrown knife landed in his neck. The Nephilim dropped to the floor, leaving all of us stunned.

"Guess we're late to the party," someone said as they advanced up the steps.

The four of us turned slowly at the sound of that voice.

It couldn't be…

Sure enough, there stood Satan, dressed in a black suit with his collar unbuttoned and no tie. Two female fallen angels flanked him as he stood just below the top step.

We all went on the defensive, reaching for hidden weapons—not firearms but knifes.

Satan raised his hands. "I'm not here to antagonize. I'm here to keep the balance."

Michael ignored him and faced Raphael. "Get him out of here," he commanded, indicating the wounded security guard.

The angel of healing lifted the man into his arms. "I won't be able to come back. Once I'm out, they won't let me back in."

"It's all right," I assured him. "We can handle this."

Raphael raced down the steps, and Uriel and I flanked Michael as the three of us stared down the three fallen angels.

"What do you want?" Michael asked Satan.

"I need the sphere—not to wield it but to destroy it."

"Why?"

"Because destroying it is the only way to keep the balance between us."

"There is no balance between us, not when you take innocent lives."

Satan crossed his arms. "And who exactly do you think I killed?"

"Sister Helen," Michael snapped.

"The nun? I didn't kill her. She was alive when I left the church."

"You mean before you blew it up!"

"I didn't blow anything up!"

The two of them were in each other's faces.

Michael's eyes suddenly were full of shock. "I knew it," he said to himself, backing down.

"What?" Satan barked.

"It's Lucifer. All of this is Lucifer. He isn't acting on your orders, is he? He's doing whatever he wants. The hounds are following his command, and he's going around claiming your moments of redemption and twisting them into sadistic glory. All to prove that he's a worthier devil."

"Watch your words, Brother." Satan sneered at him. "I wouldn't call them moments of redemption. I'm simply following the only code I keep."

"Which is?"

"Kill for purpose, not for pleasure."

The words struck something in Michael. I couldn't say what, but it visibly gave him a moment of pause.

"From what I can see," Satan said, "you need us."

Uriel scoffed. "We can handle it."

Michael raised his hand to fend off Uriel's snide comments, obviously thinking over Satan's proposition. I agreed that we were outnumbered, but allying ourselves, even temporarily, with Satan seemed like a rash decision. Yet, I would follow whatever Michael commanded, for he was the skilled warrior and knew Satan better than anyone.

"Fine," Michael said. "But we're only doing this once." He whipped off his jacket, pulling a hidden blade from the holster on his back.

Satan grinned, similarly sliding off his jacket and pulling a blade from beneath his shirt. "Agreed."

"So what, we're on the same side now?" Uriel asked, outraged.

Michael clenched his jaw. "Temporarily." He eyed me, waiting for a response.

"I don't care who we fight alongside as long as we get inside the exhibit," I said.

Another scream rang out.

"Now!" I bellowed.

The six of us advanced down the deserted hall to the exhibit entrance.

Michael reached inside his pocket and pulled out a handful of holy water grenades. "You take left, I take right."

Satan nodded. "I remember."

Michael threw the grenades on the floor, each exploding on impact. They made more noise and caused more distraction than anything, but that was the intent.

And as if nothing had happened between them, the avenging duo made an appearance again, one not seen since the days in Heaven, as Michael lured out the enemy, baited them, and Satan came in behind, ready to take them out one by one.

Gun against sword may have been shady odds for a human, but for an angel, wielding a blade was second nature. Michael was taking on more wounds than I liked, though, and while gunshots weren't fatal for any of us, they were still draining, especially when you took so many. So, like any brother, I followed him into the fray, Uriel at my side, as well as Satan's female accomplices.

We were certainly a sight to see, fallen and blessed angels fighting together for a mutual cause.

As we gained ground into the exhibit, it was hard to tell who was inside. Obviously, there were Nephilim, but there were also other people dressed in tactical gear, and they all were fighting one another.

"Find Jordan," Michael told me. "We'll deal with these guys."

Then he and Uriel launched into combat, along with Satan and his fallen angels, fighting off Nephilim and mysterious assailants alike—stunning them, wounding them, and even tying some of them up.

I crept along the edge of the battle, weaving among the alcoves until I came upon an incredible sight—Jordan laying out two of the mysterious men. Behind him, Lucifer was on the ground, defeated, as a man in a hooded cowl stood over him. Except instead of aiming his shot at Lucifer, he turned the gun and began to focus it on Jordan.

Lucifer unsteadily got to his feet and slinked away while I grabbed the fire extinguisher from the wall next to me and rushed at the man with the gun.

36

JORDAN

New York City, Present Day

The first thing I thought when I came to was, why haven't the angels arrived? The next was that the back of my head was bleeding. The last was that I had been left on the floor, completely forgotten. Odd, given that Lucifer had seemed ready to kill me.

Peering around, I wasn't entirely sure what was happening. The Nephilim were in an all-out brawl with some other group of people decked out in tactical gear, and Lucifer was fighting some man in a hooded cowl. I spotted dried blood on the handle of the man's gun. He must have been the one who had knocked me on the head. At this point, I was a mere victim in the wrong place at the wrong time, which was an advantage at the moment since it meant no one was paying attention to me.

"Help," someone whispered.

Glancing behind me into the alcove, I saw Simon Price slumped against the wall. I rushed over to him and followed the trail of blood up to his chest. He'd been shot. I placed my hands over the wound to stop the bleeding, but he pushed me aside and started taking off his jacket.

"I tried to get away…after they knocked you out…the two of them busy fighting each other…but the hooded man shot me." He sucked in a breath. "Here, take it," he rasped, handing me his jacket.

Puzzled, I asked, "Why?"

"The sphere…is in…the pocket. It's better…off with you…than them."

I hesitated. Should we really be stealing the fourteenth sphere? I guessed it was better than the alternative: letting either Lucifer or the hooded man have Lilith's power. So I took the jacket and put it on. As soon as I did, my necklace vibrated, the protective ward trying to fend off the strong energy of the sphere.

I glanced back at where Simon had been slumped, but he was already gone, his lifeless eyes staring blankly at me. I closed his eyes so he could rest peacefully. Although, I knew there was the possibility he could turn into a demon so I backed away and hid in another alcove. Settling in the corner, I inspected the jacket and discovered the garment had been specially made for the sphere, the inside pocket extra-large to fit the celestial object. Simon must have really wanted to impress Satan if he had thought through so many minute details.

"Well, well, well… What do we have here?" One of the guys in tactical gear noticed me and laughed. "Look who's shaking in his boots," he said to another.

His comrade chuckled. "Stupid kid doesn't stand a chance. Lucifer doesn't, either. Not against Lilith's army."

Lilith's army? She had an army? No wonder they were here. They wanted to recover the sphere that gave her power.

I cried out as a burning pain seared my neck. I glanced down to find my necklace taut and pulling toward the inside pocket of Simon's jacket like a magnet. What was going on? It was almost as if the sphere was trying to yank off my necklace.

Just as Lilith had done…

A freezing pain emanated from my side right where the sphere rested. Just like the cold and frozen feelings from my nightmare.

Crap! Was Lilith locked inside the sphere?

Let me out!

The words were shrieked so loudly that I wasn't the only one who heard them. One of the guys in tactical gear flinched in surprise. "Holy shit! What was that? I thought he wasn't Nephilim. They're usually the ones who can do weird tricks like that."

"How do you know? Sometimes it's not apparent," the other one argued.

My eyes widened, and I stopped. Nephilim? Was I a Nephilim? It couldn't be true... My mind panicked. Is that why I had this gift? Was I half-human, half-angel? I didn't have time to think it over as both guys lunged for me.

Jumping up, I evaded them and then turned around to dodge their punches. I roundhouse kicked one in the stomach, knocking him to the ground. The other came up from behind, grabbing me under the arms, but I reached back and yanked him over my shoulders, much like I had seen the angels do. With my opponents temporarily stunned, I breathed a sigh of relief.

Then a sharp slamming noise sounded. Turning to face it, I saw Gabriel standing above the hooded man with a fire extinguisher. He clearly had just used it to bash the man in the head, knocking him out cold.

He dropped the makeshift weapon and met my eyes. "Are you okay?"

I nodded. "I think so."

"Let's go," Gabriel said.

"Wait! I have the sphere. What do we do with it?" I asked.

"Keep it," he replied quickly. "We can't let it fall into the wrong hands."

I agreed, and while I didn't condone stealing, this object could not be left behind. Not with the damage it had caused.

"Good," Michael said, advancing toward us. "You found him."

I was shocked to see that Satan and two female fallen angels followed after him. I turned to Gabriel, about to ask what was going on, but he said, "I'll explain later," before I could get the words out.

"Where did Lucifer go?" Satan asked.

Gabriel gestured to the beaten-down security gate. "He slipped through there with the sphere."

Oh my gosh... Did Gabriel just lie? He never *lied.*

"Damn it!" Satan yelled. "I'm going after him. You two get out of here," he said to the women before departing the same way Lucifer had.

"I suggest you all leave," one of the women said. "We're going to summon a portal."

Gabriel took me by the arm and guided me out of the gallery, Michael and Uriel in tow. We went out to the hall, clamoring into the elevator instead of attempting the stairs, just as the claps of fallen thunder sounded, indicating they had summoned a portal to Hell.

"What's our escape route?" Uriel asked.

"Roof," Michael said.

Uriel looked at him. "You want us to fly out?"

Michael nodded slowly.

I smacked my hand against the buttons, pressing the top-most one, and the elevator lurched into motion. When the doors opened, we walked out into the fresh air. I hadn't taken two steps before a sharp pain in my side had me collapsing to the ground.

"Jordan!" Gabriel shouted.

That was the last thing I heard before I felt him lift me into his arms.

37

Dane

New York City, Present Day

For someone who had never held a gun in her entire life, Sophia had surprisingly good aim. The bullets she unleashed expertly hit both Penelope and Jazema, knocking the women to the floor.

Yet, Sophia didn't stop. She kept pulling the trigger, even after all the bullets had been fired, a tear running down her check.

I left Chamuel in the capable hands of the angels, and came to her side, grabbing her hand and prying the gun out. I slipped it inside my jacket.

"She's a monster! A monster!" Sophia sobbed.

"Shh," I soothed, bringing her head to my shoulder.

"Dane, we need to go," Zadkiel said. "The bullets won't stop them, only stun them. I suggest we leave before they come to."

I nodded, guiding Sophia away. "What?" she asked. "They're not dead?"

"No," Jophiel said solemnly.

Together, the two angels heaved Chamuel up in their arms. He winced as they carried him out the back door. I followed with Sophia.

In the alley, they stopped. "The van is too far. We parked it a couple blocks down thinking it'd be less conspicuous. We'll have to fly," Zadkiel said.

"I'll take him and come back," Jophiel offered, shifting Chamuel and hoisting him over his shoulder. He shot into the air so fast, it was hard to believe he had stood before us a second ago.

"What about the others?" I asked over Sophia's head. She clung to me, not quite present.

Zadkiel sighed. "Who knows? Let's hope they make it out."

"That's it?" I asked. "A hope and a prayer? Shouldn't we go back?"

"The authorities," Zadkiel began.

"I don't give a damn about the authorities!"

"We are not above the law, Dane." The angel reminded me of my words.

Our conversation was interrupted by the kitchen door swinging open. Fearing those women had come back for more, I covered Sophia with my body.

"Oh, thank god!" Dafne said.

I faced her. She seemed unharmed, although tears stained her cheeks.

"Are you all right?" Zadkiel asked.

She nodded quickly. "But Jordan…he made me leave him behind. He was convinced the others had arrived to save him, but I couldn't stay to find out. There was a woman, an assistant curator, she was shot. I helped her out of the exhibit, but then we ran into some other people fleeing and I got separated from the group. I didn't know where to go or how to find them again. This museum is a maze, but I figured you guys would either be in the kitchen or hiding out here." She stopped and sucked in a breath. "Tell me I didn't leave him for dead."

Zadkiel whipped off his sweater and draped it over her shoulders. "He won't perish. I know it."

"Were there two women inside?" I asked her.

"In the kitchen? No. No one was in there," Dafne said.

A swift breeze blew around us as Jophiel landed. "Time to leave," he said. Then he noticed Dafne. "Oh, I suppose we'll make another trip."

"Take Sophia," Zadkiel said. "We can wait."

"No, I'll wait," I clarified. "You take Dafne."

"Dane—"

"There's no time to argue!"

Reluctantly, Jophiel and Zadkiel silently agreed. They lifted the girls in their arms and took off.

I stood back and leaned against the wall, hoping no one would discover me. Then the door swung open, but this time foe, not friend, came out. He was tall, blond, and beaten up. He raised his hand to rub his temple, and I froze when I saw the ring he wore.

A black cat. A big cat. Hissing with its teeth exposed.

I had drawn that, drawn it for a police officer to identify the stranger who had posed as my father back when I was thirteen years old. Back when Jordan had saved me and I had been too resentful to realize it.

I shifted, and he detected my presence.

Squinting, he tried to see among the shadows, but I slunk deeper into them. My heart raced, and every bone in my body told me to run.

"Who lies among the shadows?" he asked. "Show your face."

Fear ran through me. Who was this guy? Why had he wanted to take me when I was a kid?

Desperately wanting answers to my questions, I stepped out from the dark. "Remember me?"

He squinted. "Should I?"

I scoffed. "Yeah, I'm the boy you tried to kidnap. You pretended to be my father."

His jaw dropped in disbelief.

I caught a glimpse of the skull tattoo etched across the back of his hand when he slid it through his hair. Why was it so familiar?

He saw me looking at it. "It's not new. I covered up it with makeup back then. I didn't want you to identify me. How do *you* remember me?"

"Your ring," I said, although I knew the tattoo, too. Just not from him. I racked my brain, trying to remember where I had seen it before.

The back door burst open again, and a figure entered. He threw himself at the guy standing in front of me, grabbing him by the collar and slamming him against the wall of the alley.

"Give me the sphere, Lucifer!"

Lucifer? No way.

"I don't have it!"

He cracked Lucifer's head against the wall. "Lies! More lies! All you do is lie!"

Lucifer sneered. "What makes you think I have it?"

"Gabriel told me you did. He saw you running off with it."

Lucifer laughed. "He lied to you, too. I don't have it." Stopping, he said, "The Sentinel ruined my plans, the bloody bastard! He turned on me!"

The guy threw Lucifer to the ground. "Now you know how it feels."

Before he could pounce on him again, he caught sight of me. His brow furrowed. "Dane?"

I tilted my head as I finally got a good look at him now that he was standing still. "Samuel?" I asked hesitantly as I faced the man who had trained me at the gym, the one who had taught me self-defense. I spied a glance at his hands, seeing the skull tattoo there.

That was how I knew it.

But if Lucifer had a matching one…

I was paralyzed.

"You're Satan, aren't you?"

He sighed. "I can explain—"

I exploded. "Explain what? How you killed her?"

"Who?" he asked.

"Sister Helen! You blew up the church with her in it!"

"Actually," Lucifer said, standing and wiping the blood from his chin, "I take credit for that." He smiled viciously before rocketing into the air.

I felt numb and crushed all at the same time. My friend was the Devil. Lucifer had killed Sister Helen. It was all too much. *Just too much.*

"Dane—"

"Leave me alone!"

"I didn't command Lucifer to do it," Satan explained. "I didn't know the church exploded. I didn't know the nun was dead."

"Her name was Sister Helen!" I screamed, the veins popping out of my neck. "She was the only one who cared!"

"That's not true."

I scoffed.

"It's not," he said adamantly. "Because I was the one who saved you."

Confused, I asked, "From what?"

"The mugging. I found you in the alley bleeding out. I brought you to the hospital. I had no idea you were connected to Sister Helen and the Sacrarium."

My mind was a whirlwind. Satan…saved me?

I glared at him. "Why?"

He shrugged. "I don't agree with senselessly killing others, and that's what they were doing to you. They had already gotten your money. They should have left it at that."

"The Devil doesn't like violence?"

"I never said that. What I don't like is killing people for no reason."

"But why train me?" All of this was too hard to comprehend.

"I don't know. When you showed up at the gym I frequented, I swore I wouldn't interfere, but you had no idea what you were doing and you couldn't pay anybody to teach you, so I did." He paused. "I felt drawn to you."

"But *why*?" I needed a concrete reason because I had always struggled between the light and the dark, and here was the darkest, evilest being to exist, telling me he had morals, telling me we had a connection, telling me he had saved my life. Me, an orphan no one loved or wanted. Me, the boy Lucifer had tried to kidnap for some reason.

Satan opened his mouth to say something, but I stopped him. "Just go."

"Dane—"

"Leave!" I screamed again.

With a solemn expression on his face, he launched into the air.

Seconds later, a swift breeze ruffled my hair. "Ready?" Zadkiel asked.

I nodded. This night was such a shit show, and I was ready for it to be over.

Zadkiel soared into the air, wind whipping at my hair. As I kid, I always had wanted the ability to fly. Now I wasn't so sure. Thankfully, the trip was quick, but by the time we landed, I felt so whiplashed, I never wanted to fly again.

Unsteady on my feet, I grabbed the back of the van for balance and pulled open the door. Inside, Chamuel lay sprawled out, Dafne and Jophiel huddled around him, trying to stabilize his leg.

"Where's Sophia?" I asked.

"In the front. She's completely checked out," Dafne said.

"Come on. Let's move." Zadkiel ushered me inside.

I hopped in the back, and he slammed the doors shut. He strode around to the driver's side and strapped himself in behind the wheel.

"Where are we going?" I asked.

"To the rendezvous point," Zadkiel replied. "In case of emergency, we agreed on a place."

I fell into silence, glancing at Dafne and following her gaze to Chamuel. He was in pain, I could tell, his eyes closed and his breathing heavy.

"Hang in there, Brother. Raphael will be here soon," Jophiel whispered.

The rendezvous point was the Hudson River Waterfront Greenway. When we arrived, it was completely deserted except for a lone figure who was waiting for us—Raphael.

"Thank the Heavens," Zadkiel said, seeing him.

As soon as the car stopped, the back of the van opened and Raphael took charge. "Clear out. I need space to set his leg."

Dafne and I did as we were told. She sat down on the curb while I ran over to the waterfront, wiped the prints off the gun and chucked it into the water. I'd still had it in my jacket, and I didn't want anyone finding it. Returning to Dafne, I sat beside her. Jophiel jumped down from the van but stayed close, and Zadkiel joined him once he turned off the car.

Raphael removed his jacket and rolled up his sleeves. He gently felt Chamuel's leg, and the angel winced.

"Well, it's a clean break," Raphael assessed. "I can set the bone, but regardless, it will take some time to heal, even for you."

"Just fix it," Chamuel pleaded.

"It's going to hurt."

"I know."

Raphael reached out, prepared to rotate it back in place, when a strong gust of wind swept by.

The other angels landed behind the van, everyone finally accounted for. However, it looked like we might need another doctor, as all three angels and Jordan were covered in varying quantities of blood.

38 JORDAN

New York City, Present Day

I awoke to muffled shouts of agony. Opening my eyes, I was wrapped in someone's arms, staring out at a road, with a slight pressure at the back of my head.

I moved, and the arms grew tighter. "Stay still," Dafne whispered in my ear.

Glancing to my right, I saw the van. Raphael was inside doing something to Chamuel.

To my left, Uriel sat on the curb next to us, digging out bullets from his arm.

"Is that really necessary?" I asked.

"Raphael's busy, and they're annoying me," he complained.

Dafne shifted me in her arms, leaning me forward and checking the rag thrown over her shoulder. "I think the bleeding's stopped."

I reached back to feel my head and winced. My fingers came away clean.

"Where are Sophia and Dane?" I asked.

"In the front of the van," Zadkiel said. "Sophia's not doing well."

"What's wrong?" I asked, lurching forward to get up and immediately falling back.

"Nothing physical," Jophiel said. "Purely mental and emotional damage."

"Oh." My head hurt too much to figure out what that meant. I brought my hand down to my side, rubbing at the dull ache. Then I realized the sphere was gone.

Panicking, I tried to move when Uriel said, "Calm down, kid. Gabriel took the sphere off you. Your necklace was trying to fight it, which resulted in abdominal pain and caused you to pass out."

If Dafne was surprised to hear we had the sphere, she didn't say anything. Then another cry of agony came from the grass where Gabriel had Michael laid out. "Hold still," Gabriel demanded.

Michael writhed on the ground. "You're missing it!"

"Fine, pry it out yourself if you're unsatisfied," Gabriel said, handing him the large surgical tweezers.

Michael glowered, obviously not in the mood. "Gabriel, please!"

I didn't blame him. It looked like he had a bullet lodged deep in his back—right between his wings.

Gabriel tried again, this time finally pulling it out.

Michael sighed in relief and rubbed his legs. "I was starting to lose feeling."

"Understandable," Raphael said, stepping down from the van and coming up behind Gabriel. "The bullet was lodged in your spine."

We all fell quiet.

Raphael sighed. "Is everyone stable?"

We all nodded, our gazes darting around the group.

"Thank the Heavens." He sat down hard on the curb, seeming completely drained from the evening.

I think all of us were.

"Raphael?" Dafne asked.

"Hmm?"

"Do you know if Bianca is okay?"

He shook his head. "I'm not sure. I figured I would go down to the hospital in the morning to check on her and the security guard."

Everyone sat in silence for a little longer until we decided it was time to return to the apartment. Dafne and I loaded into the back of the van with Chamuel and Michael, while Gabriel hopped in the driver's seat. The other angels opted to fly back.

As soon as we walked in the door, the exhaustion slammed into me. I had to take a shower before crashing, careful not to make my skull start bleeding again. Everyone seemed to feel that way, the angels washing up before settling in, too.

I crawled into bed, ready to fall into oblivion, when there was a soft knock at the door. "Come in," I said.

Dafne crept over the threshold. "Do you mind if I sleep in here? Me and Sophia were going to share the bed, but it feels weird to invade her space right now. And the couch is taken by a celestial being with a broken leg."

I glanced at the king-size bed I was snuggled in. "I don't see why not. There's plenty of room."

She walked to the side of the bed and crawled in, adjusting the pillows and pulling up the blanket.

"'Night, Jordan," she whispered.

"'Night, Dafne," I said, shutting out the light.

When I woke up the next morning, she was gone. Rubbing my eyes, I slowly got out of bed and entered the kitchen, thinking I'd find her sitting at the counter, but she wasn't there, either.

I turned to the angels sitting at the table. "Where's Dafne?" I asked.

"She went to the hospital with Raphael," Gabriel said. "But she won't be returning. Her parents want her to come home as soon as possible after what happened last night."

I deflated. "Oh." She hadn't said goodbye.

"She left you a note," Michael added. "It's on the fridge."

I strode over to the fridge and saw a pink Post-it note stuck to the door. In pretty, looping handwriting she wrote, *This isn't goodbye, DD.*

Pulling the small paper off the fridge, I smiled.

The snap of a newspaper brought my attention back to the angels. All six of them were staring at me, even Chamuel from his place on the couch.

"What?" I asked.

"You need to make up your mind," Jophiel said.

"About?"

"The girls," Michael clarified.

"I know," I said sheepishly. "I'm trying to decide how I feel. This is all new to me, and I don't know if what I'm feeling is 'I like you, let's be friends' or 'I like you, let's try to date.' You know?"

All I saw were blank stares.

"No," Uriel said, "we don't."

"But," Chamuel added, "we can try to help you navigate it."

"Hey!" Dane whisper-shouted to me from the hall. He motioned me forward with his hand.

I approached Dane, but behind my back I heard Uriel say, "My bet is on Naomi." Then Michael responded, "Not happening. It's Dafne."

When would I ever learn that expressing my feelings about girls and relationships to them was simply a bad idea?

Dane's concern erased any thoughts of Naomi or Dafne, though.

"What's wrong?" I asked.

"She wants to talk to us."

I nodded, and we entered the room.

Sophia sat up in bed, cheeks red and puffy. "I'm sorry about abandoning you last night."

Sitting on the bed next to her, I said, "You don't have to apologize."

"But I do. I don't know what came over me."

"Hey." I grabbed her hand. "Don't blame yourself for what happened."

"Why not? I put everyone in danger."

Dane shook his head and sat down on the other side of the bed. "No you didn't. An attack was going to happen whether we were there or not."

"I guess you're right," Sophia said. "Did anyone even see the sphere?"

"Oh...yeah," I said.

"Well, is it real?" she asked.

Sophia must not have been around when Dane had gotten my text at the gala. I nodded. "Yeah...and I actually, um, I took it."

Dane's eyes widened. "What? Where is it?"

I shrugged. "I think the angels have it."

He jumped from the bed and raced out of the room to confront them. Sophia and I followed.

Before Dane could say anything, though, the apartment door opened and Raphael entered.

"How are they?" I asked, eager for news.

"Both stable and expected to make full recoveries."

"Thank goodness." I sighed in relief.

"Bianca was very appreciative of your help. She told me to thank you. I also brought Dafne back to her parents so she's safe."

I nodded. "Good."

"You have the sphere?" Dane blurted out.

Gabriel sighed. "We do."

Shocked, Dane exclaimed, "I can't believe you stole it!"

"We didn't steal it," Uriel defended. "It is a celestial object, and we are celestial beings. It *belongs* to us."

"Besides," Michael added, "the best-case scenario last night was for us to walk away with it. Satan said he would destroy it, but I couldn't put that much trust in him."

Dane paled at the mention of Satan.

"You okay?" I asked.

"Yeah," he whispered.

He was acting strange, but I wrote it off as exhaustion. "How did all of you wind up fighting alongside Satan anyway?"

Michael shrugged. "We had a common enemy, and we were both outnumbered. In the moment, it was better to band together." He met my eyes. "There's something I've been meaning to tell you—all of you. He didn't kill Sister Helen."

"I know," Dane confirmed. "It was Lucifer."

"How do you know that?" Sophia asked.

Dane sighed and explained the conversation he'd had with Satan, not sparing a single detail.

"Wow, I don't know if I'm more shocked that he saved you," I said, "or that Lucifer was the one who tried to take you when we were kids."

"Yeah, I still can't figure out the why of any of it," Dane admitted.

"It has to do with the prophecy—the one of the three heirs," Sophia said adamantly. "We need to figure out what it means."

As she poured coffee for herself and Dane, I sat down in an armchair.

"Now what about you?" Dane asked Sophia. The two of them settled down in the love seat. "Are you going to tell us what happened? I mean, you shot two people."

Alarm filled my entire body. "What?"

"They were angels so she didn't kill them," Dane amended.

Still, it didn't make me feel better. "Sophia, what were you thinking?"

She was quiet as Chamuel burst out, "Not just angels! Watchers!"

"What do you mean?" Zadkiel asked. "I've been trying to decipher how those women were Watchers since last night. I figured you were hallucinating from pain."

"No! When I was fighting those women, I cut one of their sleeves, and it was plain to see the angelic script tattoo scrolling around her arm. Nephilim don't have those because they weren't created by Father and have never roamed the clouds of Heaven. I'm not crazy when I say they were Watchers! The name around her arm was Semjaza!"

Shock was splashed across each of their faces.

"The leader of the Watchers," Sophia said.

Zadkiel nodded. "Yes, how did you know?"

"I was trained as a Sacrarium Novice, remember? I learned a lot of the legends and basics."

"We never thought the Watchers were female," Gabriel said.

"Because the legends don't portray them that way," Zadkiel added. "They portray them as males who were enamored by human women."

"So is that how the Nephilim are still around?" Uriel asked. "Because they're descended from female Watchers instead of male Watchers?"

"But that's not possible. A celestial body is hardly capable enough of carrying a child," Jophiel stated.

"Which is why Geneloom exists," I said, putting the pieces together. "Dafne told me that those women were from Geneloom."

"Jazema and Penelope were their names," Dane added.

"Seriously?" Michael asked.

Dane nodded.

"Those were the names Allen Clark gave me," Michael said. "They are the ones in charge of Geneloom."

"So female Watchers are trying to create the Nephilim in a laboratory?" Raphael asked.

"Yes, because they cannot physically do it themselves," Michael said. "And I bet the male Watchers were the ones rounded up and imprisoned. The females must have escaped captivity because no one knew they existed."

"But how did no one know?" I asked.

Sophia shook her head. "Because females have been erased from history since the beginning of time. Or, in this case, their tales were spun into those of men."

"But it has to be more than that," I disagreed. "We're talking about God here. He knew what He was creating. He had to know there were female Watchers." I sighed. "Another mystery and secret to solve. How exhilarating." My tone was anything but exhilarated.

"Where did your sense of adventure go?" Raphael asked.

"I still have it," I said. "I would just rather have more answers than new secrets."

"So if Semjaza is going by the name Jazema," Zadkiel mused, "Penelope must be…"

"Penemue," Sophia said.

Zadkiel narrowed his eyes as if sensing there was more to the story. "How do you know that?" he asked.

"Because she's the woman who kidnapped me when I was five years old. She's the one who taught me how to read angelic script and showed me her tattoo to practice."

"You never told us that," I said.

"Because I don't remember a lot of it, and I don't like talking about it. But it's been coming back to me in bits and pieces. Daydreams. Nightmares. And last night, everything clicked into place."

"Everything?" I asked.

"Everything." She nodded. "And I think it's time you know it all..."

39 SOPHIA

New York City, Fourteen Years Ago

It was a bright May day. Mommy's birthday. We walked the length of the zoo holding hands, stopping to watch the animals. The seals were my favorite. How they swam, moved, and wiggled around on their bellies. I got a stuffed one from the gift shop to remember them.

When we had seen all the animals, we walked through the park and got hot dogs, pretzels, and cotton candy. Next stop was the museum. There were so many things everywhere I looked that it felt like a big wonderland. I loved the pictures painted with bright colors. Some even looked like the ones I made for Mommy.

We walked back home later in the afternoon, the sun still bright and cheery. I yawned.

"Maybe you should take a nap before dinner," Mommy said.

"Never!" I giggled, running through the front door of the apartment building and dancing up the steps.

Mommy followed me, holding my stuffed seal. She unlocked our apartment door, and I raced inside to go play with my dolls on the living room floor.

"Sophia, wash up for dinner. Preston and Gigi will be here soon."

Preston and Gigi. Blah!

Mommy's boyfriend and his mother. *Blah!* I didn't like them much. They were boring.

I went to the bathroom to wash my hands and splashed water on my face.

"Silly," Mommy said. "I didn't mean it like that." She grabbed a towel and wiped my face dry, both of us laughing.

Back in the living room, I played with my dolls, even when the doorbell rang and Preston and Gigi arrived. I decided to stay where I was. Dolls were better than grown-ups.

A loud bang came from the kitchen, followed by a thump, and I flinched. Then Gigi started screaming. "What have you done?"

Curious, I stood to see what had happened. But Mommy came in, picked me up, and whisked me out the front door. We left the apartment so fast, Mommy didn't even have her purse. All she had was her phone. I was lucky I already had shoes on because I don't think she would have waited for me to put them on.

She hailed a taxi at the curb and shuffled us inside. "New York Public Library," she told the driver.

My eyes brightened. "We're getting more books?"

Mommy smiled weakly. "Yes, sweetheart, we're getting more books."

I bounded out of the taxi when it had stopped at the curb in front of the lions. Again, I danced up the steps, holding Mom's hand and tugging her along. She took me to the children's section, and I ran to the shelves, pulling books out as I went and making a big pile. Some had pretty covers, others pretty pictures. When I found one with a seal on it, I turned to show Mommy, but she was gone.

"Mommy?" I searched the area but couldn't find her. Dropping the book, I shouted, "Mommy!"

I ran through the building, back to the front entrance, and down the big steps, stumbling as I went. Finally, I saw her in the back of a taxi. "Mommy! Wait! Mommy don't leave me!"

I started running again, but my legs wouldn't carry me fast enough to catch up. The taxi zoomed out of sight. I started to cry. I had nowhere to go, no one to come get me. The giant lions, who had felt like friends, now cast big shadows on the ground. Everyone around me was staring.

"Little girl," a lady said, "are you lost?"

"Sophia!"

I looked around for my mom, but the only woman I saw coming toward me was a blond woman. I had never met her before.

"You can't run away like that." The woman turned to the other lady. "Thank you for helping. She likes coming to see the lions more than the books."

That wasn't true.

"Of course," the nice lady said, walking away.

"Who are you?" I asked the blond woman.

"A friend. Your mom wanted me to come get you. She got called back to work."

"What's your name?"

"Penelope." She offered her hand. "Ready to go?"

40 JORDAN

New York City, Present Day

"That's where my memories start to fade," Sophia said after sharing her story. "She took me somewhere. It seemed like a lab… Now it makes more sense since it was probably an early Geneloom lab. There were other women there—scientists. They never harmed me physically. All they did was draw my blood a few times."

I just stared at her, feeling shocked, intrigued, and a little hurt that she never told me.

"But Penelope tested me mentally," Sophia continued. "Constantly. Teaching me, training me, wanting me to understand my full potential. There were other kids, strange kids, one with wings sprouting from her back. Penelope told me I could help the other kids there, but I had to let go. I still don't understand what she meant by that. I still don't even remember everything. It just comes back in waves. I remember seeing my hands full of feathers and blood at one point, though. I remember Penelope furiously yelling at me, 'Don't think about her,' trying to make me forget my mother."

She swallowed, blinking back tears. "It was easy to do because I will never forgive her for abandoning me. I tried running away once, but it didn't work. I was there for six months. I endured Penelope's verbal abuse for six months, so the woman who had left me was the last thing on my mind. I don't know what happened to my mom, and I'll never search for her. Someone filed a Missing Persons report, though, because the police got involved. They're the ones who saved me—them and the man with the St. Michael medallion."

She rubbed the pendant. "He gave me this necklace and brought me to Sister Helen. After that, I remember having to go to a courtroom a few times, but I didn't talk. The one time I did, I was called a liar so I remained quiet for a while." She looked up from the necklace. "Until we played cards at the orphanage." She paused. "Every day since, I try to shut the trauma away in a place deep in my mind, but sometimes it just comes flooding back. So when I saw Penelope last night at the gala, it triggered something—a need for revenge. I wanted to confront her, and when I saw the gun, I just grabbed it. Dane tried to stop me, but the need to cause her pain was overwhelming, so I fired the moment I had a chance. At first, it felt good. Like I had control. But then I realized I had harmed them, killed them."

"You didn't kill them," Gabriel assured her.

"I know that now, but in the moment I didn't. I panicked and retreated into my head, realizing how much Penelope still controlled me. I had nearly thrown my life away, everything I had worked so hard for, just to hurt her. What's wrong with me that I could have done that?"

"Soph, you can't dwell on the past. You didn't kill her. That's all that matters," Dane said.

"But I wanted to! That's the point! What kind of person would do that?" Sophia screamed hysterically.

"One who has faced a lot of trauma and has bottled it up for years," Chamuel said. "But the important thing is that you realize your mistake. There are ways to deal with the stress, to let out the internal pain. I can help you, if you'd like."

Sophia took a deep breath. "Yeah, that would be good."

"The man who saved you… Do you remember what he looked like?" Michael asked.

"Not really," Sophia said.

"Hmm…I wonder if it was Allen. He wore a St. Michael medallion when I met him. I also wonder if rescuing you was his first encounter with Geneloom. It might have set him on their trail."

"Sophia, I think there's something you should know," I said to her, knowing I sounded ominous.

"What?" she asked hesitantly.

She had a right to know. "We think you're the bloodline," I told her.

The angels whipped their heads to me, accusing me with stares full of *Why did you say that?*

Sophia shook her head. "No, I'm not the bloodline." She paused. "I can't be," she whispered. Then she met my gaze. "Right? I mean, why would I be the bloodline?"

"Geneloom's interest in you, for one," Michael said. "You said yourself they took some of your blood and that Penelope said you could help the others if you unlocked your full potential."

She nodded slightly.

"There's also Sister Helen and the fact that you found solace and safety with her and the Sacrarium," Gabriel added.

"And that they started training you, giving you a mission, teaching you what you needed to know," I said. "They didn't do that with me. They just threw me in headfirst when they thought it was right. I highly doubt they'd do that to the bloodline."

"Maybe you're right," she said. "But if that's true, then why would my mom leave me? Wouldn't she want to stay and protect me to preserve the line and ensure its safety?"

"She may not have had a choice about leaving you," Uriel said. "She may have thought that was the safest option. Or that woman may not have been your biological mom at all."

Sophia looked alarmed. "What do you mean?"

I shot daggers at Uriel with my eyes.

"Uh…just that the bloodline has been persecuted for a long time, and you might be the only one left so maybe they hid you with someone, a member of the society, and tried to give you a normal life. When it didn't work, they tried a different tactic."

I smacked my hand against my face at his senselessness.

"Uriel," Chamuel said.

"I know, others' feelings."

"No, we're beyond that." Chamuel shook his head. "Just be quiet."

"I don't want to think about this right now," Sophia said. "I'd rather move on, actually."

Sensing she was on the emotional edge, I changed the subject. "So what do we do now? Especially with the fourteenth sphere."

"We protect it until we figure out what it does," Zadkiel said.

"But I think I know what it does," I said.

"Really?" Michael asked.

I nodded. "When I was carrying the sphere in Simon Price's jacket,

I realized all the similarities it had to Lilith—the strong hypnotizing power, the coldness, the fact that my necklace was trying to combat it."

"You think Lilith controls the sphere?" Raphael asked.

"No, I think Lilith is locked *inside* the sphere," I said. "Before Gabriel rescued me, a voice shrieked, 'Let me out!' It came from the sphere, and I wasn't the only one who heard it. Those guys I was fighting did, too."

"But how did she get inside?" Jophiel questioned.

"I don't know. All I know is she wants to be freed, and we have to make sure that doesn't happen."

"So we destroy it," Uriel suggested.

Zadkiel adamantly shook his head. "We can't. It's a celestial object. There has to be a purpose to it."

"Its purpose is to be Lilith's prison," Dane said.

Zadkiel didn't fully agree. "Yes, but there has to be *more* to it."

"Why? That seems like a good enough purpose," Sophia commented.

"Maybe," Zadkiel mused. "But we still can't destroy it. If anything, it should be returned to Father."

"Well that's not happening anytime soon," Uriel said.

"Agreed. So in the meantime," Gabriel continued, "we protect it and regroup at the house."

41

SATAN

HELL, PRESENT DAY

I slumped in my throne, utterly defeated. Abbadona was still ill. The gala was a disaster. I didn't have the fourteenth sphere. And Lucifer was on the loose.

On top of that, there was Dane. I don't know why I saved the boy, or befriended him for that matter. Maybe because he seemed like a troubled loner and I was used to dealing with those types since all of us in Hell were troubled loners. Maybe because I had seen how vulnerable he was and how determined he was to change it. I had gone through a similar experience and could sympathize with him.

I rubbed my right underarm, then my left. Dane had been the one to tattoo my newest additions.

He couldn't pay for self-defense lessons so we'd bargained with ink. The Ace of Spades on the right. The King of Spades on the left.

But it was over now. It was time to forget him.

Sighing, I brushed my hand over my face. Since I hadn't destroyed the fourteenth sphere, my deal with Katriel was a bust. And I knew I couldn't lie to her… I mean, I *could*, but she would know I was lying since she had some weird sixth sense about such things. Regardless, I still desperately needed to find my keys. It was the only way I would be in control again.

I was back to square one. I had to hope the Sentinel was telling the truth when he said he had betrayed the Sacrarium. If he had, then he indeed knew where my keys were located, and I could use his gun to bind it to a spell that would extract the locations. But ultimately, I would have to use magic to complete the process. Abbadona was out of commission, only recently trading the hallucinations for fevers, meaning she was close to being well, yet definitely not strong or coherent enough for a spell of this magnitude. Which meant I had to rely on Astrid and Tabitha.

I sent Leviathan to summon them to the throne room.

When they came up the steps and entered, I sat up straight in my throne.

"Sir," they said in unison, bowing.

After that, they remained quiet. Our last encounter had not ended well. I had chosen Abbadona over them, and it had upset them. But I was not about to apologize. Instead, I jumped into action. "Follow me," I demanded, heading for the portal room.

But they refused to come.

"I'll give you money," I said.

"How much?" Tabitha inquired.

"However much you'd like."

"Okay," Astrid agreed, twirling about.

Finally, they trailed behind me and took their familiar seats around the central worktable in the portal room.

A loud banging started up, and I slammed my fist against the invisible barrier to my right. "Shut it, Kat! Deal's off!"

The banging ceased.

On the worktable rested the gold-plated gun I had wrestled away from the Sentinel.

"Oooh," Astrid said, picking up the gun. "Shiny." She aimed—at what I had no idea since she couldn't see—and pulled back on the trigger.

A shot rang out, lodging itself in the hard stone wall.

She giggled in delight.

Startled, I grabbed the gun from her. "This is not a toy!"

She deflated at the tone of my voice.

I looked over at Tabitha, who was unfazed by her sister's behavior. She met my gaze. "I could have told you she was insane."

Astrid giggled again at her sister's assessment.

Sighing, I pulled back the slide and unloaded the gun, placing the bullets in my pocket for safekeeping. When the firearm was no longer a danger to anyone, I set it back on the table. To be honest, I hated guns. They were loathsome pieces of technology that took the fun out of warfare. The most thrilling part about a battle was seeing the face of your opponent when you fought to the death. Guns took away that aspect. Yet, I knew many an angel, both blessed and fallen, who held a somewhat similar sentiment. None of us used guns. Perhaps some of us were now trained in how they functioned, but it was never our weapon of choice. For the Nephilim, it was a different story, their instincts tainted by their human blood.

The thought of them was a digression from the important matter at hand.

"What I need you to do," I told the sisters, "is pinpoint the locations where this gun has been."

"Has been what?" Tabitha asked. "Used?"

"No, has been physically," I clarified.

They turned to each other in confusion, trying to see if the other knew what I wanted. Obviously, neither of them did.

"Let me rephrase," I said. "I need to know where the owner of this gun has been."

Tabitha leaned forward on the table. "Now you're starting to make sense."

Astrid picked up the weapon again and ran her hands over it.

"What say you, Sister?" Tabitha asked.

"It's possible, but difficult," Astrid assessed.

"Why?" I demanded.

"This gun has been many a place," Astrid explained. "There must be something else to tie to the gun so we can pinpoint more precise locations."

"What exactly is it you're looking for, sir?" Tabitha asked.

I grappled with how much I should tell them, but I threw caution to the wind. I was getting desperate since I had no other way of finding what I wanted. "The owner of this gun has been to certain wonders of the world. I would like to go to these locations, as well."

Tabitha nodded. "What's at these wonders?"

"Why does it matter?" I asked.

"We're only trying to help, sir. The more we know, the better we can do that," Tabitha said.

Suddenly, Astrid reached out and took my hand. Instinctively, I pulled back, but she only latched on harder.

"Don't resist," Tabitha urged. "She means you no harm."

I tried to relax as Astrid touched each ring on my hand, stopping once she reached my ring from Heaven. She eased it off my finger, then dropped my hand and stroked the stone that rested on the band.

"This," she whispered. "This will do."

"Do as what?" I asked.

"To help us pinpoint the locations," Astrid said in a faraway voice. "This stone is tied to the ones you seek."

"I'm not so sure," I said, stretching out my hand to take the ring back.

Astrid deflected, spinning out of reach. Whenever she was in trance or near a trance, her senses became much more heightened.

"What's the matter, sir?" Tabitha asked, detecting a change in mood.

I composed myself to show no outward alarm. "Nothing." But inside, I was losing control. Abbadona had said not to bargain with black magic anymore. Doing a spell on the gun would have no effect on me, but if they used my ring to strengthen the spell, then there would be lasting consequences. And I wasn't sure how many more of those I could handle without it being near fatal.

"Shall we proceed?" Astrid asked.

"Yes," Tabitha said. "But not before we decide on a price."

"How much do you want?" I asked.

"A million," Tabitha revealed.

"A million!" I repeated, outraged. I didn't care about the price, as the currency in Hell held little worth or merit. What was enraging was knowing I would pay them anything to find my keys.

Tabitha shrugged. "You said however much we'd like."

"I know. But I think I'd rather give you the money without services in exchange."

"Why?" Astrid challenged, not for fear of losing the money but for fear of losing the promise of using her power. She was obsessed with her gifts, craved the feeling they brought on. It was obvious by the way she cradled the ring in her hand, anticipating the rush of the trance.

"Because I'm not comfortable tying something that belongs to me to the spell," I confessed. "Now give me back my ring, and I'll give you your money."

While I had to determine where my wonders were located, I knew this deal with Astrid and Tabitha would backfire. I *could* always wait for Abbadona. I mean, I didn't want to because who knew how long it would take for her to feel better, only delaying the process further, but I would do that if I was left with no other choice.

As soon as I thought of Abbadona, Astrid's head snapped toward me, her blind gaze venomous. "You think she's better than us! Your Abbadona! Well I'll show you!"

She squeezed her hand around the ring and let out a screeching gasp.

"Shit!" I shouted, launching myself into the air. Tackling her to the ground, I had every intention of prying my ring out of her hand and finishing off the insane seer. But before I could do either, she locked her free hand in a death grip around my neck. Our faces mere inches apart, she spat out of the words of her divination:

"Time and time again
Astrid is condemned.
Outcast, witch, and betrayer
Are the price I paid to become a slayer.

"Beaten, burned, and bruised
Astrid will no longer be abused.
It's time to face my wrath, face my might
For Astrid's spite is a great fright.

"Cursed are thee now and forever
Unless you face the threat you always lever.
Collapse, mutiny, and strife
Await you before the knife.

"So before I leave you
I have one last clue
To help you in your task
And give you what you ask.

"Two locations are what you seek.
Three in total, but one already leaked.
The first is a site of ancient stones.
May you arrive before you meet the crossbones.

"If you happen to survive
The second is a natural dive.
Along the giant's walk near the sea
May you meet your maker and hope for a plea."

Releasing my neck, Astrid returned to her normal self, though I was quite sure she remembered every word of her fateful curse, for her face still contained a defiant gleam. I slumped to the ground, drained and crestfallen, as I had paid the ultimate price, already feeling the effects of the spell.

Astrid slowly dropped my ring from her fingers, releasing it right in front of me and letting it hit the stone floor. Her hand remained outstretched. "Our money, sir."

My whole body shook, not in weakness but in rage. "Leave," I growled.

"But, sir," Tabitha intervened, "you promised."

I rose, unsteady on my feet, returning to the table. They must have thought I was retreating to get their money, but I had a far deadlier plan. In a matter of seconds, I had reached for the gun and loaded it with the bullets from my pocket. Firearms were never my first choice of weapon, but the witches' deceit had sent me into an impulsive frenzy. Turning and taking aim, I screamed, "Get out!"

"You won't shoot us," Tabitha challenged.

"Yeah, you're too spineless to make a final blow," Astrid added.

"Really?" I pulled the trigger. The bullet fired and hit Tabitha in the chest. Her face was full of shock as she slowly disintegrated.

"No!" Astrid shrieked. She stepped forward to rush me, but I trained the gun on her.

"I hope you rot in oblivion," I said.

"I hope you die at the hand of Lucifer, for he is our true king. At least my sister and I won't die in vain, knowing we trapped you according to his plans."

I pulled the trigger again and watched Astrid slowly fade away.

I picked up my ring from the floor and returned it to my finger before collapsing on one of the chairs at the worktable. I let go of the gun and rubbed a hand over my face.

What had I done? Fallen into their trap. Fallen into Lucifer's trap! This is what he had wanted!

I should have waited for Abbadona. I shouldn't have trusted them.

Trust no one.

Moving forward, that would be my new conviction. Yet, the thought did nothing to quell my anger because they still had gotten the best of me.

I placed a hand over my mouth and screamed. Be it in agony, fear, or rage, I wasn't sure. All I knew was that I was treading water, and it wouldn't be long before the current took me under.

42 SATAN

HELL, PRESENT DAY

I lay next to Abbadona on the cold stone floor of my private quarters, wallowing in my stupidity and giving in to Astrid's curse. If only I had waited.

If only…

If only…

My eyes slipped shut. When they opened again, Abbadona was gone.

Panicking, I tried to rise, but I had little strength.

No…I had to save her.

My eyes slipped shut again.

When they opened next, I was sitting on my throne. Gazing around, I had no idea how I got here, but I felt better than I had before.

I shut my eyes again, wanting to return to oblivion, when someone ran their fingers through my hair. I opened my eyes.

"My dear, what have you done?" Abbadona whispered. "I was only gone a short while, and you made a deal with those dark witches? I warned you they couldn't be trusted. I told you to call on me."

"I had no intention of tying myself to the spell. They tricked me."

"You shouldn't have let them up here in the first place."

"Abbadona." She looked me in the eyes. "What's done is done. There is nothing I can do." I reached up and covered my mouth as I coughed. Small specks of blood dappled my palm when I lifted it away.

She cradled my cheek. "The fever is setting in."

I leaned into her caress. "I know."

Her other hand came to rest on my chest. "You could take the amulet off. It may not undo Astrid's curse, but it will at least give you some strength."

"I can't."

"Why not?"

"Because I have to go to the wonders. I have to retrieve my keys. That's the only leverage I have left."

"Send someone in your stead," she pleaded.

"I can't. The keys can only be unlocked by my hand or by the holy bloodline. No one else can do it."

She leaned her forehead against mine. "I hate seeing you this way." She paused. "Lucifer will pay for what he has done."

I raised my finger to her lips to silence her. "Don't say his name."

"Let me come with you," she said instead. "I wouldn't be able to stay here knowing how vulnerable you are."

I smiled. "I'm glad you asked before I could."

"Really? You're not worried about leaving the place unattended?"

"I never said that. But I believe there are others who can watch over things, so long as they pass your approval."

A figure behind Abbadona cleared their throat. "Is this a bad time? Should we come back later? Ow!"

"Why did you have to say anything in the first place?" Nehema demanded, letting her arm drop to her side after smacking Haborym. "It was cute watching them."

Abbadona eased back and turned to assess the new arrivals. A wide smile graced her face. "So you took my recommendations to heart."

"Yes." I placed a hand on her arm, and she brought her attention back to me. "Do you trust them?"

"With my life."

I nodded. "Good. You, Leviathan, and Beelzebub will come with me. Nehema and Haborym will stay here and keep an eye on things—particularly Mammon and Asmodeus."

"What about Belphegor? Should we keep an eye on him, too?" Haborym asked.

"Yes, but I suspect Mammon and Asmodeus are the bigger issues."

"Yes, sir," she replied.

"No need to worry about anything, sir. Your home will be in good hands while you're away," Nehema assured me. "Where are you going, if you don't mind me asking?"

Bracing myself, I slowly rose from the throne. Abbadona stood from her kneeling position, close upon my heels. "I'm not sure," I said. "That's what we have to find out."

I retreated to my room, needing to look at a map. The three female fallen angels followed in my wake.

Turning my desk chair around, I sat down to gaze at the map that spanned the entire length of the wall. "There are three keys—the classic, the gemstone, and the sphere. Each was hidden at a different wonder so there are three wonders—an ancient, a natural, and a modern. My sphere was hidden at the Empire State Building, which is my modern wonder, but the sphere no longer resides there. It's now a matter of finding the other two."

"How do you know all this?" Nehema asked. "Surely they didn't reveal all this to you while you were still in Heaven?"

"No, they did not. I learned about the Union of the Spheres from Leviathan. He used to be an angel of teaching, and like many of them, he snuck around and poked through books he wasn't supposed to be reading. That's how I learned about the keys, but the locations were never disclosed. Lucifer was the one to alert me to the Sacrarium and the fact that they had my sphere."

Abbadona sighed. "Do you ever learn?"

I raised a hand to silence her. "I knew I would have to locate and retrieve the keys eventually. But I wanted the sphere more than the others because it would be the hardest item to reclaim. So I made it my mission to track the Sacrarium. Yet, after all these years, I still have not been successful, and now my hopes are futile since the archangels have it. Nevertheless, hope is not lost. There are still two keys out there, and it's finally time to uncover them."

"But you don't know where they are?" Haborym confirmed.

"Correct. And Astrid's divination will hardly help us. It was too cryptic."

"Yes, but there were clues in there," Abbadona said.

I gave her a deadpan glance. "'*A site of ancient stones.*' How is that a clue? Many of the wonders could fulfill that description."

"There's no need to get temperamental with me," she snapped.

I sighed. "I'm not. I'm just frustrated."

"Can't you do something to pinpoint the exact locations, Abbadona?" Nehema asked.

"You still have the gun, right?" Abbadona asked me.

Pointing to the wall on my left, I said, "It's over there." I had hung it among my arsenal of weapons.

She went to retrieve it and then returned to my side. Holding the gun in her hand, palm up, she hovered over it with the other, fingers twirling. A shimmering light glowed around the weapon. "Take the gun," she commanded me.

Hesitantly, I reached out my hand and grasped the gun. I was worried the light might do something, but all it did was make my skin feel warm.

Both her hands now free, Abbadona leveled them and cast them before the map on the wall. Small dots of light appeared throughout the world, highlighting locations, presumably ones where the Sentinel had been. Slowly, they started to fade until all but two were left.

The small dots of light transformed into large beams. Luckily, they were relatively close together, meaning our travels would not be extensive.

"England and Ireland," Abbadona announced. "Stonehenge and Giant's Causeway. Those are your two remaining wonders."

I weakly smiled at her in appreciation and spoke words I hadn't verbalized in centuries. "Thank you."

The three female fallen angels were all surprised by my show of grace, but luckily, they didn't draw attention to it.

"You're welcome," Abbadona replied. "Now, I think it's time we prepped for our journey."

"We need to do more than prep," I said. "We need to strategize. For these will, by no means, be easy tasks. I suspect we will be confronted when we arrive at each destination."

"By whom?" Abbadona asked.

“Lucifer, Jazema, the Sentinel, the Nephilim, and the Triune are all good guesses. I have a lot of enemies, and I’m sure any one of them would love the opportunity to crush me.”

43 JORDAN

Ithaca, New York, Present Day

When we arrived back at the house, a familiar face was there to greet us.

"Martha!" I grinned. "You're back!"

She enveloped me in a hug. "Yes, I am." She pulled back. "How are you?"

"Good. Did you see I opened the studio?"

"I certainly did! I cleaned it top to bottom, getting rid of the dust."

"You didn't have to do that. I could have."

"Jordan, I'm the housekeeper. That's my job." Her eyes trailed away from me and then grew wide. "Oh my goodness! What happened to you?" Martha rushed over to Chamuel.

He had already healed faster than any normal human would, and he had adapted quickly to getting around on crutches.

"I broke my leg," the angel told her.

"I can see that," Martha chided. "How?"

"In a fight against two fierce females."

"Don't ever stand in the way of a woman," Martha advised. "We'll take you out quicker than any man." Her eyes trailed away again. "Oh! My dears, it's so good to see you, too." She hugged Sophia and Dane. "Come inside, everyone. The house is ready for you."

We all walked through the front door. I was so glad to be home and put the gala behind us.

"Getting back to the studio," Martha said. "Did you see all your mother's paintings? I told you they were wonderful."

"They're amazing! I can't believe she had such talent and I got none of it."

Martha laughed.

After eating a quick snack, Dane, Sophia, and I went upstairs to settle in. We decided to find a new show to binge-watch, so we met in the upstairs loft.

Just as we got comfortable, Gabriel appeared. "Sorry to interrupt," he said. "We're having a group meeting in the library."

"About?" I asked.

"Next moves."

The three of us followed Gabriel downstairs. A few maps had been brought in and were laid out on the tables. All the angels were gathered around one of them, along with Martha.

"What are we doing?" I asked as we joined them.

"Making a plan to retrieve the keys," Michael said. "It's time to focus our attention on them because there are too many players trying to make power moves. The keys are no longer safe, and each of them is needed for the Union of the Spheres anyway, so it's better to get them now while we still have time."

"Can I jot down the words of that prophecy, too?" Sophia asked. "I feel like we should work on deciphering these prophecies. A lot of our answers may be in them, and I think they might connect somehow."

I reached around to the table behind me and handed her a piece of paper. "Here. We made photocopies of it."

"You digitally scanned it from *The Book of Prophecies*?" Sophia asked.

"No, Jophiel wrote it down, and we copied that," I told her.

"All right," Zadkiel said, drawing our attention. "Here's a quick lesson on the wonders of the world. There are seven ancient wonders. At these sites, our classic keys were hidden, however, many of these places were threatened long ago by various forces, driving us to retrieve the classic keys. They now are in our possession."

Simultaneously, the seven angels pulled their keys out of their pockets and placed them on the table. They were all varying shapes, sizes, and colors.

Zadkiel strode over to a map, all of us following along. "There are also seven natural wonders, and these will be the sites we are traveling to." He labeled the new map accordingly. "Our Celtic astrology signs are connected to these wonders because they're based on nature." He poised the marker over the map. "My Celtic astrology sign is Rowan and my natural wonder is Paricutín, a volcano located in Mexico." After marking the area on the map, he turned to the others, seemingly ready for them to tell us their signs and wonders.

Uriel's were Reed and Mount Everest.

Raphael's were Ivy and Victoria Falls.

Jophiel's were Vine and the Harbor of Rio de Janeiro.

Gabriel's were Hawthorn and the Grand Canyon.

Chamuel's were Willow and the Great Barrier Reef.

Michael's were Oak and the aurora borealis.

With all the locations now marked on the map, Zadkiel capped his marker and grew silent as Michael took over.

"Unlike last time," Michael said, "I think we need to travel in a more logical pattern. So starting from our current destination, it would make the most sense to go to the Grand Canyon first. From there, we go to the next closest spot and so forth, making a loop, until we end up back where we started." As he spoke, he drew his pointer finger along the map, hitting every dot Zadkiel had made.

"Also, I think we need to stick together," Gabriel said. "I know it may seem irrational for ten of us to travel to each location, but splitting up right now is not an option. We have the three of you to protect, we have the fourteenth sphere, and we will be unlocking even more powerful objects. We simply need the strength that comes in numbers; otherwise we'll be too vulnerable."

We all nodded in agreement.

Then a question came to mind. "Does each of you know the *exact* location of your keys?"

"Yes," Zadkiel said. "Before we were sent to Earth, we were told the precise place where our keys were hidden."

I sighed in relief. "That's good. At least this journey won't be as much of a guessing game as last time."

"When do we leave?" Sophia asked.

"As soon as we can," Michael said.

I turned to Dane. "Are you okay with the plan? I mean…I know you don't like giving up your job."

"Honestly," he said, "forget the job. I don't care anymore. My life is in danger. *Our* lives are in danger. Practical real-world stuff doesn't matter anymore." He paused. "I want to be upfront with everyone, though… I have money to buy food and share the cost of hotels, but I can't afford airfare."

"Speaking of that," Martha interjected, "I wasn't around last time when you all were traveling or I would have mentioned this sooner, but you have a private plane."

"Who has a private plane?" I asked. She looked at me pointedly. "Me?"

Martha nodded. "Your mother's brother, meaning your uncle, was a pilot. He owned a few planes. He left them to your mother since he had no other family. When he passed, she sold some because she had no use for them. It also reminded her too much of how he died in a helicopter crash."

"Wow…" I hardly knew my mother had a sibling, let alone that he died in a helicopter crash.

Martha's expression crumpled. "I'm so sorry! I thought you knew about him. I wouldn't have said it so insensitively."

"It's all right, Martha." While it was shocking, I would rather know the truth. Plus, there was no point in blaming her. She had no idea.

"Well, what I'm trying to explain is that your mother kept one of the planes, mainly to remember her brother. It's housed at a nearby aviation corporation. I don't know if any of you can fly." She stopped, realizing her poor choice of words. "I mean, fly a plane," she corrected.

"I can," Jophiel admitted. "Planes fascinated me when they were first being created. Flying is such a lovely and amazing experience. I thought it was a great idea to mimic it for humans. I learned on early models and kept up with it as they were adapted. Aviation technology has become so advanced, it's nothing like when it first started." He paused, realizing he was close to lecturing us on the history of planes. "Anyway, all that to say I do know how to operate and fly one."

None of us were really surprised. All the angels dabbled in technology, it just varied on what part of it they were interested in. Were they tech geniuses? No. But they each had their own skill. I simply wished Gabriel would be more mindful and remember to bring his cell phone with him. But even some humans had a tendency to forget that.

"Okay," I said slowly, still shocked by the wealth and privilege of my family. "I guess we have our own plane." Turning back to Dane, I asked, "Does that work for you?"

He grinned. "Of course."

"And what about the fourteenth sphere? We're bringing it with us?" Sophia asked.

Zadkiel nodded. "Yes, it's the best option for now. It's not safe to leave it here. It would put Martha in too much danger and be entirely unprotected. Until I can find more information about it, which has been nearly impossible so far, I want to keep it close."

"Besides," Gabriel added, "we traveled around the world once before lugging the book and Satan's sphere around—unknowingly, I will admit—but this will be no different."

"As long as you think it's safe," Sophia said, "it's fine by me. I trust your judgment."

44 JORDAN

Ithaca, New York, Present Day

The next day was a whirlwind of excitement as we packed and prepared to depart. The angels wanted to leave as soon as possible so the plan was to fly out tonight. Dane needed time to settle things at work so he had left with Jophiel this morning to attend to that. Sophia needed a few things for the trip so she went to the store with Martha and Zadkiel.

Since my bags were packed, I tried to help out around the house, but everything seemed to be under control. Laundry was done. Dishes were put away. Every surface was cleaned and polished. I knew I had to do something to keep me busy so I pulled out my phone and texted Dafne.

I'm going on a trip. Leaving tonight. Won't be back for a couple weeks. Wanted you to know.

She responded right away.

Where are you going?

I thought it over.

Pretty much everywhere.

Again, her reply came immediately. *This sounds like a celestial mission :)*

I smiled. *It is.*

I watched those three dots as she wrote back, waiting eagerly.

While you're away saving the world, I'll be preparing for the fall harvest.

Samhain will be upon us soon. The words whispered through my mind as if someone had spoken them in my ear.

The buzz of my phone brought my attention back to the moment.

I hope you take lots of pictures. Xoxo.

Sitting on my bed, I typed in my response and hit "send." *I will!*

I had been tempted to type back *xoxo* but I didn't. It seemed too… personal? Intimate? I didn't know what word I was looking for.

I was about to get up when the thought of someone else struck my mind—Naomi. I hadn't talked to her or heard from her in weeks. I should probably tell her I was leaving, too. I brought up her messages on my phone. Reading through some of them, I realized how vastly different my conversations were with her than they were with Dafne. Almost all my responses to Naomi were lies or half-truths because I couldn't tell her about my life. I couldn't be who I really was with her. It was nice being able to do that with Dafne.

Ugh!

I fell back on my bed. Why did this have to be so difficult?

I was so confused, and my feelings were swinging like a pendulum. I didn't want to be the guy who couldn't commit. In fact, all I wanted was a serious, committed relationship. So why couldn't I figure out how I felt?

Everything had been going great with Naomi. We had talked and texted and video chatted.

But Dafne…

When I'd first met her, she had seemed guarded, but I'd quickly realized it wasn't personal. She simply put up walls. Why, I had yet to find out, but Dafne's wall had started to crumble when we were in the city and she had started to open up. That had changed everything. It didn't help that we had been thrown into survival mode together, either. Or that I could talk to her about the angels. That was still a new thing, but it was a relief.

Yet, even though Naomi and I were vastly different, I felt like I had to give it more of a chance and let whatever feelings I had for Dafne go.

I tapped out a text to Naomi.

Hey! I'd love to see you. Are you busy?

I waited a few minutes, hoping she would respond.

No. I'm on campus at the library picking up some books. Meet me there?

Smiling, I typed back, *Of course! Be there soon.*

I jumped up and ran into the closet for some shoes, then dashed down the stairs. I popped my head into the library and shouted, "I need to go out! Can someone come with me?"

"Sure," Gabriel said.

We got in the car, and I took off down the driveway. Although, I didn't drive much—what, with the subway and other means of transportation—I did know how to do it. Sister Delphine had taught all of us at the orphanage once we were of age. The memory had come back unconsciously, and it made me realize just how much Sister Delphine had been around when I was younger. To be honest, if Sister Helen was ever busy, Sister Delphine was always the one to step in.

At a stoplight, I tapped my fingers on the steering wheel. Gabriel glanced at my hands, making it clear he noticed my nervous tic, but he remained silent.

I sat behind the wheel, wondering how I could find Sister Delphine.

Then I remembered Sister Helen's words: *Do not go searching for it.* At the time, she had meant her and Holy Trinity. But I imagined the same must have been true for Sister Delphine. I mean, the two of them had practically operated the same way. Plus, Sister Delphine had told me she would come back when it was time. But time for what?

I couldn't think about it anymore right now, though, because we were arriving at the university. I parked the car, and we got out.

"I'm going to meet Naomi," I told Gabriel.

"Figured as much, given your nerves. I'll be around—close but undetectable."

He walked off, leisurely striding down the sidewalk in the afternoon sun.

I tried to remember my way to the library. I headed in one direction, then realized I was going the wrong way. I backtracked and tried the other direction, but that wasn't right, either. I pulled out my phone to text Naomi.

How do I get to the library?

My phone buzzed. *I'll come to you.*

"Jordan!"

I looked up at the sound of my name. Sure enough, there was Naomi, walking toward me across the lawn.

"Hey," she said when she got closer. "How have you been?"

"Good." I tilted my head at her. She seemed different. Not as amiable somehow. "Are you okay?"

She nodded. "Wanna sit?" she asked, pointing to a picnic table.

"Sure." I followed her along the grassy lawn, and we sat down at the table in the shade.

Sighing, she said, "Jordan, do you like me?"

"Uh..." I was so taken aback by her abruptness that I didn't know what to say. Finally, I managed to form words. "Yes, of course, I like you, Naomi."

"No, I mean *really* like me."

Something was off here, so I called her on it. "What's going on, Naomi? I'd rather you say what's on your mind."

"Fine. I've been doing a lot of thinking, and I don't see us working out."

I opened my mouth to protest, but she continued. "Not because I don't like you but because I'd rather you be my friend." She paused. "This isn't coming out right. What I'm trying to say is that since the day I met you, I've felt connected to you."

I agreed. "Me too. I feel like you can read my mind sometimes."

She shook her head vigorously. "Exactly! And the times we've talked have been great. I enjoy being around you."

"But..." I anticipated.

"But when I think about taking our relationship to the next level, I start to feel all weird and confused because I realized I want you more as my friend than my boyfriend." She covered her mouth with a hand as the words rushed out. "I'm sorry!"

"There's no reason to apologize." I smiled. "I actually may be feeling the same way. I've been so confused trying to sort out my feelings for you. But now I recognize that maybe the connection we have is meant to just stay friendly."

She grabbed my hand across the table and squeezed it. "Thank you for understanding. I had been dreading this conversation for a while, but I should have known you would be so kind about it."

I smiled. "The conversation you should be dreading is the one with your parents, especially your mom. She was so determined to get us together."

Naomi laughed. "Yeah, I'll have to break it to her easy." She pulled back her hand. "I should probably get going. I have to get back to work. I only stopped over here on my lunch break to pick up some research books from the library."

"Of course. I don't want to keep you. How's it going by the way? Your internship?"

We stood together, and she reached into her purse for her keys. "Okay. I was really excited at first since it's a top-notch lab but..." She trailed off, taking her attention away from her purse and sticking it on me. "There's some weird stuff going on."

"Like what?" I asked.

"Sealed files, unidentified DNA samples, restricted areas."

All those things sounded too familiar...

Worry seeped in. "Naomi, what lab do you work for?"

"Geneloom. Have you heard of it?"

My heart sunk. "Yes, I have. But only bad things." I sighed. How did I tell her without revealing too much of the truth? But also how did I warn her that she was involved with some very dangerous people? So all I said was, "I heard they're so obsessed with genetic testing that they'll coerce people into participating."

Naomi's eyes widened. "Really? Ever since I started noticing the weird stuff that's been going on, I've been digging around with the other intern and we found this whole room that's dedicated to hundreds of thousands of blood samples, some from years ago. It's crazy how much they hold on to, like they're going to run out or something. Plus, my bosses, Jazema and Penelope, are not the nicest people. They scared most of the interns off. There are only two of us left now."

I was so alarmed, I felt like a siren was going off in my head. "Naomi, you need to quit. Those women are bad news. The whole company is bad news. You need to leave before they figure out you're sneaking around."

She shook her head. "I can't. The research I'm working on there is groundbreaking. I would never have been able to get this far without Geneloom's resources."

My head tilted back in shock. Was she part of the experiment? Was she helping the Watchers who had caused Sophia so much trauma?

Then my mind took a deep dive. What if those guys in tactical gear at the gala had been right? What if I was a Nephilim? People seemed to know my parents, but could one of them have been a Watcher, hidden in plain sight?

My name being repeated over and over again brought me back to the moment.

"Jordan, are you okay?" Naomi asked.

I nodded. "Yeah. Just be careful, Naomi."

"I will," she promised. "I should go. Maybe we can catch up again soon."

She walked away, and I remained frozen in place. I was worried about Naomi. I didn't want her to get hurt. But if she was supporting Geneloom, then I couldn't be her friend.

Gabriel crossed the lawn. "Is everything okay?"

"Not really. Do you mind driving?" I handed him the keys.

He took them without asking any further questions.

When we returned home, Gabriel parked the car and I raced inside. I couldn't get the word *Nephilim* out of my mind, and I felt like I was on autopilot. I heard voices and saw the shapes of figures as I headed for the hall bathroom, but I didn't stop to listen to them or even register who they were. Without closing the door, I whipped off my shirt and tried to see my back in the mirror. I twisted this way and that, extending my arms behind me and touching the skin to see if there were any sign of wings or feathers sprouting. Nothing.

"Jordan, what's going on?" Michael asked.

Wild-eyed, I glanced at the doorway where nearly everyone stood, concern splashed across their faces. I must have looked like I'd lost it.

Dropping my arms, I said, "Yeah, I had a bad itch, and then I thought it might be a bug so I freaked out, but there's nothing there."

"O-kay," Dane said.

Somehow Gabriel knew I wasn't telling the truth. "What happened with Naomi?"

I sighed, pulling my shirt back on. "We've decided to just be friends."

"Oh no!" Sophia said, grabbing me in a hug. "I'm so sorry."

Behind her back, I saw Michael stick out his hand to Uriel and say, "Pay up."

Furious, Chamuel swung one of his crutches at them. "Do any of you have any consideration for a human's feelings?"

"It's okay," I said, stepping away from Sophia. "I realized that I didn't want to take things further, either." I paused. "Especially now."

"Why?" Sophia asked.

"Because Naomi works for Geneloom. I warned her how bad they are, but she refused to leave because she needed the opportunity whether she liked what they're doing or not."

Chamuel stopped hitting them with his crutches. "What? That sweet girl is on their side?"

"I don't know," I said. "It didn't seem like it."

"How did Geneloom come up?" Michael asked.

"Weeks ago, she had told me she was interning at a lab, and with her major in biomolecular engineering that made sense to me. But today, I asked her about her internship, and she actually told me which lab she works for."

"Maybe it is for the best, then," Raphael agreed. "You don't want to be wrapped up in that."

"Yeah, it's just..." I paused. "I'm worried about her and I don't want her to get hurt. But how do I convince her to leave? And if she's adamant about staying, how can I trust her? I mean, for all I know, Jazema and Penelope might want something and force her to do it."

"I see your point. Maybe it's not *what* they want, though," Gabriel suggested, "but *whom*. The seven of us and the three of you are certainly something Geneloom might be interested in, and her connection to us is something they could exploit."

My eyes widened. "You're not making this any better."

"Sorry," Gabriel said, falling quiet.

Dane tapped his finger against his chin. "Why don't you tell her parents? They might force her to quit if they knew she was in danger."

Thinking it over, I said, "I could. But then I would be betraying her."

Sophia sighed. "There's no perfect solution, Jordan. It's a matter of what you care about more. Betraying Naomi to her parents but ultimately protecting her, or letting her stay at Geneloom and possibly getting hurt."

Neither seemed like good options in my opinion, but maybe I was overreacting. Naomi was safe at the moment, and she seemed like she knew what she was doing. Besides, if I said anything, it would only draw attention to her. Staying silent might be the best idea in this case.

I looked over my shoulder and glanced at my bare back in the mirror.

I should tell them my suspicions. I knew I should. But I didn't. I could handle a lot—angels, hellhounds, Satan. The one thing I couldn't was the Nephilim. I didn't want to be one. So I remained silent on all accounts, hoping it was the right decision to make.

45 SATAN

SALISBURY, ENGLAND, PRESENT DAY

Setting foot anywhere near Stonehenge in the month of June was a foolish mistake. There were people everywhere—some average tourists, others wannabe witches—all excited for midsummer, even though it was three weeks away. While I hated humans meddling in my business, time wasn't on our side so we didn't have a choice but to suffer through it. Luckily, the four of us blended in nicely with the stranger and more peculiar crowd: Beelzebub big and burly, Leviathan quiet and cunning, Abbadona fierce and powerful, and me stubborn and moody.

"How do we do this exactly?" Beelzebub asked.

"Not sure. I think I need to touch the stones," I said.

Leviathan and Beelzebub looked over the crowd.

"No one's allowed near the stones, sir," Leviathan said.

"Which is why you're here," I reminded them, "to create a distraction while I go wander among them."

"Or," Abbadona said, "we take an easier path." She closed her eyes and raised her head to the sky.

It was a bright, sunny day, but clouds started to roll in—rather quickly, in fact. The sky darkened and lightning struck the air. Fat drops of rain fell down on our heads, and it soon turned into a downpour. The humans started racing inside, some screaming in panicked delight.

I cradled Abbadona's wet cheek. "What would I do without you?"

Eyes still closed and head still turned to the sky, she smiled wide. "Go before this turns into something I can't control."

Her power to manipulate water and energy was captivating, but I forced myself to step over the short stanchion running the length of the path and trod through the wet grass to approach the stones. The rain was the perfect deterrent. Leviathan and Beelzebub stood guard, one close to Abbadona, the other following me.

"Do we need to check every stone?" Beelzebub asked.

I coughed, temporarily stopping my search—too much exertion—and I choked on my blood, all because of Astrid's curse. "Yes," I hissed out.

Beelzebub roamed among the stones. "If your key is so important, wouldn't it be in an important stone?"

"Are you even looking?" I yelled at him.

He stopped. "No."

"Damn you! Get out of my sight!"

"Sorry, sir. I'll be over here, keeping guard." Beelzebub withdrew a few feet away.

While I never liked listening to his logic, Beelzebub had a point. That meant there was only one option: the Altar Stone. I strode to the middle of the circle.

"Boss! We got trouble!"

My head snapped around at Beelzebub's warning. "Who is it?" I demanded.

"Not sure. They don't have guns, though, so it can't be Nephilim."

"Shit! That's even worse."

"Why?"

"Because then it's the Triune!"

I crept closer to the spot where I knew the Altar Stone rested, but it wasn't there. Another stone had fallen atop it, pushing it into the ground. *Damn it!*

A figure dropped down from the sky, landing in front of me and not missing a beat as she swiped her sword at me. My reflexes slow, I pulled back but not in time. The blade grazed my chest, cutting my shirt and drawing a thin line of blood.

"We're at this again, I see," she said.

I chuckled. "Aziza, did you really expect me to give up?"

Another figure landed next to her, sending a punch right to my face.

I raised my hand and felt the blood upon my lip. "Nice to see you, too, Yadira." I coughed again.

Aziza squinted. "What's wrong with you?"

"Nothing that can't be fixed."

Yadira raised her hand again for another punch.

"If you value the life of your comrade, I would suggest you back down," I threatened.

Aziza sprang forward and grabbed me by the shirt. "Where is she? We know you've had her all these years."

I smirked. "I can't tell you where she is, but I assure you Kat's rotting away, still hoping for rescue."

Her fist tightened, and her eyes shot daggers at me. "It's time to meet your end."

Whacked from behind, Aziza fell to the ground; however, she was a nimble and agile one, using the fall to roll over and spring up again.

She drew a second sword from behind her back. Abbadona faced her, the fallen angel's staff positioned in a fighting stance. Then they both sprang, a clash of black and white wings.

Yadira swung at me again, this time with her war hammer. I barely had time to dodge it as the weapon came down and collided with the earth. Effortlessly lifting it, she prepared to swing another blow, but not before Beelzebub ran into her and tackled her to the ground. Their muscular forms wrestled over the rock and grass.

With all attention drawn away from me, I splayed my bloodied hand on the ground and braced myself to rise. A force pulsated through me so strong it was as if I had been struck by lightning. Looking down, I saw my hand rested on a rock completely submerged in the earth. Before my eyes, the Ophiuchus symbol appeared faintly on the stone in a combination of blood and light. Something slowly rose from the stone's core, finally taking shape just beneath the surface. It was a key. *My key.* The key Michael had ripped from my neck after the war.

Once it was free, I picked it up. At last, I was reunited with what was mine. After all these years of tracking and searching and compromising, only to be betrayed and deceived, I was finally victorious. I rose, ready to finish off the Triune and depart.

In the air above me, Abbadona and Aziza fought, rain still pouring down.

"Sir, we need to go!" Leviathan said, running through the rocks toward me. "Our cover is blown."

"Have the human authorities arrived?"

"Yes, and there is no holding them back."

I outstretched my wings, preparing to fly. "We need to assist the others before we can leave."

"It's better to get you out of here. I can come back."

As the words left Leviathan's mouth, Abbadona came spiraling to the ground and careened into the earth.

Dazed, she screamed, "Watch out!"

Aziza came down on my back, digging her knives into my wings and tearing the feathers. I roared and knocked her off. Adrenaline pumping, I elbowed her in the ribs, took hold of her arm, twisted, and pried one of her knives free, only to feint and sink it in her thigh. She screamed and scampered back.

Leviathan and Abbadona grabbed my arms and forced me to move. The pain was so intense it numbed my entire body.

"Beelzebub, take him!" Abbadona demanded.

I was lifted over his shoulder, and he quickly launched us into the air, Abbadona and Leviathan flanking us as we made our escape.

I'd thought I would never return to the quiet solace within me, the place in my mind where I had gone when I had first fallen. Yet, that was where I retreated to, a place where I could curl into a ball and let my weakness wash over me.

46 JORDAN

Tusayan, Arizona, Present Day

Fun fact: the Grand Canyon has its own airport. I didn't think I would have learned that if we had flown here traditionally, but since we were using my uncle's plane, we had needed somewhere to land, preferably near our destination.

Another fun tidbit: Jophiel was an exceptionally skilled pilot. He had taken off so expertly and effortlessly, I had hardly felt the transition from ground to air. Even now, he landed smoothly, providing a pleasant end to the first leg of our trip.

Since we had left Ithaca around midnight, it was now 3:30 AM. By cover of darkness, we exited the plane with our belongings and got transportation to one of the hotels close by.

Sophia, Dane, and I went right to sleep when we arrived at the hotel room. Gabriel wanted to get an early start since we had to hike a short distance to the precise location where his gemstone key was hidden.

In the morning, the three of us ate a quick breakfast downstairs in the hotel dining area while Chamuel decided to stay in the room for the day since his leg was still healing and it was hard for him to move around.

Once we finished eating, we were off, packs full of supplies slung over our shoulders.

"Did everyone put on sunscreen?" Sophia asked, smearing even more over her arms.

"Yes, we did. Now stop before I take it away from you," Dane told her.

"I'm just trying to avoid anyone getting sunburn," Sophia defended.

We entered the trail, boots crunching over rock and dirt as we walked. I glanced at Gabriel at the head of the group. This was the first time I'd ever seen him in a T-shirt and cargo pants. It was a surprise to see him in anything but a suit, really. I was glad he had dressed for the occasion, though, because on our last journey, he hadn't, constantly wearing a suit even as we traveled through hot and humid climates.

"Where is it that we're going again?" Uriel asked.

"Angels Window," Gabriel said.

"Is that a coincidence?" I wondered aloud.

"Probably not," Gabriel responded. "But wait until you see it. The view is beautiful."

The majority of our hike was spent in companionable silence. I would stop occasionally to take some pictures, either of my breathtaking surroundings or some selfies with Sophia and Dane. I had learned last time that pictures with the angels were essentially forbidden so I didn't ask them. Although, I hoped to coax them into taking one at some point.

As we crested a ridge, I sucked in a breath at the incredible view. Red rock surrounded me as far as the eye could see, expanding all the way to the horizon. Trees lined the cliffside, and the white puffy clouds in the sky looked so close I could reach out and touch them.

"That's Angels Window," Gabriel said, pointing at a rock formation.

It was long, almost like a bridge, and stretched out into the middle of the canyon. There were a few people milling about the viewing deck on top. Yet, a few feet down, in the middle of the rock, was a hole naturally carved into the stone. "That hole is the window?" I asked.

Gabriel nodded. "We'll need a slight distraction."

"I'll go with you," Michael said. "Just in case."

We hiked the remaining distance to the viewing deck, and the rest of us went to work.

"Oh my gosh!" Sophia exclaimed. "Did you see that eagle?" She ran over to the edge of the railing, looking out into the canyon. "It had an animal in its mouth!"

The few strangers around us were immediately interested.

"There it is!" Raphael said, pointing in the complete opposite direction Sophia had.

Everyone followed his indication.

Out of the corner of my eye, Gabriel and Michael climbed over the railing and then completely dropped into thin air.

Leaning over the railing, I tried getting a glimpse of them.

"I must be seeing things!" I heard Sophia call out. "I swore it was a bird!"

From my viewpoint, I could just make out what Gabriel was doing. He ran his hand over a small tree rooted just underneath the hole. Without being by his side, it was hard to tell what happened next, but it seemed like whatever he had done worked because I saw him curl his hand around something.

Suddenly, a shadow flew overhead, and I looked up. The people on the viewing deck, myself included, stood in awe as a large eagle crested through the air. Flapping its wings, it gained altitude and glided along on the slight breeze.

"All done," Gabriel said at my side.

I jumped in surprise, then looked to Michael. "The bird was your handiwork, right?"

"Eagles are my messengers," he said, the bird swooping low and ruffling his hair.

The small crowd oohed and aahed.

"I told you it was a bird!" Sophia said. She came over to me. "How did I do?"

I chuckled. "Perfect."

We hiked back down the path and stopped halfway for a break. That's when we all gathered around so Gabriel could show us his gemstone key. He opened his hand, and in the middle of his palm sat a clear triangular-cut danburite stone. I had to refrain from reaching out and touching it. The stone had a simple beauty to it, but a pulsating energy radiated off the gem.

Gabriel reached inside his pocket for a velvet pouch, in which he carefully placed the gemstone for safekeeping.

Sophia and Dane found a spot to sit down and opened their packs.

"Hey, guys," I said to them, "what are you doing?"

"Lunch break," Dane responded, taking some food out of his bag.

"But we just got started. And we need to keep a steady pace," I told them. "We shouldn't stay here long."

"Look at the view, though!" Sophia said, biting into her sandwich. After swallowing, she said, "Given everything we've seen and been through, I need to take in some beauty."

"Cleanse the palate," Dane agreed, his mouth full.

While I loved them both dearly, Sophia and Dane were really cramping the style and flow the angels and I had grown used to when traveling.

Don't get me wrong, we had taken breaks, but most of the time we had been on the move.

I looked at the angels. They shrugged as if to say, *Why not?*

I sighed but joined them in the shady spot they had found. I pulled out my sandwich and dug in.

"So I've been thinking over this prophecy—the three heirs one," Sophia said between bites.

"Did you discover anything?" Jophiel asked.

"Maybe." She reached inside her backpack and took out the paper with the prophecy on it. From here, I could see she had marked it up with notes. "Look at the first stanza: *'Bloodlines tied betwixt you three / Threads sealed and woven in a tree. / Find the one destined to thee / Your family tree you cannot flee.'* To me, it seems like the fates of the three heirs are sealed together, potentially within the tapestry, but also within physical trees. Then the next stanza is, *'In boughs of cypress, spruce, and oak / Lies the blade you must uncloak. / Assume your role, discover your power / For you will need it at the fateful hour.'* The physical family trees are the cypress, spruce, and oak, one for each heir. I think maybe there are actual trees we need to find and inside each of them is a blade, sort of like the keys being hidden in the wonders of the world. Now, the blade could literally be a knife or it could be a leaf. It's hard to say, but there's *something* in the tree that will help us discover who we are."

Sophia had really put some thought into this. I was impressed.

"The third stanza," she continued, "reads, *'Children raised together / Must follow the feather. / Red, green, blue in hue / They will guide you anew.'* This is what made me believe we were the three heirs because we were raised together. The feather part is what I think will lead us to the physical trees, although it seems we each have a different color feather to follow. Finally, the last stanza, *'Wisdom, blood, and balance / Will each be challenged. / Not one, not two, but three shares / So goes the Prophecy of the Three Heirs.'* This part I'm not entirely sure what it's getting at other than the three heirs will have to share what is to come equally."

Sophia broke off, and we all sat in silence, thoughtful expressions on our faces.

"Your interpretations are very logical," Zadkiel said. "There is another thing I would add, but it's not in the prophecy itself, rather an inkling I picked up on since the three of you reunited." He paused trying to grasp the right words. "It seems like there is some higher work going on here—something your families did or your parents, even. And that it's something you must continue or finish."

"Or change," I added.

Zadkiel nodded.

"I think you're right," Dane said. "I also think that whenever we find these trees from the prophecy, we'll not just know who we are, but we'll also know the answers to all our parents' lingering secrets."

"I agree," I said. "First we need to discover what specific trees we need to find, though."

"I feel like we won't be able to do that without the other part of the tapestry," Sophia said.

"So where could it be?" Jophiel asked.

"Well, the only room still locked at the house is the office," Gabriel commented.

"Why hide the two parts in one place?" Michael asked. "It would make more sense to separate them."

We each faded off into thought again. It was hard to say where the rest of the tapestry could be.

Once the three of us were done eating, we all hiked the rest of the way back and returned to the hotel to freshen up. We checked out quickly after that, going back to the plane to prepare for our next stop.

47

JORDAN

Uruapan, Mexico, Present Day

When we landed again, this time at Uruapan International Airport, I grabbed Michael by the arm as we got off the plane. "Don't you think it's strange we haven't encountered any opposition? Especially since we're carrying the fourteenth sphere around? This seems too easy."

Our eyes met, then slowly shifted to the backpack Zadkiel was wearing. "Yes, I do," Michael said, "which is why we're setting a quick pace. Apparently, no one knows we were the ones to leave the gala with the sphere. So I think we need to get in and out of these key locations as fast as possible, especially now. Geneloom has several locations throughout Central America so, in a way, we're in enemy territory. Anyone could be working for them. We have to keep our guard up."

I nodded. "I'll let Sophia and Dane know."

We exited the airport and found a car for Gabriel, Chamuel, and the three of us to take to the hotel while the others flew ahead. We stayed on a main four-lane road, passing tiny stores and restaurants, and then the urban section of the city gave way to a more rural one.

Stepping out of the car, I was hit by a wave of humidity, the air thick with moisture. Sophia immediately pulled her mane of waves into a ponytail while I covered mine with a baseball cap.

Inside, we were quickly situated in a set of adjoining rooms. "Let's rest and start again in the morning," Zadkiel said. "We have to begin the hike early in the day because we don't want to be on the trail when it gets dark."

"You're starting to scare me with this hike," Dane confessed.

"Don't be scared. We just have to trek through the forest and across a lava field," the angel of teaching explained.

We all stared at him wide-eyed, even the other angels.

"Oh, yeah, don't worry about the lava field," Uriel commented sarcastically.

"It's not active," Zadkiel clarified.

"Still, I wonder if the kids should remain here with Chamuel and the rest of us fly in," Gabriel suggested.

"No," I said.

"Speak for yourself," Dane whispered.

But I was adamant. "I'm going." The whole part of the journey was experiencing it, not watching from the sidelines. The more I experienced, the more I'd learn, and then the more prepared I'd be for whatever was coming. My motives may not have made things easy, but they were valid.

The next morning, Chamuel stayed in the hotel again after Zadkiel had assured him another hike was in our future—this time more extensive and strenuous. Thankfully, the angel was almost healed, which was not only good because we needed all the manpower we could get but also because he obviously hated missing out on our excursions. When Gabriel had showed him the gemstone key, Chamuel had admired it for a few moments, turning it over in his hand and letting the light catch the stone so it glimmered and gleamed.

The rest of us took the bus from Uruapan to the beginning of the trail. There were a few people congregating around, preparing to make the trek in groups, either on foot or on horses, all of them with guides.

"Do we need one?" Dane asked.

Zadkiel shot him a look as if to say, *I am your guide.*

Dane held up his hands in surrender. "Just asking. I don't want to get lost."

"We won't get lost. Now let's go." Zadkiel set out, the rest of us following.

When we entered the forest, it wasn't as scary as Zadkiel had made it sound. There was a designated path to follow, marked with a border of wood. I did understand why he wanted to get back before dark, though. Even on the path, the forest at night was not a place I would want to get stuck.

Groups on horseback passed us, their steeds becoming skittish.

"Why couldn't we have ridden horses?" Sophia asked. "That would have been fun."

"Horses are uneasy around us," Raphael said. "It takes a lot to calm them down."

"Unless you're Uriel," Jophiel added. "He's the horse whisperer."

The group with the horses continued on the path while Zadkiel led us a different way.

"Shouldn't we follow them?" Dane asked, skeptical of Zadkiel's sense of direction.

"That's the long way. This is the short way," he explained. "Plus, the horses can't go across the lava field."

Sophia halted. "I'm really trying to be open-minded here and not to complain, but if the horses can't go over the lava field, should *we* be going over the lava field?"

Zadkiel sighed. "It's not active hot lava. It's just a landform from the previous eruption."

"That doesn't make it any better!" Dane exclaimed.

"The long way is fourteen miles. This way is only eight. Take your pick," he compromised.

"Let's do the lava field," I said, forging ahead of Zadkiel.

Laid out before us was a wasteland of black, ashy, uneven rock. And straight ahead loomed the dome of the steaming volcano. Now I stopped. "Zadkiel," I hissed, "I thought you said Paricutín was inactive."

He huffed. "It is."

"Then why is it steaming?"

"Because it's *a volcano*. Whether it's active or not, there are still things happening beneath the earth. I promise you, though, we will not be dealing with an eruption. And if we do, you have your own rescue helicopter in each of us."

Halfway across the lava field, my feet started to ache, mainly because of the uneven ground. When we finally reached the base of the volcano, I looked up at the steep hillside.

"It'll take about a half hour to get to the top," Zadkiel said. "The incline will be difficult terrain. Do you want to attempt the trek?"

"We came this far," Sophia said.

Midway, the three of us took a short break to pant and heave our breath in and out.

"Whose...genius...idea...was...this?" Dane wheezed.

Sophia and I looked at each other, wanting to place the blame on the other. Then we both said, "Ours."

"Maybe...we should...stop...here," Dane suggested.

Sophia shook her head. "No." She stepped forward and continued on.

Three of the angels were ahead of us while the three others were behind us, forming a protective circle even as we hiked. None of them seemed to be struggling, though, their bodies created and conditioned differently from ours. Once we finally made it to the top, the three of us collapsed on the ground, sweating and barely able to breathe. I chugged some water and tried to stabilize myself. Gazing out from our perch, I took in another breathtaking view. Forests covered every inch of the earth, and rolling hills and mountains spread out before us.

Caught up in where I was, I didn't realize Zadkiel and Jophiel had left until they were gone. I glanced down at the volcano, my mouth dropping open in shock as the two missing angels were levitating over a tree that was rooted a few feet down from the top of the volcano. Zadkiel seemed to be doing whatever Gabriel had done last time, placing his hand among the branches and drawing out a gemstone. Where exactly the stones came from was still a mystery, but I was sure we would find out soon enough. Right now, I was more concerned about the fact that their wings were out in public.

"Uh, shouldn't they be a little more cautious?" I asked.

"No one else is around," Michael said.

I scanned the hilltop. "Okay, but there are people down *there*," I said, pointing down the side of the volcano.

"They'll be done by the time those people make it to the top," Uriel said. "No one will see them."

Sure enough, Zadkiel and Jophiel were already flying toward us, gemstone retrieved. We all gathered around as they landed, and Zadkiel opened his hand. In his palm lay a purple square-cut amethyst.

"Wow." Sophia sighed. "It's so pretty."

Zadkiel smiled and, just as Gabriel had, reached into his pocket for a velvet pouch to safely secure the stone.

Dane leveled him with a menacing glance. "And now we go back?"

I placed a hand on his shoulder. "Don't try to find logic in the way we travel. There never is any."

"Besides," Zadkiel said, "we offered to come without you." He strode over to the other side of the volcano. "Going down is a lot more fun than coming up, though."

We followed him to the edge to see people sliding down through the black sand of the hillside.

"I'm game!" Dane said, sitting down on the volcano ledge.

My face brightened. "Race you!" I challenged, dropping down and sliding off.

"Hey! Wait for me!" Sophia and Dane yelled in unison.

The three of us glided down the hill so fast, it only took about two minutes. When we reached the bottom, we were filthy, black ashen sand caked to our clothes and faces. Still, the three of us couldn't stop laughing from the exhilaration of the moment.

48 SATAN

Bushmills, Northern Ireland, Present Day

When I opened my eyes, the first thing I saw was a card sitting on a bedside table that read, WELCOME TO THE SMUGGLERS INN. On it was a pirate with a hook for a hand.

Rolling over in the bed, I instantly screamed in pain. Hands latched on to my arms, turning me back onto my stomach. The pain slowly receded. I took a deep breath, bringing on a spasm of coughs.

I wiped the blood from my mouth and glanced over my shoulder at Abbadona. She watched me in horror, knowing full well I was deteriorating too fast. Especially now with my new injury.

"Where the hell are we?" I asked.

"Northern Ireland. In a town just a few miles from Giant's Causeway."

"Where are Leviathan and Beelzebub?"

"They're downstairs keeping watch." Abbadona stroked my bare shoulder. "You can't go on. We must return to Hell."

I laughed sardonically. "Then why did you bring me here?"

Her expression grew defensive. "Because if I had done what I had wanted to—bring you back to Hell and tear that amulet from your neck—you would have never forgiven me, and I would rather face your wrath than your scorn."

I quickly sat up and caressed her cheek, kissing her full on the lips. At first, she was surprised, but then she fell into the kiss, deepening it. There was enough passion between the two of us, I'm sure we could have gone on for hours if it hadn't been for my ill condition.

I needed to take a breath of air so I had to pull back, only to lose myself to a coughing fit yet again. When I stopped, I dropped my forehead to hers. "I'm sorry."

She stroked my neck. "Don't be."

"I had to do it. I had to kiss you before—"

She silenced me by putting a finger to my mouth. "Don't say it."

I gently pried her hand away. "Before I perish. We both know how this ends."

She adamantly shook her head. "There is a way. There is *always* a way."

"To what? Break a curse?"

Abbadona nodded.

"Well, I don't think Astrid was being very forgiving this time." I pulled away from her and tried to glance at my back. "How bad is it?"

She pursed her lips. "You can't fly. Aziza put multiple holes in your wings, and you're not healing." She turned my head back to look at her. "Let's get this stone and go back to Hell so we can take that amulet off you."

I nodded and stood up. Abbadona retrieved a new shirt for me and helped me get dressed, easing the garment around my wings. Feeling slightly more fortified, I grabbed my jacket, taking her hand in mine as we went downstairs.

Leviathan stood watch in the lobby, lounging in one of the chairs with a newspaper by the front door to blend in.

"Where's Beelzebub?" I asked him.

"In there." He pointed to the attached pub.

Nearing the entrance, the whole pub was singing an Irish tune. Beelzebub sat at the bar, pounding his fist on the bar top and singing at the top of his lungs.

I sighed and rolled my eyes. "Retrieve him."

Leviathan entered, walked up to the fallen angel, and pulled him away by the arm.

With our ragtag group reunited, we left the inn and headed to Giant's Causeway. Today, it was naturally gloomy, the sky gray and the clouds heavy. The sound of waves and seagulls filled my senses as we landed upon a clifftop. Beelzebub set me down, and I drew close to the edge, peering over at the basalt columns below. An army awaited us down there, Nephilim milling about the tourists with watchful eyes. Their hands lurked near their waistbands, ready to draw their weapons at the first sign of danger.

The Sentinel must have told Jazema the locations of my keys, and subsequently, she had dispatched a team of Nephilim to hinder my attempt at retrieving them. Meanwhile, the Triune seemed nowhere in sight, but they had miraculously appeared at Stonehenge so I wouldn't be surprised if they arrived at some point.

"What's the plan?" Leviathan asked.

Abbadona snaked down the path. "Free coffee and hot drinks in the café!" she yelled. "Get them while you can!"

The humans raced one another back up the cliff for the fake offer. The simple creatures were so predictable.

All that remained were the Nephilim. They drew their guns and pointed them at her.

I tensed and advanced forward, but Beelzebub grabbed my arm and hauled me back.

A figure, sitting in the middle of the stone formation, rose and faced Abbadona.

Lucifer.

I tried going down there again, but this time both Beelzebub and Leviathan restrained me.

"Did he send you after the disaster that was Stonehenge?" Lucifer asked Abbadona.

She didn't reply.

"Or is he here, alive? I'm guessing it's that because no one can retrieve the gemstone key but him."

"Neither." She drew closer to him. Every Nephilim followed her with their guns as she moved.

"Stop," Lucifer demanded.

Abbadona halted.

"What are you here for, then?"

She bowed low, her hand falling beneath her skirt. "To bestow my loyalty to you."

I smirked from my hiding spot. *Oh, she was good.*

Lucifer grinned. "Drop the guns."

They were lowered.

"Is that what you stole the river water for?" Abbadona asked, glancing at the guns. "To create the bullets Satan never would?"

"Yes." Lucifer examined her face. "You're a lot smarter than I thought you were. Certainly an asset."

She nodded, her hand slowly inching out from her dress. "The water I control," she said, smiling mischievously.

Lucifer blanched.

Abbadona moved fast as she drove a knife into Lucifer's foot, kicked him back into the sea, and raised her hands to stop the bullets.

Recognizing our cue, the three of us raced down the cliff, Beelzebub and Leviathan taking flight to meet the fight first. The Nephilim dropped their guns as the bullets turned to water in their chambers, Abbadona whispering some spell to reverse their creation. My fallen angels engaged the Nephilim in combat, fists ready and punches rolling.

The Nephilim had spent too long relying on guns instead of their physical prowess. My fallen angels had not.

I crept through the melee down to the rocks where Abbadona stood.

"This is it. The Wishing Chair." She indicated the spot where Lucifer had sat, a natural seat among the stones in the shape of a throne.

Ready to end this terrible adventure, I reached out my hand, only to be blindsided by a boot to the face. Spitting out blood, I glanced over my shoulder at a sopping-wet Lucifer.

He grinned and motioned me forward with a taunting gesture. I braced myself and rose from my knees, ready to face the fight even though I knew it would be my end. But Abbadona engaged him first, her staff swinging.

"I guess she fights your battles for you now!" Lucifer roared, dodging her blows.

"Just finish this!" she screamed at me, smacking him in the face.

While his taunts grated along my skin, I ignored them and listened to Abbadona. It was time to finish this.

Stumbling back to the Wishing Chair, I dropped to my knees and reached out to place my hand on the seat. Again, the stone thrummed beneath me and the gemstone key rose from the depths of the basalt stone until it sat gently upon the surface. I picked it up to observe the black square-cut onyx.

Raising my gaze, I saw a blade speeding through the air, end over end, its mark the fierce angel I had come to adore. Everyone thought the Devil couldn't love, couldn't feel. Yet, my entire existence had been built on pain—not just on enacting it but bearing the burden of it. And if I was forced to feel pain, then I sure as hell could feel other emotions, which is why my heart squeezed in my chest at the thought of losing Abbadona.

No! Not her!

I jumped off the rocks, down to the edge of the sea, pushing her out of the way as the cold metal tore through the skin of my chest.

"No!" Abbadona screamed, scrambling to my side. She lifted me in her arms, pulling the knife free and placing her hand over the wound. She was giving me her energy to heal, but I didn't want it.

Prying her hand free, I demanded, "Abbadona, stop! You need to summon a portal to get us out of here. We can deal with my wounds later."

She composed herself, pressed her fingers to the ground, and shouted, *"Inferos!"*

Thunder clapped through the sky as the portal to Hell was summoned. But rather than take me, it only took Abbadona and my two fallen angels. Lucifer had grabbed me before I could go through.

The thunder receded, and the portal closed, whisking away the only allies I had left. I collapsed to the ground as a bloody foot and a pair of painted toes appeared before my eyes.

"Let's end it," Lucifer suggested, drawing a knife.

"No." Jazema stayed his hand. "Let's take him back to the lab."

49 DANE

Rio de Janeiro, Brazil, Present Day

"What do you think about this one?" Sophia asked me, slinging a silk scarf around her neck. It was the third one she had tried on, and honestly, she looked beautiful in all of them.

"It's great," I said, scanning the street.

She pouted. "You didn't even look."

"Will you just make up your mind already?" Uriel blared.

Sophia glared at him. He crossed his arms and fell quiet.

I glanced at her, and my eyes widened. "That one. Get that one."

"You think?" She looked at herself in the small mirror the stall lady handed her, forgetting about Uriel.

Coming closer, I fingered the pale-blue silk. "Absolutely. Blue is your color."

God, how I wished I could draw her. Every inch. Every curve. Every shadow.

Our eyes met, and I dropped my hand. Looking at the stall lady, I asked, "How much?"

She told me the price, and I reached for my wallet.

"No way! You're not buying this for me," Sophia protested.

"Why not? I want to." I handed over the money.

Her eyes softened. "Thank you," she whispered. "Dane—"

"There she is again!" I exclaimed, cutting her off and moving past her.

"Who?" Uriel asked, turning around.

"The girl from the gala. I swear she's been following us through the market all day."

"Really? Maybe we should go back," Sophia suggested.

I nodded. "Let's find Jordan."

We retraced our steps through the market, the sun beating down on us.

After our slide down the side of the volcano in Mexico, we had trekked back through the forest, washed up at the hotel, and hopped on the plane, embarking to our next location, Rio de Janeiro.

Jophiel's gemstone key was hidden in Guanabara Bay, the giant harbor just northeast of the city. The angels had gone off this morning to find a boat and sent the three of us to the market. With Chamuel and Uriel as escorts, of course. Chamuel's leg had finally healed, but the others still wanted him to take it easy so he had been put on babysitting duty. Uriel had tagged along to take a break from carrying the backpack with the fourteenth sphere, but he obviously was annoyed with this task, too.

"There he is!" Sophia exclaimed.

Jordan was at a textile stall, arms full of fabric. Chamuel stood by his side, admiring the patterns Jordan was picking.

We approached them. "What are you doing?" I asked.

Jordan ignored me as he talked to the stall owner.

"He's buying fabric," Chamuel stated the obvious.

Sophia shrugged. "Yes, but why?"

"Why do you think?" Chamuel wiggled his eyebrows.

Sophia's face lit up, and she covered her mouth with her hands. "I thought he didn't like her," she whispered.

"Oh, he likes her," Chamuel assured Sophia.

"Can you please stop talking about me like I'm not here?" Jordan asked, turning away from the stall.

"Sorry," Sophia said. "I'm just really excited! You and Dafne are perfect!"

Jordan sighed. "Let's not talk about this."

"That's it!" I yelled, taking off through the market.

"Dane!" they all shouted, chasing after me, their feet making loud thumping sounds as they hit the pavement.

The raven-haired girl was back, and she was totally following us. As soon as she saw me coming, she turned tail and ran. I pushed and shoved my way through the crowd, trying to keep her in my line of sight. She was fast, so fast it was almost superhuman.

She skirted down a small side street, scaled the wall of a building, spread her brown speckled wings, and took flight.

Holy crap!

The others joined me, chests heaving.

"Did you see that?" I asked them.

Jordan nodded in shock.

"Yeah," Sophia said. "Better yet, I've seen her before, and not just at the gala. When I came out of that underground tunnel after Sister Helen was attacked—" her voice broke on the words but she regained her composure "—she was on the street staring at me."

"What does she want?" Jordan asked.

Sophia shrugged. "I'm not sure."

"I think it's time we leave," Uriel said.

The five of us walked back to the harbor, hoping the others had found a boat. Sure enough, they stood on the dock, preparing to embark.

"You've arrived just in time," Gabriel said. "What's wrong?"

We told them about the Nephilim girl.

"She had wings?" Jophiel asked. "Real, functional wings?"

"Yes," Chamuel confirmed.

"She must be descended straight from a Watcher," Michael said. "We better get going before more trouble finds us. Uriel, you're good with the bag?"

Uriel nodded, donning the backpack and pulling the straps tight. The Nephilim weren't following us for the angels' keys. They wanted the fourteenth sphere, and while I wasn't one-hundred-percent sure how they had found us, I suspected it had to do with Lilith. For all I knew, she was purposely leading everyone to us since it would improve her chances of being released.

Setting our worries about the girl aside, we all climbed into the boat.

"So where are we going?" Jordan asked.

"To a small island in the middle of the harbor," Jophiel said.

Chamuel stood behind the wheel. "I love driving a boat. It reminds me of my time in Venice. It's the only easy way to get around there," he commented, turning the key. The engine hummed to life. "The streets are a maze. Even a seasoned Venetian can get lost among them after a few glasses of wine. Besides," he added, "it's not much different from driving a car…usually."

"Boy, are we happy you're back," Uriel said. "Although, I think Martha's rubbing off on you with these wild tales."

Ignoring him, Chamuel raised the throttle and eased us out into the harbor. Jophiel got up from his seat and approached Chamuel's side, giving him directions to the island.

My hair whipped in the sea wind, something I was not particularly fond of since I meticulously styled it every morning. Sophia put her arm around my shoulder and said, "Smile!" I leaned in as she snapped a picture of us on her phone.

It really was a beautiful day to be out on the bay. The sky was clear with just a few fluffy clouds. The sea itself was a gradient of blue, the deepest depths a dark lapis and the shallow parts a light periwinkle. I reached into my bag for my sketchpad and jotted down the landscape around me.

"Have you done that everywhere we've been?" Jordan asked.

"Yep," I said, not taking my eyes off the paper.

Sophia touched my arm, and a zing of electricity shot through it. "It's wonderful."

I didn't know if she meant my drawings in general or how accurately I was capturing the scene around us. Either way, I said, "Thanks."

"Can I see?" Gabriel asked.

Surprised by his curiosity, I showed it to him.

"It's beautiful. You have a true gift," he said. "And trust me when I say that. I've seen more pieces created by angels than anyone else, and your talent surpasses theirs."

"Wow…thank you." My face heated, a little embarrassed. No one had ever praised my artistry like that before.

We sped through the water for a few moments longer before slowing down near a tiny island—so tiny, in fact, that there was absolutely nothing on it except for some trees. It probably didn't even have a name.

"Can we come this time?" Jordan asked. "I want to see the key retrieval up close, and it was impossible to do that before."

"Sure," Jophiel said.

After storing my sketchpad, I hopped off the boat with the others. We followed Jophiel to an outcropping of trees where he stopped abruptly. He crouched down in front of a patch of vine, placing his hand among the leaves.

"The keys aren't always in the trees themselves," the angel explained. "But rather rise up from the earth or through a rock. Either way, the keys are hidden in the natural elements of this world and sense our celestial energy when we arrive. Right now, I feel a thrum in my hand. That's the thrum of the Earth. It's the thrum of energy and life."

A beam of light appeared, tracing a symbol in thin air.

"What's that?" Sophia asked in pure fascination and awe.

"That is the ogham rune for Vine, my Celtic astrology symbol. They're very similar to the zodiac symbols, except these are based on a medieval Irish language rather than the language of the stars." He withdrew his hand from the vine and unfurled his fist. Inside his palm sat a yellow oval-cut citrine. Jophiel smiled at the looks on our faces. "It's truly extraordinary what the Earth can do, if only we would cherish it and allow it to take its natural course."

Jophiel took a velvet pouch from his pocket and placed the gemstone inside. We stood up and walked back to the boat.

"Success?" Uriel asked.

Jophiel held up the pouch. "Success."

That was, until the raven-haired girl swooped down and snatched Uriel by the backpack.

Michael immediately launched into the air after her, followed by the others. Jordan, Sophia, and I just stood there, stunned. Panic rose in my chest as I tried to figure out what had happened. That girl must have had a death wish, taking on six archangels by herself.

50 MICHAEL

Rio de Janeiro, Brazil, Present Day

The air was hot and dry as I flew through the sky, the humidity thick on my skin. My eyes were trained on the Nephilim girl as she soared on feathery wings with Uriel in her clutches. My brother was loudly cursing as his wings were trapped beneath the backpack. He could do nothing more than try to pry her fingers off, a hard task when she was looming above him out of reach.

Swooping down, I collided with the girl. She let go of Uriel as we free-fell through the air, doing everything in her power to beat the crap out of me—swinging punches, kicking ribs, pulling hair, even biting fingers.

Finally, I let her go before we hit the water. She rocketed back into the air, pursuing Uriel again. Except this time, he had freed himself from the backpack and was clutching it to his chest.

Gabriel was the next to trail her, the rest of us close behind, following her erratic movements as she tried to lose us in the sky. Unfortunately for her, there were no clouds to hide behind or zip through. That would have been the easiest way to evade us.

Then a slight breeze swept along the bay, and the girl used it to her advantage, spanning out her wings and letting the small gust increase her speed. It allowed her to surge through the sky, closing the distance between her and Uriel in seconds. She grabbed hold of the bag again, but this time they fought over it. Unlike me, who had been hesitant to harm the girl, Uriel had no qualms doling out a few punches and kicks. They dropped altitude fast, more focused on fighting than flying.

Suddenly, the girl swung the bag, both of them letting go as Uriel went plummeting into the ocean. She smiled viciously and swooped down to seize the backpack before it could sink into the watery depths.

The others chased after her, and I followed once I saw Uriel surface and climb aboard the boat with Chamuel and the kids.

I refocused on the situation at hand. This girl had been calculated in her attack. Now we needed to be, as well.

I drew close to Gabriel's side. He snapped his attention to me. "Fly around this rocky hill, and attack her from the front. We'll keep pursuing from behind. We need to catch her off guard to get the bag back."

Nodding, he broke away from the group.

Raphael, Jophiel, and Zadkiel followed my lead as we flanked her on either side, converging together in the air to form a square, one that gradually grew smaller and smaller in size until all four of us had her trapped in the middle with nowhere to go.

She was about to burst through a small gap in front when Gabriel approached from that direction. Panicking, she threw the bag up in the air and dropped low.

I snatched the bag and searched inside, knowing she wouldn't have given up that easily. Sure enough, she had taken the sphere.

"Zadkiel, Jophiel, stay in the sky!" I commanded. "Gabriel, Raphael, follow me!"

We dived for the rocky hill she seemed to be moving toward. Since she had a head start, she landed on the ground and ran for the cover of the trees. The three of us followed her into the forest. The cool shade was a pleasant change from the hot sun and humid air, but I hardly took notice, my mind too focused on getting the sphere back.

I'd known it was ridiculous to bring it with us, but we couldn't leave it at the house. That would have forced us to split up, and we couldn't do that, either. I had debated holding off on retrieving the keys until we figured out what to do with the fourteenth sphere, but the only idea Zadkiel had was to return it to Heaven, which was just not possible as none of us had a way of going back. Either the Seraphim would have to come to us or we would have to be summoned by them, and trying to convince them would only take more time, time we didn't have. So there was no point delaying our journey.

I was determined to protect the sphere from falling into the wrong hands, but after this, seeing how easy it was for someone to take it from us, I was starting to wonder if destroying it was the best option. But we had to get it back before we could consider doing that.

It was hard to tell what direction the girl had gone as there were no broken branches or footprints to give us clues. Clearly, her Nephilim skills were kicking in since she covered her tracks so masterfully.

We remained quiet, slowly easing deeper into the forest. It wasn't big so I would search the whole thing if I had to, and if she decided to take to the sky again, my intent was that Zadkiel and Jophiel could intercept her.

We came upon a small stream and decided to let it guide us through the trees. It was there that the girl chose to reveal her secret hiding place as she dropped down from one of the trees and brought Raphael to the ground. They wrestled in the stream as she tried to wound our brother with a sharp knife. He gripped her hand forcefully, attempting to immobilize her.

I came from behind and grabbed her by the back of collar, pulling her off Raphael. She kept swiping the knife at nothing.

"Will you give up already?" I shouted. "You're outnumbered!"

She sheathed her knife in the holster she wore on her thigh and suddenly twisted around, jabbing the pressure point in my shoulder with her fingers.

The sharp pain in my arm forced me to release her. She kicked me in the abdomen, sending me flying to the dirt. She turned to get away but not before Gabriel swung the biggest tree branch I had ever seen and blindsided her. It sent her sprawling to the ground.

He threw the branch aside and bent down to retrieve the sphere from her small backpack.

She blinked a few times and raised herself up. "I will never stop! Geneloom will never stop! Now that I know you are the ones who have the fourteenth sphere, we will not let you rest!"

Even though her speech held strength, she no longer did. She tried getting to her feet but collapsed a few times. Gabriel probably had given her a concussion.

"What do we do with her?" Raphael asked.

I turned to look at my brothers and sighed. "I don't know."

"We can't let her go back," Gabriel said. "She's right. No one knew we left the gala with the sphere. If she returns and tells them, we'll have everyone on our backs."

"So what do you want to do? Keep her?" I asked. "That won't be easy."

"Guys," Raphael said wearily. "I don't think it's an issue anymore."

Gabriel and I brought our attention back to the girl, but she was gone. It was as if she had disappeared into thin air, not making a single sound.

Great. The one moment we were finally ahead of everyone, and we blew it.

I rubbed a hand over my face. We couldn't stop now. We had to finish what we started and deal with the consequences.

"At least we have the sphere," I said. "Now let's get back to the others."

The three of us rejoined Zadkiel and Jophiel and then headed back to the plane. By the time we returned, it was already evening.

I placed the sphere inside the backpack and paused, wondering again if I should just destroy it. It would be the easy way to handle things—smash it right now and let all our worries go away.

Unfortunately, angels never did anything the easy way.

51 DANE

Rio de Janeiro, Brazil, Present Day

As we clambered onto the boat, Uriel fell through the sky with the girl, the two wrestling each other for the backpack. Clever and keen, the girl let go, the bag soaring through the air and Uriel crashing into the water. She swiftly glided after it, snatching it from the air and racing off as the other angels pursued her.

"Follow them!" Jordan yelled.

Chamuel shook his head. "It's my job to keep you safe so I'm taking you back to the plane. Besides, we'll never be able to trail them. Aerial chases are full of haphazard movements that are impossible to follow in a boat."

Spewing water, Uriel surfaced and cursed. "Damn girl!" He swam over to us and climbed aboard, shaking out his feathers.

"Hey! Watch it," I said, droplets splashing all over me.

Sophia's brow furrowed. "Aren't you going back?"

"Not if I don't get my wings dry," Uriel said. "It's too hard to fly with wet wings."

"So water is your kryptonite?" I asked.

"I said *hard*, not impossible," Uriel clarified.

Chamuel lifted the throttle and turned the boat around.

"Seriously?" Jordan shouted, frustrated. "You're taking us back?"

"Unless you'd like to sprout some wings and go after them," Chamuel joked.

Jordan grew quiet, ending the argument. I marveled, yet again, at how I came to be on an adventure with actual archangels.

At the dock, Chamuel returned the boat to its owner and thanked him for allowing us to use it. Then he herded us back to the plane like a mother hen. Uriel came with us, not wanting to leave Chamuel alone if we were attacked. "We may have our differences, but I'll always have his back," Uriel told us. "We're brothers."

We waited on the plane for the others to return. Sophia read a book, and I sketched while Jordan paced the length of the aisle, doing a poorer job hiding his worry than the rest of us.

"Looks like Gabriel's rubbing off on you," Uriel said.

Jordan stopped. "You're not concerned they're not back yet?"

"Of course I am," Uriel stated bluntly. "But my job right now is to make sure you three survive."

"Speaking of which," Chamuel added, "I'm going out to grab you all some food. I'll be back soon."

Jordan huffed and finally sat down.

About an hour later, Chamuel came back with bauru sandwiches, rice, and roasted vegetables. The three of us ate in silence, mainly because Sophia and I knew Jordan was anxious and nothing we said would take his mind off the angels.

Night fell, and they still hadn't returned.

"What if they're hurt?" Jordan exploded just as the plane door opened.

The five angels strode onboard in various states of dishevelment—some dirty, some bruised, some wet.

"Did you get it?" Uriel asked.

Michael placed the backpack down and collapsed in a seat. "Yes."

"Who was that girl?" Sophia asked.

"Beats me. She's strong, though, and it was like she completely vanished into thin air," Raphael observed.

"She'll be back," I assured him. "I saw the gleam of excitement in her eye. She revels in the chase. She probably took the bag just to taunt you and test the waters."

"Regardless," Michael said, "we have to be on our guard more than ever. This was just the beginning of their attacks now that they know for sure that we have the sphere. I can feel it."

In the short time I had known him, I had learned to listen to Michael's gut instincts, because everything he'd had a "feeling" about so far had been right.

I said a silent prayer and continued sketching.

52 JORDAN

Victoria Falls, Zimbabwe, Present Day

Putting our setback in Brazil behind us, we were all determined to finish our mission. Jophiel resumed his role as pilot, taking off into the night and commencing our flight to Africa.

Raphael's stone was next, hidden at Victoria Falls, one of the largest waterfalls on Earth. Jophiel landed us in the city of Livingstone, and we took a helicopter to the town of Victoria Falls. I was a little uneasy about boarding the helicopter ever since Martha had told me that's how my uncle had died. So even though the ride gave us a fantastic aerial view of the immense waterfall, I was tense the whole time.

"That's Devils Pool!" the pilot shouted to us.

I looked down at a spot where the cascading waters fell over a steep cliff. A rainbow hovered over it from the refraction of light against the moisture in the air.

What a fitting name, since the steep drop looked like it could take you right into the pits of Hell.

When we got off the helicopter, I took a moment to let out a sigh of relief, followed by a huge yawn as jet lag started to set in.

"Don't!" Sophia complained. "Yawning's contagious." She twisted her mouth around, fighting the urge to yawn, too.

Once we found a hotel and got some rooms, we settled in for the evening. Between our exhaustion and the angels' disappointment, we all needed a fresh start.

In the morning, we ate breakfast and met the angels outside the hotel.

"So is the gemstone key actually hidden in the falls?" I asked.

"Not too far down," Raphael said, "but definitely submerged in the waters."

"Meaning we can't go with you," Sophia said.

Raphael shook his head. "Not for the key retrieval."

"We rented this safari car for the day, though," Zadkiel said. "That way, no one has to hike."

"Over the flat plains of Africa?" Dane chimed in. "That would have been easy."

Zadkiel laughed at his grumpiness.

Gabriel sat behind the wheel, ready to depart, so we all climbed inside. The drive to Victoria Falls was pleasant. As Dane had noted, the terrain was flat, the plains spread out before us with plenty of bushy foliage and trees. I was glad to get back to the place where my mission trip would have been. On my previous excursion, when I had first met Raphael, it had been so tempting to just stay here and explore the continent and help its people. Back then, we had been attacked by the Fallen so our time here was cut short more than any of us would have liked. Even now, I couldn't say we would be staying long, but at least we were back.

The road we were on skirted the waterfall, and I tried to catch a glimpse of it through the trees. It wasn't until we came around a bend that the falls stood before us in plain view. It had been amazing to see the waters from the sky, but it was an entirely different feeling to have them only a few feet away from you. You could hear the gush and rush of water, feel the force of the falls, see the rainbow right before you, smell the scent of mist, and taste the salty air in your mouth. Seeing sights like these made you appreciate the beauty of Earth, made you feel connected to its energy.

Raphael and Uriel exited the car. "We'll be back."

"Good luck!" Sophia called after them.

"We'll watch out for the girl," Michael assured them.

He and Gabriel slipped out of the vehicle, too, keeping watch over land and sky while Raphael and Uriel went to the waterfall's edge and disappeared over the side. Since Victoria Falls was so large, there were numerous spots where people could stop and gaze upon the wondrous sight. We had chosen one of the seemingly deserted areas so as not to attract any attention.

I braced my hand on the car door latch, ready to open it.

"Where are you going?" Zadkiel asked.

I frowned. "Out there. To see the waterfall."

He shook his head. "Everyone stays here. We have to contain the risk."

"I'll just be a sec," I said in disbelief, leaving the car.

"Jordan, come back here!" Zadkiel yelled, following me.

I reached into my pocket for my phone so I could snap a picture when I was completely swept off my feet and into the air. Thinking it was some kind of cruel joke, I said, "That's enough, Zadkiel! I get it!"

But looking up, I didn't see my friend. I saw the venomous gaze of the raven-haired girl.

"Jordan!" I heard my name screamed from the earth below.

She held me beneath my arms, soaring higher and higher—far higher than I would have liked to go outside an airplane. I looked down, my stomach roiling into knots. On my last trip with the angels, I was constantly dealing with bouts of motion sickness; however, I had never traveled much prior to that. Since then, I had gotten more accustomed to traveling, but nothing had prepared me for this. The Nephilim girl looped around the sky, making me dizzy. Then she erratically starting weaving through the air to avoid the pursuit of the angels coming to my rescue. She was purely taunting them now by capturing me.

She started to descend, low over the treetops of the rainforest, suddenly dropping me among the trees. I was thankful to be on the ground, so much so I didn't realize where she had released me.

Glancing over my shoulder, I saw the familiar outline of a hell-hound. I scrambled to my feet only to see five more. She let out a whistle as she flew off, signaling them to attack.

I booked it through the jungle, jumping over fallen branches and ducking beneath low-hanging vines. Somehow, one of the hounds had circled around in front of me because one jumped at me head-on, sending me tripping over my feet and sliding down a hill.

And this time it wasn't fun. It was bumpy and rough.

At the bottom was a river of shallow water. I jumped up and ran through the water, my feet splashing and shoes getting soaked through. The hounds paused briefly to sniff the river, ensuring that it wasn't holy water they were about to cross, and then came bounding after me. I guessed my trick of getting wet to prevent their chase was a myth since they kept coming.

The more I ran, the more I realized where I was going: right toward the falls.

Across from me, on solid land, was the car and my friends. All that remained between us was Devils Pool.

They must have noticed me—who wouldn't when I was making such noise?—and started yelling my name again. I was running out of land, but there was no stopping. It looked like I was going over the falls. The angels saw me, I knew they saw me, and they would certainly come rescue me the moment I jumped. I swallowed, praying I was right.

Zadkiel and Jophiel seemed to deduce my intent, for they leaped out of the car and surged into the air.

When I neared the edge, I didn't miss a beat, and I sailed over the side, free-falling through the mist. One of the hellhounds stopped just at the edge, its jaws snapping. On my way down, I thought I passed Raphael and Uriel because I could distinctly hear Uriel curse.

And while all these angels knew I was falling, I had yet to be saved.

Closing my eyes, I tried to succumb to my fate. It had been my own stupid decision.

Until a side swipe knocked the breath out of me and I opened my eyes again to find I was rising through the air.

This time, when I looked up, Gabriel's amber eyes met mine, yet they held a note of anger in them.

"I'm sorry!" I yelled through the wind.

"What were you thinking?"

"Operation Free Fall," I joked. He grimaced. It was a little too soon apparently.

We landed a few feet in front of the car, and the moment Gabriel released me, I dropped to my knees and vomited in a bush. Too many aerial maneuvers for one day.

Lifting my head, I saw the raven-haired girl swooping down again, but this time at Gabriel. "Watch out!" I yelled.

She tackled Gabriel to the ground, the two of them rolling through the dirt. It seemed like she wanted revenge for some reason because she kept bashing him in the head.

Before he could do anything, Sophia came running past me and leaped at the girl, pushing her off Gabriel. Now they wrestled in the dirt, and to my surprise, Sophia landed a few punches, moving with a quickness I didn't realize she possessed.

Sophia kicked her, and the girl clawed at Sophia's face, but Sophia dodged the sharp nails as the rest of us drew closer to the fight. Instead of retaliating, the girl launched into the air and took off.

After a moment, Sophia composed herself and helped Gabriel up.

Michael landed near us and came to investigate. When he saw me sitting on the ground, he released a breath. "Oh, thank the Heavens. I lost you in the jungle, and then I saw the hounds retreat. I thought they got you."

"No, I'm here," I said.

"We did see you jump over the falls, right? That wasn't my imagination?" Uriel asked.

I nodded. "Yes, you did."

"You what?" Michael exclaimed.

"Jumped over the falls," I verified. "Poor decision, I've come to realize."

"When would it ever be a good decision?" Michael barked back.

"You still haven't taught me what to do when I encounter a hellhound, so give me a break. I improvised!"

"You were told to stay in the car," the angry angel countered. "If you had done as we asked, you wouldn't have needed to fight off the hellhounds or kamikaze yourself over the edge of the waterfall."

I opened my mouth to argue, then snapped it shut. He had a point. How could I explain I had only wanted a picture of the natural wonder when so much was at stake?

"Does anyone care to see the gemstone?" Raphael asked, switching subjects.

"I do!" Dane and Sophia said together.

I joined them to admire the green rectangular-cut emerald. Raphael slipped it inside his velvet pouch and placed it in his pocket.

We all climbed back in the car, and I suddenly could feel all the celestial energy radiating through it. And I didn't mean the angels. With the fourteenth sphere and now four gemstone keys, the force was so strong it was noticeable. At least for me.

As we drove down the road, I couldn't help but think about how much we had accomplished in such a short amount of time. Another gemstone retrieved and only three more to go.

53 Satan

Location Unknown, Present Day

I had fallen into darkness, this time one I'd thought would be more permanent, except my eyes were opening again. Angels didn't typically lose consciousness, so I figured my sudden ability to do so was on account of Astrid's curse. But instead of waking up in a bed with Abbadona at my side, I woke up with my head resting against my chest and my hands chained to the wall. By now, Lucifer and Jazema must have known my Hellfire was gone because someone had to touch me to chain me here.

I pulled on my bonds, testing their strength—or possibly my strength since I could barely pull them taut. The wound on my chest from Jazema's knife was still bleeding slowly. Abbadona had done enough to ease the flow, but eventually, it would end me if it wasn't treated. And I highly doubted anyone here was going to help me.

I looked around at the cell I was being held in. It was a fancy, sterile white one with clear walls, like a fish tank where I could be observed.

Outside my bubble, I could tell there was a more expansive lab since I saw a handful of people walk past, one carrying files, another pushing a cart with vials. I sat back against the wall, wondering if

Abbadona, Leviathan, and Beelzebub had made it back to Hell, and if so, what had lain in wait for them there. At least they could assemble reinforcements and prepare before Lucifer came back and attacked.

A beeping noise sounded, and a door to my left opened. I glanced over to see Lucifer, Jazema, and another woman enter the room.

"So this is our Lord Satan," the mysterious woman said.

I flounced my hands and made a bowing gesture from where I sat on the floor. "Yours truly," I rasped.

"I'm Penelope. I don't believe we've met."

I ignored her and gazed at her bare arm, reading the angelic script branded there. My eyes trailed to Jazema, doing the same with her exposed skin.

Chuckling and wheezing at the same time, I said, "Well shit. You're not Nephilim. You're Watchers."

"Why do you think I kept telling you to ally with them?" Lucifer sneered.

"Lucifer." Jazema placed a hand on his arm. "He's not worth it."

It compelled him into silence.

I shook my head. "And you were taunting me about who fights my battles."

Lucifer launched himself at the glass between us, furious. "Let me in there! I want to make him pay! Especially now without his Hellfire!"

"I don't think so," Penelope said. "If you can't control yourself, I suggest you leave."

"Besides, why beat a cat when they're down?" I teased. "Our battle would be much better if I were at my full strength."

"You haven't been at your full strength since a snake bit you in the hand," Jazema said. "I'm surprised you don't resent Lilith like everyone else does. I mean, she stole the most from you."

"Who says," I slurred, fighting the sudden effects of Astrid's curse and forcing myself to keep my eyes open, "I don't resent Lilith?"

"Fine. Maybe you do. Maybe we have a common enemy. But it doesn't change anything," Jazema said.

"What…do you want?"

Jazema grinned. "I already got what I want." She opened her palm to show me my keys—the two I had just retrieved myself.

I weakly tried to fling myself at the glass.

She laughed at me. They all did.

No. This couldn't be happening. Everything that was supposed to give me leverage, give me power, was gone. My stake in the prophecy was lost. I had no more bargaining chips.

As my eyes slid shut, I desperately wished I would be taken away into oblivion.

54 JORDAN

Queensland, Australia, Present Day

Our next stop was Australia, which meant we had to endure a terribly long flight. Unlike the last time I had been there, though, there was no ridiculous eighteen-hour drive across the Australian outback to follow. This journey was actually much more pleasant. I think being in our own plane helped a lot since we weren't crammed in a cabin full of strangers and we could walk about if we wanted. Of course, I realized how uncommon a situation that was. I was just appreciative to experience it at least once.

We flew into the Hamilton Island Airport on a small island off the coast of Queensland near the Great Barrier Reef. That was our precise reason for being here since Chamuel's gemstone key was hidden inside one of the coral reefs.

"Heart Reef, to be precise," he had told us, which was a coral reef that had naturally formed into the shape of a heart.

Once we landed, we found a hotel and took a short nap since we had arrived around 6:00 AM. With a few hours of much-needed rest in us, Dane, Sophia, and I were ready to assist the angels in any way we could. Which was hardly at all. They had already found a boat for us to use and had rented scuba gear to make the dive into the water.

I boarded the boat and found a place to sit and enjoy the view. Clear, aqua-blue water spanned out before us, and I couldn't wait to be in the middle of it to see all the fish and other sea creatures. We never knew when danger would strike so I didn't want to miss an opportunity to enjoy the beauty of the world while I could.

Gabriel came over and slipped a life vest over my head.

"Why do I need this? I didn't in Brazil."

"That was different. We didn't know we would be attacked by a freakish Nephilim girl, you weren't jumping off cliffs, and quite honestly, I hadn't thought about it."

He stepped away from me and did the same to Dane and Sophia.

At least, I wasn't getting special treatment.

Chamuel stood at the helm dressed in a diving suit. He pushed up on the throttle, and we zipped out into the ocean. Heart Reef was about thirty-seven miles from where we were so I settled into the ride and marveled at the sea below.

When the boat slowed, I noticed Jophiel putting on some diving gear.

"You know how to dive, too?" I asked him.

He nodded. "I've saved countless artifacts this way."

While the angels certainly preferred old-school methods, they had adapted exceptionally well to modern means, especially in the jobs they had held in their time on Earth.

Chamuel anchored the boat and gave everyone a warning. "Do not touch the anchor, do not touch the wheel, do not touch *anything* until I return."

"We have absolutely no inclination to do any of those things," Michael assured him. "Right, Jordan?" he added.

"Just because I decided to jump off a waterfall, all of a sudden I'm untrustworthy?"

They all stared at me in silence.

"I promise I won't do anything stupid," I vowed.

"Good." Chamuel smiled, then sat on the edge of the boat and strapped on a tank. Jophiel sat next to him ready to go. They inserted their mouthpieces and leaned back, falling into the sea.

I watched as they sank below the surface and began to swim through the water. Looking down, I could see the coral reefs, the colorful structures creating a beautiful rainbow. There were plenty of fish, too, big and small, as well as giant clams, sea anemones, and best of all…

"Sea turtles!" I exclaimed.

"Where?" Sophia asked.

She and Dane ran over to me, and I pointed at the water. Sophia and I admired two turtles as they swam by.

Dane, on the other hand, was looking over his shoulder. "Uh… who are they?"

Sophia and I followed his gaze. Michael had, too.

There was a speedboat heading our way—fast. I knew we were in trouble as soon as I saw it, but when bullets started flying, there was no question.

Gabriel grabbed the three of us and pushed us to the floor of the boat, shielding us with his body. The other angels took cover, Michael being the first to chance it. He rose, clearly intending to launch into the air, but a bullet flew at him and lodged his arm. He hissed in pain and dropped low again.

Grimacing, he said, "This isn't good."

Raphael inspected his wound. "Hold still."

"I can't! It hurts!" Michael winced.

"Really?" Zadkiel asked. "Bullets don't normally hurt us that much."

"It feels like it's stinging through my skin," Michael explained.

Raphael quickly grabbed a set of surgical tweezers and removed the bullet from Michael's arm. "That's because they're not normal bullets."

"Is Geneloom making angel-killing weapons now?" Zadkiel asked.

"Yes, and we have every intention of wiping you all out," said the Nephilim girl, who had raised our anchor and now kicked the throttle forward. She stretched her wings and flew into the air as the boat took off unmanned.

Uriel scrambled forward, grabbing the wheel and lowering the speed. "Why did the sailor have to be the one with the aquatic wonder? Separating operator and boat is such a bad idea!" He clutched the wheel and tried to bring us to a stop, but it wasn't working. "I don't know what I'm doing!"

Zadkiel ran over to assist, but all he did was speed up the boat again.

"You're not helping!" Uriel complained.

"I read a boating manual once," Zadkiel defended.

Uriel pressed his lips into a firm line. "What, from the eighteenth century?"

The other boat full of Nephilim had taken our place, trying to trick Chamuel and Jophiel into thinking our boat was still there.

"We need to go back!" I shouted. "The others are in danger!" As we'd learned, it didn't take the angels long to recover the keys so Chamuel and Jophiel would be surfacing any minute.

Gabriel turned to me, placing his hands on my shoulders. "Promise me you'll stay on the boat."

"I promise. Now go!"

He and Michael took off, ambushing the Nephilim. I could hear shots being fired and hoped none of them had hit their mark.

Sophia came to Uriel's and Zadkiel's aid, opening the glove box and finding the operator's manual. *"Step one,"* she read, *"put the key in the ignition."*

Uriel cried, "Oh, Lord in Heaven! You're just like him! Can we skip to step fifteen, please?"

"She's trying to help," Zadkiel defended.

While the three of them bickered, Dane and Raphael were quietly assembling a weapon. They had taken Raphael's knife and attached it to a flagpole, mimicking a harpoon. "What are you going to use that for?" I asked.

"To strike the Nephilim girl the next time she comes flying around," Dane said.

I looked at Raphael. Violence of this kind wasn't something he usually condoned. "We need to defend ourselves," he justified.

Glancing up, I saw Chamuel and Jophiel surfacing right into the middle of a gunfight. We were out of time so I made another rash decision. I dashed to the steering wheel, avoided the three of them who were fighting over the instruction manual, and gunned the throttle. The boat shot forward, knocking them to the deck.

"What are you doing?" Sophia screamed.

"Saving them!" I steered the boat into the Nephilim one. Everyone on both decks was jolted. So much so that I fell into the water.

My act created the perfect distraction, though, allowing Gabriel and Michael to disarm a few Nephilim.

Chamuel and Jophiel swam over to our boat, and Raphael and Uriel helped them onboard while Zadkiel and Sophia fished me out of the water.

I was back on deck only for a few seconds when Dane started aiming his makeshift harpoon. "Here she comes!" he warned. "Chamuel, take cover!"

The angel barely had time to take his tank off before the Nephilim girl swooped at him. He dodged her and hit the deck. Dane patiently waited, trailing the girl with his eyes, analyzing her moves before he made his. I had never realized how cunning and calculating he could be, but in that moment, wicked determination was written all over his face.

He locked in on his target and threw the harpoon through the air. It landed exactly where he'd intended it to, not hitting her body but tearing her wing.

She fell from the sky and landed in the water with a splash.

Gabriel and Michael flew back over to our boat. "Do you have the key?" they asked in unison.

Chamuel shouted, "Yes!" and gunned the boat in reverse, separating our boat from the Nephilim's.

"There was a reverse?" Uriel shouted in exasperation.

Sophia slapped the manual at him. "Page forty-five. That's what you get for skimming."

When the two boats detached, it left a gaping hole in theirs. The boat slowly sank, but we zipped off without a backward glance knowing there was no way the Nephilim could overtake us, even if they swam the thirty-seven miles to shore.

We rode back to the dock in silence, exhaustion taking its toll.

Gabriel sat next to me, examining my wet hair. "I thought I told you to stay on the boat."

"I did! I fell off!"

"After crashing it into the other one," Gabriel admonished.

"I was trying to help. They needed our help. *You* needed our help."

"I know," Gabriel conceded, "which is why I want to thank you." He looked at Sophia and Dane. "All of you."

Despite the danger, they beamed under his gratitude.

When Chamuel returned the boat and diving gear, we had to pay a large fine for the damage. Since I was the one who had crashed it, I'd insisted on paying it myself.

Afterward, we all gathered around on the dock so he could show us his gem. It was rose quartz in the shape of a heart.

"How perfect for the angel who loves to take care of others," Sophia said, giving him a side hug.

He returned the gesture. "I couldn't agree more."

55

JORDAN

Lukla, Nepal, Present Day

When Uriel had told us his natural wonder was Mount Everest, my mind hadn't fully registered what that meant. When he told us again after leaving Australia, I flat-out laughed because I thought it was a joke. But it wasn't. I immediately grew serious, knowing the journey to the peak was perilous, and us mere humans were nowhere near conditioned for it.

"Obviously, you can't come," he told Sophia, Dane, and me.

We nodded in agreement. None of us had any desire to make that trek. Many climbers never came back.

"I'll be flying up. Raphael is coming with me, just in case anything happens."

I knew he wasn't worried about attackers as much as he was worried about sustaining an injury during the journey.

And it was our hope, at least, that the next time the Nephilim attacked us, it would be someplace the angels had more control.

Jophiel landed the plane at Tenzing-Hillary Airport in Lukla, the closest town nearest the mountain. We found lodging at Yeti Mountain Home and settled in since we would be there a few days. Although

Uriel and Raphael were flying, the journey to the peak could still take longer than most key retrievals, as they would have to deal with the changing climate.

The two angels, bundled in warm clothes, hiked out of town on foot. They'd duck out of sight once they found a secluded area. I was worried about them, though. I think we all were, but apparently, no one wanted to voice their concerns.

Luckily, the hotel provided lots of amenities to keep us occupied throughout the day, like a library, greenhouse, and museum. There were also some yoga sessions, which Sophia really enjoyed. It was one remedy Chamuel had suggested for her to relieve the stress of her past trauma.

In addition to enjoying the indoor activities, there was a lot to appreciate outdoors, too. The hotel was surrounded by sweeping forests and, of course, the snowcapped mountains of Everest and other tall points in the distance. The whole setting was serene and quiet, a welcome atmosphere after the adrenaline-filled, heart-pounding adventures we'd just had.

Dane spent most of his time outside with Jophiel, enjoying the scenic material around him and conveying its beauty on paper. His art was truly fantastic, and he seemed to thrive when he was out in nature.

Two days had passed since Uriel and Raphael had left. I was nervous that something had happened to them, but I tried to be optimistic. Sophia did a good job distracting us by sharing her interpretations of the prophecies again—this time the Union of the Spheres. The angels and I had guessed at some of its meaning already, but Sophia was convinced she, Dane, and I had a part in it.

"I know these two prophecies are connected, and I *know* we're involved," she kept saying, staring at the printouts.

"Sophia, no matter how many times you say it, it won't make the meaning magically appear," I told her.

She read it over again. "I still think it's the three of us. It's like some kind of feeling or intuition I have."

Dane and I shrugged as we continued our game of cards. All of us were seated in the lounge near the hotel entrance. When the door creaked open, none of us looked up because we had grown used to visitors, other guests, and staff walking through. It wasn't until I heard, "They didn't even miss us," that my head snapped up.

Uriel and Raphael stood in the doorway, covered in snow and ice.

We all jumped up and welcomed them back, drawing them closer to the fire in the hearth.

They thawed out their hands and feet, describing all that had happened on their journey.

"The wind was rough—cold, icy, whipping. It was hard to fly in any one direction without getting lost," Uriel said.

"And we saw so many people out there hiking on this minuscule path. I don't understand why anyone would want to do that. There's no fun in it," Raphael commented.

"So…?" Sophia asked.

Uriel anticipated her question and drew out the gemstone. It was a rectangular-cut ruby.

"These never cease to amaze me," Sophia said. "Each one is so unique."

"They are pretty cool," Dane admitted.

"And we only have one left." I wiggled my eyebrows at Michael.

56 SATAN

Location Unknown, Present Day

A few days had probably passed, so I wasn't sure why I hadn't died by now. I was more than ready to drift off.

The door to my left opened, and Jazema walked in. She stopped next to Lucifer, who had remained in the room the entire time, staring at me, and asked him, "Have you really stayed here watching him?"

"I want to have the satisfaction of seeing him die," he told her.

"What did you do to him that's making it take so long?" she demanded.

"I did nothing," Lucifer said. "It was that insane seer. She cursed him to suffer."

I chuckle-wheezed again. "You just want to see me die so you can return to Hell and claim the glory of killing me, claim the glory of my throne, when you actually had no hand in my demise."

"Is that true?" Jazema asked.

Lucifer nodded. "Yes, one cannot move positions in Hell unless there is a vacancy. Usually, the only way for that to occur is to kill someone."

"I meant, is it true you had no hand in killing him?" she pressed.

Lucifer grew quiet. "Possibly."

"Then you're no better than he is," she spat. "Neither of you have the gall."

"Excuse me?" Lucifer asked, offended.

"You heard me."

"If you would just let me in there, I could finish him off now!" Lucifer defended.

Jazema crossed her arms. "You had your chance. Plenty of them. Besides, if you killed him now, it would be a petty and unjust move. He can hardly fight back."

Lucifer sighed.

Then a thought occurred to me. "All these years you've been asking for my blood and DNA. Why not take it now? I'm here and I can't put up a fight, as you mentioned."

"Because your blood is now tainted by Astrid's curse. We wanted it when it was strong and thriving." She walked around the back of the cell to kneel down next to me. Only a glass barrier stood between us—one I could have demolished in seconds if my Hellfire still worked.

She smirked and whispered, "Besides, what I really want is the Hellfire, and there are other ways to get that."

My eyes widened. How? I was the only one with it running through my veins.

Unless her experiments…

"Jazema! What did you do?" I shouted.

But she just laughed and sauntered out of the room.

57

SOPHIA

Senja Island, Norway, Present Day

In my opinion, the best wonder was saved for last. The aurora borealis was our final stop, and it truly was a destination on my bucket list. I was also excited because the night we planned on seeing the ethereal lights in the sky was Dane's birthday. I made sure to tell the others so we could surprise him, although Jordan already knew.

We flew into Bardufoss Airport and took the bus transfer to the Aurora Borealis Observatory. It was a place that offered lodging and viewing of the aurora borealis all in one. We had reserved one of the apartments to fit all of us comfortably. It had a panoramic view, but I'm sure all of us would be out in the cold, staring up at the lights as Michael retrieved the final gemstone key.

After settling in, the angels joined us for dinner at the observatory's restaurant, where we were celebrating Dane's birthday.

"This is delicious," Jordan said, finishing off his last bite.

Dane laughed. "You think everything is delicious."

"Isn't that the truth," the angels agreed in unison.

The waiter came to clear the dishes, and once they were gone, he brought out a slice of cake and placed it in front of Dane.

"Happy birthday to you!" I sang.

He grinned at me as Jordan and the others joined in on the song. When we stopped, he blew out the single candle. The waiter brought over two more slices for Jordan and me.

"I can't believe it's July," Jordan said. "We've been gone a month."

"Hopefully, we'll be home for the fourth," Dane commented. "Seeing the fireworks off the lake in your backyard would be really fun."

"It would," Jordan agreed.

"We should definitely do it," I said, grabbing Dane's hand under the table.

He stopped chewing and looked at me. I smiled.

"There's something I should tell you all," Michael said. "I don't want to disappoint you, but we probably won't see the lights tonight."

Jordan dropped his fork. "Why not?"

"Well, like you said, it's July. The sun barely sets up here in the north this time of year, and the only way to see the lights is if it's dark," Michael explained.

"But then how do you get the stone?" Dane asked.

"Whether we can see the lights or not doesn't matter. It's more about the timing. I just have to be out there during the midnight sun."

I was quiet because I was disappointed. I had hoped to make this night special for Dane.

When we were done with dessert, we all went back to our rooms at the apartment. Since there was nothing to see outside, I decided to stay in mine for the rest of the night. I supposed I should have noticed something was up with the lights given how few guests were here. That should have been a tip-off. Glancing at my bags, I realized I'd forgotten to give Dane his present.

Grabbing the gift, I was about to leave to go give it to him when I heard a soft knock on my door. I opened it to find Dane standing before me.

"Do you mind if I come in?" he asked.

"No, I was just about to come find you. I forgot to give you your gift." I handed it to him.

We sat down on the bed, and he reached inside the bag and pulled out a sketchbook.

"I thought you might need another one. Plus, I saw you looking at it when we were in the market. But instead of buying it, you bought me the scarf."

Nodding, he slid his hand over the cover. "Thank you. For all of this. I know you were the one who remembered it was my birthday and made some plans to celebrate it."

I lay back to look at the view out the window. He followed suit.

"It's incredible, isn't it? To think we're here," Dane said.

I turned my head on the pillow and looked at him. "Yes, especially with you."

He met my eyes and hesitantly reached out a hand to touch my cheek. "I think about you so much. You're constantly on my mind."

"Then why haven't you said or done anything?"

"Like what?" he asked.

I tapped my lips.

He smiled. "I've wanted to…"

"But…?"

"But I didn't think you liked me. I thought I would never have a chance with you. I thought I was too damaged for you."

I tried to contain myself, even though I was freaking out on the inside. Dane had just confessed that he liked me! I had so many emotions right now, giddy and ecstatic being two of them.

I grabbed his hand resting on my cheek and took it in both of mine. "Are you crazy? Why would you even think that? Especially after what I told you happened to me."

"Well I didn't know that initially. Recently, I actually thought maybe you felt something, too, since you seemed to like spending time with me."

"I do," I whispered, brushing his cheek with my lips.

He shivered at my touch and latched on to my hand. "Spending these last few weeks with you, I feel more like myself than ever before. You support me and my dreams. No one has ever done that—taken an interest in me or what I like."

I scooched closer to him. "I feel the same way. Every time you look at me, I feel like I can let my guard down and be the real me. Not the perfectionist or the brainiac. Just me."

We were so close our faces were practically touching. He cupped my cheek and closed the distance, bringing our mouths together in a kiss. It was innocent at first, both of us testing the waters. Then I pulled him closer and lost myself in him.

58

MICHAEL

Senja Island, Norway, Present Day

It was almost midnight so I figured it was time to check on the kids to see if they wanted to join me outside for the key retrieval. I knew it wouldn't be nearly as exciting without the lights, but it was still nice to offer.

I approached the boys' room first and knocked on the door. No answer. I knocked again. "Jordan? Dane?" Again nothing.

Worried, I tried the handle. It turned open, but neither of them was inside. Really panicked now, I raced over to Sophia's room and knocked on the door. "Sophia? Are you in there?"

I heard voices on the other side, and a brief moment passed before she opened the door, Dane at her side.

"Is everything all right?" she asked.

"Do you know where Jordan is?"

"In our room," Dane said.

I shook my head. "But he isn't."

"You sure?" Dane frowned. "I don't know where else he would be."

"We need to find him." I glanced at the two of them. "Follow me."

They grabbed their coats and shoes, and trailed after me.

I barged into the room I was sharing with Gabriel. "We have a problem."

He startled. "What is it?"

"Jordan's missing."

Gabriel's jaw tightened. "I thought he was sleeping."

I stared at him pointedly.

"You think he had a vision?"

Nodding, I said, "I don't know why else he would vanish. The sphere is still here, right?"

Gabriel crossed the room and dug inside the bag with the sphere. He nodded. "Yeah, it's still here."

"I guess we can rule out the Nephilim, then," I said.

Gabriel looked at the clock. "You're running out of time. Go retrieve the key with Chamuel. The rest of us will look for Jordan."

I couldn't care less about the key right now, but he had a point. We had come this far; there was no sense in wasting it.

We regrouped with the others outside. Chamuel and I headed for the beach while everyone else canvassed the area, searching for Jordan.

It was still light out as we walked along the sand. At exactly midnight, we came upon the spot where the key rested among large boulders and rocks strewn about the beach. I placed my hand atop one of them and felt the stone thrum. The ogham rune for Oak appeared in a beam of light. The gemstone key rose from the depths of the stone and came to rest on the surface. I picked it up and showed it to Chamuel, the two of us gazing at the deep-blue pear-shaped lapis lazuli.

"How precious." The sound of a gun being cocked drew our attention away, and we turned around.

The hooded man from the gala stood before us. He had a gun pointed at me, but in the crook of his other arm, he held Jordan by the neck. The boy had a gash on his brow and a swollen eye. There was a gag in his mouth, and I imagined his hands were tied up, as well. He looked scared.

"What do you want?" I asked, shoving the gemstone key in my pocket.

He chuckled. "I like you. Cutting right to the chase, not even caring who I am."

"What do you want?" I repeated, much more forceful this time.

He met my eyes. "I want the sphere." He moved the gun away from me and placed it under Jordan's chin. "Or the boy dies." Jordan's eyes widened in panic.

"I don't have it, not on me," I said. "It's in my room."

The hooded man jabbed the weapon harder into Jordan's chin. Instead of more fright, though, a look of determination now crossed Jordan's eyes.

"I'll give it to you," I said, "but I have to go get it."

"No one's going anywhere!" the man yelled.

"Then how are we supposed to give you what you want?" Chamuel asked.

Suddenly, Jordan wiggled out of his gag. "You aren't!" he shouted, biting the man's hand.

Before the man could recover, Jordan pulled his head back, then slammed it into his assailant's nose, breaking it. Blood gushed out, and the man let go of Jordan and recoiled in pain.

I glided through the air as Jordan fell to the ground. I was about to sweep him away when a shot sounded and a bullet hit the sand just to the left of me. I grabbed the kid and rolled behind a boulder for cover.

That's when our reinforcements arrived. Arrow after arrow flew through the air, hitting their mark each time as Uriel executed an expert assault on the hooded man.

Bringing my attention back to Jordan, I broke the bindings around his hands. "Are you all right?"

He rubbed his wrists. "Yeah, I was sleeping when that guy came in and punched me in the face. It was an awful way to wake up. I didn't know what was happening or where I was. Then he tied me up and gagged me. Told me to be quiet and follow his orders." He sighed. "I'm *so* done with sneak attacks."

I peeked around the boulder and noticed the attack had ceased.

Raphael and Jophiel were a short distance away, barricading Dane and Sophia behind another large rock.

Rising, I approached the man, who had a few arrows planted in him. Kicking away his gun, I analyzed him, trying to find some hint as to who he was. His face was entirely covered, and his clothes had no distinctive marks. Then I zeroed in on his right hand, where he wore a black ring with a gold double helix engraved on it.

It couldn't be… He was the Sentinel, the man who had been chasing Allen Clark.

"Gabriel, stop! What are you doing?" Zadkiel cried.

"Destroying this thing!"

"But we can't just obliterate a celestial object. There will be consequences," Zadkiel stated.

"I don't care! Not this time. I need to do what's right, not what's practical," Gabriel said. "This sphere has done more harm than good, and what's the point of keeping it if Lilith's inside? She needs to be vanquished!"

Unlike Zadkiel, I supported Gabriel's decision and had been prepared to destroy the sphere myself if I had to. While I hadn't told the others, clearly Gabriel and I had been thinking the same thing.

Behind me, the Sentinel laughed. I turned around and saw that he was snapping the arrows from his body, preparing to fight once again. Those wounds should have been fatal. How he was able to stand there like nothing had ever struck him was beyond me. He must have been invincible. And that meant he wasn't fully human.

Gabriel stepped on top of one of the large boulders, the fourteenth sphere in his hand. Raising it above him, he paused a moment, the sunlight catching the sapphire and creating a strong glow. Then he brought it down hard and smashed it against the rock.

"No!" Zadkiel shouted.

Upon impact, a large shock reverberated, sending everyone to the ground.

Then an evil, maniacal laugh filled the air.

A woman sat among the rocks, dressed entirely in black rags. Her long, black hair hid her face, but when she pushed it back, there was no denying who it was. *Lilith.*

She smiled mischievously. "Why, thank you for freeing me, Gabriel."

Horror swept over my brother's expression. "It was supposed to destroy you."

Lilith tsked. "A blessed angel sealed me in the sphere so a blessed angel can't destroy it. Only a fallen one can."

The Sentinel stood and drew close to her side. He reached out a hand to help her up. "It's been a long time, my dear," she said.

"Anything for you, mistress."

"Good." She leveled her gaze on us. "Let's finish them off."

She raised her hands, about to do something, but I didn't stick around to find out what. Instead, I glided through the air, picked up

Jordan, and kept going. The others followed, Raphael carrying Sophia and Jophiel carrying Dane.

We didn't stop until we were back at Bardufoss Airport, where we quickly boarded the plane and retreated as fast and as far away as possible. Lilith was now on the loose, and we had no surefire way of stopping her.

59 LILITH

Senja Island, Norway, Present Day

I clenched my hand in a fist and watched those pitiable angels retreat. I could have brought them down with one flick of my wrist. I could have followed after them on my own wings. But I didn't. Their time would come. Right now I had to focus on bigger matters. Like regaining my strength, reuniting with my army, and planning an attack against my greatest enemy. Oddly enough, I had become the epitome of patience. Living centuries and never getting what I wanted had only taught me to wait for the opportune time to strike. Well, now would be my time. A reckoning was coming. And no one was safe.

I fixed my gaze on the Sentinel, taking in his hooded cowl. It was certainly a better disguise than what he had originally worn—a fedora hat and face mask. He wasn't complete, though. He wasn't mine when he still wore Jazema's mark, the double helix ring. It was about time I fixed that and tied up loose ends.

"Where's Lucifer?" I demanded.

The Sentinel crossed his arms. "Gone. He's not on your side anymore. He's not on Satan's, either. Right now he's with Jazema. Until he exhausts their partnership, too."

I pursed my lips. "So Lucifer never completed his task?"

"Unfortunately not. As you can see, the boy—Dane, I think—is with the angels and his friends."

I let out a scream of rage. "That's not how it was supposed to be! Lucifer was supposed to get him for me. He was supposed to keep him until I returned!"

"Lucifer is an incompetent fool," the Sentinel said.

My irritation turned on him. "Then why didn't you do anything? Why didn't you intercede and complete the task yourself?"

"Because I was infiltrating Geneloom. It hasn't been easy. I needed to gain Jazema's trust, and there's one person from my past who has made that difficult."

"Still playing cat and mouse with Allen Clark? That's what he goes by now, right?"

"How do you know that?"

I smirked. "Because I know everything, darling."

His eyes turned to slits, but he didn't voice his feelings. Instead, he asked, "What do we do about the boy?"

"Leave that to me," I said. "He's mine to deal with now."

The Sentinel shrugged. "Fine. We should leave, then. Before we are discovered."

"I have a better idea." I stepped forward, meaning to close the small gap between us, but my balance was unsteady. He noticed and grabbed my arm to support me.

"My transformation can wait until you're strong again," he said, anticipating my intentions. "I've waited nineteen years. I think a few more days won't hurt."

Adamantly, I shook my head.

"You need rest," he continued. "None of your plans will work if you don't give yourself time to recover. You've been locked in that sphere—"

"Enough!" I bellowed. "I'm not weak! And I will not have you commanding me about!" I pulled my arm from his grasp, seething.

"I'm sorry, mistress. All I want is your success."

"If that's what you want," I ground out, "then you will obey my wishes."

"All right." He paused. "What must I do?"

I sneered. "First off, take out those ridiculous colored lenses."

Obediently, he raised his hands to his eyes and expertly extracted the chestnut-colored lenses to reveal what lay beneath—bloodred irises.

"It was the only way to hide in plain sight," he explained. "To throw off Jazema and make her think I was hers. If she saw my eyes, I would have been compromised. They're a dead giveaway that I'm yours."

I drew close to his side. "I understand the lengths you had to go to, but you no longer have to uphold any illusions. Now that I'm back, you can be free to express your true self, especially once you're whole."

He went to toss the lenses to the ground, but I reached out and stopped him before he could. "We need those," I said.

"For what?"

"For your transformation. We'll need items to bind the spell." He made a fist and shoved them in his pocket. Slowly, I glided my hand along his arm up to his shoulder. "The uncanny strength, the ability to regenerate, and the red eyes were only three-quarters of the process. We must finish you." My hand trailed down farther to rest at his shoulder blades. "It's time to give you your wings."

He tensed under my touch and slowly turned to face me, red eyes searching mine.

"Meet me in the forest. You'll know where to find me." I slipped a knife free from his belt. "Bring a sacrifice, and be prepared to feel pain." I sauntered off without even observing his reaction and disappeared into the trees.

I picked up fallen branches as I walked until I came to a clearing and piled them up in the center. I sat down on the ground in front of them, closed my eyes, and began chanting. Soon, the branches ignited before me, the heat warm against my skin.

Eyes still shut, I drew out the blade and sliced the palm of my hand. Squeezing my fingers, I let the blood drip down my arm. I placed the knife next to my foot and then dipped my fingers in the blood oozing from my palm, using the liquid to draw symbols along my arms and legs and across my face. As soon as I traced the spot in the middle of my forehead, my eyes flew open as the power within me ignited and surged. I smiled from the thrill of it.

When I was locked in the sphere, I could only feel the power living inside me. I couldn't tap into it. Eventually, I had discovered a way to use the lesser extents, mainly telepathic deceptions, but never the good stuff—the blood magic.

Now I was ready.

I stood and walked around the fire, a trail of blood following in my wake, creating a binding circle.

I heard the Sentinel approach before I saw him. "Kneel," I commanded, facing him. He was covered in blood and held out the heart of some animal. I took the sacrifice and placed it just outside the binding circle. He dropped to his knees before the fire, and I loomed behind him. I pulled the hooded cowl from his head and discarded it to the side, knowing he would need it again. "Take off your shirt." He obeyed. "And give me the lenses." He reached into his pocket and handed them to me.

Once again, I used the knife to slice my palm and dipped my fingers in the blood to trace similar symbols on his arms, abdomen, and face. When I reached the spot between his eyes, I pressed my thumb firmly to the skin and chanted the guttural command that I knew would start the spell.

Immediately, he screamed.

The words of the dark incantation easily formed on my lips as I continued the spell. It wasn't until the fire raged that I stepped away from the Sentinel and advanced toward the inferno.

"I call to thee, Qliphoth, to grant me a transmutation."

The flames roared audibly in response.

"This man's soul," I began, throwing in the chestnut-colored lenses. The fire flared briefly but didn't explode against the binding circle as I had intended. The spell needed something more, something stronger.

Without hesitation, I strode back to the Sentinel and reached for the ring at his hand, slipping off the double helix band and tossing it in the fire. He was in so much pain, my action went unnoticed. But I finally received the result I wanted from the blaze. It burst into the air, fighting against the invisible edges that bound it.

The Sentinel started screaming again.

"Combined with the dark offering he seeks," I continued. Turning to the Sentinel, I demanded, "Tell Qliphoth what it is you desire."

He was writhing and breathing heavily, but he managed to get out the words. "I desire…to have wings."

The fire erupted forcefully, much more strongly than I had

anticipated. It nearly broke the binding circle, but before it could, I grabbed the heart and pitched it into the flames, knowing the sacrifice would appease the dark force I had summoned.

Now it was time to seal the spell.

I grasped the knife and freshened the wound on my hand. Then I raised it to the Sentinel's lips. Even though his whole body was tense with pain, he was still lucid enough to give me a questioning look.

"For this to work, you must consume my blood."

He was wary. His hesitation revealed that. But something must have urged him on because he drew my hand to his lips and let my blood wash over his tongue.

Seconds later, I drew back and flung the remaining droplets into the fire. It burst one more time and changed from a fiery orange to a deep black.

With the knife blade raised, I brought the tip of it to the edge of the fire. "First bound in blood, now bound to blade, let this man's desire be made." I pierced the binding circle with the knife, almost like popping a balloon, except the fire didn't escape and explode outward. Instead, it drew inward, pulling all the black flames into the knife.

I smiled as a quiet lull fell over the forest.

There was only one thing left to do now.

I approached the Sentinel from behind and slashed him across the back, not deep enough to inflict a fatal injury. But enough to draw a slight well of blood and have gargoyle-like wings unfurling from his vertebrae.

He cried out in agony and hunched over as the transmutation took its full effect.

I stood by, my work done. It would be some time before he finally stopped writhing and shrieking.

My vision danced before me.

Perhaps I needed the time to recover, too.

Then, in my mind's eye, I saw all my plans come crashing down as I realized the angels would alert Heaven about my escape from the sphere as soon as they could.

I wouldn't let that happen.

I stood tall and summoned the little strength I had left. *"Novissimum!"*

An invisible surge of power poured out of me and into the world, ready to block any calls or warnings to Heaven.

Collapsing to the ground, I remained conscious but was completely drained. With time I would get better, stronger. I just needed to reorient myself because my work was only beginning. And the hardest, yet most satisfying, part was still to come.

60 JORDAN

Ithaca, New York, Present Day

We made it home before the Fourth of July but only because the angels had refused to stop until we were safely back at the house.

When we'd all crossed the threshold, the ten of us deflated. It was hard not to feel dejected when we had just unleashed Lilith on the world.

Once we'd settled in and Sophia, Dane, and I had gotten some rest, we all reconvened in the library. The ten of us sat there in silence.

Dane finally broke the tension. "Now what do we do?"

"We have to alert Father and the Seraphim," Zadkiel said.

"No, we can fix this," Uriel assured us.

"How?" Gabriel exploded. "The sphere was the only thing that trapped her, and now it's gone because of me!"

"Gabriel, don't self-destruct," Michael advised.

"Easy for you to say. You didn't unleash our biggest threat."

"No, but I wanted to," Michael said, then backtracked. "What I mean is, I wanted to destroy the sphere, too, and the outcome would have been the same if I had. None of us knew that only a fallen angel could destroy it."

"Except Satan. He was actually telling the truth," Gabriel said.

"I will admit that we have a problem on our hands," Raphael commented, "but we also need to address what we accomplished. We successfully retrieved all the gemstone keys."

"Yes, but what do we do about Lilith?" Chamuel asked, coming back to the urgent matter at hand.

Jophiel rubbed his jaw. "Maybe we do send a message to Heaven."

"How?" Sophia asked.

I looked at Gabriel. "Get the horn. You need to do it."

"Horn? Like an instrument?" Dane asked.

I nodded.

Gabriel left the library and retreated downstairs to the music room. We followed in his footsteps, especially as he opened the back patio doors and stepped out onto the lawn. He raised the long, gold Horn of Assembly to his lips and blew.

All I heard was a somber tune, but I knew an important message was being conveyed in it, one the Heavens would know how to respond to.

When the Fourth of July actually arrived, we fulfilled our goal and watched the fireworks along the lake from the backyard. The three of us and Martha truly enjoyed the experience. The angels did, too, but I could tell they were in a state of constant worry. There had been no answer to Gabriel's message. Granted, it had only been two days, but they were eager for a call to action.

While we waited, I figured now was the time to handle my "gift." There were no more distractions. The necklace had kept the visions at bay, but at the cemetery, Sister Delphine had said I would have to either wear it forever or master my abilities—whatever those were since I wasn't quite sure—if I wanted peace. I was willing to learn how to control it as long as I found a teacher…and as long as I didn't sprout wings and turn into a Nephilim.

We had encountered many of the half-human, half-angel creatures at the museum and on our trip, and I had come to learn that most of them didn't have wings. Only the ones who had descended directly from Watchers did. Most of them only had gifts, be it high intelligence, superstrength, or speedy reflexes. Perhaps if I was a Nephilim, I wasn't one descended directly from a Watcher. Perhaps I just had a small fraction of Nephilim blood running through my veins. I wish I knew.

And right now, Sister Delphine seemed like my best shot at getting an answer so I called the church I knew she belonged to. But no one seemed to know who I was talking about. It was as if she didn't exist.

Had I imagined her?

I shook my head. That was a ridiculous thought. Dane and Sophia knew her. The angels had met her. She had to be somewhere.

Sophia and Dane, as well as the angels, assisted in the search. The angels, in particular, needed something to occupy them since they still hadn't heard from Heaven. But all our efforts came back without any leads. If I couldn't rely on Sister Delphine, who else could help me?

I supposed Dafne was a possibility. She had told me she was an ally. I had texted her when we had returned to let her know I was home, but I hadn't heard anything back.

The rest of July and August passed quickly with no word from Dafne or Sister Delphine.

Sitting in front of my laptop one day, I sighed.

"No luck?" Martha asked, looking up from clipping coupons at the kitchen table.

I shook my head. "No." Then an idea struck me. Martha had been the housekeeper for years, meaning she might know more than I thought about my family. "Martha, do you know anything about my father?"

She furrowed her brow. "Not much. He was a kind and quiet man. Absolutely adored your mother. And boy, did he have a brain. He loved history, and the majority of the books in the library are his."

I nodded. "Do you know anything about his family? I hear so much about my mother and the Sinclairs."

She paused, thinking. "If I recall, your father had two siblings, a brother and a sister, both older than him."

"What happened to them?"

Martha shrugged. "I'm not sure." She paused. "I do know that the Conways didn't approve of your mother, which led to an estrangement between your father and his parents. He was only close to his siblings after that. The Sinclairs had been wary of the match between your parents, too, but they came to accept it."

"I wonder why there was so much animosity," I said.

"There are a lot of feelings running within a family, bonds cherished and built. But when you start to blend it, introduce new people into it, those feelings become more pronounced. It might just be that the Conways felt like they were losing your father when he met your mother, that he had changed in some way, and it was hard for them to face that change."

While Martha hadn't told me much, she had told me enough. It seemed like my father had family ties and connections. If he had been a Watcher or a Nephilim, I didn't think that would be the case. Right?

"Thanks, Martha."

"Anytime."

I focused my attention back on the laptop when the doorbell rang. I didn't move to get it, since the angels insisted on being the only ones to open the door. They were worried someone might track us down and try to attack.

A few moments later, Michael walked into the kitchen with a small envelope and handed it to me.

"What's this?" I asked.

"It was left at the door. It had your name on it."

Sure enough, my first name was written in cursive along the front. Flipping it over, I noticed the wax seal—not a fleur-de-lis but a tree.

Nervous excitement ran through my veins as I pried open the envelope. I pulled out a small note card, and read what it said aloud.

"'All of you must come see me. Tomorrow at noon. 1055 Applegate Road.'"

"See who?" Martha asked.

I looked up, smiling. "Sister Delphine."

61 JORDAN

Ithaca, New York, Present Day

I could hardly sleep knowing we would be seeing Sister Delphine soon. She had told me she would find me, and I had doubted her, but in the end, she had kept her word.

The homes along Applegate Road, which was surprisingly close to my own house, were spread out from one another on large pieces of land. It was the beginning of September, and the leaves were already changing.

I sat in the back seat of the van with Sophia and Dane, their hands interlocked. I was glad they had found each other in all this. Especially now, as Sophia had made the difficult decision to take the fall semester off. While online classes were a possibility, she thought it was a little impractical to be juggling school right now with everything that was going on.

The two of them had made a lot of sacrifices ever since they had gotten involved in this battle between good and evil. Hopefully, after today, we would get some answers and their losses would not have been in vain.

When we pulled up to the house, I was surprised to see a large Tudor-style mansion. Raphael parked the car, and we all exited the van together and hesitantly approached the door.

Clearly, I wasn't the only one who was nervous.

Sophia reached out and rang the doorbell.

We waited a few moments before someone answered. It was Sister Delphine. Seeing her in plain clothes—a simple sweater and jeans—was odd, but it made me realize how she wasn't anywhere near as old as Sister Helen had been. They had to have at least a ten-year gap between them—Sister Helen in her sixties, Sister Delphine in her fifties. I analyzed Sister Delphine some more, noticing her dark-brown hair that was pulled back in a bun and just beginning to gray at the roots. Her emerald-green eyes held a sharp wit, and her angular jaw and high cheekbones conveyed a sophisticated beauty.

"Welcome," Sister Delphine said. "I'm glad you received my message. Why don't you all come in?"

We entered the house, and I had to gasp and admire my surroundings. The interior was beautiful, everything covered in dark wood, from the floors to the walls. There were paintings and decorative trinkets everywhere you looked. It was a home full of heirlooms and family history—you could just feel it.

Sister Delphine led us to a sunroom where she had lemonade and small sandwiches waiting for us. We all sat down on the comfy couches and chairs, gazing out at an amazing view of the forest.

Sophia, Dane, and I didn't pick at the food. We were too anxious to hear what Sister Delphine had to say.

"I'm sure you all want to know why I called you here so I'll get right to it," Sister Delphine said. "I didn't invite you here just to discuss Jordan's gift. It's part of the reason, but I really wanted to talk with all three of you because you're all special and it's time you knew who you are."

Sophia was sitting between Dane and me, and she latched on to both our hands.

"Before that, though, let's address Jordan's visions," Sister Delphine went on.

I nodded.

"As you probably know by now, your necklace acts as a barrier to ward off the visions. It was originally your mother's, and she wore it for protection."

"From whom?" Michael asked.

"Lilith," Sister Delphine answered. "She tried desperately to control your mother by invading her mind, and the necklace was the only way to protect her from it. The necklace had been created for her by angels." She folded her hands in her lap. "But your visions have nothing to do with Lilith's mind games, or even your mother's side of the family. It has to do with your father's."

Oh no... Please don't let my suspicions come true. Please don't let me be a Nephilim.

"The Conway family is one of ten families connected to a group of angels known as the Ishim," she continued. I swallowed, remembering how the Ishim were once Watchers. "These angels were sent to Earth to teach their knowledge to humans, and they chose the ten families who would receive it and ultimately pass it along through thousands of generations. The Conway bloodline is particularly important because it is imbued with an ancient gift, that of the Sight. With the Ishim's teachings, the gift only became more powerful among your ancestors, manifesting differently in each person and, in some cases, not manifesting at all. Soon, the Conways became chief of the ten families, for their wisdom was far-reaching."

"So my father wasn't a Nephilim or a Watcher, then?" I clarified.

"Heavens, no! He was fully human. Just a human with a great gift of the Sight."

I sighed in relief.

"How do we help Jordan learn to harness his gift, though?" Zadkiel asked.

"He will have to undergo spiritual and meditative training. But not before he is unbound."

I scrunched up my nose. "Unbound?"

Sister Delphine grew serious. "Yes. In fact, you three must *all* be unbound."

"What does that mean?" Dane asked.

Sister Delphine stood. "Let me show you."

She brought us upstairs to a two-story library, the massive room full of books, more wood paneling etched with an ornate design, and an excellent view of the land and woods. I didn't know what the library had to do with us being unbound until I took in row upon row of tapestries hanging from the upper deck walls.

My eyes finally landed on one with a large rectangular hole in the middle of it. The hole was surrounded by flora and fauna—lilies and birds.

Just like the piece we found in my mother's studio...

My feet carried me closer, brushing past the others and even going so far as to mount the steps to the upper deck to get a better look. I reached out my hand, but nothing happened. Everything was muted. Glancing down at the necklace, I yanked it off, and suddenly my mind was flooded with images.

The red feather of a cardinal. The red petal of a spider lily. The red tree of cypress. *Dane.*

The blue feather of a jay. The blue petal of the lily of the Nile. The blue tree of spruce. *Sophia.*

The green feather of a swallow. The green petal of a Madonna lily. The green tree of oak. *Jordan.*

Then there was a lone figure sitting before a loom, weaving the tapestry together. But instead of seeing my mother as I'd expected to, I saw Sister Delphine.

So goes the Prophecy of the Three Heirs…

I was forcefully smacked back, landing on the heavy carpet. Everyone surrounded me with looks of concern on their faces—everyone but Sister Delphine.

"What did you do?" I asked.

She grimaced. "I made the tapestry. I bound the three of you so you wouldn't know who you truly are."

"Why?" Sophia demanded, her outrage dripping from the single word.

"Because you three come from powerful bloodlines, and neither Sister Helen nor I wanted any of you to carry on their legacies, for they were lives full of hardship and strife. So we thought it would be better for you all not to know your lineages, to forget who you were and to live normal lives. But someone didn't agree with our choice, and he tore the tapestry apart, planting a piece of it in your house, knowing you would find it one day and want to discover its secrets."

"Who did that?" I asked.

Sister Delphine met my gaze. "Your uncle, Aeron Conway. It was his last act before he disappeared. No one knows where he is." She paused. "I never tried to recover the tapestry piece because, by that point, I'd realized that no matter what I did, it was inevitable. I could not shield you from your destiny forever. I had acted rashly those years ago, hoping to spare you from what your parents had suffered through, but it is simply impossible. You must learn from their mistakes and carry on where they left off."

Dane crossed his arms. "All right, but why can't you just tell us who we are? Why do we need to unbind ourselves?"

"When I made the tapestry, I had to connect the prophecy to something in order for it to survive among the threads. So I tied it to my life. If anyone tells you who you are, I will die."

"Isn't that a little drastic?" Uriel asked.

"No," Sister Delphine said seriously, "not when you come to know the truth and how much of a burden they must bear. Then you will understand why I did what I did, why I thought it was right. But I can say nothing more, not until they are unbound."

"How do we unbind ourselves?" I asked.

She turned to me. "You must repair the tapestry and follow the instructions it gives you. I cannot repair it for you since I would fall ill as a result. But I can teach you how to do so."

Sophia's eyes were full of determination and her voice eager as she said, "All right, when can we start?"

"Whenever you'd like," Sister Delphine replied.

"Weaving prophecies into tapestries isn't common practice," Gabriel said. "How did you have the power to do it?"

She faintly smiled, then looked at me. Our eyes locked. "Because I'm a Conway, too. I'm your aunt."

62 SATAN

Location Unknown, Present Day

More days passed. Weeks, even. And I was still here.

Why was I still here?

Anyone else would have perished by now with the amount of blood I was losing.

I slumped against the wall, and my breathing rattled in and out. I could hardly keep my eyes open, but something kept shifting in and out of focus. I forced my eyes to hold still for a few seconds to gaze upon the chain resting on my chest.

I chuckle-wheezed. Astrid had cursed me to die, but her amulet was keeping me alive.

"What's so funny?" Lucifer asked.

I ignored him. Maybe I should pull it off and end it. Is that what would happen? Or would I be sucked back to Hell? The amulet allowed me to walk the Earth so if I took it off, would I be stuck here, would it send me back to Hell, or would it just obliterate me with pain where I sat?

I supposed I could find out.

"Hey! Are you listening to me?" Lucifer demanded.

"Not really," I rasped.

He was about to say something else when the door opened and Jazema and Penelope came marching in. "He *still* hasn't perished yet?" Penelope asked.

"I could end it quickly if you let me in there," Lucifer remarked.

"No, we've been over this already," Jazema said.

Penelope drew close to the cell, analyzing my face. "You're stronger than I thought you were. Those two made it seem like you were some pathetic angel with no sense of how to rule."

I grinned weakly. "I'm glad I could change your mind."

"Did you know you don't have to use Watchers to create Nephilim? Any angel will do. Even an archangel. All we need is blood or hair—whatever works with the means we have, really. They're not all scientific." Penelope stared at me. "If only you weren't tainted…"

Another buzzing noise sounded as someone else entered the room. It was a girl. She looked beaten-up. She looked…familiar.

I sat straighter. "You're the girl from the Empire State Building." I turned to Lucifer. "The one you let attack Beelzebub."

"And if you hadn't interfered, he would be gone, the buffoon," Lucifer remarked.

Jazema stroked the girl's hair. "What happened to you, Rajani?"

"I was bested by an infuriating boy!"

"And what of the sphere?" Penelope clearly couldn't care less about Rajani's well-being.

"The Sentinel showed up for it. But one of the angels tried destroying it," Rajani informed them.

"Tried? What happened?" Lucifer asked.

Rajani vehemently barked out her next words. "Lilith was unleashed."

Oh shit. I had to get out of here.

"Let me go!" I yelled.

They all laughed at me.

Jazema focused on her manicured nails. "Why would we do that?"

"You're dead! Do you hear me? You're all dead!"

"That's rich, coming from someone who is chained and bleeding," Rajani mocked.

"Besides, how exactly do you plan on killing *us*?" Lucifer teased.

Thunder boomed overhead.

I smiled. "You'd be surprised."

A portal opened behind them, and grenades came sailing through—the real kind, not the holy water kind. My enemies took cover before the grenades exploded.

Another portal appeared in my cell. "Rescue squad has arrived!" Nehema shouted, looking thrilled. "Sorry it took so long. This is place is fortified."

She swung a pickax through the air, and the blade met my chains. They fell to the ground, broken. She came closer and pulled a hairpin from her long tresses. After inserting it in the lock, she shimmied and twisted it, and then *pop!* My bonds snapped open.

I rubbed my wrists as another figure came through the portal.

Abbadona.

She grabbed my arm to support me, and I touched her cheek. "I missed you."

She smiled.

"Who sent the grenades?" I asked.

"Haborym. She likes blowing things up." Nehema bowed low. "After you, sir. Belphegor can only seal the doors for so long."

"He's helping?" I asked, slowly stepping over to the portal.

"He hacked into the system. I don't know how it works," Abbadona said, exasperated. "Just go through so we can get you back."

She said the words as a door opened. Except this time, it wasn't the exterior door but my cell door. Lucifer raised a gun and fired a shot just as the three of us went through the portal back to Hell.

63

SATAN

HELL, PRESENT DAY

We came out the other side and crashed into my portal room. Nehema and Abbadona looked at each other to see who had taken the hit.

I roared in pain, the bullet lodged in my abdomen.

"Damn it!" Abbadona yelled.

Leviathan and Beelzebub came running in from the throne room.

"Get him on the table!" Abbadona demanded.

Leviathan swept an arm across the worktable, scattering everything onto the floor. Then Beelzebub lifted me in his arms and deposited me on the cold stone top.

Another shot rang through the room, hitting the wall behind us. It was a warning shot, and it had come from the entranceway to my throne room. Mammon stood there, gun aimed in Abbadona's direction. "Back off and leave him be!" he yelled. "Or I will shoot you!"

Asmodeus stood next to him in the doorway, unarmed and standing proud.

Haborym quietly approached from behind them and jumped on Mammon's back, forcing his gun arm in the air as he tried to level another shot. Beelzebub ran and tackled Asmodeus, who fell to the ground with a big *oof*.

"You're ruining my coat!" he complained.

Unfortunately, they weren't our only concern as Murmur and Mulciber stepped inside.

"We got this!" Nehema said, nodding to Leviathan.

She and Haborym engaged the new assailants so Abbadona could work on me. Placing her hand over my chest, she finished the work she had started on Jazema's knife wound. Then she reached down and grasped my amulet, preparing to yank it off. Before she could, someone smacked her from behind, sending her to the ground. Lucifer had come through the portal, his devious expression making it clear that he was itching to finish me off.

Abbadona got to her feet and struck him, distracting him and taking his attention off me. They fought, bringing the battle out into the throne room.

Now that I was alone, I knew I had to end this. I dug my fingers in my bullet wound, screaming until I found the small piece of metal and pried it out. Thankfully, it was a normal bullet because I don't think I could have handled the ones Lucifer had created from the river water. I rolled off the table and landed on my feet. I grabbed the amulet, pulling it free. It turned to dust in my hand. Briefly, I fell to my knees as my injuries started healing. My wounds closed up, and the holes in my wings sealed.

A banging to my left commenced, and I shouted, "Shut up, Kat!"

I didn't need to deal with her stupid attempts at distraction right now. I coughed, blood coming up. Wiping my mouth, I knew I was still dying, but I had regained some of my strength and my ability to fly. There was only one unknown that remained. Placing my hand on the foot of the table, I summoned the fire inside me. The Hellfire ignited along my skin, obliterating the stone foot and sending the worktable collapsing to the ground.

I smirked. Now it was time to make Lucifer pay.

I rose and strode through the archway into the throne room, advancing through the melee and then connecting a roundhouse kick straight to Lucifer's stomach. He lurched backward, away from Abbadona, temporarily stunned. Before he could regain his footing, I ran and tackled him over the Pit. We fell through the air, punching, kicking, ramming into rocky walls, and through it all I made sure not to touch his bare skin. He didn't know the Hellfire had returned, and I would keep it that way until I needed it.

Essentially, we beat the shit of out each other. But rather than take this fight to Misery for all the spirits to see, I flew through the entryway cave into the Eighth Cavern where the rivers awaited us.

As soon as I arrived, the whispering started. I ignored it, landing in an open space among the five rivers. Lucifer met me there, and we fought each other with our bare hands. I connected my blows to his clothed body, not ready yet to reveal my secret weapon.

Each of us let out our rage and hate for the other. I think his hatred of me originated from my mere existence while mine was from how his deception and betrayal had stung.

Did it sting as bad as Michael's?

The voice distracted me, and Lucifer sent me sailing with a kick. I careened against the rocky ground.

You chose someone who looked like him on purpose. You wanted your brother back.

I pounded my fist against the ground. I didn't know what Lucifer was hearing, but I could tell the voices were talking to him, too. Except it didn't seem to distract him. It seemed to egg him on.

He jumped on me, wrapping his hands around my throat in an attempt to strangle me. He screamed as the Hellfire burned the bare skin of his palms, but he didn't let go. A manic gleam had entered his gaze. I reached a hand up to his face and pushed my thumb into his eye. He roared. Yet, his grip still remained viselike.

"Just die already!" he growled savagely. "So I can have what's yours!"

Suddenly, he released my neck as he was pulled back by a strong force. The river had enclosed around his ankle, ready to drag him under.

"Let me go!" he shouted to the water. "We had a deal!"

"But you never paid," it responded in a guttural tone.

Abbadona arrived on the scene, reaching out a hand to influence the water. But Mammon appeared behind her, and he smacked her in the head. She fell to the ground and struggled to rise, exhaustion seeming to settle in. He took her arms and tied her up. She tried to fight him but to no avail. Mammon stuck a gag in her mouth so she couldn't speak any spells, either.

"You want your payment?" Lucifer yelled. "Then take him!"

I had just gotten to my feet when the water wrapped around my abdomen and pulled. Falling to my stomach, I tried gripping anything in sight to stop the strong backward tug and grasped on to a rock.

"He'll do nicely," the river purred.

Another stream of water came to curl around my feet.

I held on to the rock as tightly as I could, drawing blood.

"Don't resist. It's better to come freely," the water rasped.

I heard Abbadona's muffled scream, saw the agony in her eyes, as she helplessly watched my demise.

Lucifer knelt in front of me and smiled. "To the rivers with you," he said, using the words I had always used when sentencing someone for punishment.

He pried my fingers off the rock one by one, not caring that the Hellfire burned him.

As soon as there was nothing left holding me back, the River of Hate swallowed me whole. I splashed into its cold, dark depths, and as I fell through the bottomless waters, I knew this fall would be worse than my fall from Heaven.

64 JORDAN

Ithaca, New York, Present Day

September had turned into late October. Sister Delphine and Sophia were nearly done repairing the tapestry, the two of them working on it every day for more than a month and a half and forming an inseparable bond over that time. Chamuel stayed with them at Sister Delphine's house to act as a watchful eye and an admiring observer of their work.

Meanwhile, Dane and I beat the crap out of each other every day. We needed to hone our self-defense skills, and what better way to do that than sparring. Plus, I enjoyed practicing with him because we pretty much had the same skill set. The angels were fantastic teachers, but it was hard to learn things sometimes when they anticipated every single one of our moves.

"Ah!" I yelled as Dane flipped me on my back. I lay there on the mat, sweaty and exhausted, refusing to get up.

"Are we done for today?" Dane asked.

"Yeah, I can't handle anymore."

"Good. We have to pick up Sophia's birthday cake before she comes back."

"Got it."

Dane's phone rang, and he answered it.

I stared up at the ceiling, daydreaming, when I heard Dane say, "We'll be over soon."

He hung up and looked at me. "Hit the showers. Sophia and Sister Delphine finished the tapestry, and they want us over there as soon as possible."

I jumped up and raced upstairs to get ready.

Dane and I took the fastest showers ever. Then we clambered into the van with the angels to head to Sister Delphine's house. On the way, we stopped at the bakery to pick up Sophia's cake, which took longer than expected since it was Halloween and everyone wanted sweet treats.

When we arrived at the house, we left the cake in the kitchen and then headed straight for the library. As soon as we entered, I gasped. It was magnificent to see the tapestry whole. It actually seemed to glow now that the threads were connected again. The colors were more vibrant, as well, making the tree seem alive as it danced before my eyes. Weaving was not an easy art, and I was proud of Sophia for learning it. You wouldn't even know it had been repaired by a beginner, that's how perfect it looked.

The angels stayed in the lower level of the library while Dane and I ascended to the upper deck. Their presence, support, and protection had continued in the months since we'd returned home from traveling, but they all seemed a little distant. I imagined it was because they had never heard back from Heaven and were still wondering if Lilith was at large. There was no way to know if their comrades had taken action without them.

Sister Delphine joined the angels below, leaving the three of us standing in front of the tapestry alone—Dane on the left, me in the middle, and Sophia on the right. The colors of the tree determined our formation since, in my vision when I'd first seen the second piece of the tapestry, Dane had symbolized red, I had symbolized green, and Sophia had symbolized blue.

I took off my necklace and placed it in my pocket. I was still wearing it every day to keep Lilith and the visions away until we unbound ourselves and I was able to train with Sister Delphine. But in a moment like this, when everything depended on knowing the prophecy's instructions, it was vital that no protective wards stood in the way.

The three of us grasped hands, ready for a revelation. Then Dane and Sophia touched their free hands to the fabric.

Once the connection was made, words came pouring out from the tapestry. I could hear them in my mind.

When Samhain falls, so shall thee.
The three heirs must find the trees.
Follow the birds, it has begun.
The twentieth year can't be outrun.

An image flashed before my eyes, revealing a huge sprawling tree—I assumed it was the site where I could be unbound—and its location.

Each of us opened our eyes and unclasped our hands. We looked at each other in awe and surprise.

"Whoa," Dane said. "Did you see it, too?"

"See what?" I asked.

"The tree."

I nodded. "I saw *a* tree, but I think we each saw a different one."

"Mine was the Lone Cypress in Pebble Beach, California," he told us.

"That sounds a lot better than mine," Sophia commented. "Mine was the Tree Root Cave in Forks, Washington."

"What about yours?" Dane asked me.

"The Angel Oak in Johns Island, South Carolina."

Suddenly, there was birdsong and pecking at the window nearest the tapestry. The three of us approached to see a red cardinal, a violet-green swallow, and a blue jay.

My eyes widened.

"What do they want?" Dane asked, his voice full of shock.

"They want us to follow them," Sophia said. "It's happening. We're going to be unbound today. It's Samhain, as well as my birthday, and I'm the first of the three of us to turn twenty. It makes sense with the new piece of the prophecy."

The birds pecked at the glass again, as if to confirm Sophia's theory.

"We have to be at our locations before midnight." I could see it in my mind's eye. The moon glowing over the branches of each tree.

We looked at one another, nodding in agreement.

We descended to the lower level of the library and discussed with the angels how best to proceed.

"There's no choice but to split up this time," Michael said. "We have to be at three locations at once."

"I suggest we fly the kids in personally," Gabriel added. "There's no point taking a commercial flight, and we only have one private plane and are already working on limited time. The fastest way to do this is if we take them ourselves."

"All right. Then let's get ready," Raphael said.

"Before you do that," Sister Delphine added, "please promise me you'll be careful."

"Of course we will," I assured her.

"And one more thing." Dane kissed Sophia. "Happy Birthday."

She blushed. "Thanks."

With that, we split into groups and each went our separate ways.

65

LILITH

Hell, Present Day

It had been a long time since I walked the depths of these caverns. Everyone complained that I was so elusive, yet I had been hiding in plain sight for years in the one place where no one wanted to go. Walking among the rivers of the Eighth Cavern, I closed my eyes and relished in their cheers. They had missed me, my sweet, sweet pets. And now it was time to play again, time to finish what we had started.

The Sentinel waited upon the bank of the River of Pain. His hooded cowl was gone for now since it was only the two of us here. He was immune to the waters, just like all my creatures were, a simple blood magic spell running through their DNA.

I approached him, placing a finger on his neck and running my pointy nail down the length of it. He was by far my finest specimen, although not my most powerful.

"Your forces are ready, mistress," he said. "They await you on the other side."

"Excellent. It's about time they were put to good use."

I stepped into the water, descending farther and farther into the River of Pain until my head was submerged. Then I swam, knowing the way to the other side. When I surfaced, I had arrived at the barren wastelands of Purgatory.

Thousands were assembled there, my army ready and waiting to strike. They banged their weapons against their shields, chanting and cheering for my return.

The Sentinel appeared at my side, hooded once again, having surfaced from the river's edge, as well.

Looking up at the cloudy sky, I said, "It's time. Is the attack team assembled?" I wasn't about to waste my entire army on a skirmish with Heaven when a bigger battle still loomed before us.

"Ready and waiting for your command, mistress," the Sentinel said, stepping aside to reveal a small group of soldiers.

"Good. Let's go."

Leathery, gargoyle-like wings eased out from my back, from all our backs, and we ascended into the air.

With an arsenal of weapons strapped to my body, I felt confident taking on my most desired enemy. I was dressed in my finest—leather pants, heeled boots, corset top, and serpentine jewelry—for how else did you arrive at the gates of Heaven but looking your best?

It was time for revenge, and those angels had no idea what was about to hit them.

66 DANE

Pebble Beach, California, Present Day

We arrived at Pebble Beach just shy of midnight. Raphael landed a few feet away from the tree, placing me gently on the ground while Jophiel set down beside us. It was hard to see my surroundings at night, but I could hear the crashing waves and feel the wind against my skin. A bird landed on my shoulder, and I flinched in surprise. I knew it was a cardinal when it quickly flashed its red wings at me, flitting away to sit in the boughs of the tree.

Swallowing hard, I trekked over to the tree and stood before it, unsure what to do. The cardinal flew from his perch to one of the tree roots and crawled inside a small hole. I got to my knees and peered in the hole, but it was hard to see anything. Raising my hand, I hesitated. Did I really want to put it in there without knowing what awaited me?

I summoned the courage and reached forward. At first, I felt nothing but leaves and stone, yet as my hand brushed over a rock, I felt something sticking out of it. Grasping whatever it was, I pulled it free and brought it out. It was a dagger, black as night with engravings carved in the hilt and sheath—a flower of some kind.

Spider lilies.

A female voice spoke, resonating through my mind. It was Sister Delphine, speaking the words of the prophecy from the night she bound us.

Taking the hilt in my hand I pulled the dagger from its sheath to gaze at a bloodred blade. When the moonlight caught it, the wind gusted and my head flung back.

Daniel Samael Cross.

I heard the name spoken in my head, and while I was familiar with my first and last name, I never knew I had a middle name.

Son of Satan, King of Hell.

Son of Lilith, Mother of Blood Magic.

The heir of the unholy bloodline.

Take thy blade, wet thy hand, unleash thy power from within, for your truth resides inside.

Something threw me forward, and my hands hit the ground, my head lowered.

The blood rushed through my veins, cold as ice, leaving me numb and in shock. Satan was my father? And that psycho woman, Lilith, was my mother? It couldn't be…

But my whole body trembled as the horror of it all struck me. I was an evil abomination after all. No wonder the dark always tried to drag me under.

Taking the dagger, I sliced my hand without thinking, as if I knew instinctively what to do. I screamed in pain, not from the cut but from the sensation of heat that enveloped my body, as if all my skin was on fire.

The angels raced to my side, but two figures dropped down from the sky before they could make it to me. I swiped my dagger at one of them, forcing the person to jump back. The angels engaged the other figure, and I shoved the dagger in my jacket for safekeeping as the pain in my body grew worse, horrendously worse.

"Dane! Run!" Raphael shouted.

I had every intention of doing so when my feet fell out from under me. My body grew numb as the pain became so overwhelming, I couldn't move.

A face appeared close to mine, but I couldn't make out who it was. "We meet again," a girl said.

Then a sudden burst of light had everyone staggering to the ground. Lying among the leaves, I looked around. The angels had disappeared.

Shit! Where did they go?

My assailants recovered, stepping forward in the moonlight.

Jazema and the girl with the raven hair.

The girl lifted me under the armpits. "It's payback time," she whispered in my ear.

We launched into the night, my future uncertain. One indisputable fact was clear, though. I was in Geneloom's clutches.

67 SOPHIA

FORKS, WASHINGTON, PRESENT DAY

I'd admit, I had been such a *Twilight* fangirl in middle school that the thought of coming to Forks, Washington, was extremely exciting. But I tucked my inner book nerd away for the night and focused on the task at hand.

When Chamuel landed on the beach, he set me down gently next to him on the sand. Uriel silently drifted to the ground on my other side, and the three of us eyed the Tree Root Cave.

"That is the scariest thing I've ever seen," Uriel commented.

Chamuel shot him a glare.

"Sorry, but it's true."

"Maybe I don't have to go in there," I said.

A blue jay flitted past us right into the tangled, hanging roots.

I sighed. "Or maybe I do."

The tree sat on a short overlook, yet there was no solid ground supporting it underneath, its roots completely exposed and forming the top of the cave. In the dark of night, it was creepy to look at, but I didn't think broad daylight would have helped much.

Taking a deep breath, I strode forward. I stopped before the entrance to the cave, staring into the dark. It reminded me of the tunnel Sister Helen had sent me down.

The thought brought me back to that place, back to the panic and fear I had felt.

No. I shook the idea away. *I can do this. I am one of the three heirs. Possibly the bloodline. It is time I face my fears.*

I crept into the cave, the inside damp and cold. An earthy scent permeated the air, and while I could tell the interior wasn't deep, it was still hard to see anything. Luckily, the bright feathers of the blue jay guided my way until it rested atop a stone at the back wall of the cave. When I stood in front of the stone, the bird flew away, out of the cave and into the night.

I knelt down and ran my hands over the rock. What was I supposed to do with a rock?

My left hand bumped into something, and I curled my fingers around it and pulled. A dagger came loose. The hilt and sheath were gray, covered with engravings of a flower.

Lily of the Nile.

Sister Delphine's voice resonated through my mind, and I suddenly knew what to do.

Grasping the hilt, I separated the dagger from its sheath and admired the deep-blue blade. As the clouds outside parted, a beam of moonlight shone over my shoulder, gleaming against the dagger. The wind gusted, and my head flung back.

Sophia Helene Conway.

The name was spoken in my head.

It couldn't be. I was related to Jordan? And I had a middle name?

Daughter of Aeron Conway, the father who always wanted you but never could.

Daughter of Penelope Grigori, the Watcher known as Penemue, who always wanted you but never should.

The heir of the Nephilim bloodline.

Take thy blade, wet thy hand, unleash thy power from within, for your deceit lies without.

My body projected forward, and I hit the ground, hands splayed, head lowered.

Oh my god… I wasn't the holy bloodline. I was a Nephilim.

I sliced my hand with the dagger. The cut didn't hurt, but the searing agony of splitting skin across my back made me cry out.

The angels raced to the cave, but there was a sudden burst of light and they were gone.

The pain along my back forced my eyes shut. Then a comforting hand rested on my shoulder. "Don't worry, sweetheart. Your mother's here to protect you."

Grimacing, I pried my eyes open to see Penelope's face.

No… Not again.

My eyes shifted down to splatters of blood and feathers on the ground. I glanced over my shoulder, finding a hunch of wings sprouting from my back.

I screamed in horror and shock. My memories had been trying to tell me all along that I was a halfling creature.

Penelope placed her fingers under my chin to turn my head. "I told you all along you had potential."

Tears streamed down my face.

"It was just a matter of forcing it out of you."

My lip trembled as if I were my five-old-year self again.

"How about you come with me?"

She asked it as if I had a choice, when in reality, I knew I was heading to Geneloom whether I wanted to or not.

68 JORDAN

Johns Island, South Carolina, Present Day

The cold breeze of fall slapped my face as Gabriel flew through the night. Luckily, our journey to South Carolina wasn't long, thanks to his celestial speediness. We landed in the woods, and Gabriel set me down. Michael and Zadkiel stood on each side of their brother, their wings shifting behind their backs. We all stood before the massive Angel Oak Tree. Its trunk was thick and its branches so huge they crawled to the ground and spanned the earth like giant arms.

A swallow flitted to my shoulder.

I leaned my head toward it and whispered, "Lead me."

It sprang to life, flying through the air and into a hovel in the tree. Advancing forward, I followed. Without fear or hesitation, I looked inside and saw a stone resting within the tree, a dagger sticking out of it.

The time to learn who I was had come. I reached out and gripped the small hilt, pulling the blade free. Flower engravings marked the pure white hilt and sheath.

Madonna Lily.

I would have recognized the voice that spoke in my head anywhere. It was Sister Delphine.

I drew the dagger from its sheath and saw the dark-green blade. As soon as it came free and the moon shone on it, a gust of wind sent my head flying back.

Jordan Anson Conway.

My full name was spoken aloud, the middle one a revelation to me.

Son of Arthur Conway, sage and seer of the Sefirot.

Son of Evangeline Sinclair, sacred and sublime scion.

The heir of the holy bloodline.

Take thy blade, wet thy hand, unleash thy power from within, for your journey is obscure.

I flew forward, bracing myself against the ground with my palms.

All this time… It had been me all this time.

Taking the dagger, I sliced my hand. I barely felt the cut, but a sudden headache thundered through my brain, and I screamed in pain. Voices, songs, and prophecies flooded my mind at once. My fleur-de-lis necklace was still in my pocket, but I had to fight against the noise to reach it.

I looked up at the angels. Rather than coming to my aid, they stood their ground and withdrew their weapons. Figures crept out from the woods, weaving through the branches and tree trunks. It was a truly haunting sight.

And that's when I realized the thundering hadn't just been a sensation exploding through my head. It had been the fallen claps of thunder, a sound my ears had grown accustomed to after being exposed to it so many times.

Fallen angels, their black wings on full display, kept pouring forth from the woods. I hardly recognized a single face among the infernal crowd, yet I knew the angels were looking upon their former brothers and sisters.

A figure stepped forward. I recognized him as Mammon since he had attacked me during my first trip with the angels last fall. "Give us the boy," he said.

Michael drew his sword. "Never."

My three friends charged into the horde as one.

I shoved the dagger into my jacket pocket and forced the voices to calm down as I fought off a few fallen angels who tried to snatch me. We were severely outnumbered, and while we had been in similar situations before, I didn't think there was any miracle that would save us now.

Reaching for the Angel Oak, I intended to climb its branches to seek solace and a better vantage point when a sudden burst of light leveled everyone to the ground, myself included.

I stared up at the canopy of leaves, then rolled over to see that the angels had disappeared.

What? Where had they gone? Who had taken them? Were they all right?

A menacing chuckle loomed over me. Looking up, I saw Mammon's ghoulish face. "Remember me."

His fist slammed into the side of my face. Dazed, I fumbled along the ground, meaning to push myself up. Before I could, a branch connected with the back of my head.

Eyes spinning, I dropped to the bed of leaves beneath the tree.

"Take him."

A burly figure appeared and lifted me. It wasn't the usual burly member of the Six but a new one. He dragged my feet along the ground as he marched through the woods until we reached a clearing.

Thunder roared through the night as a portal was summoned. As I was hauled backward, the last thing I saw was the beautiful, sprawling tree before I descended into Hell.

Reference Guides

CAST OF CHARACTERS

HUMANS

Aeron Conway: Jordan's uncle

Allen Clark: an informant who alerts Michael to Geneloom's operation

Angelica: Tony and Francesca's granddaughter

Arthur Conway: Jordan's father

Bianca: Simon Price's assistant at the Met

Claudia: Tony and Francesca's daughter

Dafne Delucci: Sophia's best friend and roommate at Harvard

Dane: an orphan; grew up with Jordan and Sophia; Jordan's roommate at Holy Trinity

Deborah Barnes: Naomi's mother

Enzo: Tony and Francesca's grandson

Evangeline Conway: Jordan's mother

Francesca: Tony's wife

Gigi: Preston's mother

Jordan Conway: an orphan; grew up with Dane and Sophia

Laila Barnes: Naomi's sister

Martha O'Reilly: Jordan's housekeeper; Sister Helen's biological sister

Mr. and Mrs. Delucci: Dafne's father and mother

Naomi Barnes: Jordan's neighbor; set up to date Jordan by her mother and Martha

Nonna Bea: Tony's mother; real first name is Beatrice

Peter Barnes: Naomi's father

Preston: Sophia's mother's boyfriend

Simon Price: curator of the Department of Ancient Art and Antiquities at the Met

Simone Barnes: Naomi's sister

Sister Delphine: a nun who helped run Holy Trinity with Sister Helen

Sister Helen: Head Sister at Holy Trinity; Martha O'Reilly's biological sister; member of the Sacrarium, Alpha classification; full name is Helen O'Reilly

Sophia: an orphan; Jordan's best friend; training to be a member of the Sacrarium; grew up with Dane and Jordan

Tony: a friend of Gabriel's; Gabriel's "assistant"

Heaven

Father: ruler in Heaven; creator of all angels; otherwise known as God

Angels

Araziel (AH-RAZZ-EE-EL): a male Angel; an angel of music

Ariel: a female Archangel; an angel of power; member of the Council of Archangels

Cassiel: a male Archangel; an angel of power

Chamuel (CHAM-U-EL): a male Archangel; an angel of the home; member of the Council of Archangels; lives on Earth; alias is Cam Angel

Gabriel: a male Archangel; an angel of music; member of the Council of Archangels; lives on Earth; alias is Gabriel Maestro

Griel (GREE-EL): a female Angel; an angel of music

Haniel (HAN-EE-EL): a female Archangel; an angel of healing

Jophiel (JOE-FEE-EL): a male Archangel; an angel of art; member of the Council of Archangels; lives on Earth; alias is Jo Crane

Justice: a male Virtue

Metatron: a male Archangel; an angel of teaching; member of the Council of Archangels

Michael: a male Archangel; an angel of power; member of the Council of Archangels; lives on Earth; alias is Michael Lyons

Raphael: a male Archangel; an angel of healing; member of the Council of Archangels; lives on Earth; alias is Dr. Raphael Wolf

Raziel (RAZZ-EE-EL): a male Archangel; an angel of teaching; member of the Council of Archangels

Sandalphon (SAN-DAL-FON): a male Archangel; an angel of nature; member of the Council of Archangels

Seraphiel (SER-REF-EE-EL): a female Seraphim; Head Seraphim

Tzaphkiel (ZAHF-KEE-EL): a female Archangel; an angel of the home; member of the Council of Archangels

Uriel (YOUR-EE-EL): a male Archangel; an angel of nature; member of the Council of Archangels; lives on Earth; alias is Uri Reed

Zadkiel (ZAHD-KEE-EL): a male Archangel; an angel of teaching; member of the Council of Archangels; lives on Earth; alias is Zak Leid

The Triune

Aziza (AH-ZEE-ZAH): a female member of the Triune; represents Islam

Katriel (KAT-TREE-EL): a female member of the Triune; represents Christianity; otherwise known as Kat

Yadira (YAH-DEER-AH): a female member of the Triune; represents Judaism

Hell

Abbadona: a female fallen angel; resides in the Eighth Cavern; the only angel not affected by the Rivers of Hell; practices the healing arts

Asmodeus (AS-MO-DEE-US): a male fallen angel; member of the Six; leader of Lust

Astrid: a spirit; a witch; one of the Witchcraft Sisters; practices black magic; blind; Tabitha's sister

Balberith (BALL-BURR-RITH): a male fallen angel; attends to spirits in the throne room by watching them, recording their requests, and escorting them back to where they belong

Beelzebub (BILL-ZE-BUB): a male fallen angel; member of the Six; leader of Gluttony

Belphegor (BELL-FA-GOR): a male fallen angel; member of the Six; leader of Laze

Cerberus (SIR-BER-US): three-headed dog in Hell; Leviathan's "pet"

Haborym (HA-BORE-RIM): a female fallen angel; helped Satan manipulate divine light to create his portals, barriers, and shields; forges the weapons in Hell

Leviathan: a male fallen angel; member of the Six; leader of Envy

Lilith: the snake in Eden who bit Satan; the mother of blood magic

Lucifer: a male fallen angel; member of the Six; leader of Pride; Satan's second-in-command; alias is Luc Helton

Mammon: a male fallen angel; member of the Six; leader of Greed

Mulciber (MUL-SIB-BURR): a male fallen angel; escorts spirits from Misery to the city they will reside in

Murmur: a male fallen angel; interrogates spirits in Misery to determine what city they will reside in

Nehema (NAH-HE-MA): a female fallen angel; promoted to leader of Misery

Satan: a male fallen angel; the ruler of Hell; leader of the Six; leader of Elysium; former Archangel; former angel of power; former member of the Council of Archangels; given name was Samael (SAM-MY-EL); alias is Samuel Cross

Tabitha: a spirit; a witch; one of the Witchcraft Sisters; practices black magic; Astrid's sister

Connected to Nephilim Operations

Jazema Grigori (JAZZ-EM-AH GREH-GOR-EE): owner of Geneloom; Penelope Grigori's sister

Parvati Irin (PAR-VAH-TEE EYE-RIN): former owner of Giant Heart Healing Center; died in a lab accident

Penelope Grigori: current owner of Giant Heart Healing Center; Jazema Grigori's sister

Rajani (RAY-JON-E): a teenage Nephilim girl with speckled brown wings

Salma Amir: a doctor and geneticist hired by Jazema; died in a lab accident

Sentinel, the: a person employed by Jazema to kill people and tie up loose ends

OTHERS

Angelo: works in Gabriel's apartment building
Benny: a footman in Gabriel's apartment building
Daisy: Uriel's coworker
Dr. Parr: Raphael's colleague
Dr. Reynolds: Raphael's colleague
Doug: a mailman
Emily: presumed Sacrarium member
Ethan: Jordan's former coworker
Marcus: Jordan's former boss
Margaret: a student at Oxford
Matthew: Uriel's coworker
Sheila: Uriel's coworker
Umberto: maître d' of the restaurant where Chamuel worked

Glossary

1055 Applegate Road: The address of Sister Delphine's house.

34 Central Park West: The address of Gabriel's apartment.

Alpha: The highest classification for a Sacrarium member; distributes information to all other members; has taken oath to protect the holy bloodline; there is only one Alpha, and this designation is given to Sister Helen.

amulet: The necklace Astrid and Tabitha created for Satan so he can travel to Earth.

ancient wonders of the world: Locations around the globe from the ancient world; many no longer exist; where the classic keys are hidden.

angel of art: Angel that possesses the capability to create artistic works or inventions.

angel of healing: Angel that possesses the capability to heal.

angel of music: Angel that possesses the capability to play any musical instrument.

angel of nature: Angel that possesses the capability to protect and care for nature.

angel of power: Angel that possesses the capability to fight.

angel of teaching: Angel that possesses the capability to teach and learn.

angel of the home: Angel that possesses the capability to nurture and care for the home.

angelic script: Language of angels that is mainly written.

Angels: Ranked nine out of nine classifications in the Celestial Hierarchy; part of the Third Choir; known as Heaven's messengers; reside in Low Heaven; duties are to act as guardian angels.

anointing oil: Holy oil used to rub on the body for ceremonial purposes.

Archangels: Ranked eight out of nine classifications in the Celestial Hierarchy; part of the Third Choir; known as Heaven's messengers; reside in Low Heaven; duties are to watch and protect humankind.

astrological constellations: Twelve (formerly thirteen) star signs; otherwise known as the zodiac; a member of the Council of Archangels represents each sign.

barriers: Divine light that has the ability to barricade things; made by angels of art with God's permission; otherwise known as divine light barriers.

Beta: The second classification for a Sacrarium member; given covert duties and aware of almost all confidential information; has taken oath to protect the holy bloodline.

black magic: A dark type of magic practiced by Astrid and Tabitha.

blood magic: A force stronger than black magic; created and mainly used by Lilith.

Brooklyn Heights: A neighborhood in Brooklyn, New York, where Holy Trinity Home for Disadvantaged Youth is located.

Castle Key, the: An item that went missing from Heaven; needed to open the tower of the castle in High Heaven.

castle: The structure in High Heaven where the Seraphim, Cherubim, and Thrones reside.

cathedrals: Two structures in Low Heaven where the Principalities and Angels reside.

celestial energy: Holy energy emitted by anything divine; usually undetectable by most humans.

Celestial Hierarchy: The classification system in Heaven that organizes different types of angels and their duties.

Celtic tree astrology: Similar to astrological constellations but based on trees and nature instead of stars; a member of the Council of Archangels represents each sign.

chakram: A sharp, disklike weapon that separates into two identical pieces.

Cherubim: Ranked two out of nine classifications in the Celestial Hierarchy; part of the First Choir; known as Heaven's counselors; reside in High Heaven; duties are to provide input on decisions made by God and relay messages to the Second Choir.

circle of vocation: A grouping system for angels in the Third Choir that determines their skill set; there are seven circles of vocation in total.

classic key: A metal key that was hidden at the ancient wonders of the world; this key is needed for the Union of the Spheres; each member on the Council of Archangels has one.

Council of Angels: Consists of a group of Angels appointed by God; implemented for order.

Council of Archangels: Consists of a group of Archangels appointed by God; implemented for order; thirteen members in total until Satan fell.

Council of Cherubim: Consists of a group of Cherubim appointed by God; implemented for order.

Council of Dominions: Consists of a group of Dominions appointed by God; implemented for order.

Council of Powers: Consists of a group of Powers appointed by God; implemented for order.

Council of Principalities: Consists of a group of Principalities appointed by God; implemented for order.

Council of Seraphim: Consists of a group of Seraphim appointed by God; implemented for order.

Council of Thrones: Consists of a group of Thrones appointed by God; implemented for order.

Council of Virtues: Consists of a group of Virtues appointed by God; implemented for order.

dark beings: Humans that are infected with dark matter but are still alive.

dark energy/dark matter: An evil substance that can infect and pollute humans; lethal to angels and the Fallen.

dark energy weapon: A weapon that has been created from the river water in Hell and sanctified in dark matter; otherwise known as a dark weapon; lethal to humans, angels, and the Fallen.

deadly sin rings: A piece of jewelry worn by Satan and the Six.

demon cash: A currency in Hell.

demons: Humans that were turned into dark beings that are now dead.

divine light: A type of energy that comes from God.

divine markings: Another name for angel tattoos.

divine wisdoms: All knowledge contained in Heaven.

Dominions: Ranked four out of nine classifications in the Celestial Hierarchy; part of the Second Choir; known as Heaven's governors;

reside in Middle Heaven; duties are to uphold laws and relay messages to the Third Choir.

Eden: The Garden of Eden; created by God and located on Earth.

Eighth Cavern, the: Eighth level of Hell; where the five rivers reside; Abbadona dwells here since she is immune to the tempting whispers of the waters.

Elysium: First city in Hell ruled by Satan; otherwise known as the Royal City; where fallen angels reside.

Envy: Third city in Hell; run by Leviathan; where spirits that succumbed to envy reside.

fallen claps of thunder: The sound heard when the Fallen travel to and from Hell; can impair the hearing of humans.

fallen forces/Fallen, the: A term used to describe Satan and his army of fallen angels and demons.

First Choir, the: A hierarchical designation that contains the highest level of angels—the Seraphim, Cherubim, and Thrones.

fleur-de-lis: A three-pronged symbol associated with the Sacrarium.

Flood, the: The biblical story of how God sent a massive storm to wipe out the Earth so that He could create it again.

Forge, the: The place in High Heaven where all divine objects are made.

fourteenth sphere, the: A gemstone sphere whose true existence is unknown.

Gamma: The third classification for a Sacrarium member; only called upon when needed and informed on a need-to-know basis; has taken oath to protect the holy bloodline.

gemstone key: A gemstone that is hidden at the natural wonders of the world; needed for the Union of the Spheres; each member on the Council of Archangels has one.

Geneloom: A genetic-testing company that conducts secret experiments.

Giant Heart Healing Center: A rehab facility that works with Geneloom for the same aims.

Gluttony: Fourth city in Hell; run by Beelzebub; where spirits that succumbed to gluttony reside.

Greed: Fifth city in Hell; run by Mammon; where spirits that succumbed to greed reside.

Hall of Law: A structure in Middle Heaven that contains all heavenly laws; where one of the stolen objects was placed.

halls: Three structures in Middle Heaven where the Dominions, Virtues, and Powers reside.

Head of Council: A designation given to Metatron that signifies he is the leader of the Council of Archangels.

Head Seraphim: a designation given to Seraphiel that signifies she is the highest angelic authority.

Heaven's counselors: A designation for the type of angelic duties given to the First Choir.

Heaven's governors: A designation for the type of angelic duties given to the Second Choir

Heaven's messengers: A designation for the type of angelic duties given to the Third Choir.

Heavenly Gates: An entrance located in High Heaven that leads to another heavenly realm.

heavenly light: A type of energy that comes from angels.

Hellfire: a mixture of heavenly light and divine light; the angels of art accidentally created Hellfire by mixing together mass quantities of heavenly light and divine light, creating dark matter; the type of fire that rages in Hell; Satan's punishment; lethal to almost everyone and everything.

hellhounds: Dogs in Hell that guard caves between cities.

High Heaven: Where the Seraphim, Cherubim, and Thrones reside.

holy bloodline: A living descendant of Jesus and Mary Magdalene; also known as the heir.

Holy Trinity Home for Disadvantaged Youth: The orphanage where Jordan, Sophia, and Dane grew up; more commonly known as Holy Trinity.

holy water grenade: Clear glass balls filled with holy water.

holy water: Sanctified and purified water that is lethal to the Fallen.

Horn of Assembly: A long, gold horn used to send messages to angels or Heaven.

incarnation: A person meant to represent a deity.

inferos: Latin word meaning "Hell;" the Fallen must place a hand to the ground and say this word in order to open a portal to travel back to Hell.

Ishim, the: Angels who were once Watchers; also known as good Watchers; sent to Earth to teach humans and pass along their wisdom; five in total; much of their knowledge is gained through visions and conditioning of the mind.

Keys, the: Nickname for the classic keys and the gemstone keys.

Laze: Seventh city in Hell; run by Belphegor; where spirits that succumbed to laziness reside.

leader of the army: A designation given to Michael that signifies that he is in charge of the heavenly army.

light energy/light matter: A pure substance that is lethal to humans, angels, and the Fallen.

light energy weapon: A weapon that has been created from divine light and sanctified in light matter; otherwise known as a light weapon; lethal to humans, angels, and the Fallen.

Low Heaven: Where the Principalities, Archangels, and Angels reside.

Lust: Sixth city in Hell; run by Asmodeus; where spirits that succumbed to lust reside.

Metatron's Cube: A formation of circles linked together; created by Metatron; the placement required for the Union of the Spheres.

MetroCard: A New York City public transportation pass.

Middle Heaven: Where the Dominions, Virtues, and Powers reside.

Misery: located in the ninth cavern of Hell; where all spirits must complete their sentence of torment before they can move into a city; all spirits who succumb to anger remain here eternally.

modern wonders of the world: Locations around the globe from the modern world; many are not necessarily modern but are popular tourist sites; where the spheres are hidden.

natural wonders of the world: Locations around the globe that are natural phenomena; where the gemstone keys are hidden.

necessary evil: Something unpleasant that must be done to achieve a particular outcome; in the context of this book series it is the notion that evil was intentionally created by God.

Nephilim, the: Half-human, half-angel beings; their forefathers were Watchers and their mothers were mortal women.

neque heredis exponere: Latin phrase meaning "Do not expose the heir;" the motto of the Sacrarium.

Novice: The lowest classification for a Sacrarium member; taught rudimentary information in preparation for taking the oath to protect the holy bloodline; a member must remain at this level for five years to determine their dedication and trustworthiness before they take their oath.

novissimum: A Latin word meaning "hinder."

Operation Pure Form: The secret experiment Geneloom is conducting to achieve the untainted genetics of the Watchers.

Pit, the: A large, dark void that spans throughout Hell and is sometimes used as punishment by Satan.

portal room: A room in Hell connected to Satan's private quarters where his portal to Earth resides; also where Satan keeps prisoners.

portals: Divine light that has the ability to transport things; made by angels of art with God's permission.

Powers: Ranked six out of nine classifications in the Celestial Hierarchy; part of the Second Choir; known as Heaven's governors; reside in Middle Heaven; duties are to uphold laws and relay messages to the Third Choir.

Pride: Second city in Hell; run by Lucifer; where spirits that succumbed to pride reside.

Principalities: Ranked seven out of nine classifications in the Celestial Hierarchy; part of the Third Choir; known as Heaven's messengers; reside in Low Heaven; duties are to interact with members and institutions of the church.

Prophecy of the Three Heirs, the: A foretelling of how Jordan, Dane, and Sophia can discover who they are.

pure form: A term Geneloom uses to signify the untainted genetics of the Watchers.

Purgatory: A realm between Heaven and Hell.

Qliphoth: A realm of evil where dark forces reside.

red blaze, the: A term Satan uses for Hellfire.

Rivers of Hell, the: Located in the Eighth Cavern of Hell; five rivers in total—the River of Pain, the River of Lamentation, the River of Forgetfulness, the River of Fire, and the River of Hate; the waters tempt beings into their depths for eternal punishment.

Royal City, the: A nickname for Elysium.

Sacrarium: A secret society meant to protect the holy bloodline.

Sacred Heart High School: The high school that Jordan, Sophia, and Dane attended.

sanctuaries: Seven structures in Low Heaven, each designated for a circle of vocation.

Sanctuary of Art: A structure in Low Heaven that houses the angels of art; the symbol to represent this circle of vocation is an artist's palette.

Sanctuary of Healing: A structure in Low Heaven that houses the angels of healing; the symbol to represent this circle of vocation is a caduceus.

Sanctuary of Music: A structure in Low Heaven that houses the angels of music; the symbol to represent this circle of vocation is a music note.

Sanctuary of Nature: A structure in Low Heaven that houses the angels of nature; the symbol to represent this circle of vocation is a tree.

Sanctuary of Power: A structure in Low Heaven that houses the angels of power; the symbol to represent this circle of vocation is a helmet.

Sanctuary of Teaching: A structure in Low Heaven that houses the angels of teaching; the symbol to represent this circle of vocation is a scroll.

Sanctuary of the Home: A structure in Low Heaven that houses the angels of the home; the symbol to represent this circle of vocation is a hearth flame.

Second Choir, the: A hierarchical designation that contains mid-level angels—the Dominions, Virtues, and Powers.

Sefirot: A realm of wisdom where light forces reside; where the teachings of the Ishim originated.

Seraphim: Ranked one out of nine classifications in the Celestial Hierarchy; part of the First Choir; known as Heaven's counselors; reside in High Heaven; duties are to provide input on decisions made by God and relay messages to the Second Choir.

Seventh Day Gathering: A celebration in Heaven meant for camaraderie.

shields: Divine light that has the ability to cloak things; made by angels of art with God's permission.

Sight, the: An ancient gift that gives a person the ability to have visions.

Six, the: Satan's fallen angels that execute his bidding—Lucifer, Leviathan, Beelzebub, Mammon, Asmodeus, and Belphegor.

skull ring: A piece of jewelry worn by Satan and the Six.

skull tattoo: An identifier of the Six; Satan and each member of the Six has it on the back of their hands.

Son of God: Signifies God's incarnation on Earth; mainly used in reference to Jesus.

Sovereign's Orb: The orb that is created during the Union of the Spheres; the thirteen spheres combine to make it.

Sovereign's Scepter: A scepter that holds the Sovereign's Orb; needed for the Union of the Spheres.

spheres: Round stones the size of a grapefruit; thirteen in total; needed for the Union of the Spheres; each member on the Council of Archangels has one.

spirit coin: A currency in Hell.

spirits: Deceased people in Heaven or Hell.

St. Michael medallion: A small pendant worn on a necklace that depicts Archangel Michael.

storage chest: A large, rectangular case that an angel travels with.

terra: Latin word meaning "Earth;" the Fallen must place a hand on a portal and say this word, along with their intended location, in order to travel to Earth.

The Book of Prophecies: A book from Heaven that contains prophecies and other divine wisdoms; it was also an item that went missing from Heaven.

Third Choir, the: A hierarchical designation that contains the lowest level of angels—the Principalities, Archangels, and Angels.

throne room: A room connected to Satan's private quarters where he receives visitors.

Thrones: Ranked three out of nine classifications in the Celestial Hierarchy; part of the First Choir; known as Heaven's counselors; reside in High Heaven; duties are to provide input on decisions made by God and relay messages to the Second Choir.

Tree of Good and Evil/Tree of Knowledge, the: Located in Eden.

Tree of Life, the: A symbol of growth and ancestry for Jordan, Dane, and Sophia.

trial of trust: A task given to a Sacrarium Novice to prove they are dedicated and trustworthy; occurs after their training is finished; a novice can take the oath to protect the holy bloodline upon successful completion of a trial of trust.

trinity: A Christian notion meant to signify the three parts of God—Father, Son, and Holy Spirit.

Triune, the: A group of angels meant to protect the holy bloodline and anything related to it; connected to the Sacrarium.

Union of the Spheres, the: The process of combining thirteen spheres into one in order to make the Sovereign's Orb; the ceremony gives the wielder immense power.

Virtues: Ranked five out of nine classifications in the Celestial Hierarchy; part of the Second Choir; known as Heaven's governors; reside in Middle Heaven; duties are to uphold laws and relay messages to the Third Choir.

Watch Towers: Three structures in Low Heaven; one contains the Council of Archangels, and the other two are where Archangels stand watch over the world; where Archangels reside.

Watchers, the: A group of angels sent from Heaven to Earth in order to teach humans; fell in love with mortal women and produced the Nephilim; now considered fallen angels.

wonders, the: A nickname for the ancient, natural, and modern wonders of the world.

ACKNOWLEDGMENTS

I won't lie. This one was rough. I started and stopped writing about three or four times because I didn't know where the story began, scrapping thousands of words each time. I struggled to balance writing with life as new changes and responsibilities presented themselves. I flat-out procrastinated for months until I was hit with a solid deadline that left me to write 50,000 words in a week (I swear I'm not even exaggerating), forcing me to pull my first ever all-nighter. I stretched myself thin, pushed myself to exhaustion, and yet I wouldn't undo any of it because this book made me a better writer. Granted, I would never approach another project this way, and have definitely learned my lesson to change my ways for the future.

Through it all, my biggest champion was my mom, so the first round of thank-yous must go to her. She rode this roller coaster with me, cheering me on when I needed it as well as forcing me to discipline myself. I cried tears on her shoulder and shared laughs with her too, all to finally make it here where the book is actually finished and complete. Thank you, Mom, for always being there.

Next up is my partner in crime, my brother, Anthony. Thank you for being the best person to bounce ideas off of. Our brainstorming and dream casting sessions are always my favorite conversations that fill me with excitement for this series and inspire me to move forward and keep writing.

As always, thank you, Dad, for being there and supporting me through everything. I think it's time to address publicly that you single-handedly make every pin that goes out to readers worldwide, so that in itself is a commitment and dedication that I will be forever grateful for.

My family—the unit as I like to call them—are my rock. They are the first three people who read my books, the ones I hold drafting meetings with to discuss edits. When I'm not writing, they're the ones I'm enjoying life with, so I will say this every time: I don't know where I would be without you all. I love you guys.

Now on to the people who dove deep into this story and helped me pull it together. Danielle, you are my savior. Thank you for your amazing editing skills, but more importantly thank you for being the kindest, most awesome human being. You stuck with me as I struggled, and pushed me to evolve into a better writer. Shannon, thank you for working with me to develop the plot of this manuscript into an intricate story. Even though the structure was there, you really helped me polish the little details that made a big difference. Overall, a big round of applause to the Double Vision Editorial (www.doublevisioneditorial.com) team for being so stellar.

Thanks to Jessica, my fantastic mapmaker at Lizard Ink Maps (www.lizardinkstudio.com). You brought my worlds to life right before my eyes and made them look incredible. Once again, a shoutout to

Adrianne (www.adriannetamararachne.com) for inspiring the symbol artwork for this book. I'm so excited about our current collaborations, and am really looking forward to seeing all your wonderful work.

To Franklin, thank you for producing another awesome book trailer. You make the process so easy, and always produce a high-quality product that everyone can enjoy. While on the topic of videos, thanks to Zach (www.zachhoffmanvoice.com) for providing the voiceover. Your skills truly push it over the edge.

Thank you to every tour company that hosted me for my first book (YA Bound Book Tours, MTMC Tours, Prism Book Tours, Bewitching Book Tours, Literary Bound Tours, Storygram Tours, MLC-Mágico Libro Casa Tours, Indiegram Book Tours, Starlight Tours, and Divine Book Tours). You all were truly amazing, and I wouldn't have been able to get the reach I did without you.

Thanks to everyone who did a live event with me last year (Albert, Reeka, Mary Jo, Jennie, Missy, Sara, Cortnye, Kimmie). Chatting with you all was so much fun, and I cannot thank you enough for taking the time to participate.

Michael at Print Partners (www.print-partners.com), thank you for being such a wonderful person to work with. I'm really excited about our collaboration, and that I can support a local business.

And finally, the readers! THANK YOU for reading, reviewing, unboxing, posting...thank you for everything. Your support has been phenomenal, and I wouldn't be where I am today as an author without each and every one of you. I can't wait to see your reactions to this book, and I really hope you enjoy it.

Wings up!

CPSIA information can be obtained
at www.ICGtesting.com
Printed in the USA
BVHW032047180821
614567BV00011B/8/J

9 781732 516236